D0384742

COMICS SQUAD

LUNCH!

☆ **COMICS BY** ☆

CECE BELL

JEFFREY BROWN

CECIL CASTELLUCCI & SARA VARON

NATHAN HALE

JENNIFER L. HOLM & MATTHEW HOLM

JARRETT J. KROSOCZKA

PEANUTS

JASON SHIGA

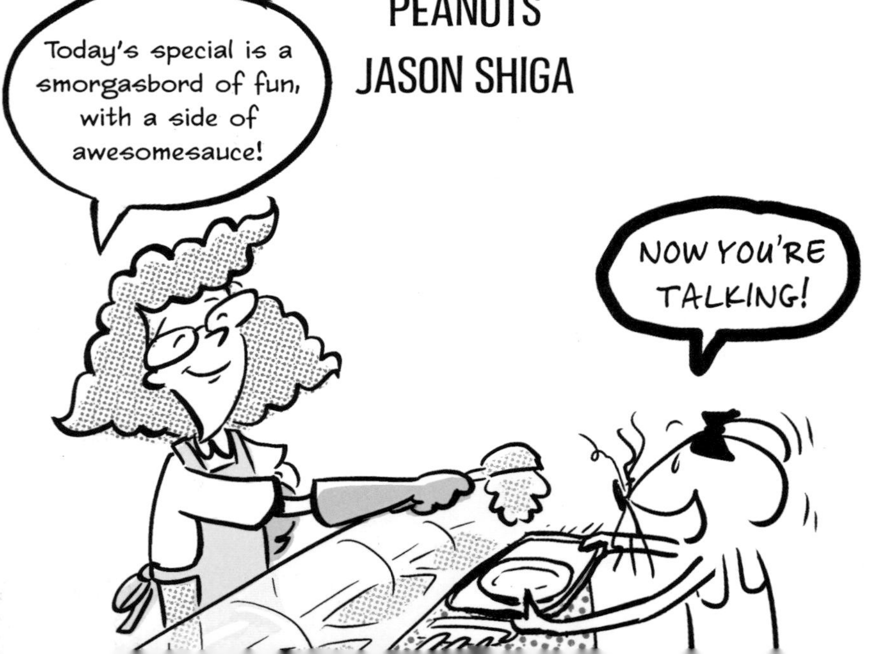
Today's special is a smorgasbord of fun, with a side of awesomesauce!
NOW YOU'RE TALKING!

COMICS SQUAD

LUNCH!

· EDITED BY ·

JENNIFER L. HOLM, MATTHEW HOLM & JARRETT J. KROSOCZKA

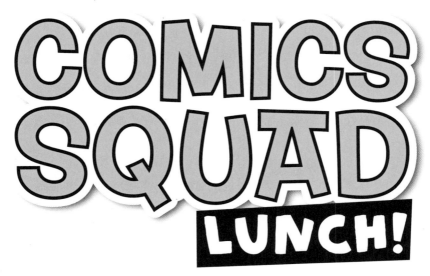

Fortified with eight essential vitamins!

WAIT—WE DON'T HAVE TO **EAT** THE BOOK, DO WE?

RANDOM HOUSE 🏠 NEW YORK

FOR EVA, ROBIN, AND SCOTT— COMICS SQUAD SUPERHEROES!

They're scrumptious!

This is a work of fiction. Names, characters, places, and incidents either are the product of the authors' imagination or are used fictitiously. Any resemblance to actual persons, living or dead, events, or locales is entirely coincidental.

Compilation copyright © 2016 by Jennifer L. Holm, Matthew Holm, and Jarrett J. Krosoczka

"Crazy Little Thing Called Lunch!" copyright © 2016 by Cece Bell. "Snoopy in . . . Lunchtime Beagle" copyright © 2016 by Peanuts Worldwide LLC. "Babymouse: Lunch Table Champion" copyright © 2016 by Jennifer L. Holm and Matthew Holm. "The Case of the Missing Science Project" copyright © 2016 by Jason Shiga. "Pikput & Cullen in . . . Worst Day Ever!" copyright © 2016 by Cecil Castellucci and Sara Varon. "Lucy & Andy Neanderthal: Cave Soup" copyright © 2016 by Jeffrey Brown. "Lunch Bomb 1943" copyright © 2016 by Nathan Hale. "Lunch Girl and the Ominous Origin" copyright © 2016 by Jarrett J. Krosoczka.

Cover art copyright © 2016 by Jennifer L. Holm and Matthew Holm, Jarrett J. Krosoczka, Cecil Castellucci and Sara Varon, Cece Bell, Jason Shiga, Nathan Hale, Jeffrey Brown, and Peanuts Worldwide LLC

All rights reserved. Published in the United States by Random House Children's Books, a division of Penguin Random House LLC, New York.

Random House and the colophon are registered trademarks of Penguin Random House LLC.

Visit us on the Web! randomhousekids.com

Educators and librarians, for a variety of teaching tools, visit us at RHTeachersLibrarians.com

Library of Congress Cataloging-in-Publication Data is available upon request.

ISBN 978-0-553-51264-9 (trade) — ISBN 978-0-553-51265-6 (lib. bdg.) — ISBN 978-0-553-51266-3 (ebook)

MANUFACTURED IN CHINA

10 9 8 7 6 5 4 3 2 1

First Edition

Random House Children's Books supports the First Amendment and celebrates the right to read.

★ CONTENTS ★

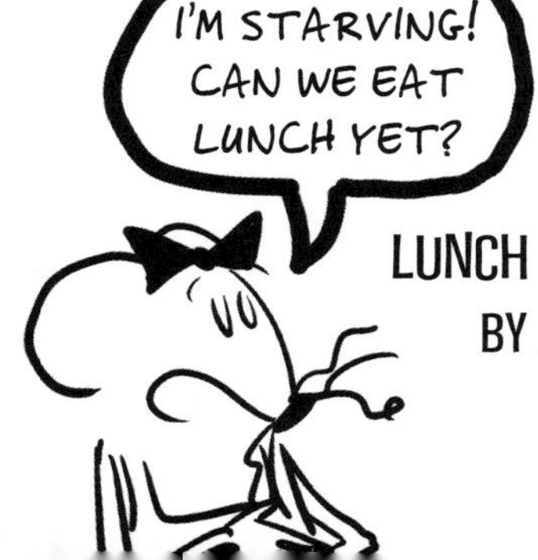

I'M STARVING! CAN WE EAT LUNCH YET?

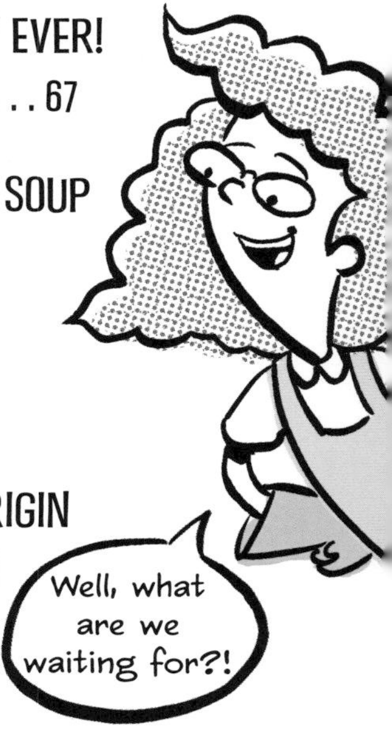

Well, what are we waiting for?!

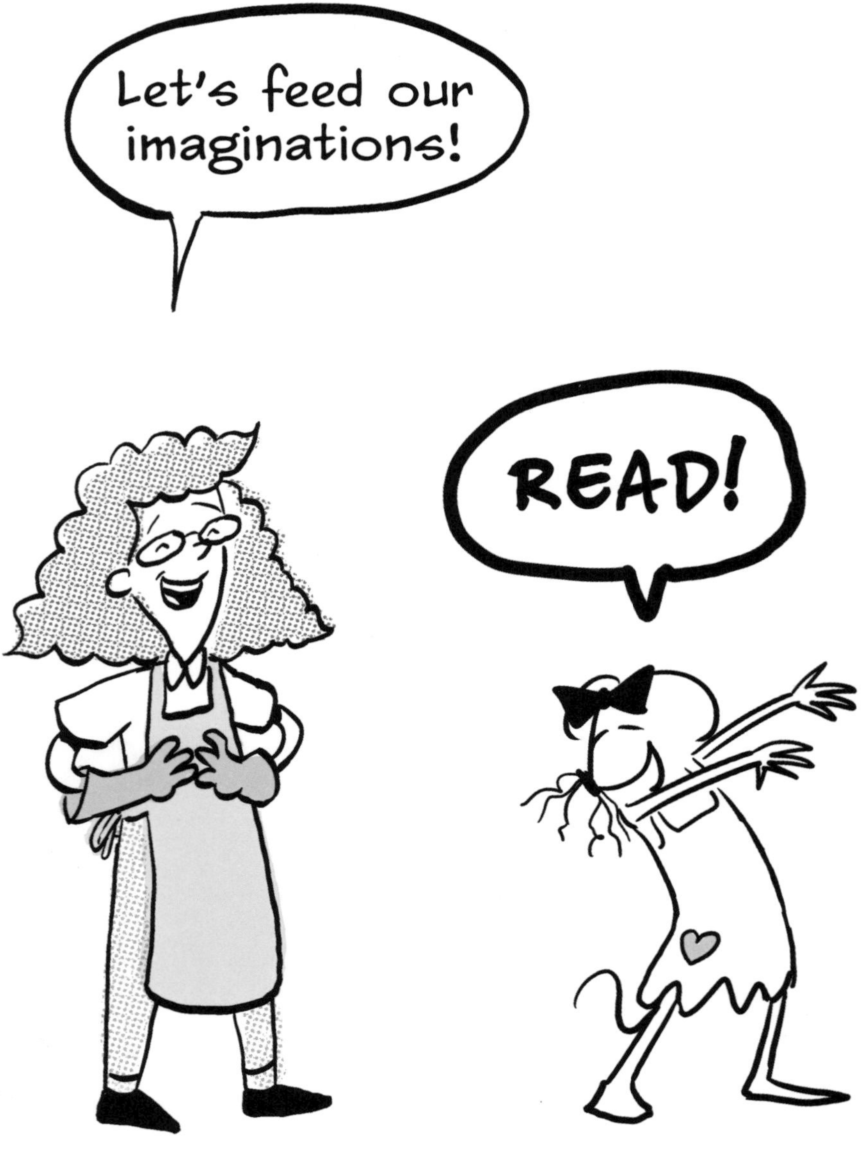
Let's feed our imaginations!
READ!

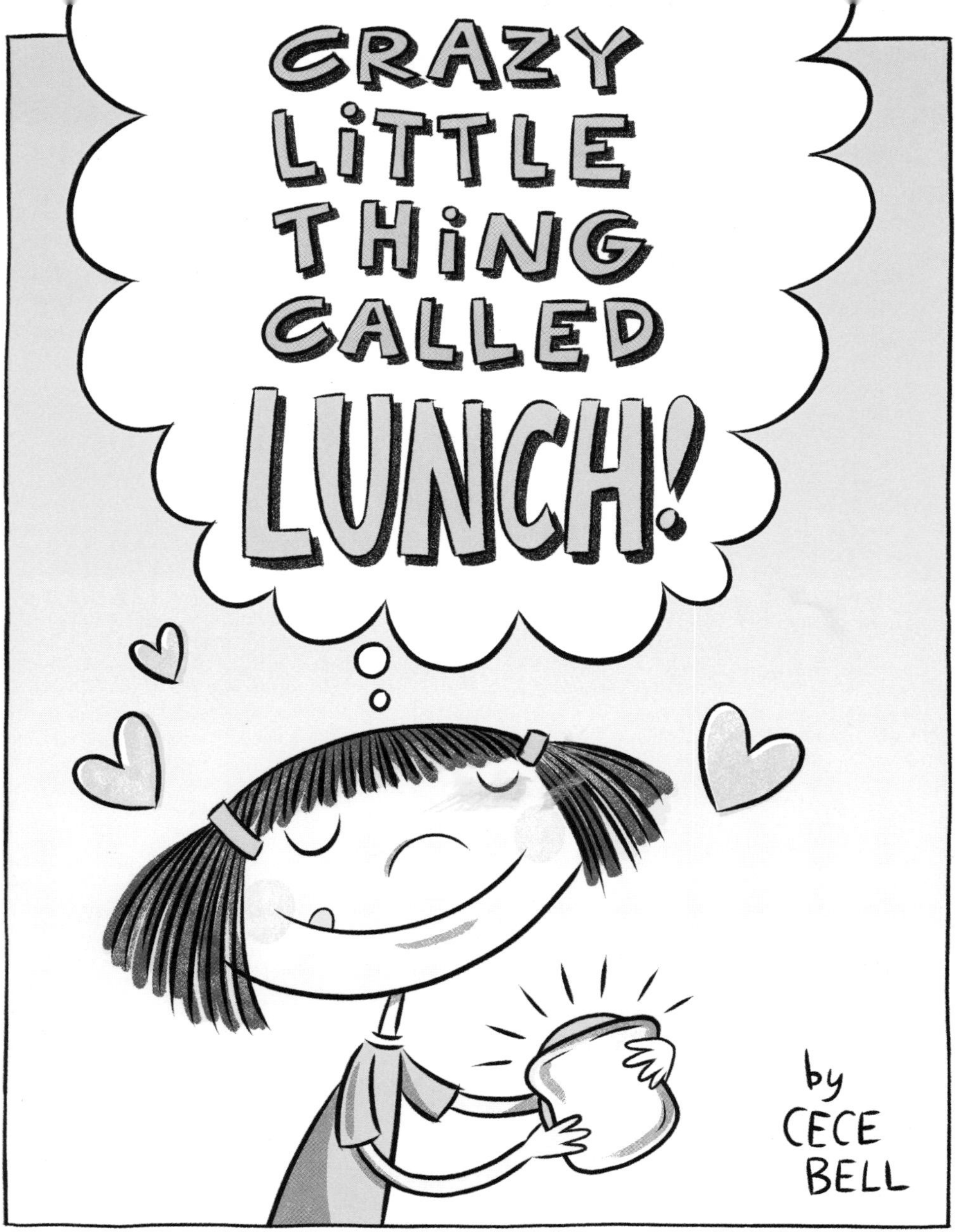
CRAZY LITTLE THING CALLED LUNCH!
by CECE BELL

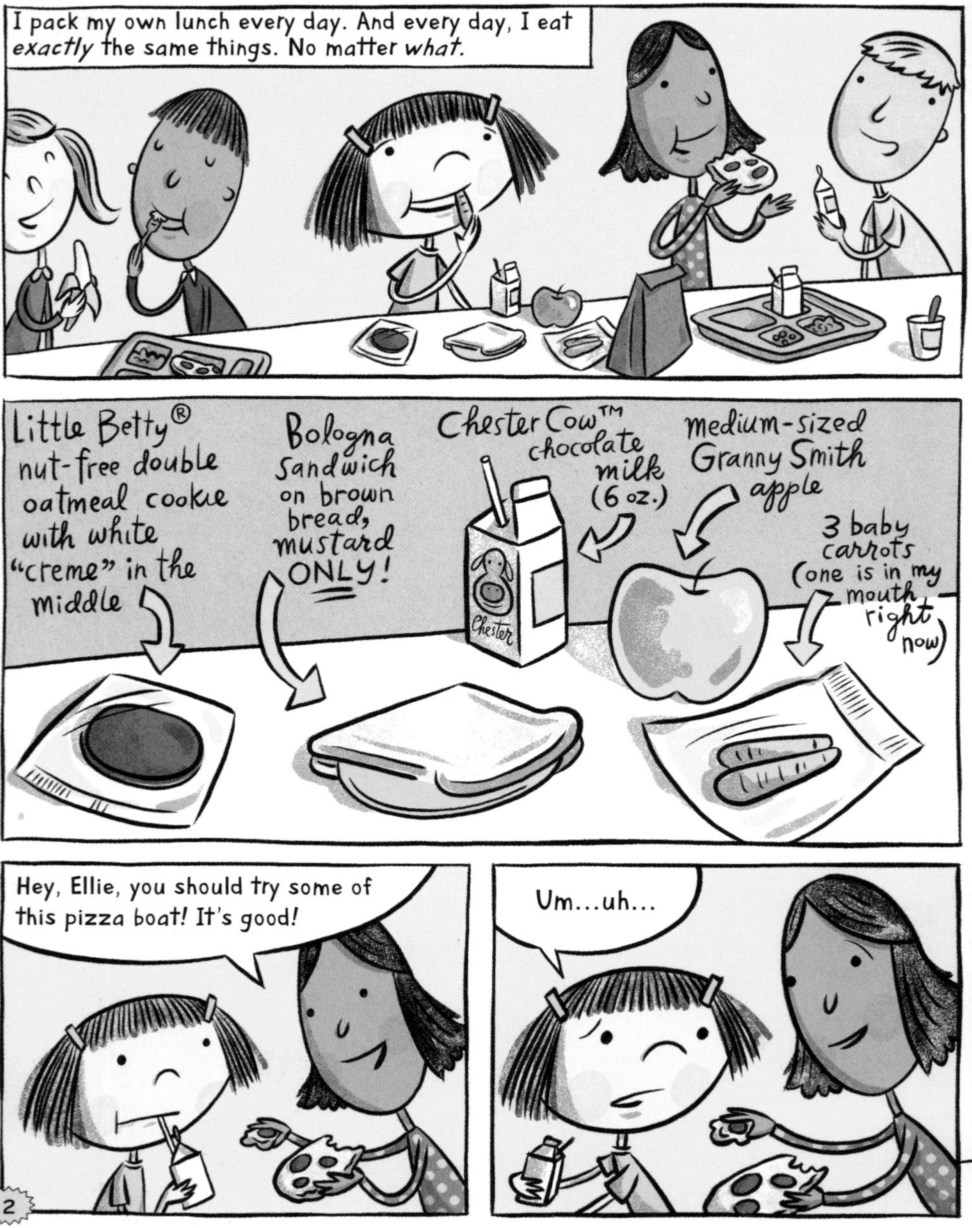
I pack my own lunch every day. And every day, I eat *exactly* the same things. No matter *what.*
Little Betty® nut-free double oatmeal cookie with white "creme" in the middle
Bologna sandwich on brown bread, mustard ONLY!
Chester Cow™ chocolate milk (6 oz.)
Chester
medium-sized Granny Smith apple
3 baby carrots (one is in my mouth right now)
Hey, Ellie, you should try some of this pizza boat! It's good!
Um...uh...

I *like* having the same thing to eat every day. I mean, what if I change my lunch, and crazy things start happening? I know it's not that simple, but—*what if?*

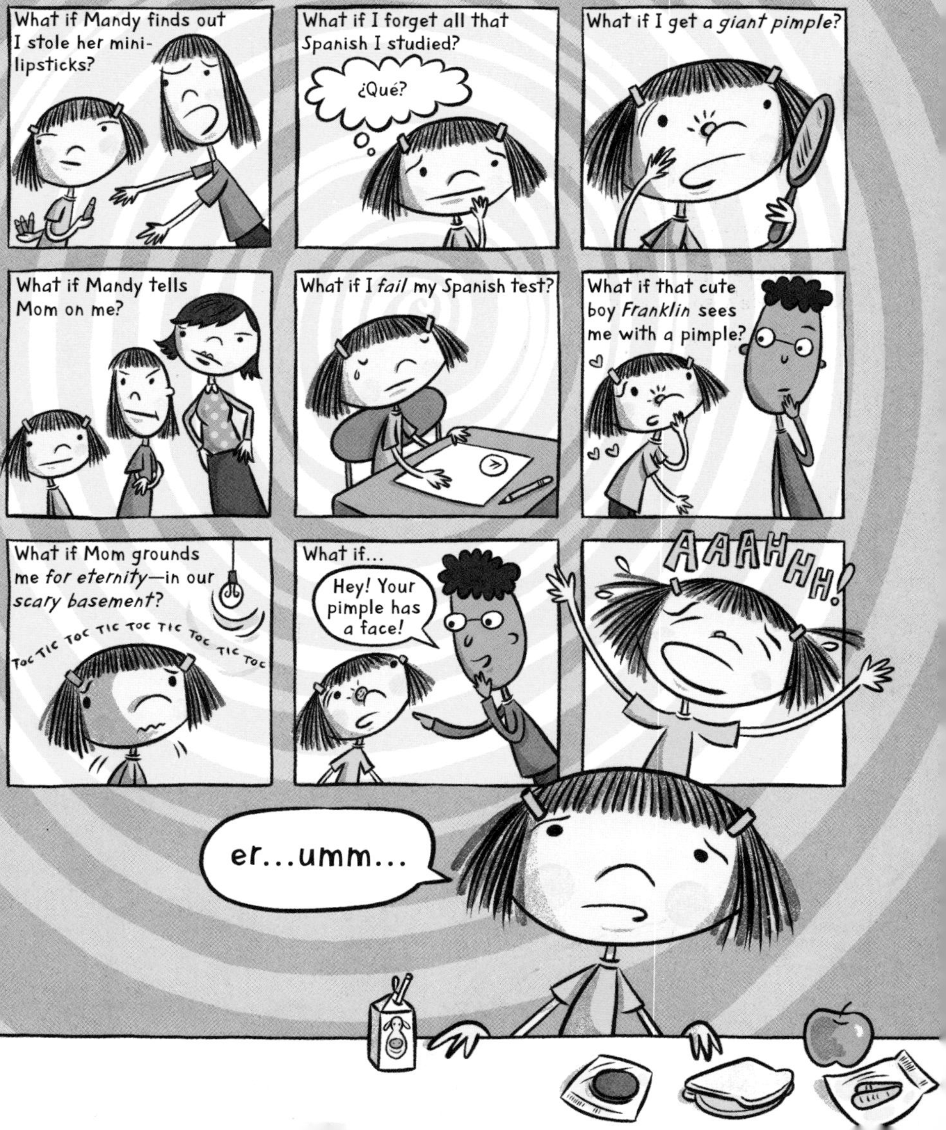
What if Mandy finds out I stole her mini-lipsticks?
What if I forget all that Spanish I studied?
¿Qué?
What if I get a *giant pimple*?
What if Mandy tells Mom on me?
What if I *fail* my Spanish test?
What if that cute boy *Franklin* sees me with a pimple?
What if Mom grounds me *for eternity*—in our *scary basement*?
TOC TIC TOC TIC TOC TIC TOC TIC TOC
What if...
Hey! Your pimple has a face!
AAAHHHH!
er...umm...

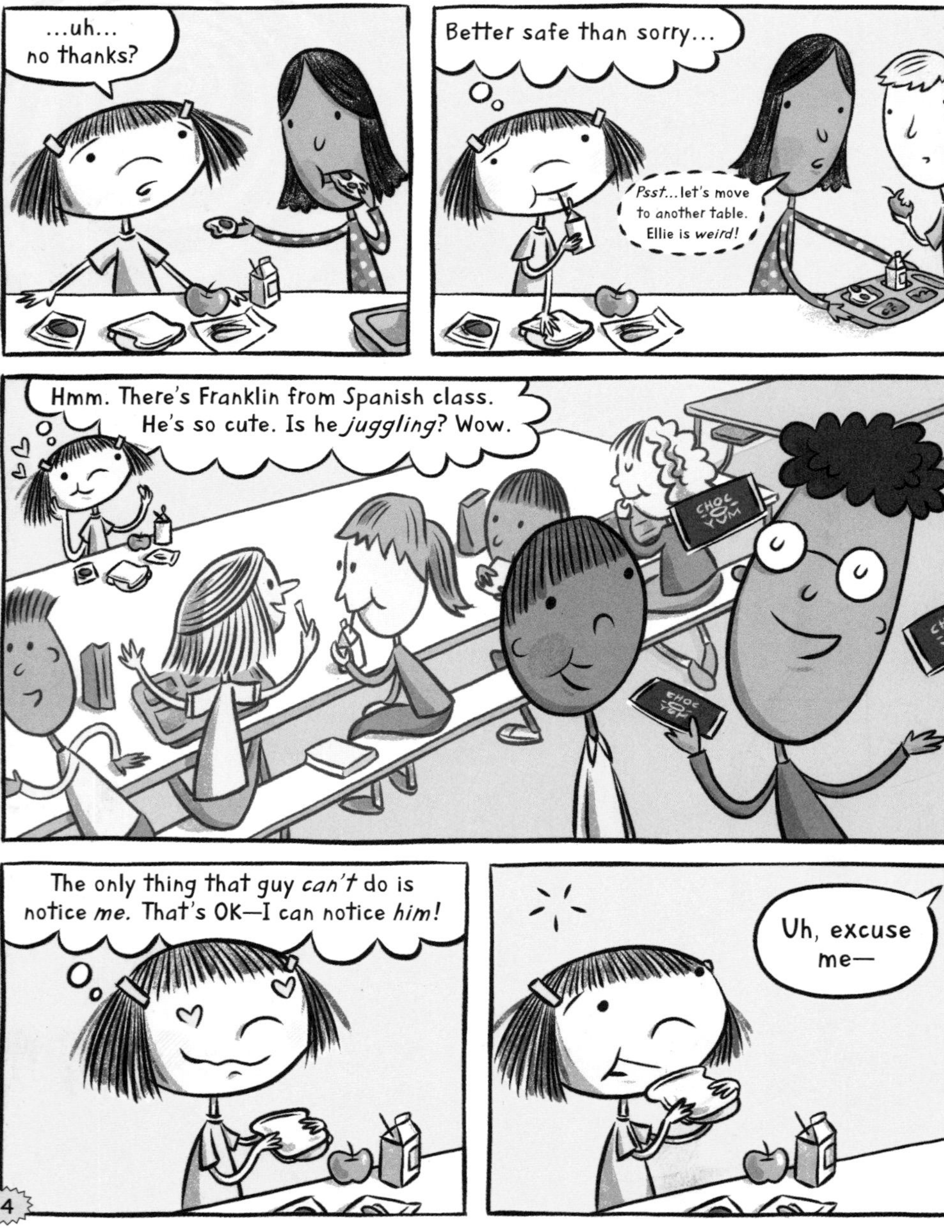
...uh...
no thanks?
Better safe than sorry...
Psst... let's move to another table. Ellie is weird!
Hmm. There's Franklin from Spanish class. He's so cute. Is he juggling? Wow.
CHOC O YUM
The only thing that guy can't do is notice me. That's OK—I can notice him!
Uh, excuse me—

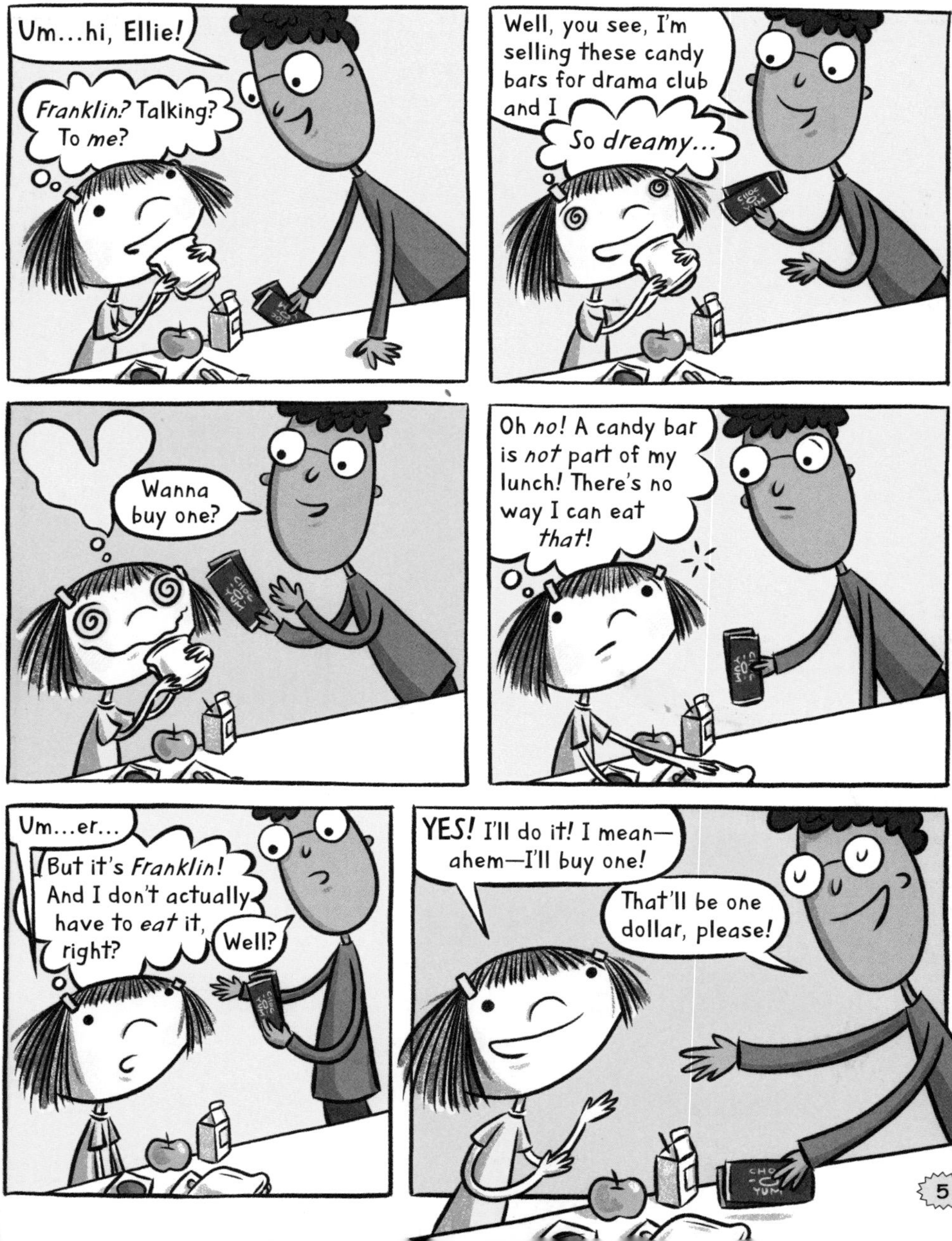
Um...hi, Ellie!
Franklin? Talking? To me?
Well, you see, I'm selling these candy bars for drama club and I
So dreamy...
Wanna buy one?
Oh no! A candy bar is not part of my lunch! There's no way I can eat that!
Um...er...
But it's Franklin! And I don't actually have to eat it, right?
Well?
YES! I'll do it! I mean—ahem—I'll buy one!
That'll be one dollar, please!

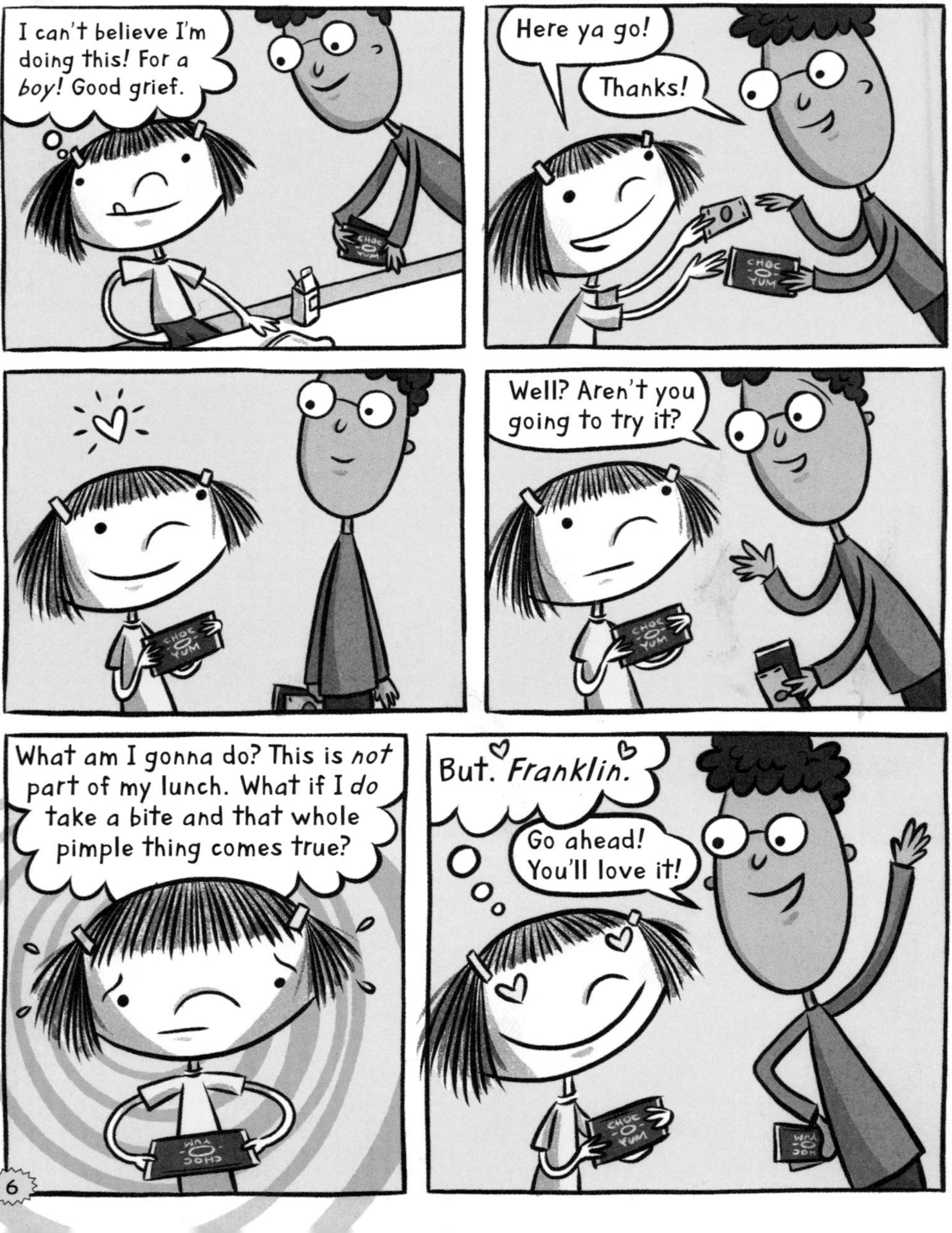
I can't believe I'm doing this! For a *boy*! Good grief.
CHOC-O-YUM
Here ya go!
Thanks!
CHOC-O-YUM
CHOC-O-YUM
Well? Aren't you going to try it?
CHOC-O-YUM
What am I gonna do? This is *not* part of my lunch. What if I *do* take a bite and that whole pimple thing comes true?
CHOC-O-YUM
But. *Franklin.*
Go ahead! You'll love it!
CHOC-O-YUM

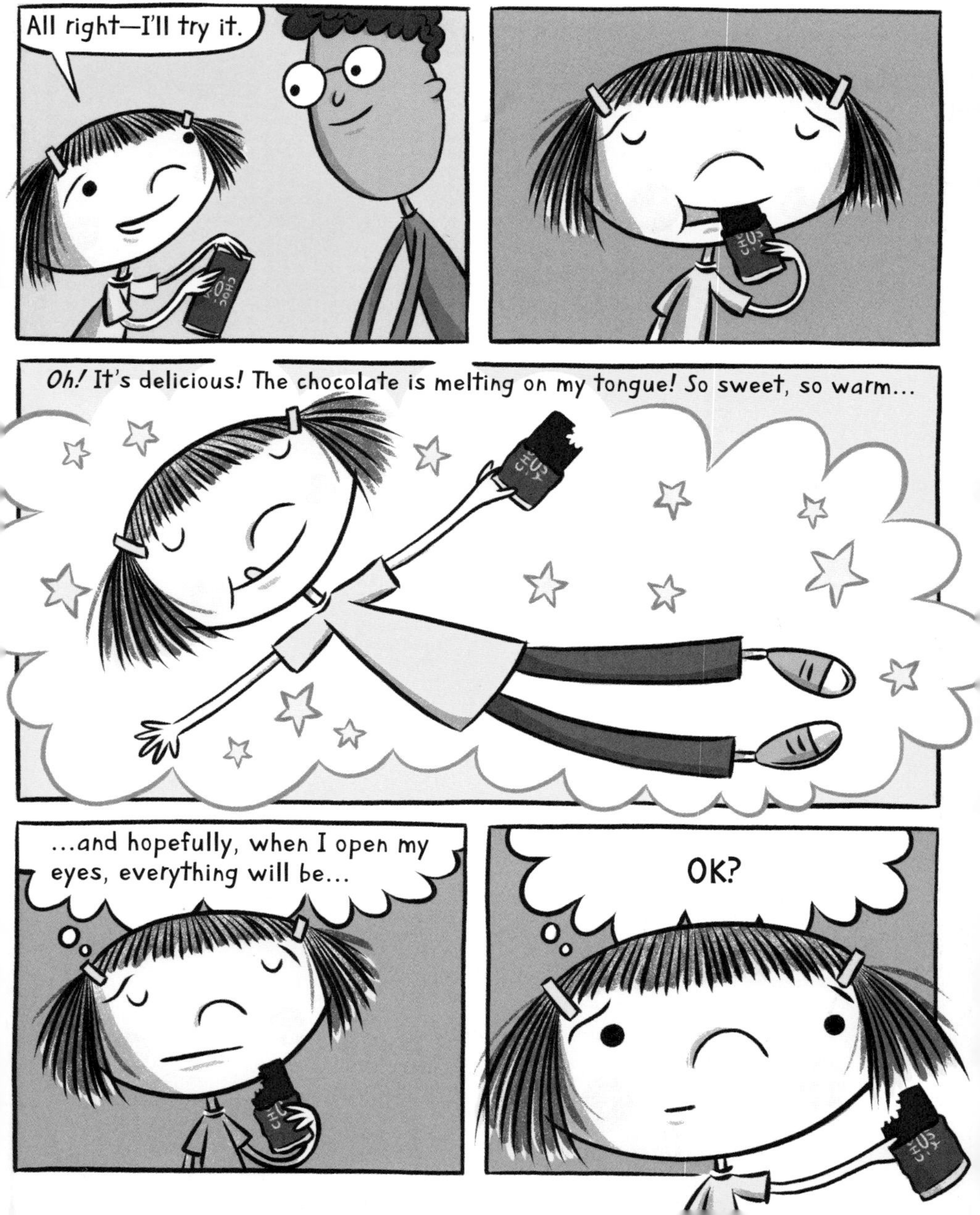
All right—I'll try it.
Oh! It's delicious! The chocolate is melting on my tongue! So sweet, so warm...
...and hopefully, when I open my eyes, everything will be...
OK?

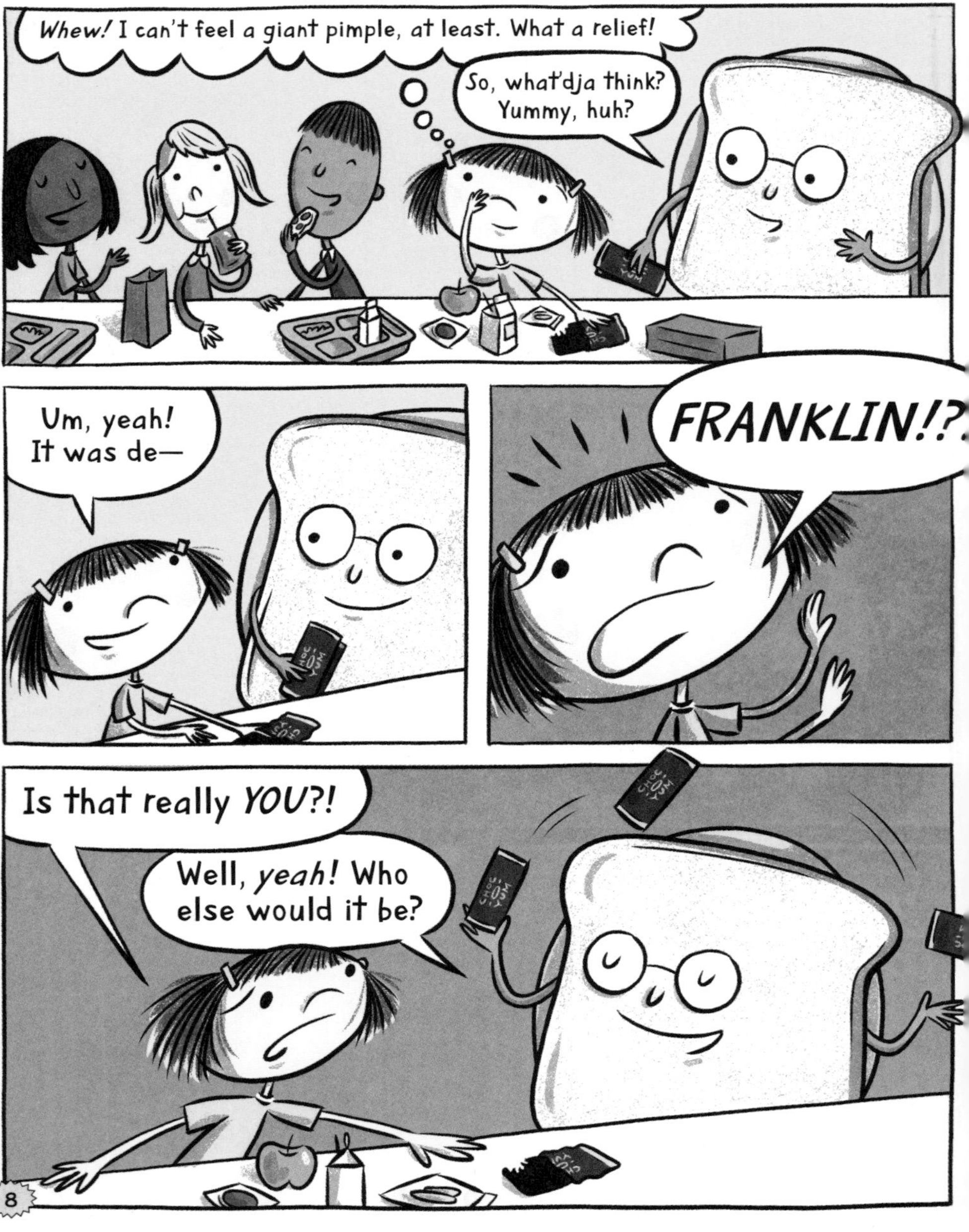
Whew! I can't feel a giant pimple, at least. What a relief!
So, what'dja think? Yummy, huh?
Um, yeah! It was de—
FRANKLIN!?
Is that really YOU?!
Well, yeah! Who else would it be?

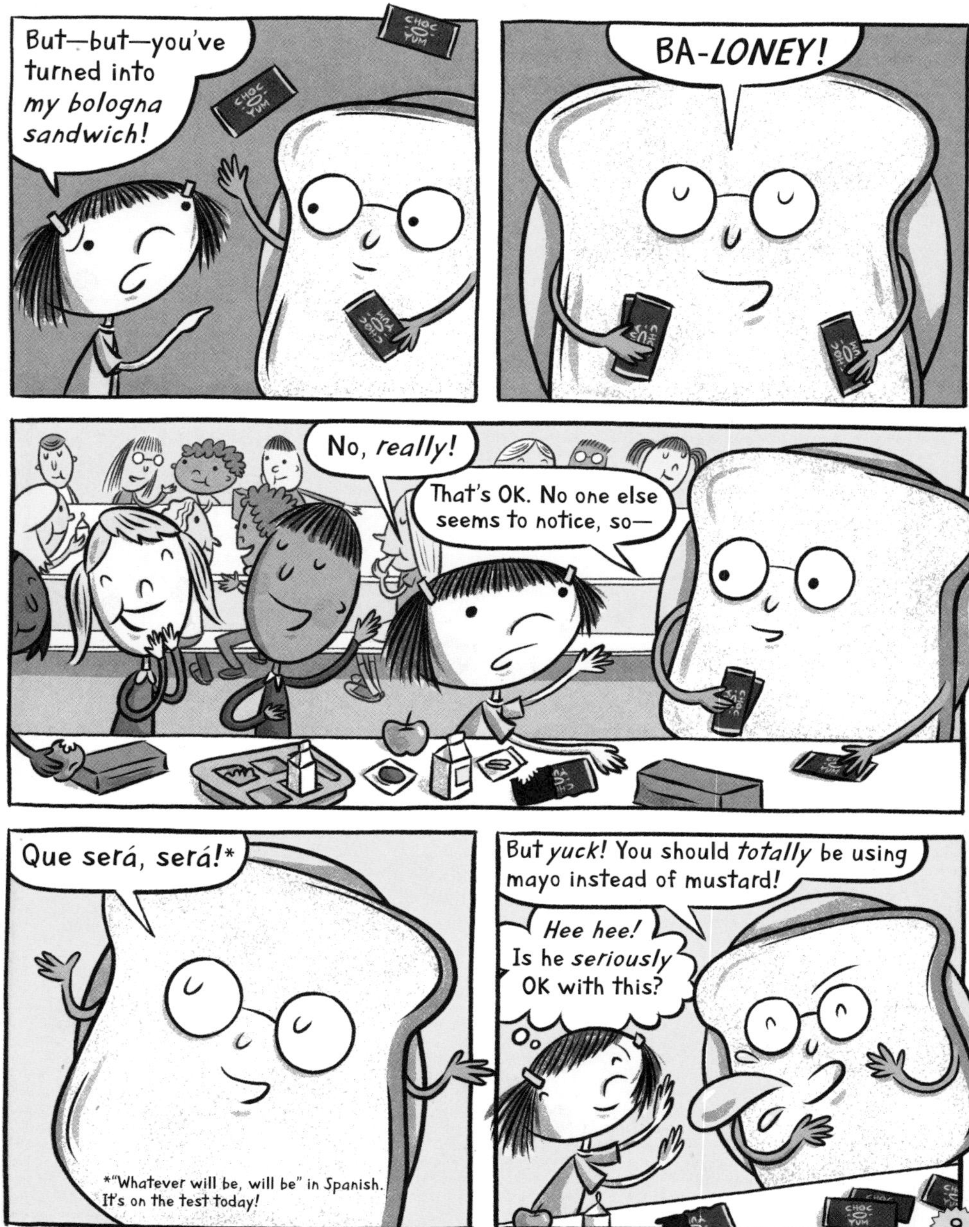
But—but—you've turned into *my bologna sandwich!*
CHOC O YUM
BA-*LONEY!*
No, *really!*
That's OK. No one else seems to notice, so—
Que será, será!*
*"Whatever will be, will be" in Spanish. It's on the test today!
But *yuck!* You should *totally* be using mayo instead of mustard!
Hee hee! Is he *seriously* OK with this?

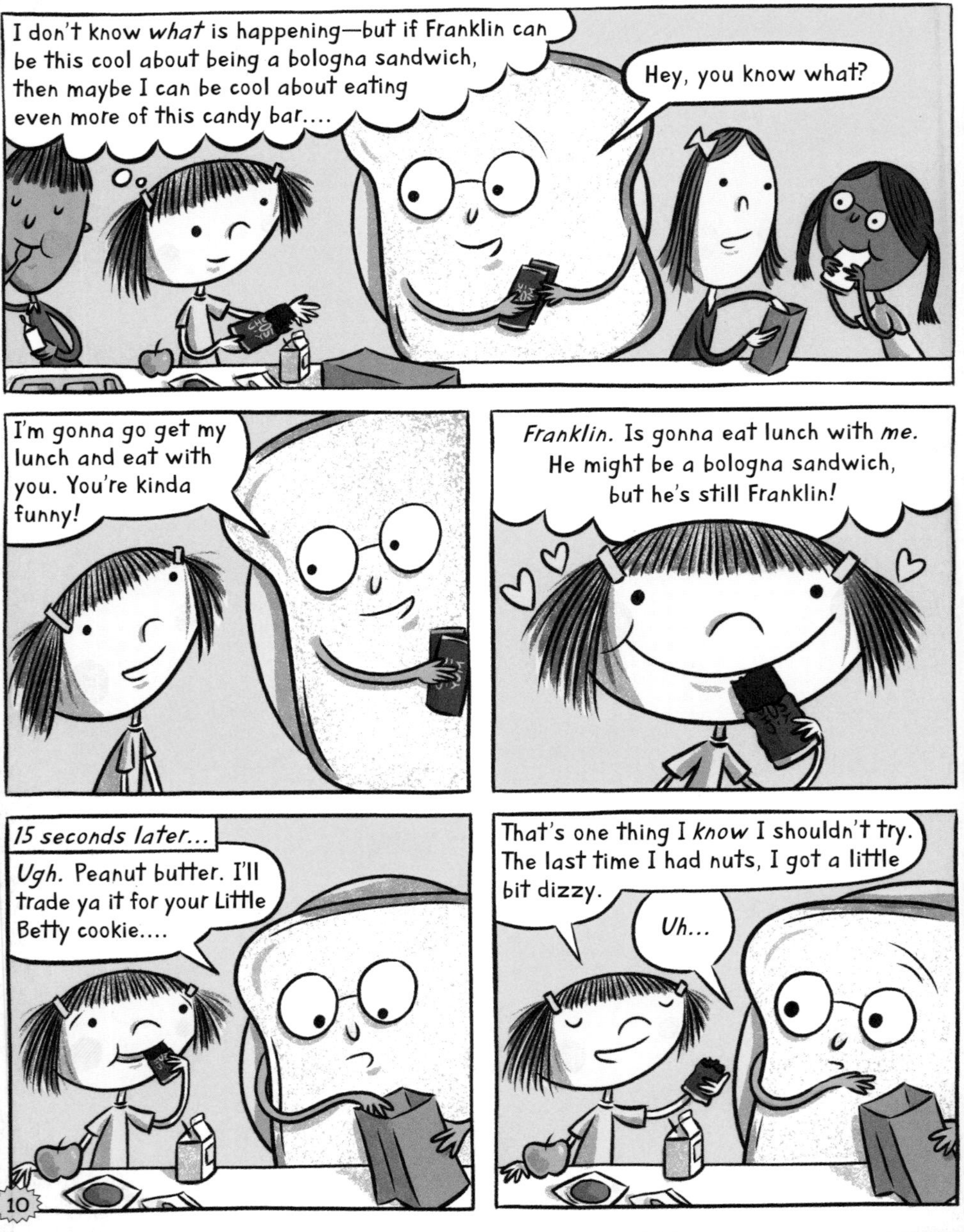
I don't know *what* is happening—but if Franklin can be this cool about being a bologna sandwich, then maybe I can be cool about eating even more of this candy bar....
Hey, you know what?
I'm gonna go get my lunch and eat with you. You're kinda funny!
Franklin. Is gonna eat lunch with *me.* He might be a bologna sandwich, but he's still Franklin!
15 seconds later...
Ugh. Peanut butter. I'll trade ya it for your Little Betty cookie....
That's one thing I *know* I shouldn't try. The last time I had nuts, I got a little bit dizzy.
Uh...

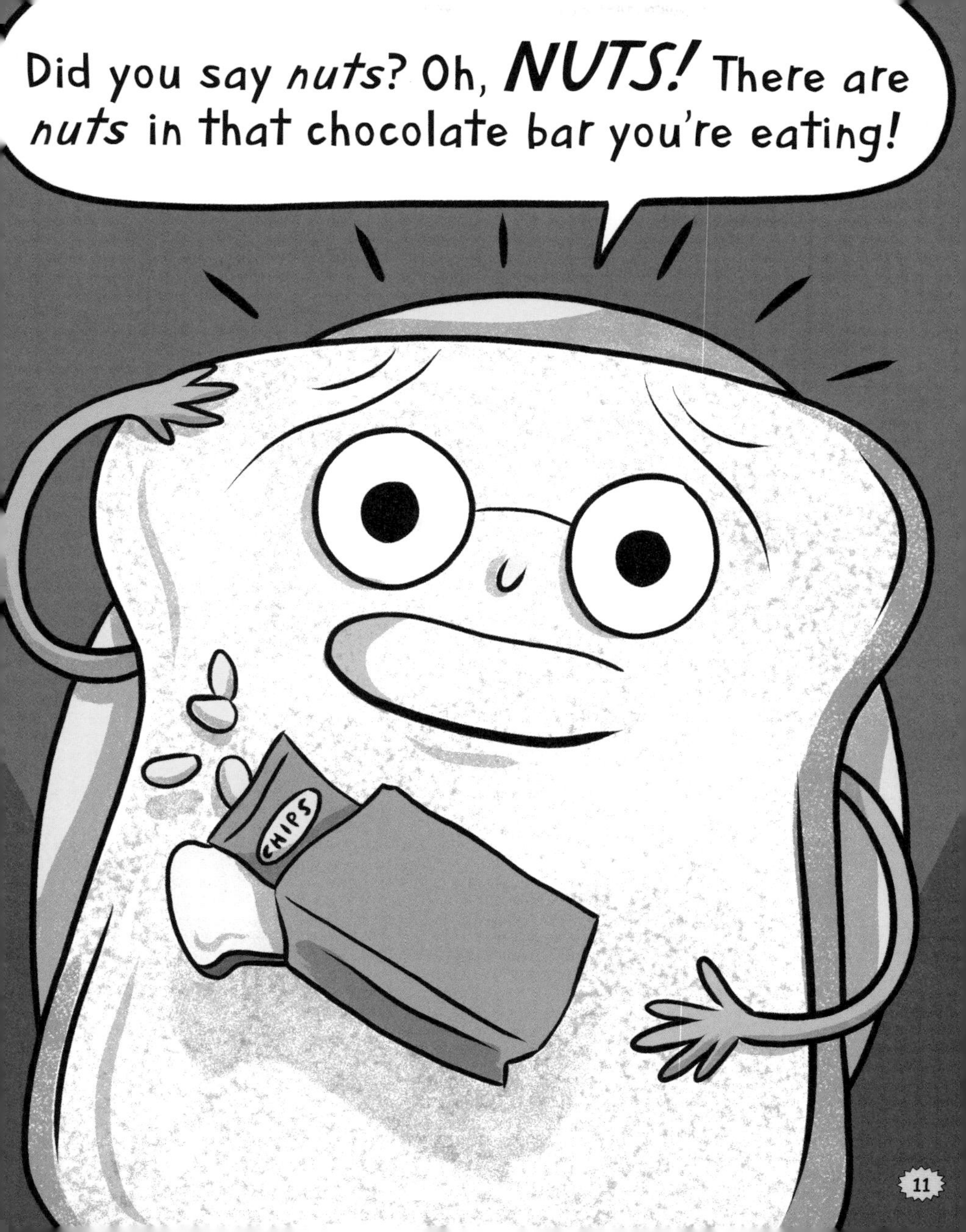
Did you say *nuts*? Oh, ***NUTS!*** There are *nuts* in that chocolate bar you're eating!
CHIPS

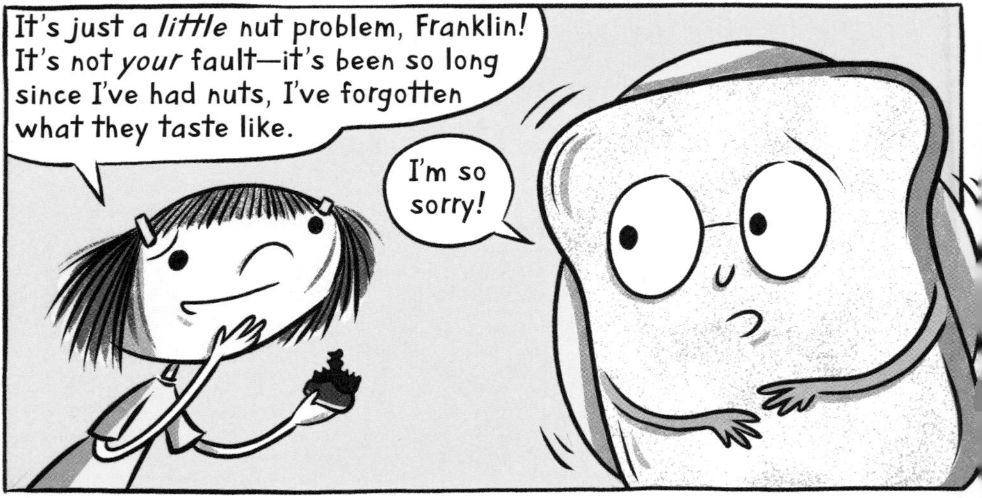
It's just a *little* nut problem, Franklin! It's not *your* fault—it's been so long since I've had nuts, I've forgotten what they taste like.
I'm so sorry!

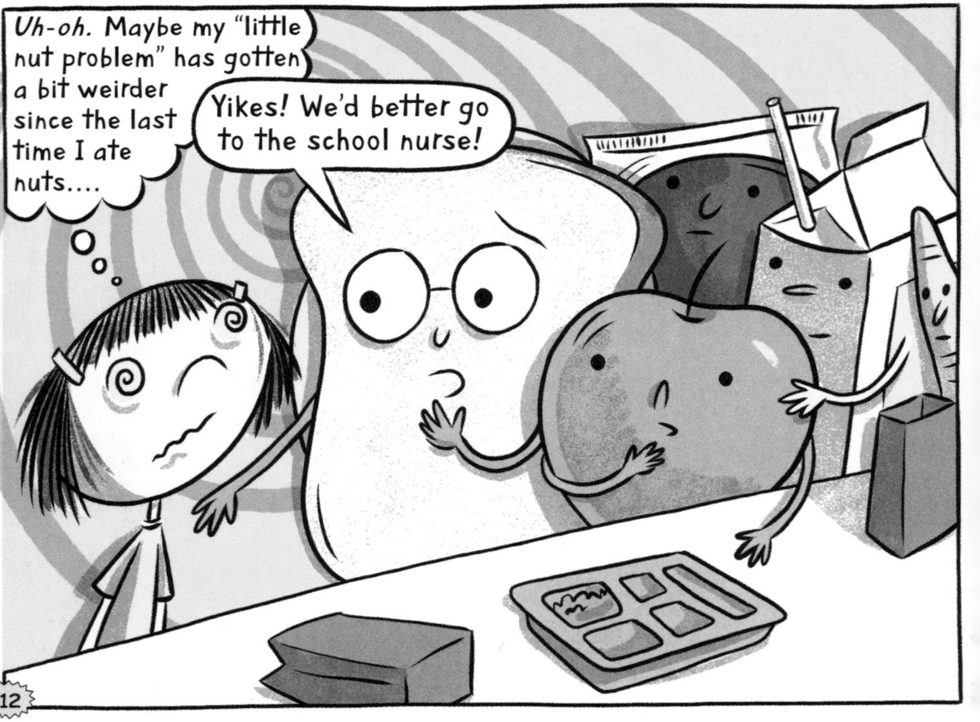
Uh-oh. Maybe my "little nut problem" has gotten a bit weirder since the last time I ate nuts....
Yikes! We'd better go to the school nurse!

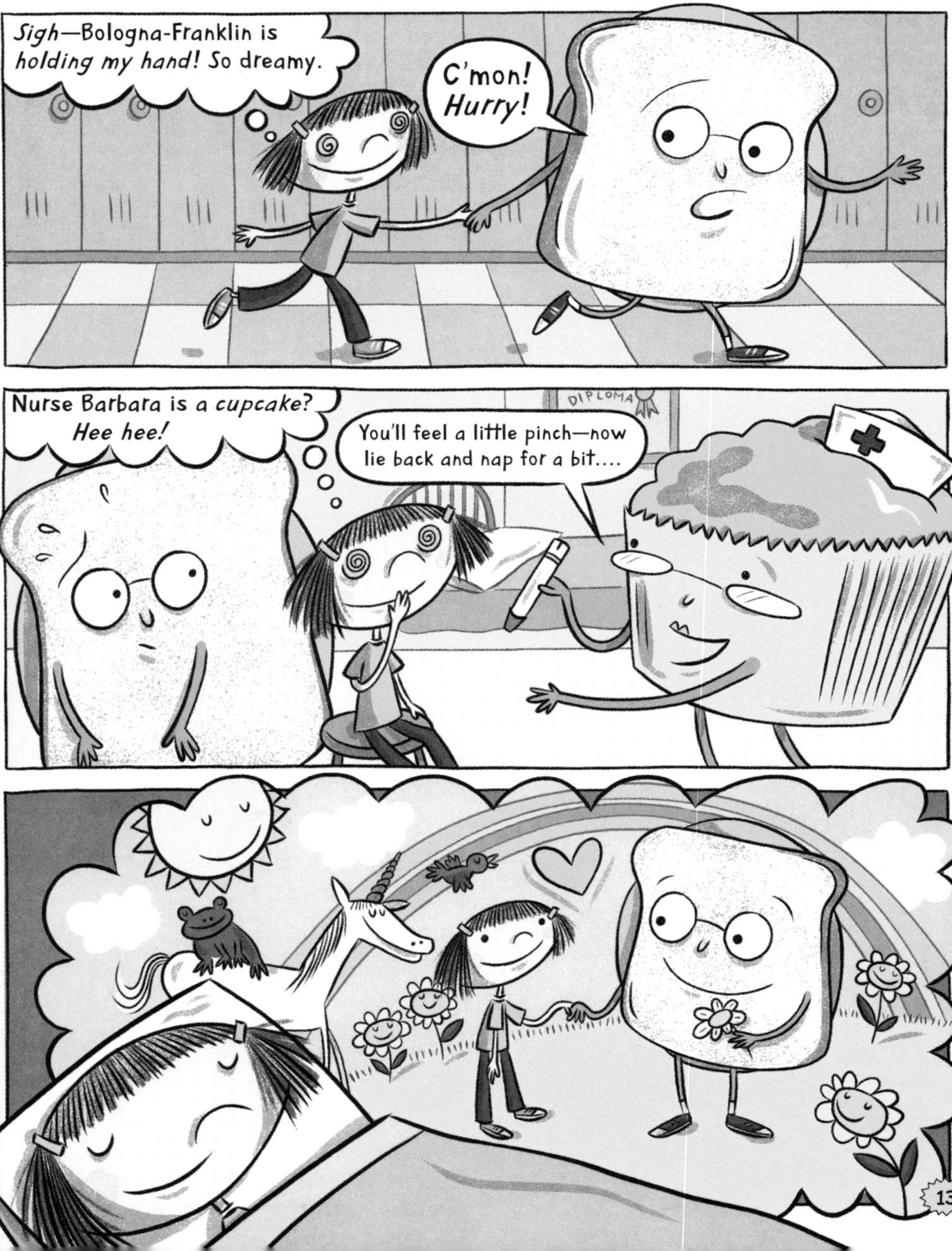
Sigh—Bologna-Franklin is holding my hand! So dreamy.
C'mon! Hurry!
Nurse Barbara is a cupcake? Hee hee!
DIPLOMA
You'll feel a little pinch—now lie back and nap for a bit....

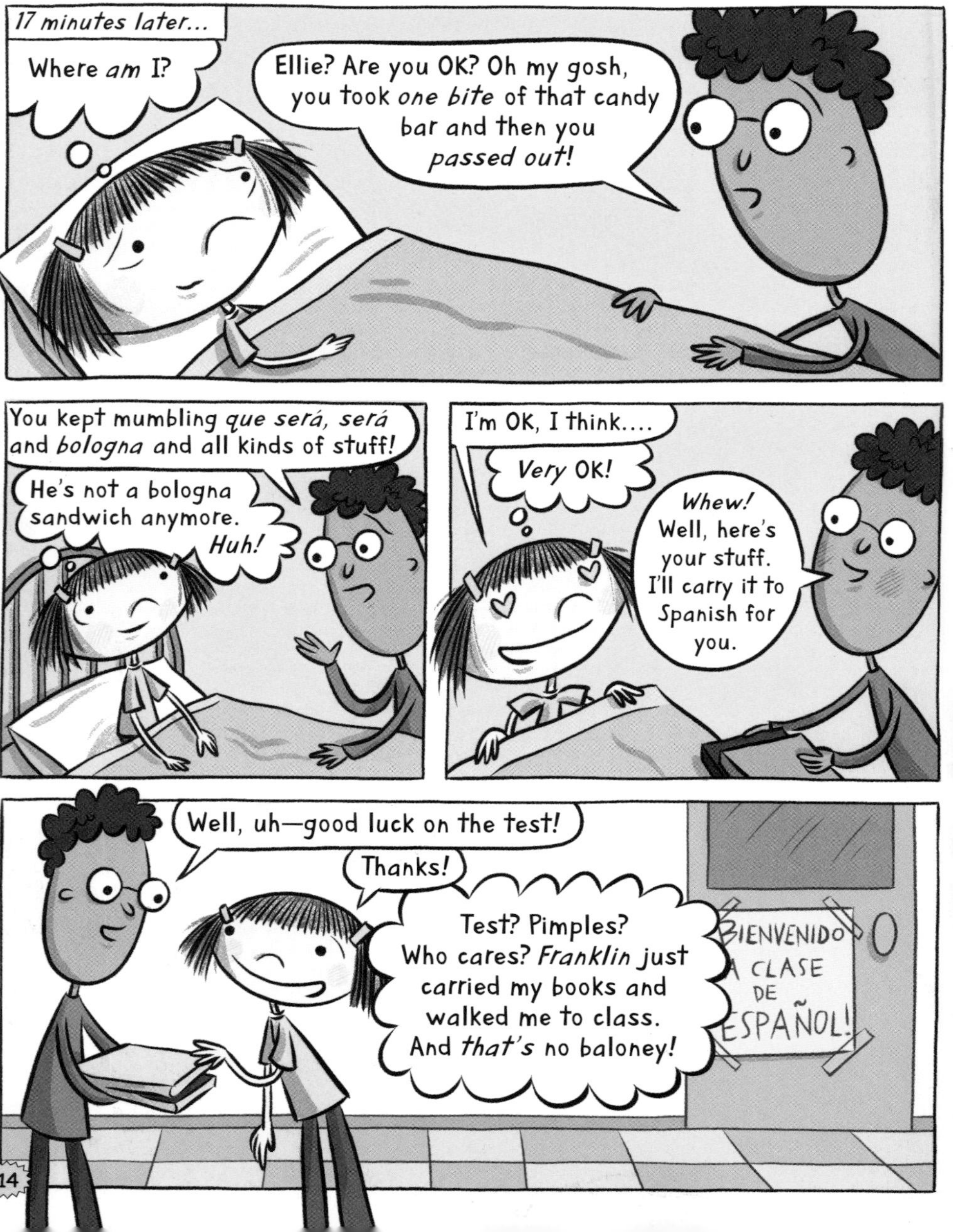

17 minutes later...
Where *am* I?
Ellie? Are you OK? Oh my gosh, you took *one bite* of that candy bar and then you *passed out*!
You kept mumbling *que será, será* and *bologna* and all kinds of stuff!
He's not a bologna sandwich anymore. *Huh!*
I'm OK, I think....
Very OK!
Whew! Well, here's your stuff. I'll carry it to Spanish for you.
Well, uh—good luck on the test!
Thanks!
Test? Pimples? Who cares? *Franklin* just carried my books and walked me to class. And *that's* no baloney!
BIENVENIDO A CLASE DE ESPAÑOL!

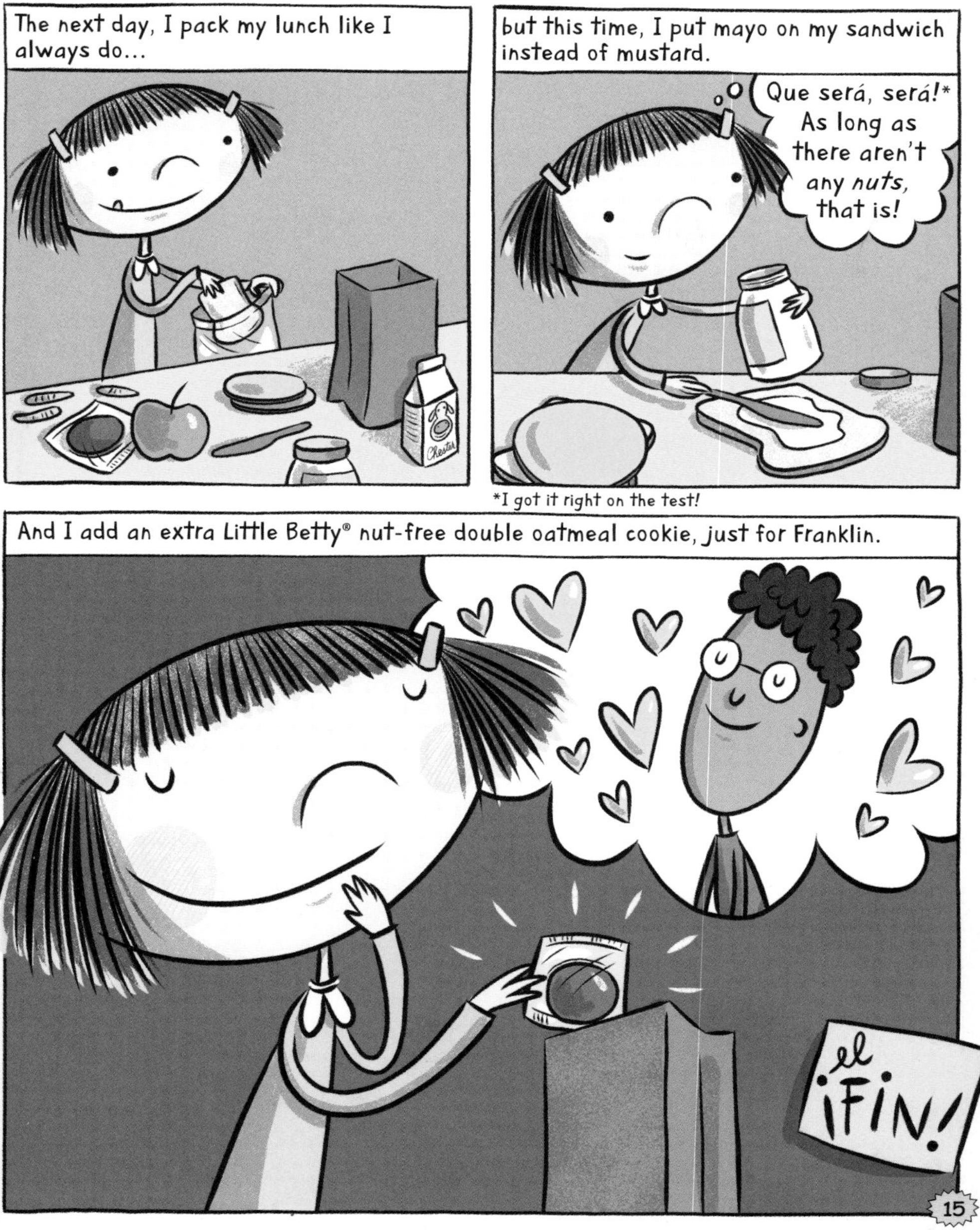
The next day, I pack my lunch like I always do...
Chester
but this time, I put mayo on my sandwich instead of mustard.
Que será, será!* As long as there aren't any *nuts*, that is!
*I got it right on the test!
And I add an extra Little Betty® nut-free double oatmeal cookie, just for Franklin.
el ¡FIN!

MASH-UP MADNESS!

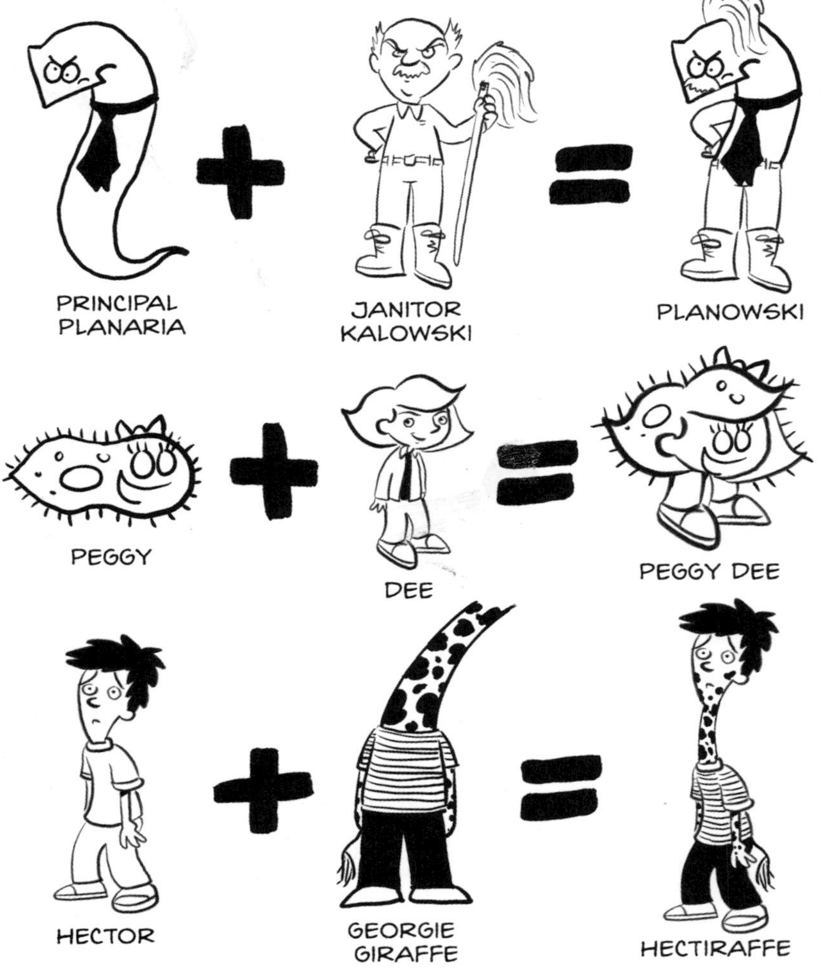
PRINCIPAL PLANARIA
JANITOR KALOWSKI
PLANOWSKI
PEGGY
DEE
PEGGY DEE
HECTOR
GEORGIE GIRAFFE
HECTIRAFFE

NOW GO TRY DRAWING YOUR OWN MASH-UPS!

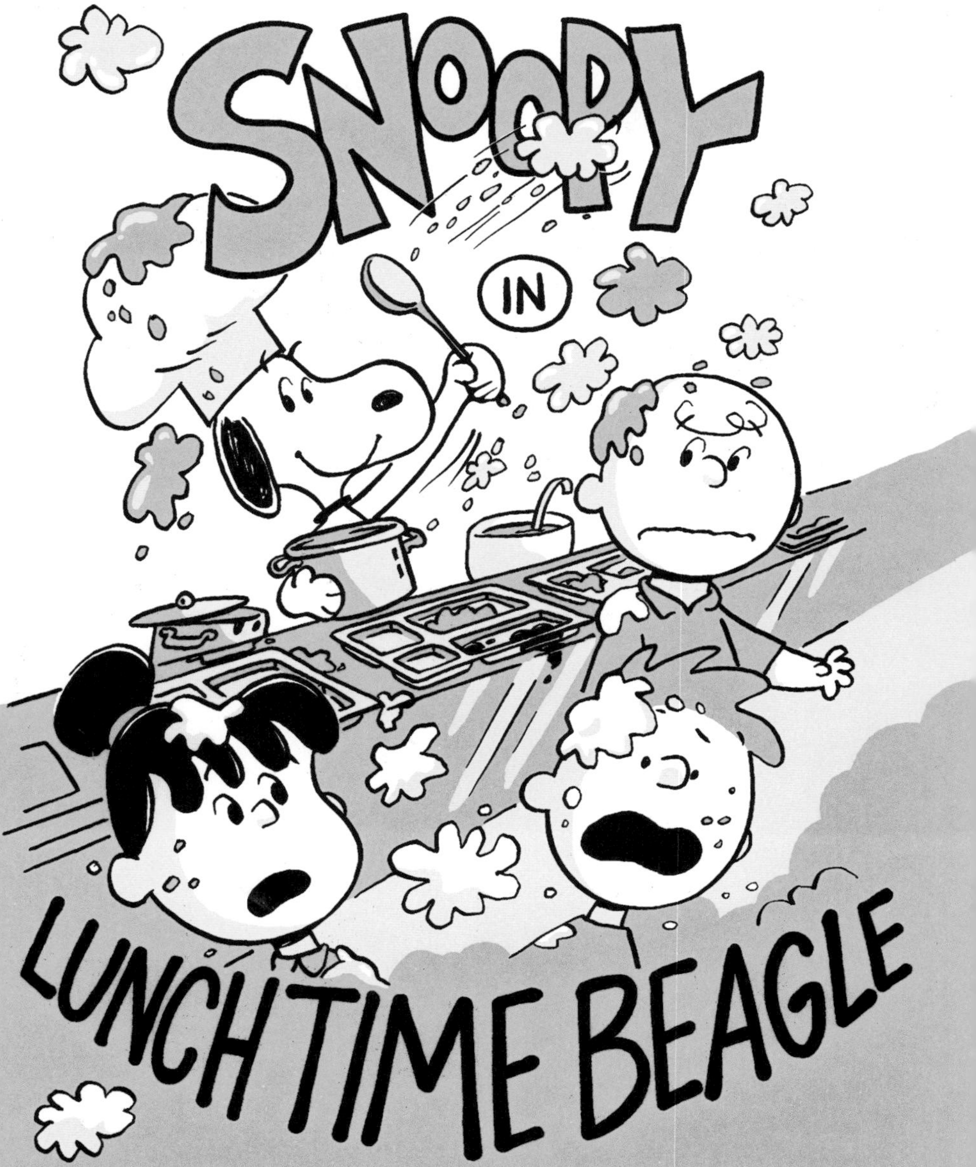
SNOOPY
IN
LUNCH TIME BEAGLE

PEANUTS CREATED BY CHARLES M. SCHULZ

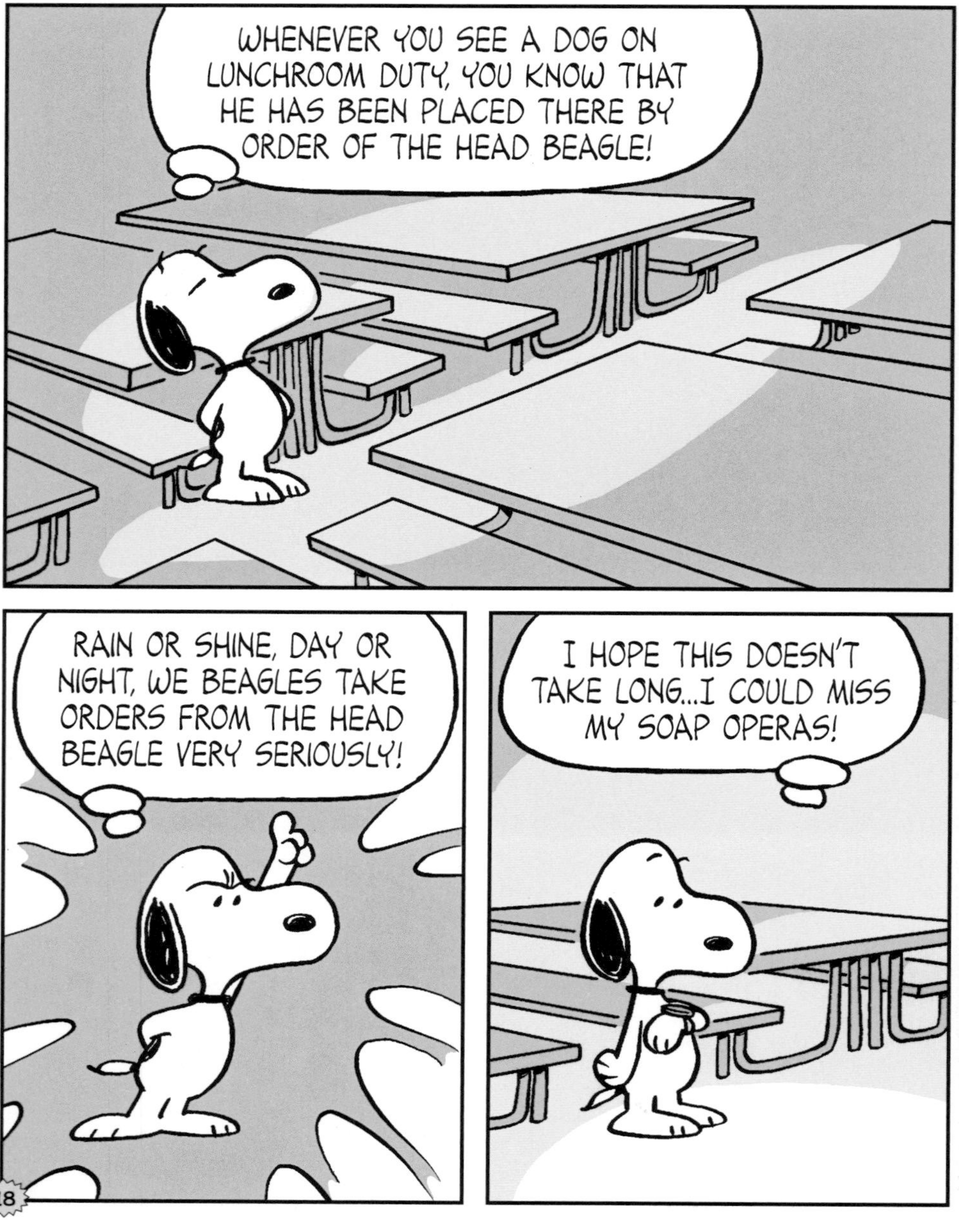
WHENEVER YOU SEE A DOG ON LUNCHROOM DUTY, YOU KNOW THAT HE HAS BEEN PLACED THERE BY ORDER OF THE HEAD BEAGLE!
RAIN OR SHINE, DAY OR NIGHT, WE BEAGLES TAKE ORDERS FROM THE HEAD BEAGLE VERY SERIOUSLY!
I HOPE THIS DOESN'T TAKE LONG...I COULD MISS MY SOAP OPERAS!

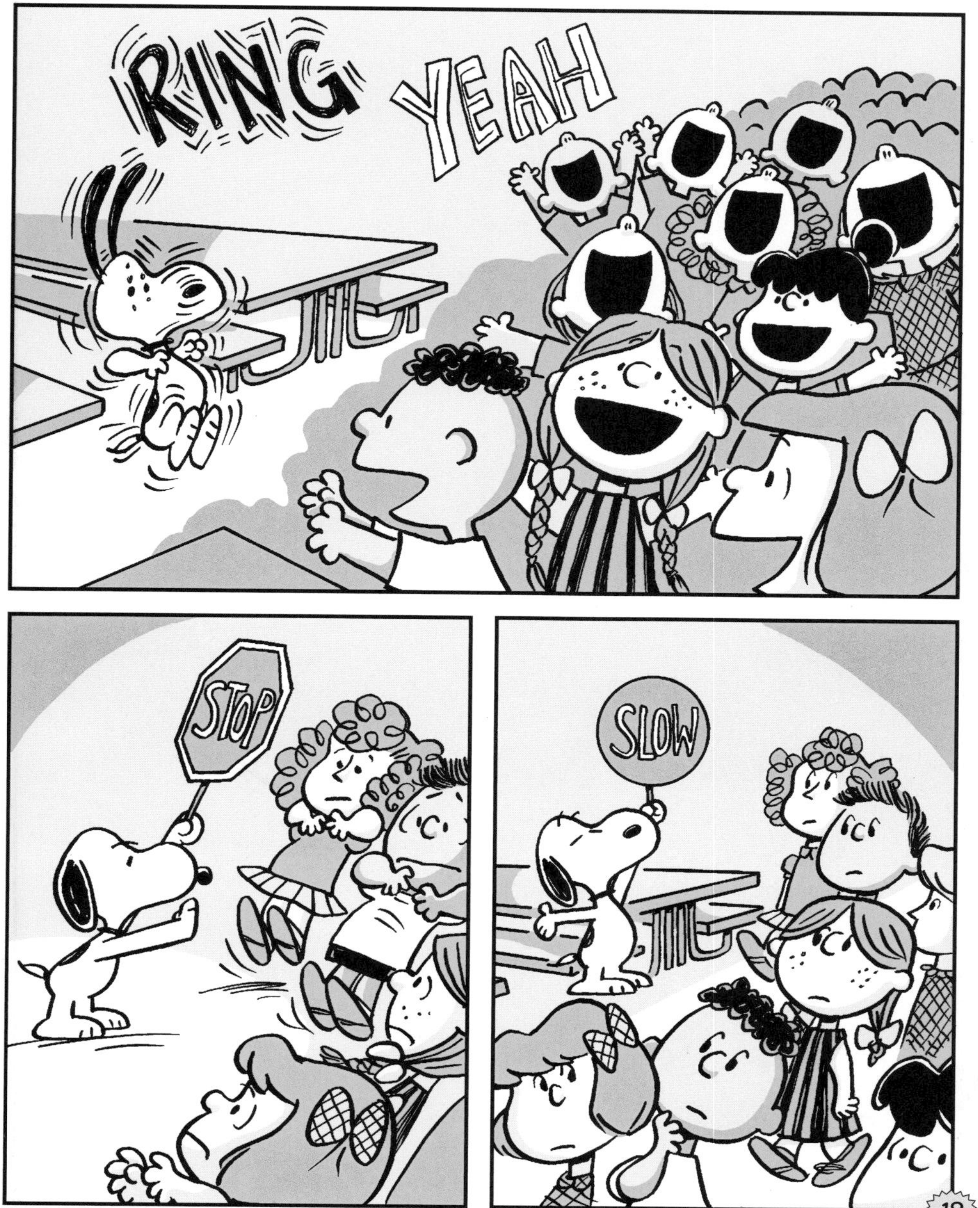
RING
YEAH
STOP
SLOW

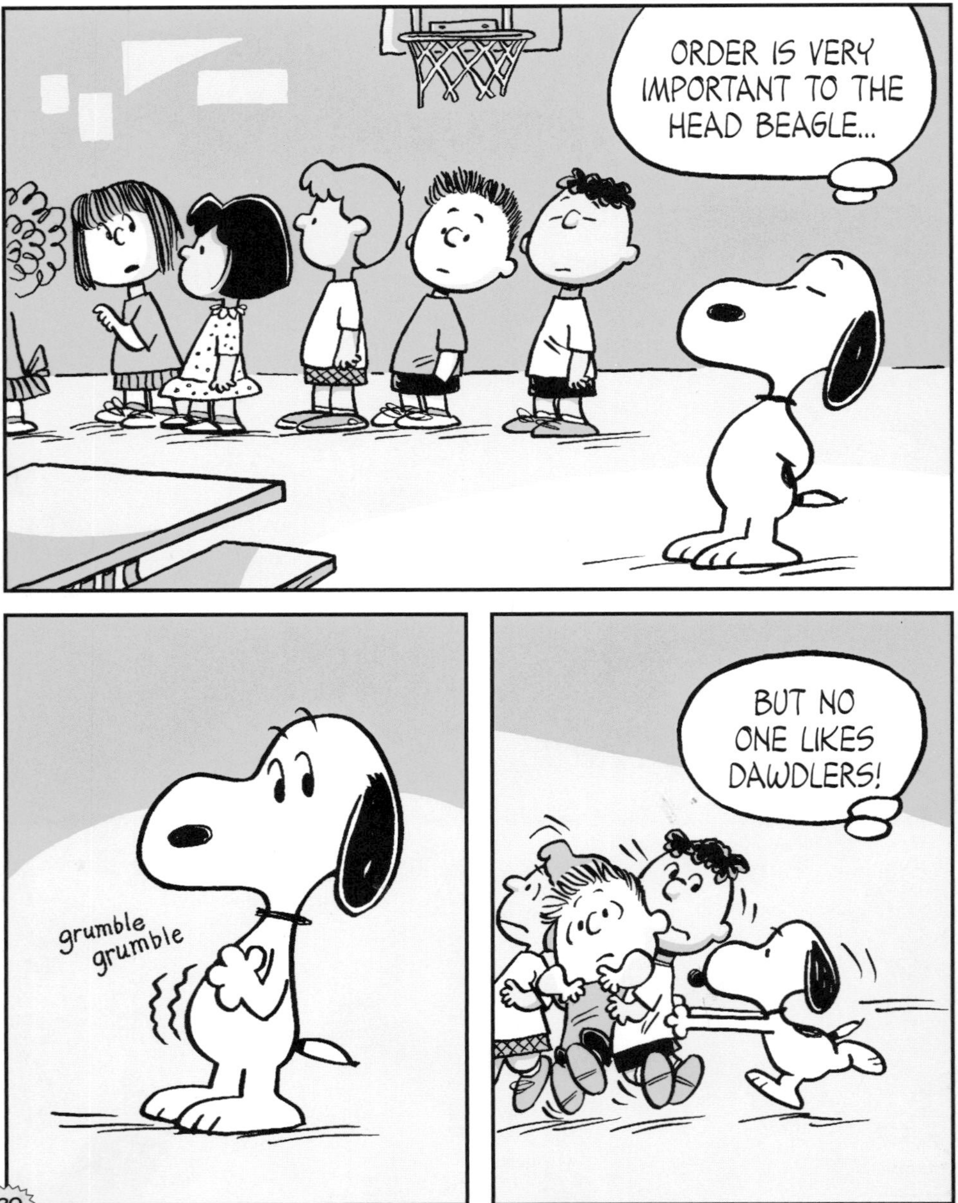
ORDER IS VERY IMPORTANT TO THE HEAD BEAGLE...
grumble grumble
BUT NO ONE LIKES DAWDLERS!

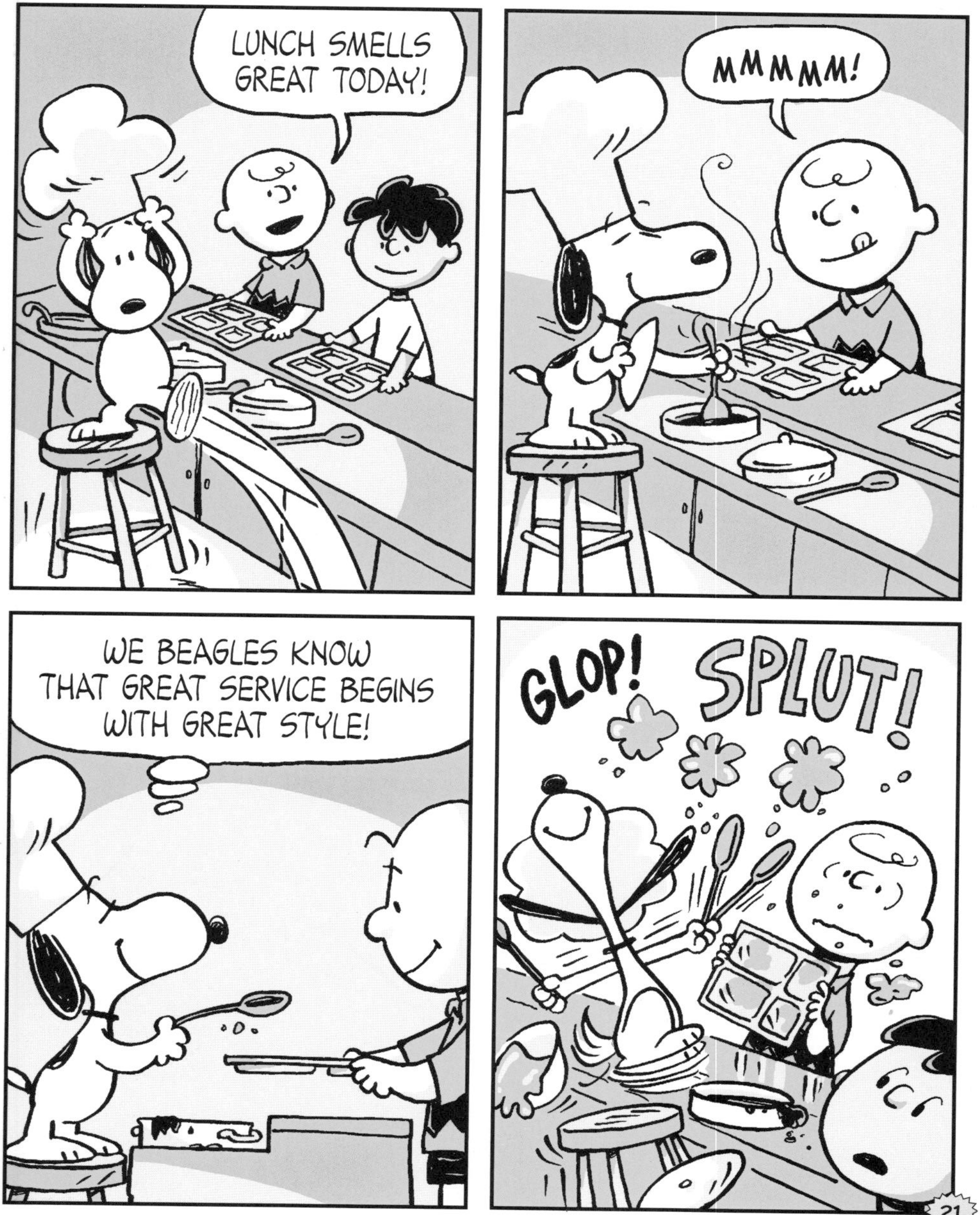
LUNCH SMELLS GREAT TODAY!
MMMMM!
WE BEAGLES KNOW THAT GREAT SERVICE BEGINS WITH GREAT STYLE!
GLOP!
SPLUT!

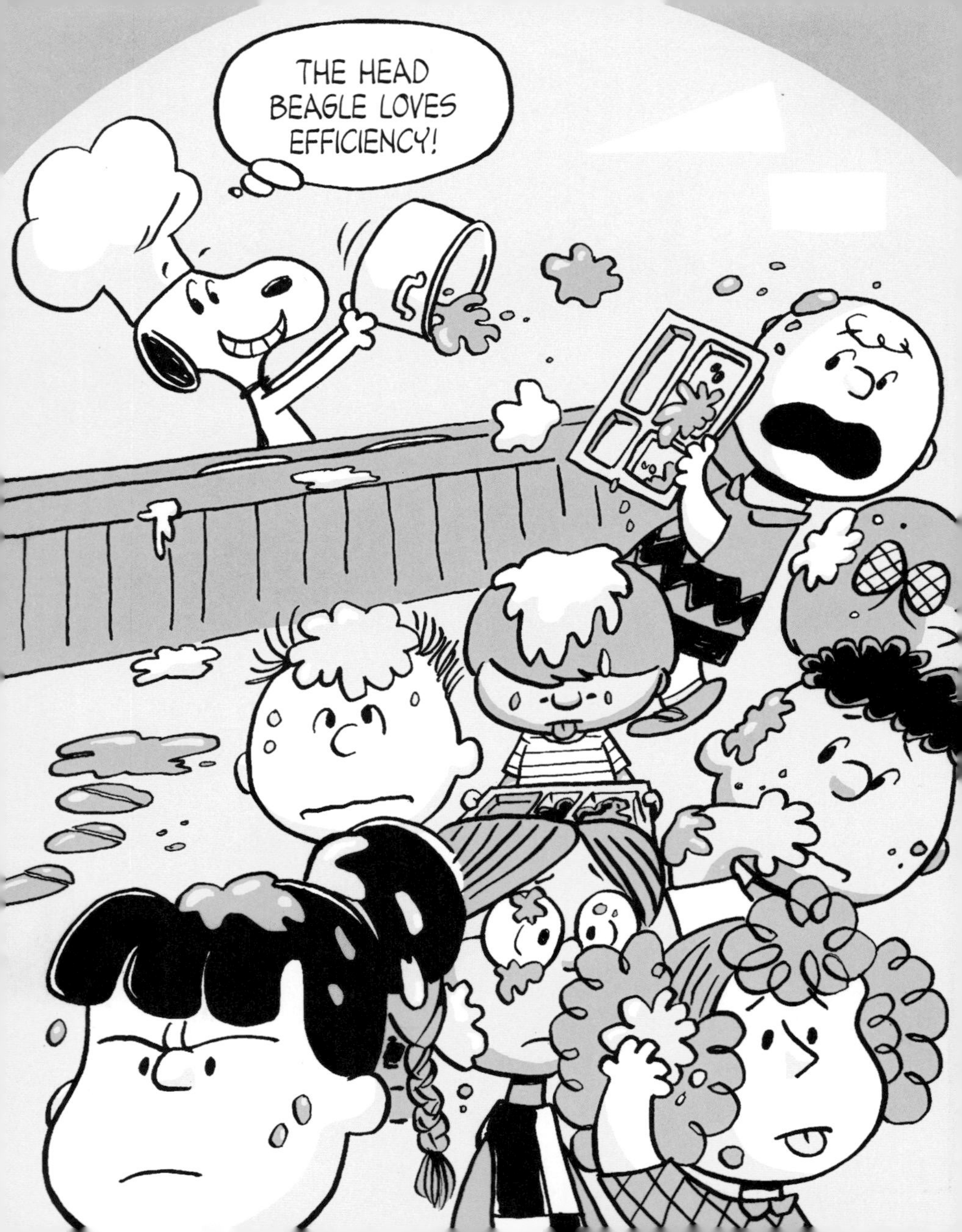
THE HEAD BEAGLE LOVES EFFICIENCY!

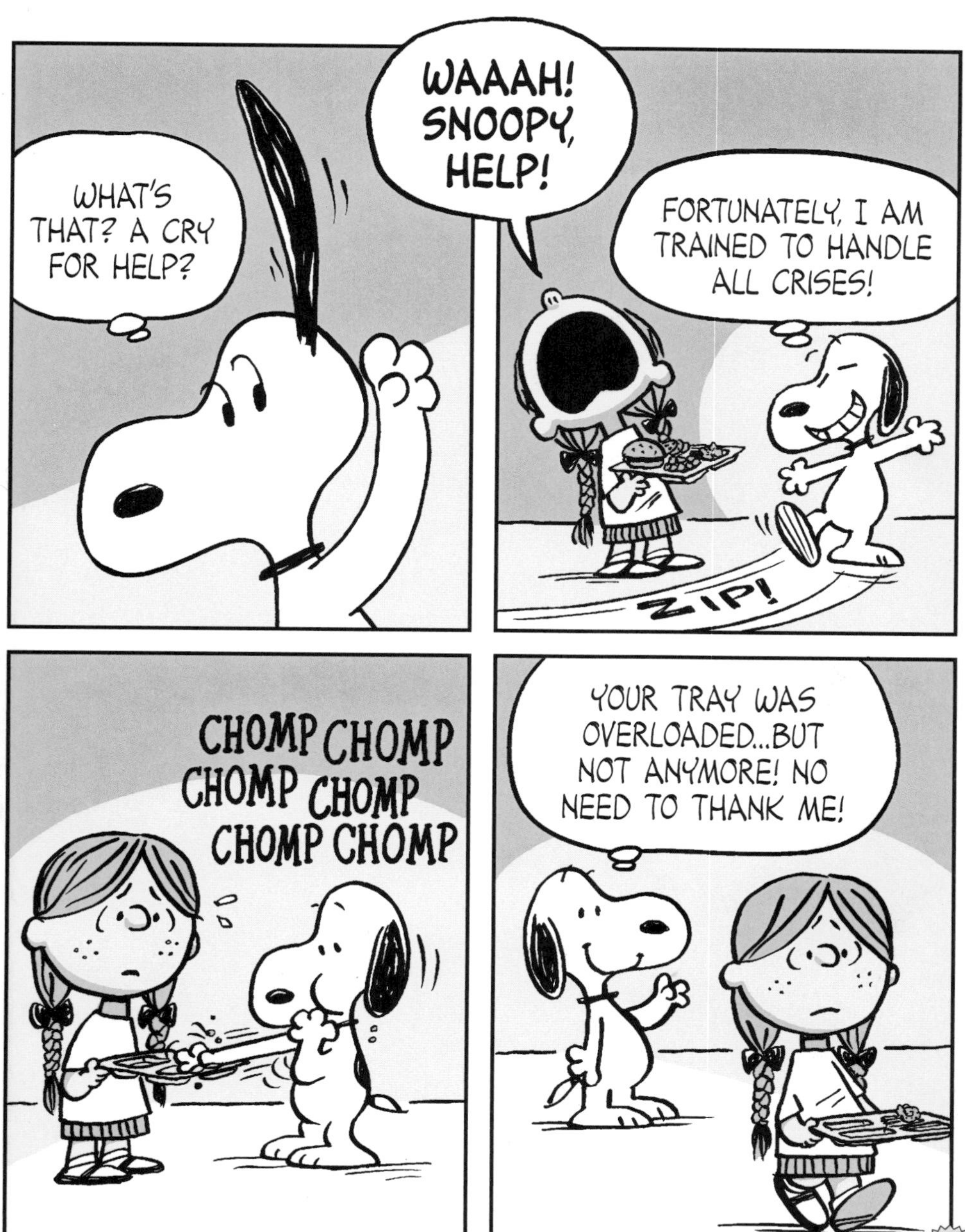
WHAT'S THAT? A CRY FOR HELP?
WAAAH! SNOOPY, HELP!
FORTUNATELY, I AM TRAINED TO HANDLE ALL CRISES!
ZIP!
CHOMP CHOMP CHOMP CHOMP CHOMP CHOMP
YOUR TRAY WAS OVERLOADED...BUT NOT ANYMORE! NO NEED TO THANK ME!

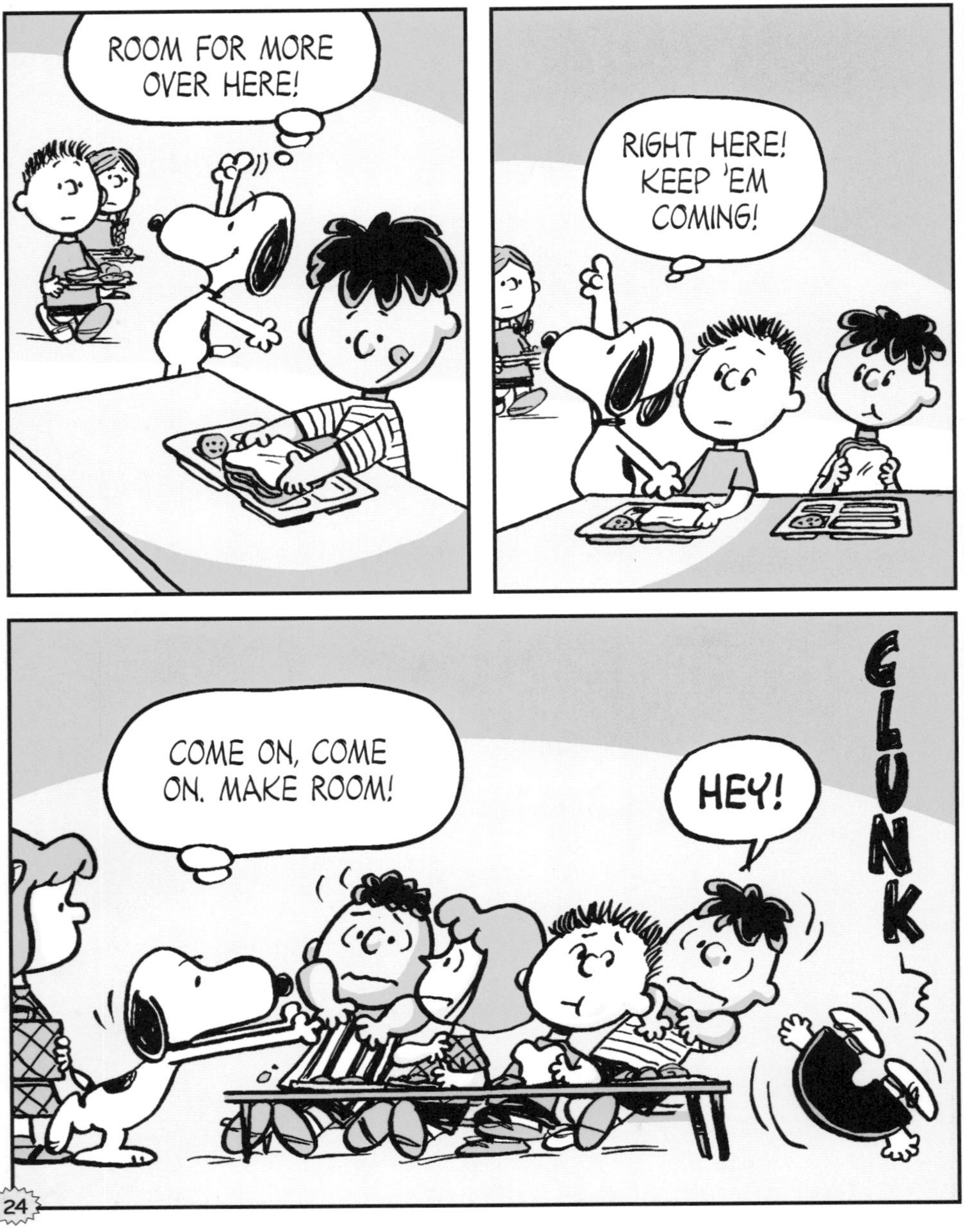
ROOM FOR MORE OVER HERE!
RIGHT HERE! KEEP 'EM COMING!
COME ON, COME ON. MAKE ROOM!
HEY!
CLUNK

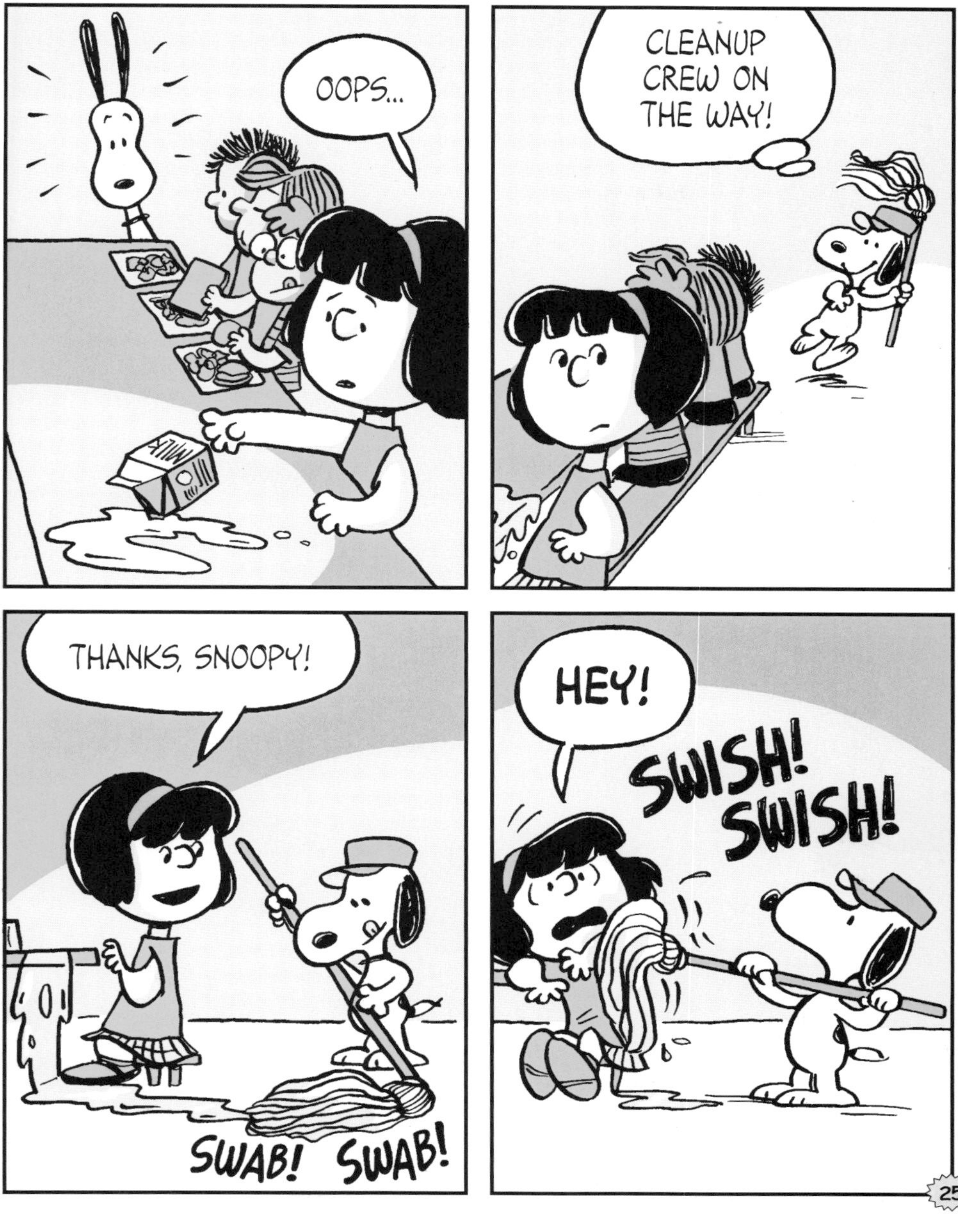
OOPS...
MILK
CLEANUP CREW ON THE WAY!
THANKS, SNOOPY!
SWAB! SWAB!
HEY!
SWISH! SWISH!

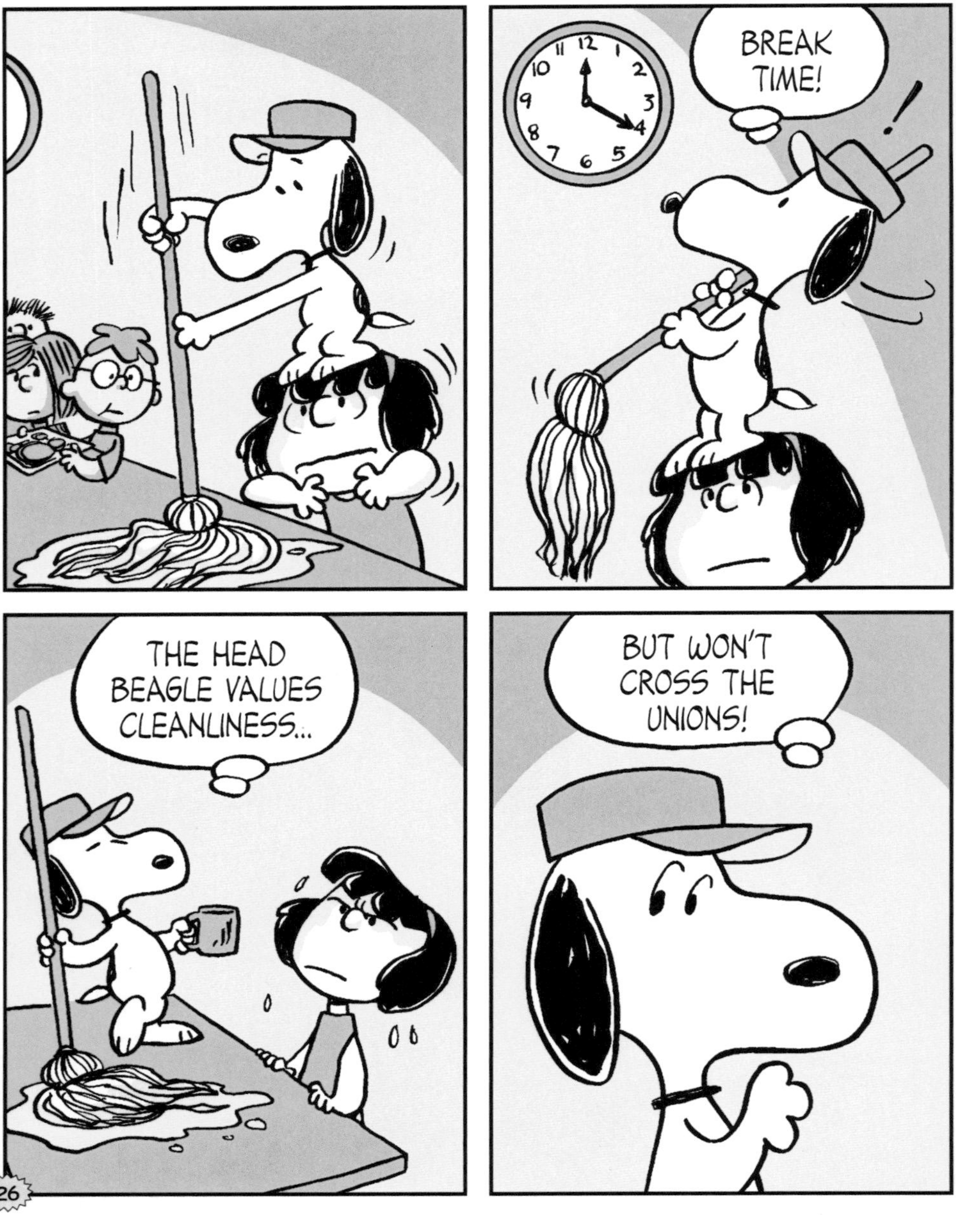
BREAK TIME!
!
THE HEAD BEAGLE VALUES CLEANLINESS...
BUT WON'T CROSS THE UNIONS!

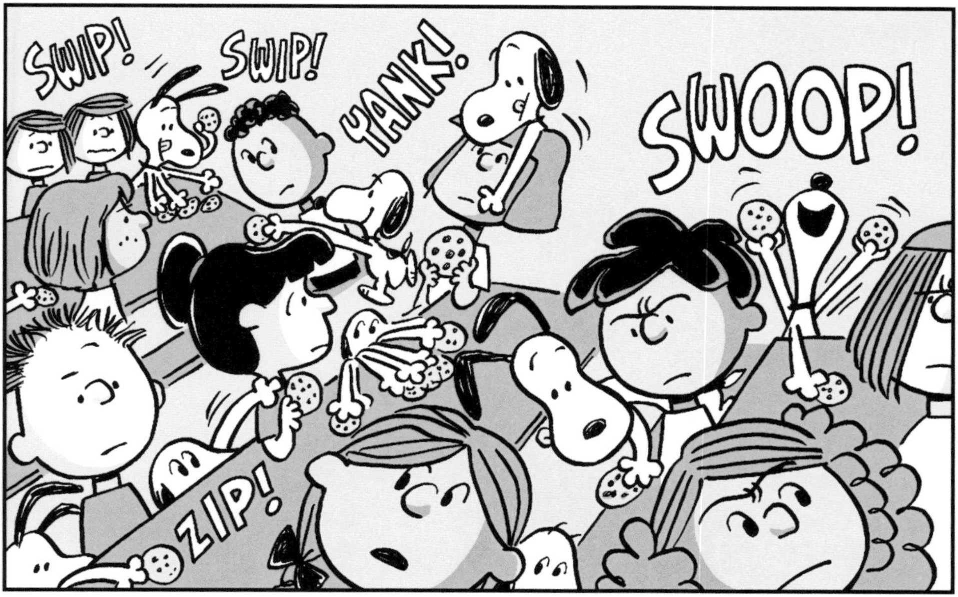
SWIP!
SWIP!
YANK!
SWOOP!
ZIP!

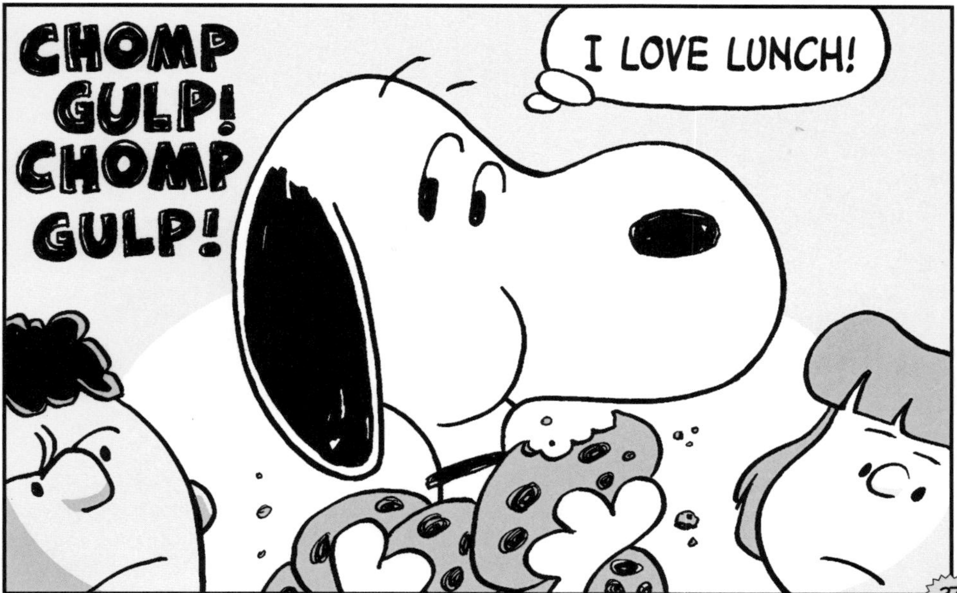
CHOMP
GULP!
CHOMP
GULP!
I LOVE LUNCH!

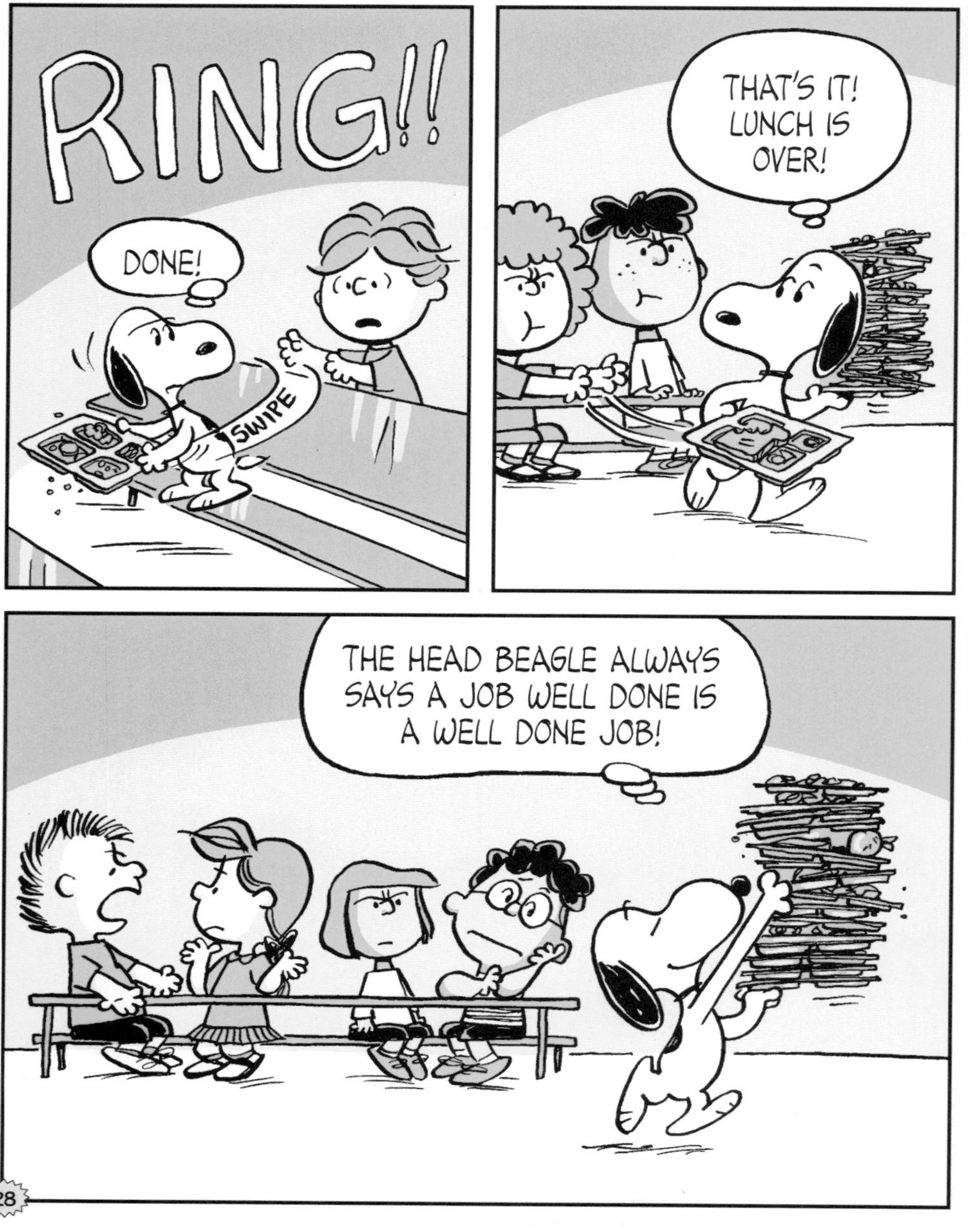
RING!!
DONE!
SWIPE
THAT'S IT! LUNCH IS OVER!
THE HEAD BEAGLE ALWAYS SAYS A JOB WELL DONE IS A WELL DONE JOB!

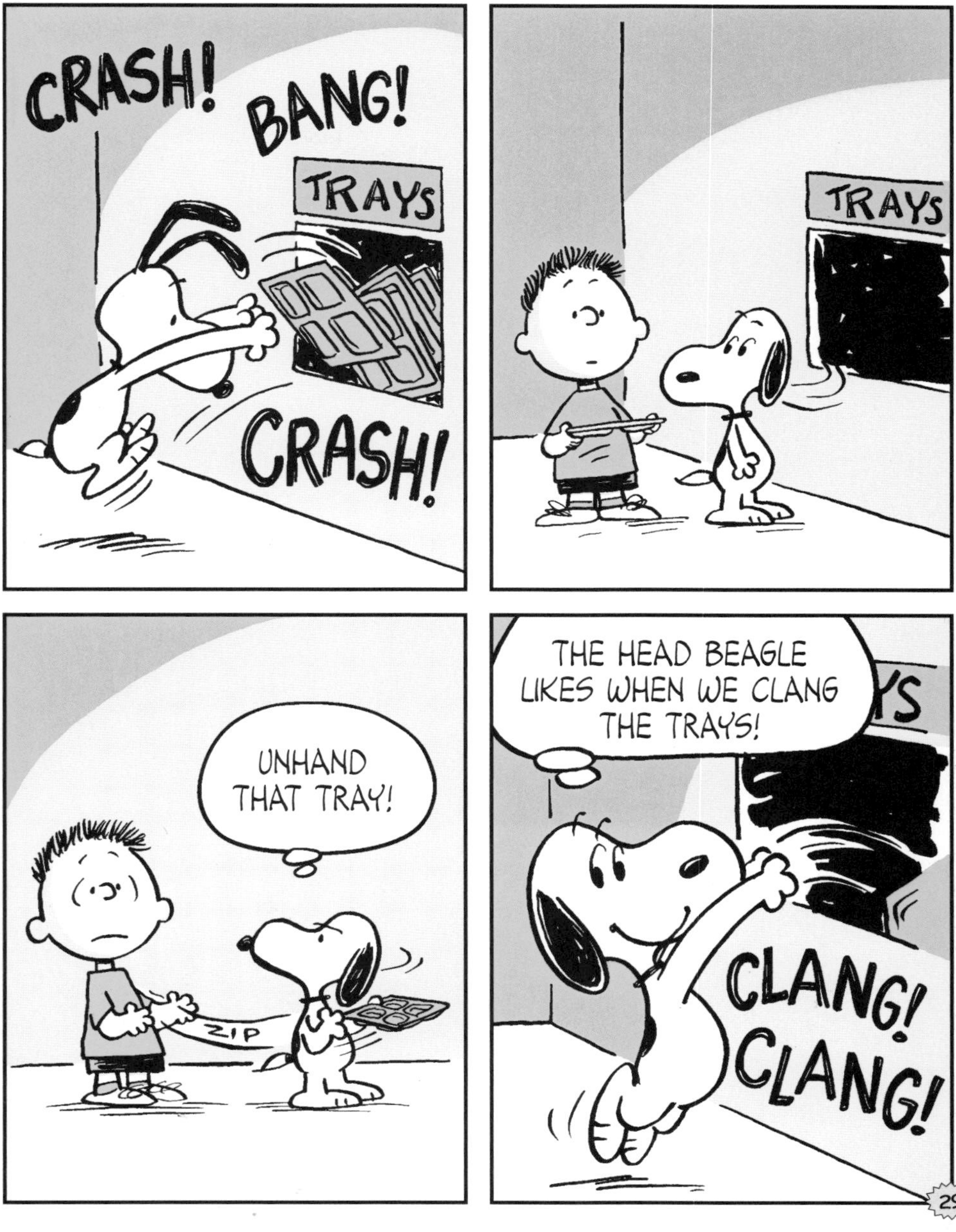
CRASH!
BANG!
TRAYS
CRASH!
TRAYS
UNHAND THAT TRAY!
ZIP
THE HEAD BEAGLE LIKES WHEN WE CLANG THE TRAYS!
CLANG! CLANG!

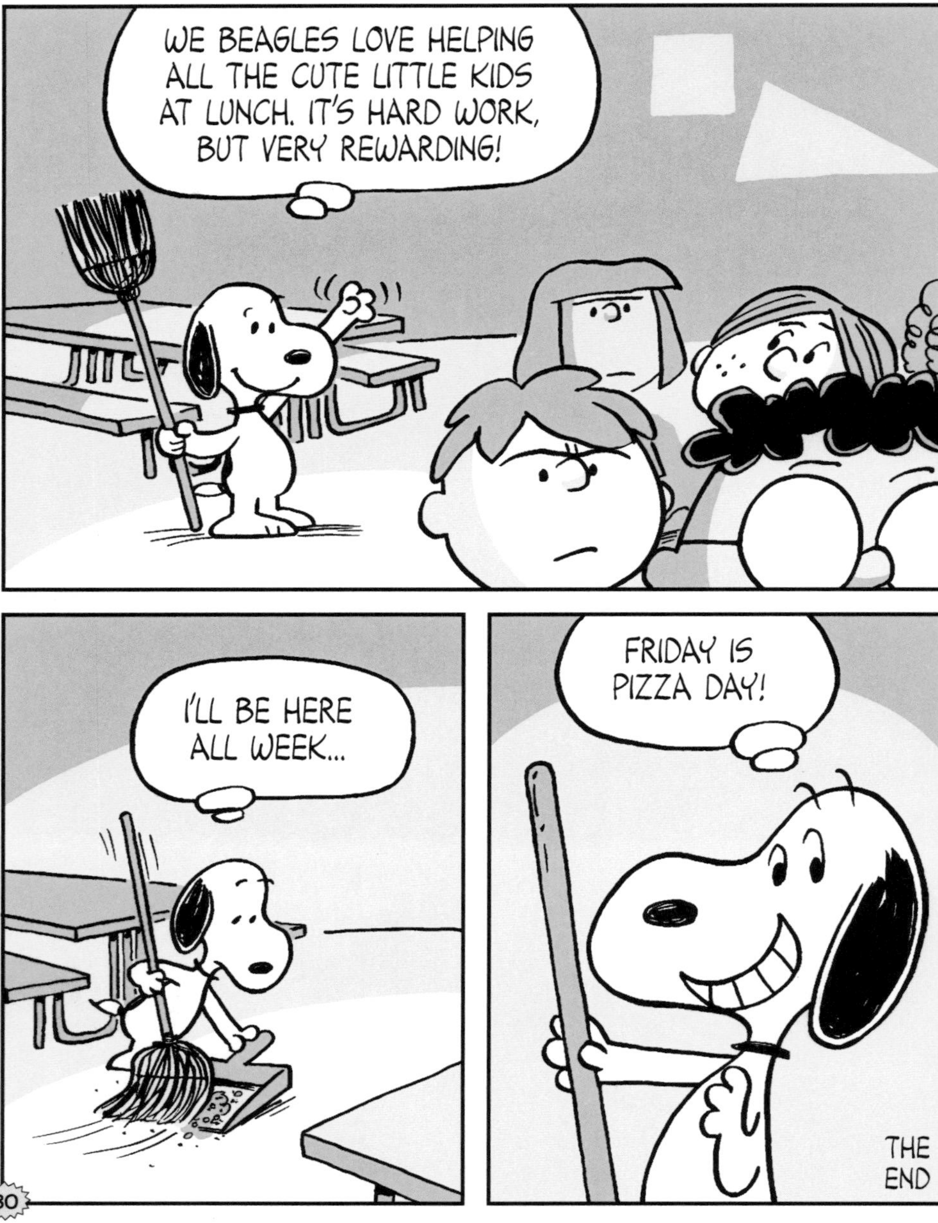
WE BEAGLES LOVE HELPING ALL THE CUTE LITTLE KIDS AT LUNCH. IT'S HARD WORK, BUT VERY REWARDING!
I'LL BE HERE ALL WEEK...
FRIDAY IS PIZZA DAY!
THE END

BABYMOUSE

LUNCH TABLE CHAMPION

BY JENNIFER L. HOLM & MATTHEW HOLM

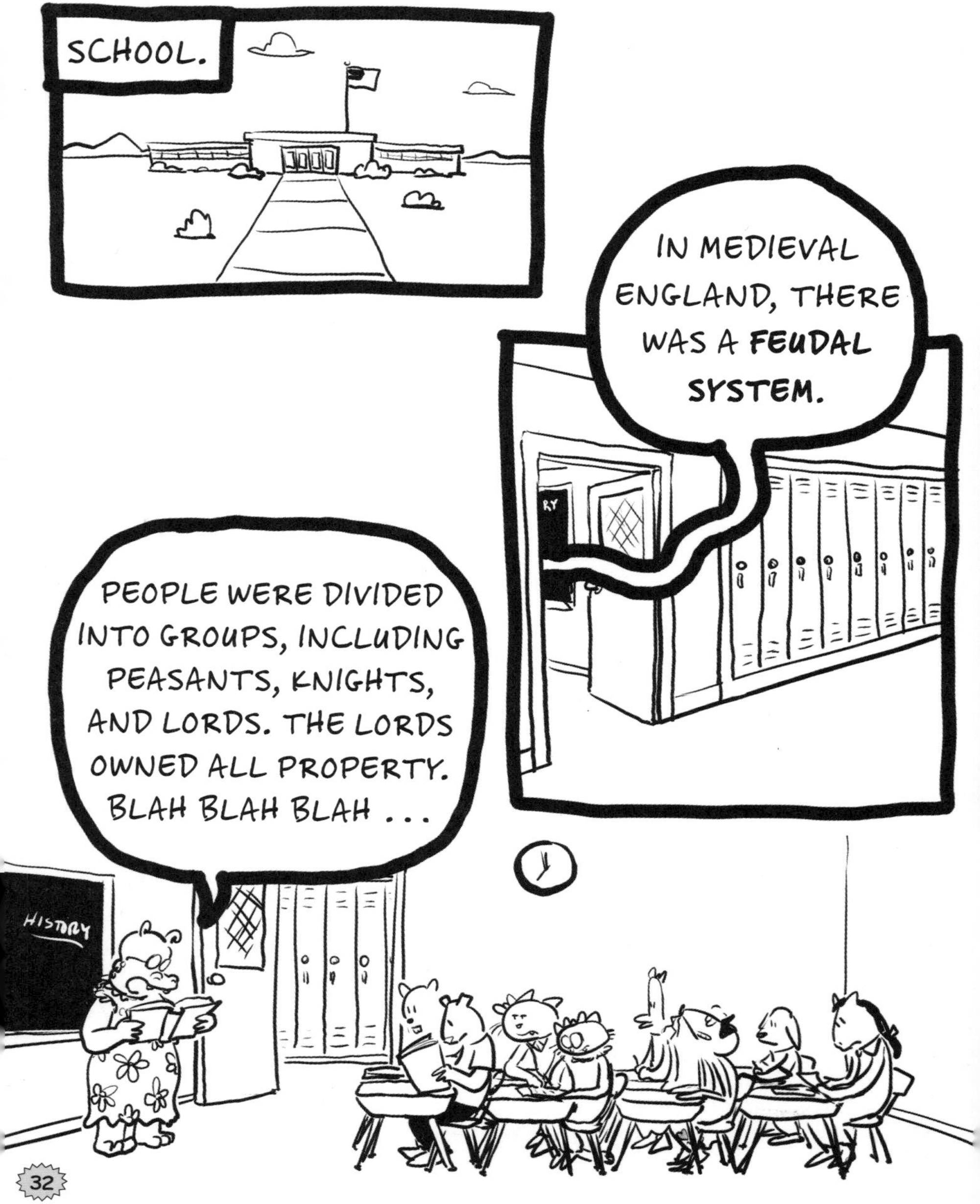
SCHOOL.
IN MEDIEVAL ENGLAND, THERE WAS A **FEUDAL SYSTEM.**
PEOPLE WERE DIVIDED INTO GROUPS, INCLUDING PEASANTS, KNIGHTS, AND LORDS. THE LORDS OWNED ALL PROPERTY. BLAH BLAH BLAH . . .
HISTORY

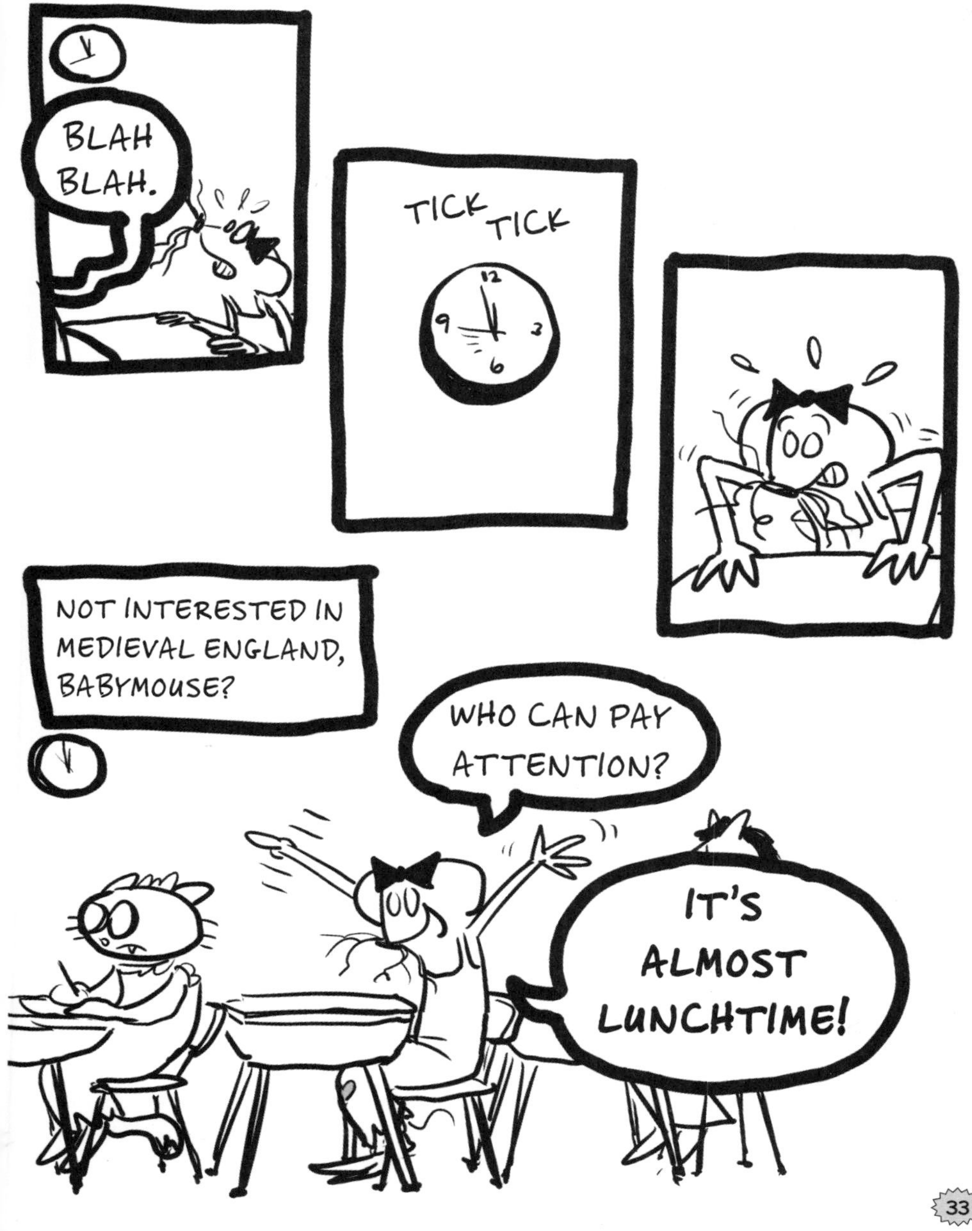
BLAH
BLAH.
TICK TICK
12
9
3
6
NOT INTERESTED IN MEDIEVAL ENGLAND, BABYMOUSE?
WHO CAN PAY ATTENTION?
IT'S ALMOST LUNCHTIME!

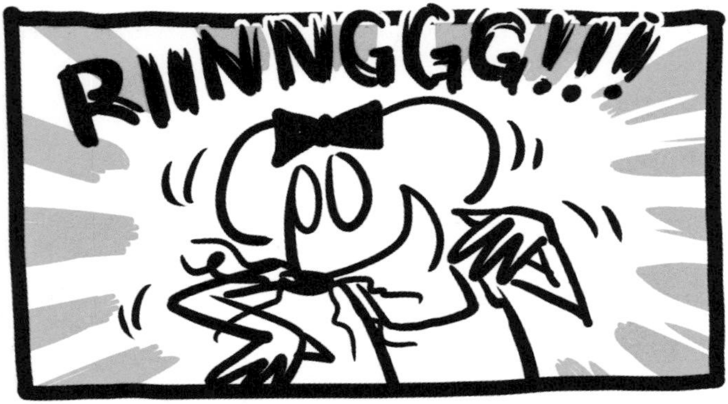
RIINNGGG!!!

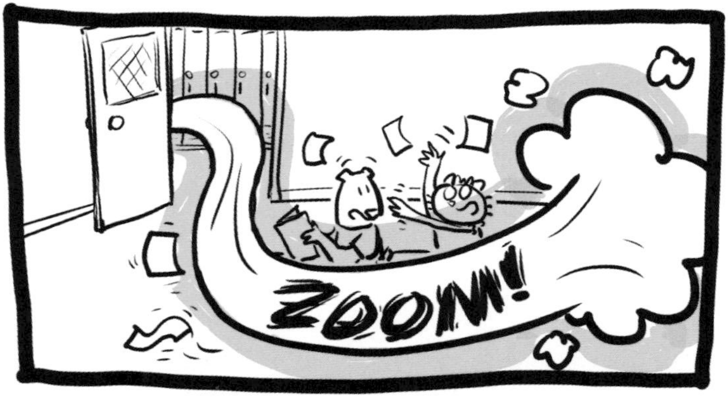
ZOOM!

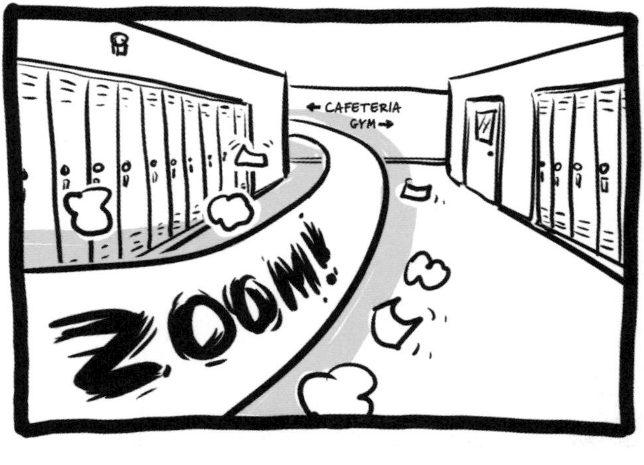
← CAFETERIA
GYM →
ZOOM!

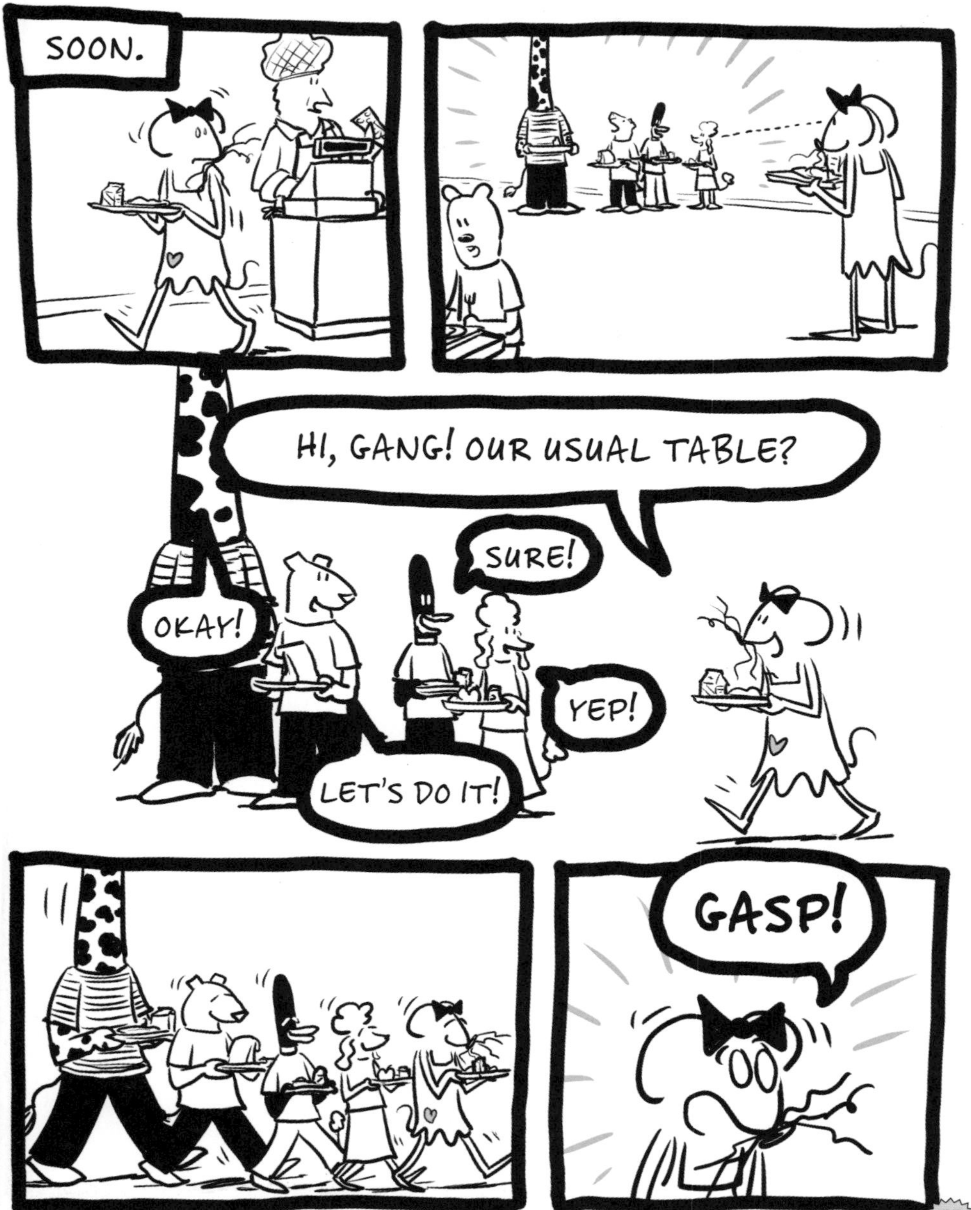
SOON.
HI, GANG! OUR USUAL TABLE?
OKAY!
SURE!
YEP!
LET'S DO IT!
GASP!

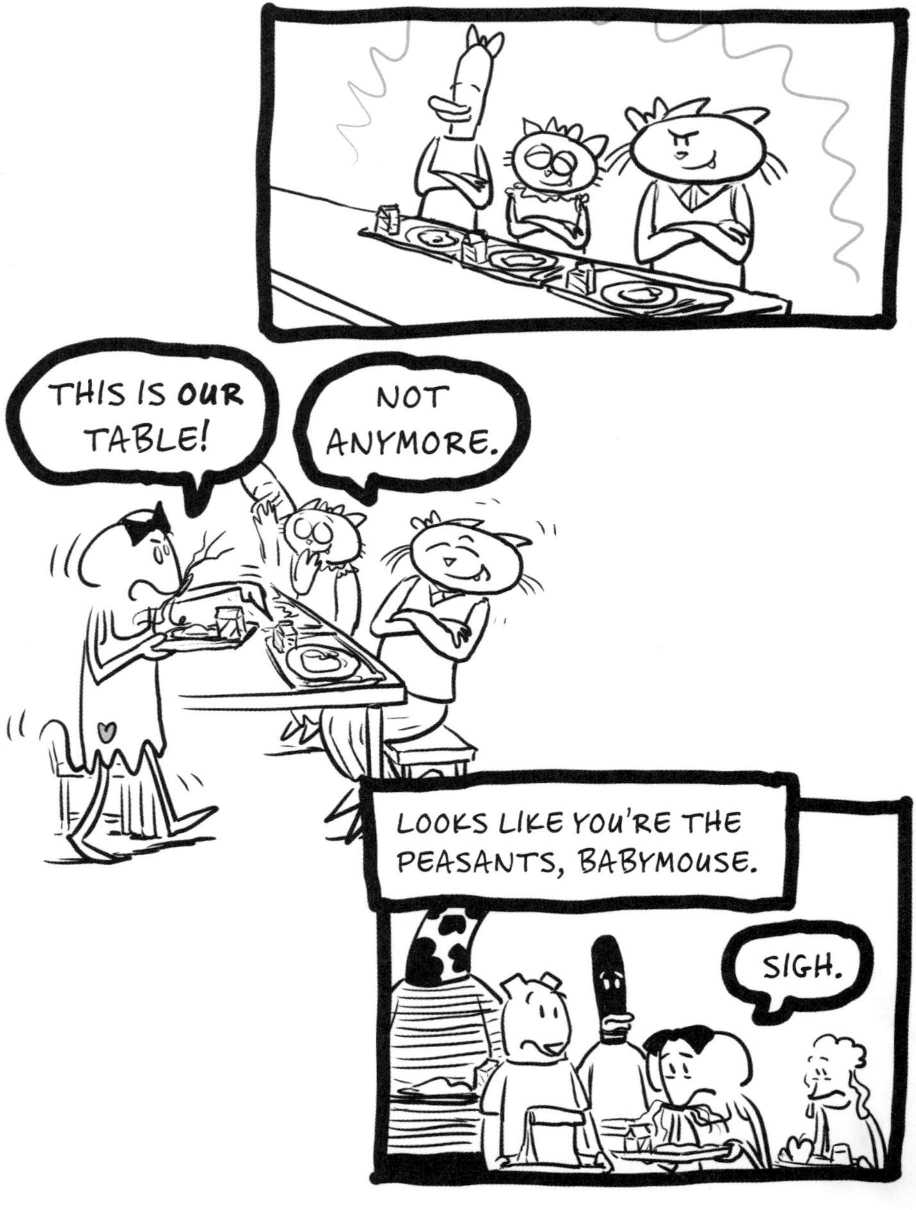
THIS IS **OUR** TABLE!
NOT ANYMORE.
LOOKS LIKE YOU'RE THE PEASANTS, BABYMOUSE.
SIGH.

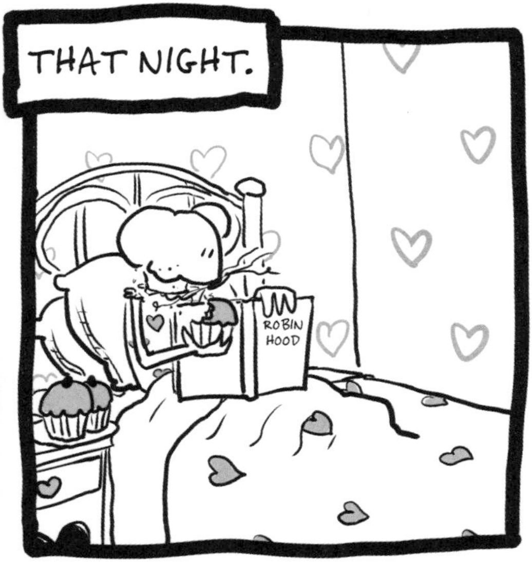
THAT NIGHT.
ROBIN HOOD

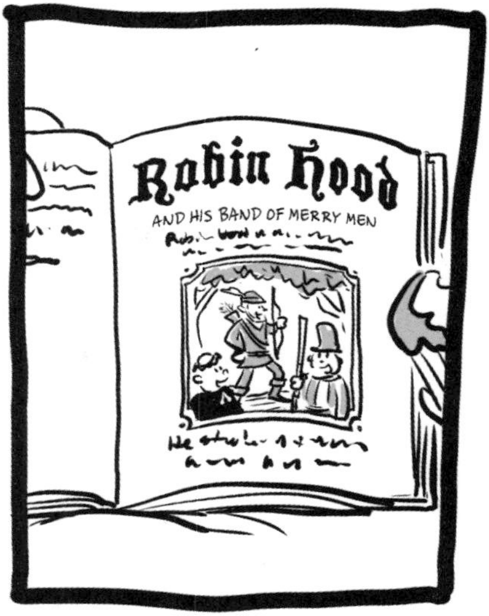
Robin Hood
AND HIS BAND OF MERRY MEN

ROBIN HOOD WAS THE
CHAMPION OF THE PEASANTS!

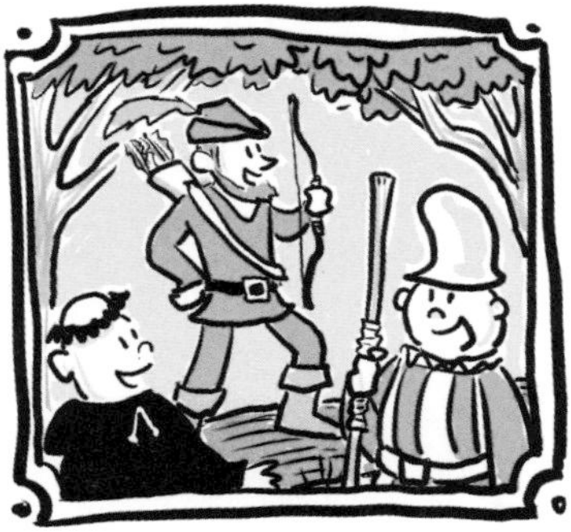

HE STOLE FROM THE RICH
AND GAVE TO THE POOR.

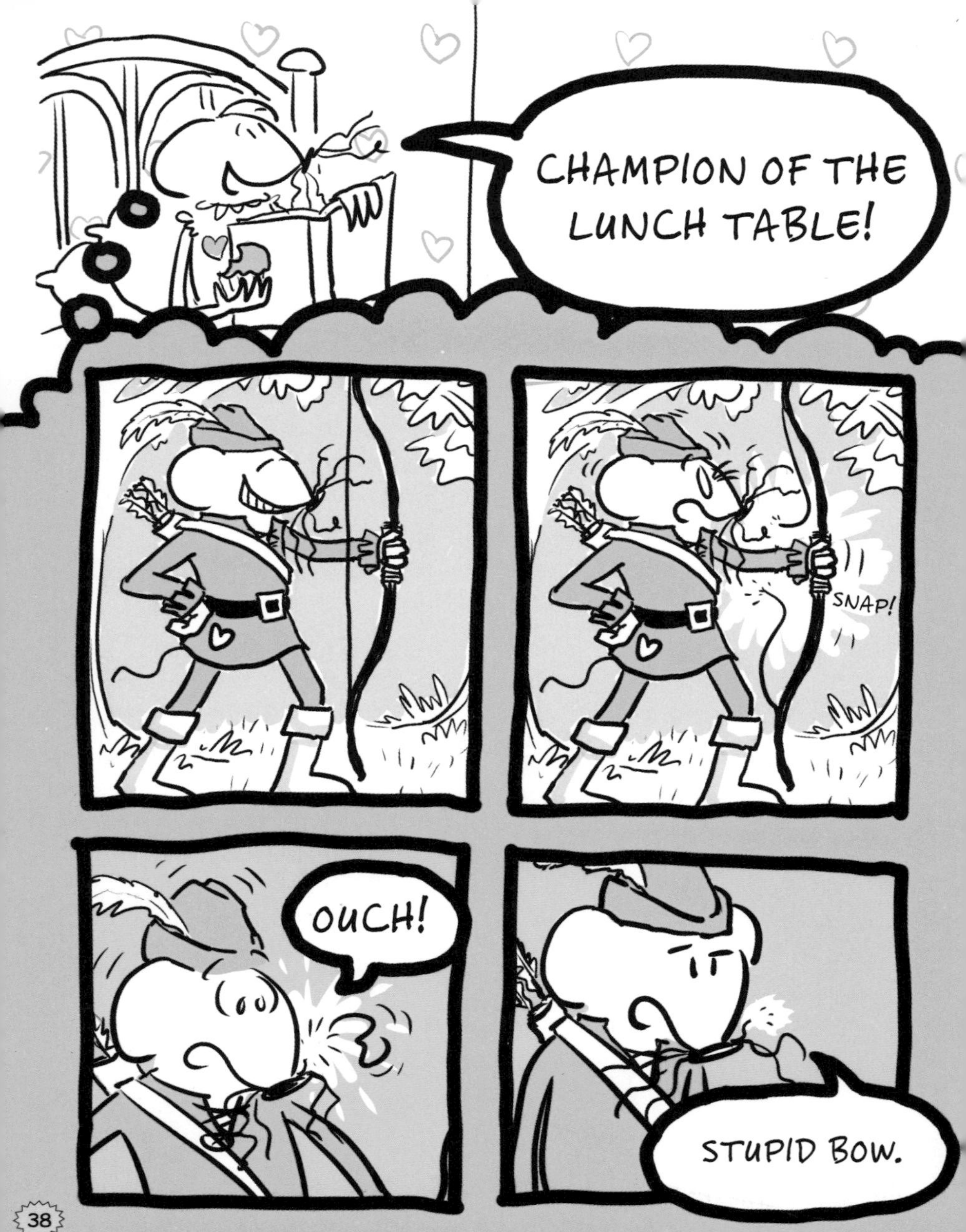
CHAMPION OF THE LUNCH TABLE!
SNAP!
OUCH!
STUPID BOW.

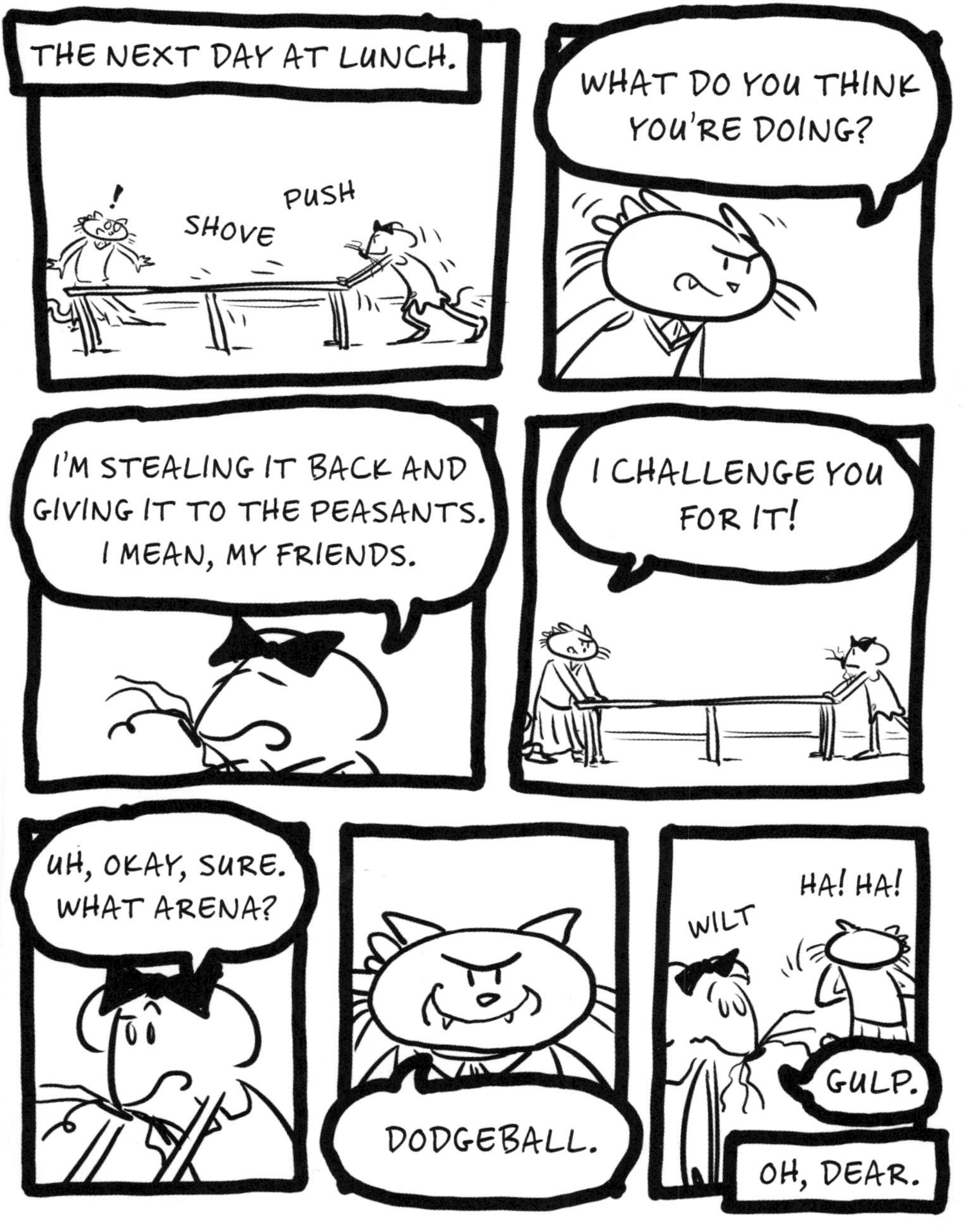
THE NEXT DAY AT LUNCH.
PUSH
SHOVE
WHAT DO YOU THINK YOU'RE DOING?
I'M STEALING IT BACK AND GIVING IT TO THE PEASANTS. I MEAN, MY FRIENDS.
I CHALLENGE YOU FOR IT!
UH, OKAY, SURE. WHAT ARENA?
DODGEBALL.
HA! HA!
WILT
GULP.
OH, DEAR.

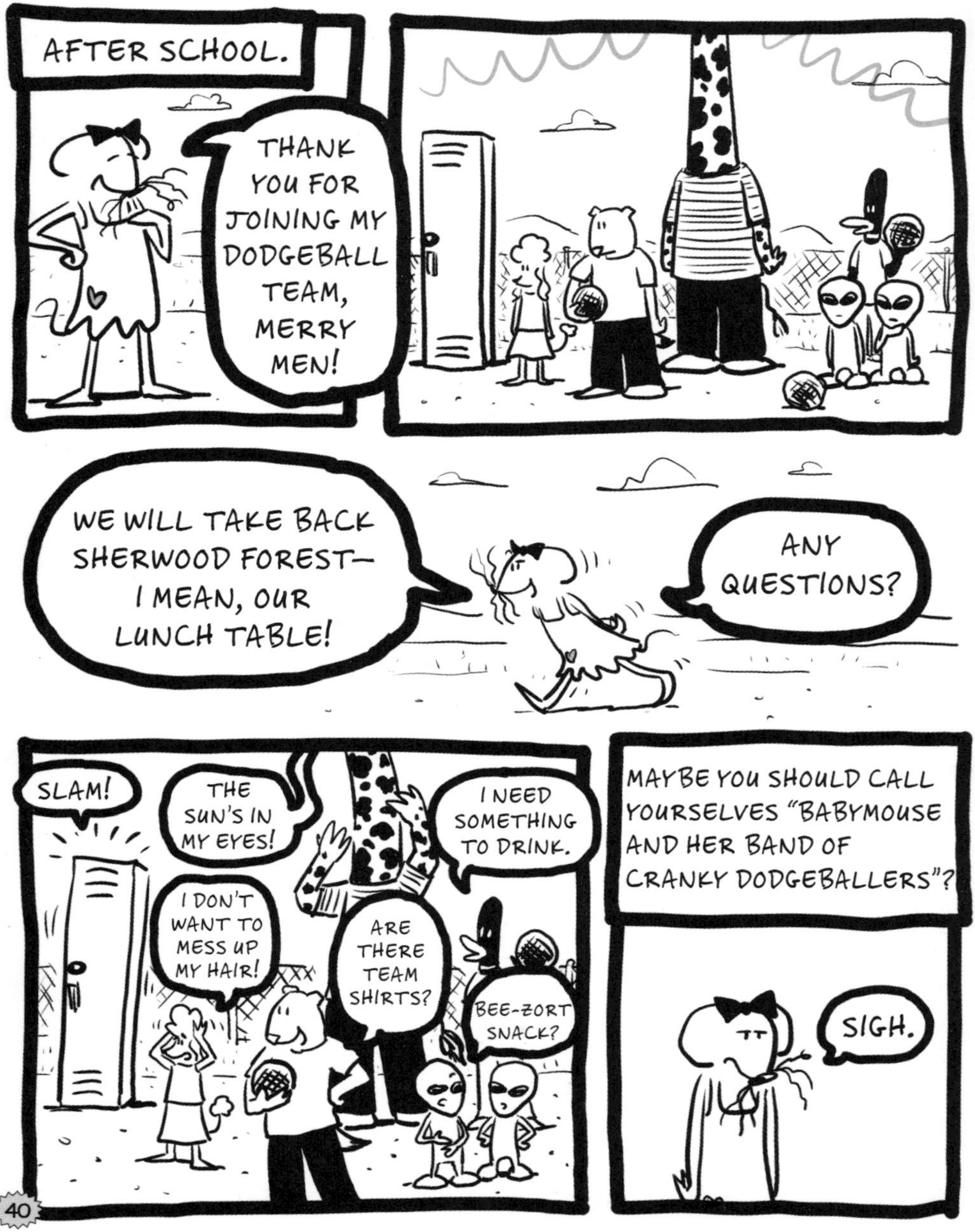
AFTER SCHOOL.
THANK YOU FOR JOINING MY DODGEBALL TEAM, MERRY MEN!
WE WILL TAKE BACK SHERWOOD FOREST— I MEAN, OUR LUNCH TABLE!
ANY QUESTIONS?
SLAM!
THE SUN'S IN MY EYES!
I NEED SOMETHING TO DRINK.
I DON'T WANT TO MESS UP MY HAIR!
ARE THERE TEAM SHIRTS?
BEE-ZORT SNACK?
MAYBE YOU SHOULD CALL YOURSELVES "BABYMOUSE AND HER BAND OF CRANKY DODGEBALLERS"?
SIGH.

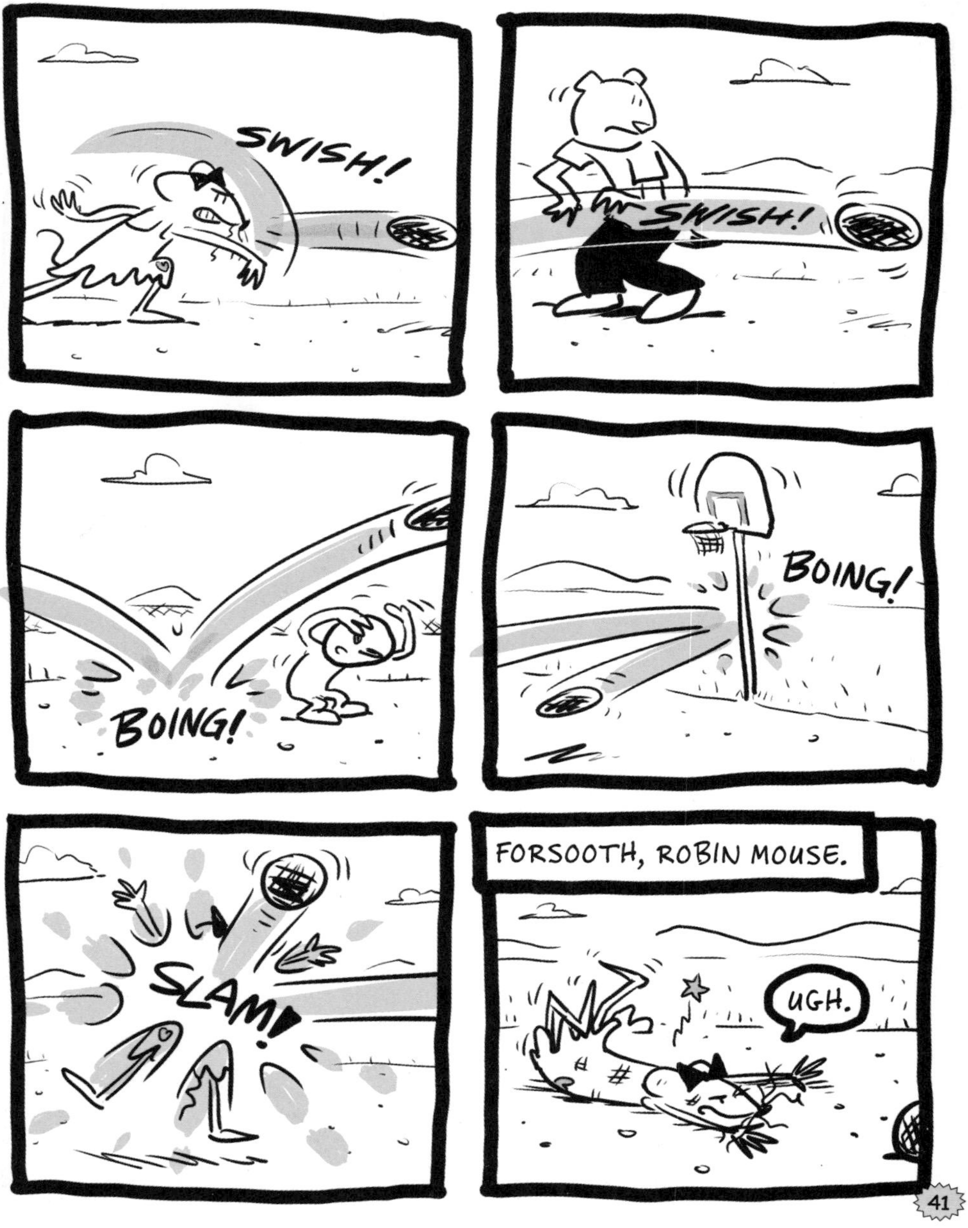
SWISH!
SWISH!
BOING!
BOING!
SLAM!
FORSOOTH, ROBIN MOUSE.
UGH.

THE DAY OF THE CHALLENGE.

PREPARE FOR DEFEAT!

NOT LIKELY.

SHRUG

TWEET!

SWOOSH!

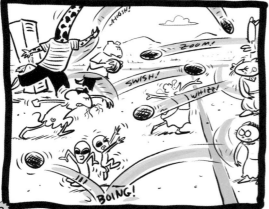

WHOSH!

ZOOM!

SWISH!

WHIZZ!

BOING!

WE CAME ALL THE WAY FROM ALPHA CENTAURI TO DODGE UNIDENTIFIED FLYING OBJECTS?!

ZOOM!

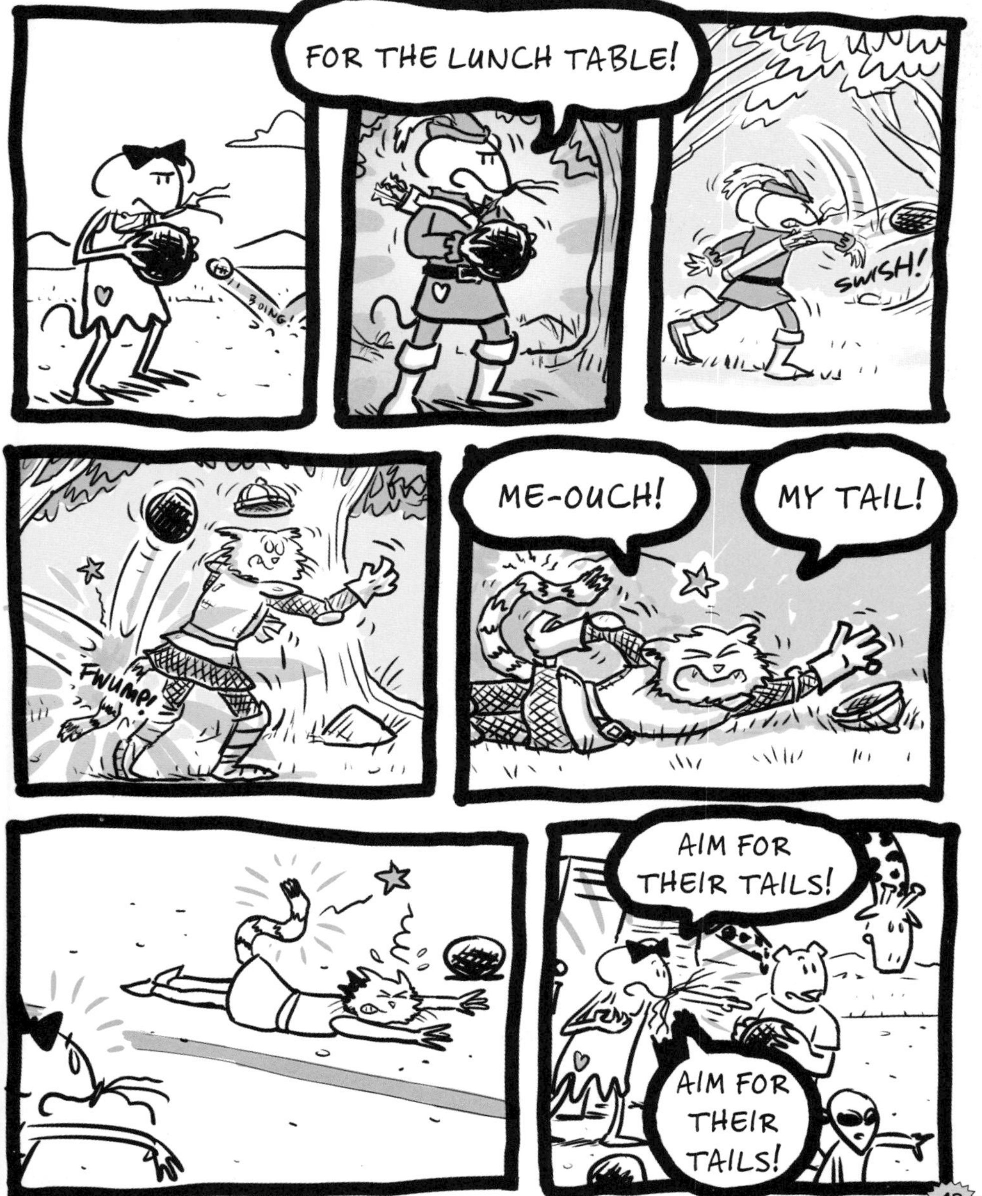

BOING!
FOR THE LUNCH TABLE!
SWISH!
FWUMP!
ME-OUCH!
MY TAIL!
AIM FOR THEIR TAILS!
AIM FOR THEIR TAILS!

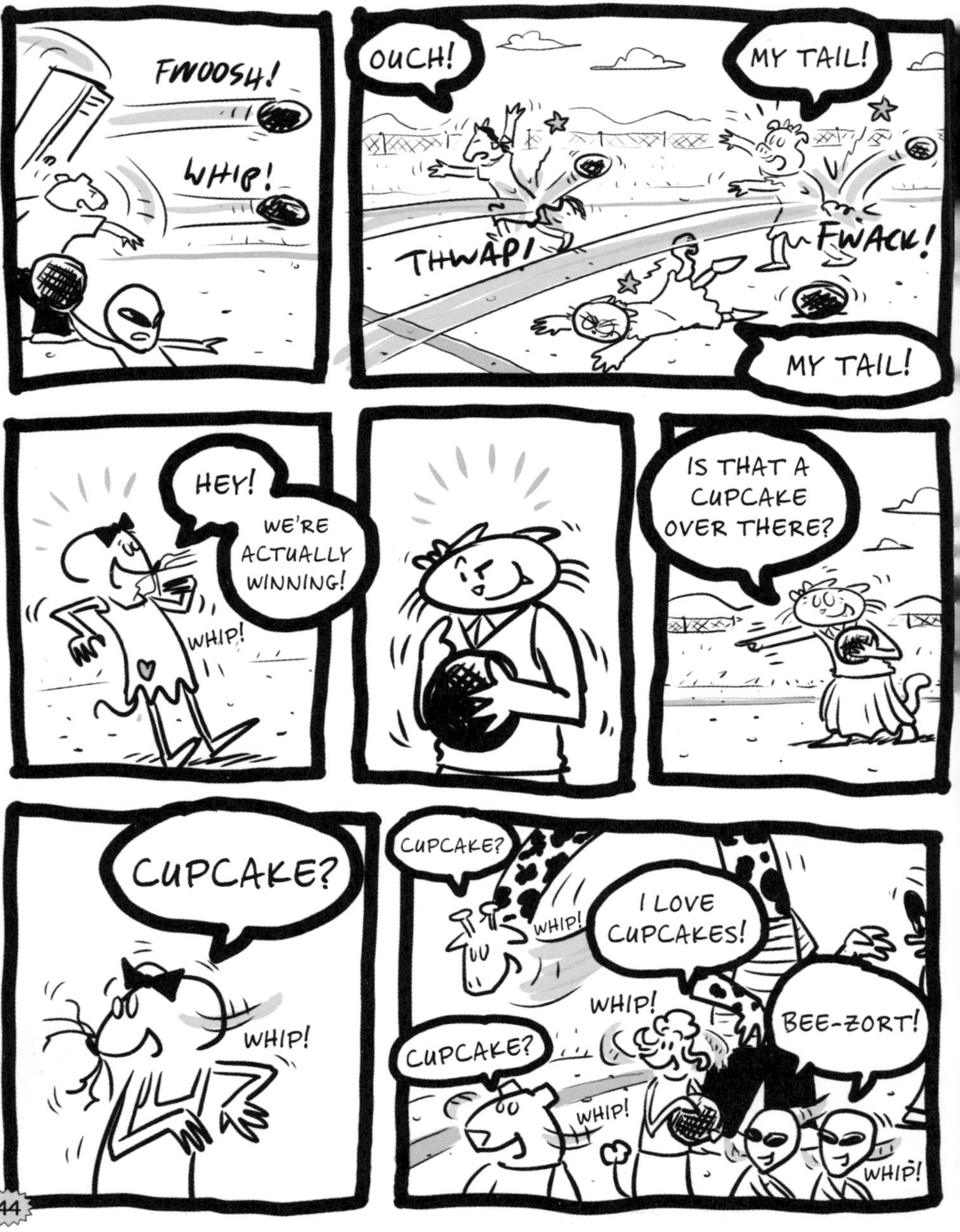
FWOOSH!
WHIP!
OUCH!
MY TAIL!
THWAP!
FWACK!
MY TAIL!
HEY!
WE'RE ACTUALLY WINNING!
WHIP!
IS THAT A CUPCAKE OVER THERE?
CUPCAKE?
WHIP!
CUPCAKE?
WHIP!
I LOVE CUPCAKES!
WHIP!
BEE-ZORT!
CUPCAKE?
WHIP!
WHIP!

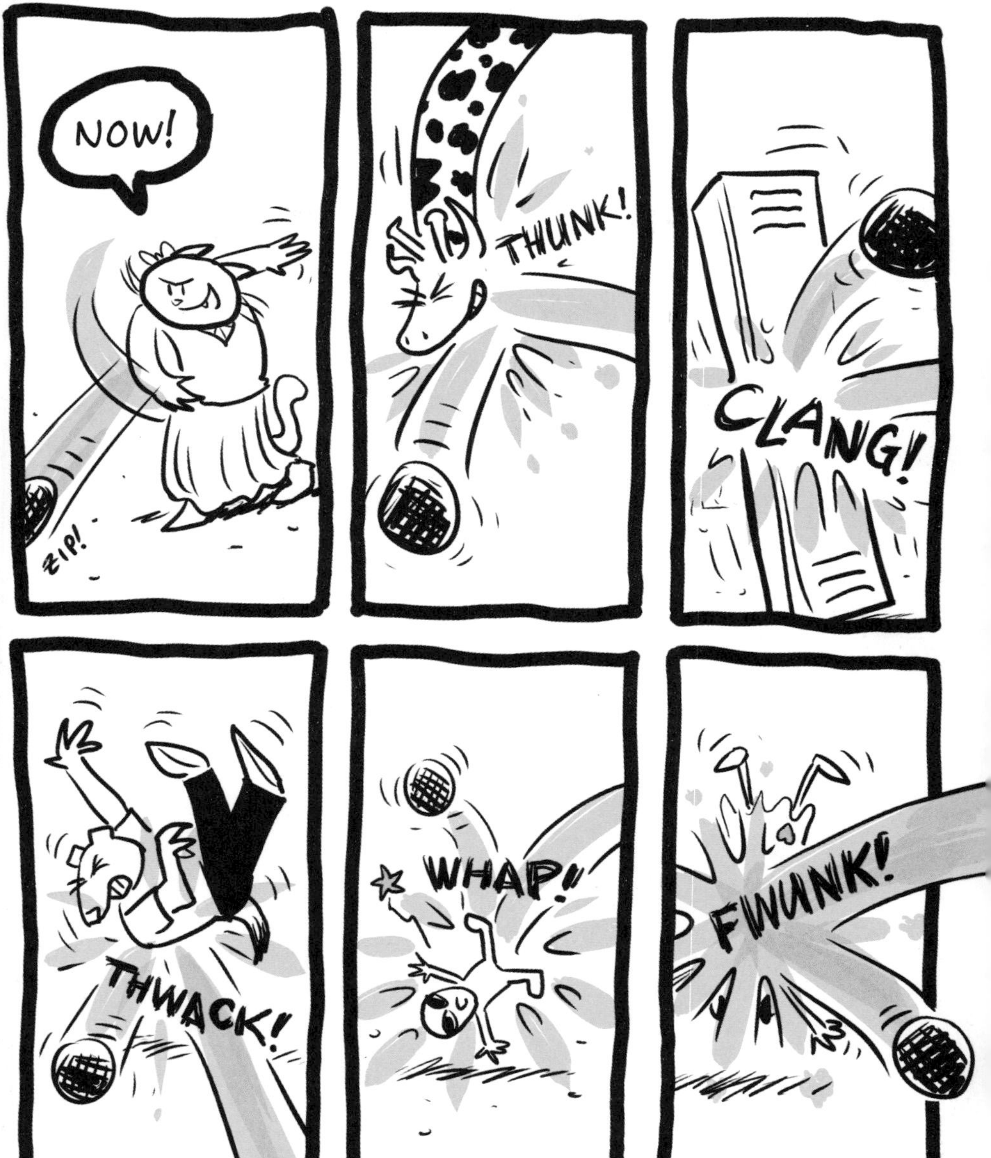
NOW!
ZIP!
THUNK!
CLANG!
THWACK!
WHAP!
FWUNK!

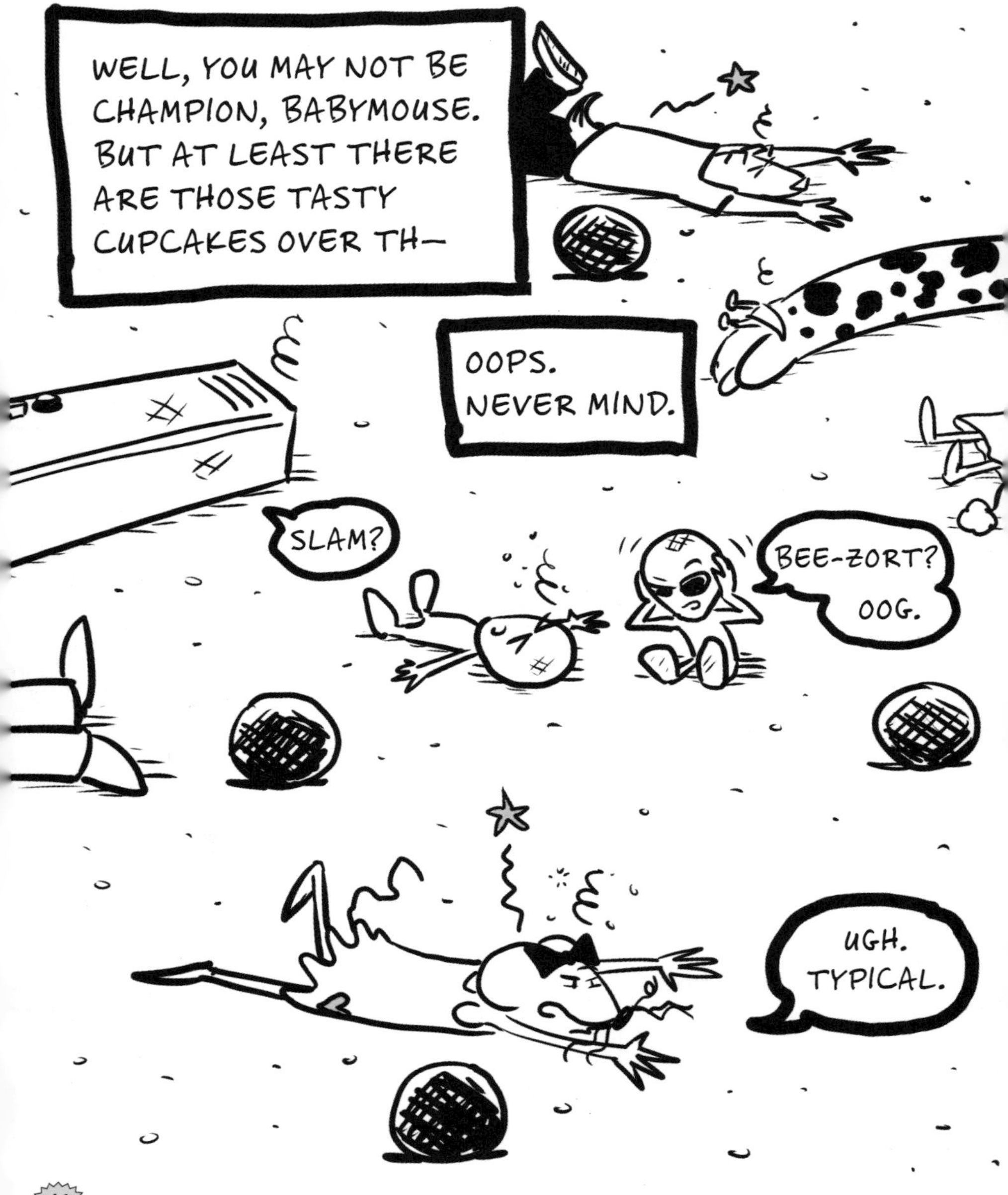
WELL, YOU MAY NOT BE CHAMPION, BABYMOUSE. BUT AT LEAST THERE ARE THOSE TASTY CUPCAKES OVER TH—
OOPS. NEVER MIND.
SLAM?
BEE-ZORT? OOG.
UGH. TYPICAL.

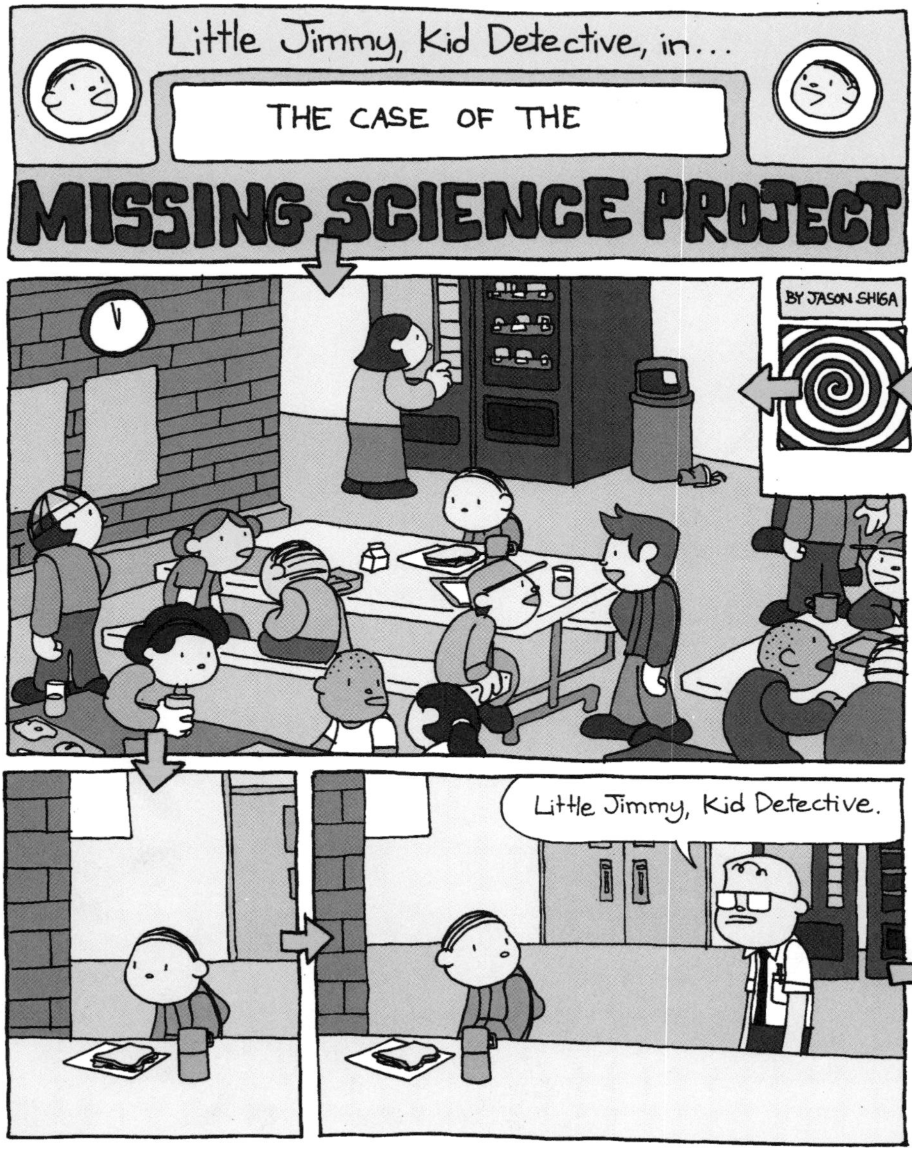
Little Jimmy, Kid Detective, in...
THE CASE OF THE
MISSING SCIENCE PROJECT
BY JASON SHIGA
Little Jimmy, Kid Detective.

How did you get to this panel? You did it by turning the page and reading from the top like in a normal comic. But this is not a normal comic.

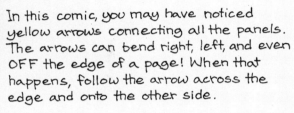

In this comic, you may have noticed yellow arrows connecting all the panels. The arrows can bend right, left, and even OFF the edge of a page! When that happens, follow the arrow across the edge and onto the other side.

Further in the story, arrows can even split in two or more directions. At that point YOU, the reader, can choose which branch to follow. And by making the right choices, YOU help Jimmy solve the Case of the Missing Science Project.

Oh, hello, Filbert.

Jimmy! I'm so glad I found you! You're my last hope.

Are you okay?

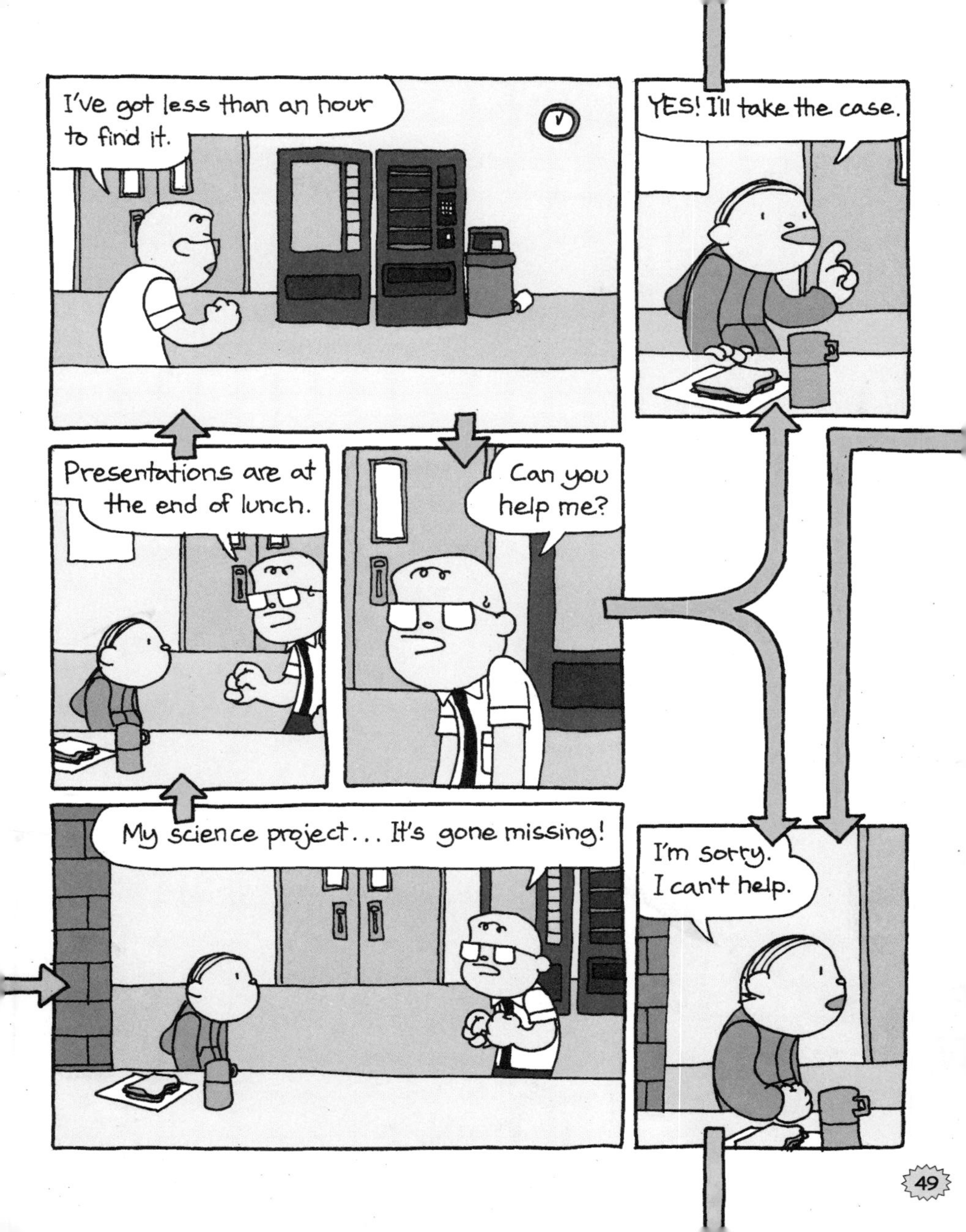
My science project... It's gone missing!
Presentations are at the end of lunch.
I've got less than an hour to find it.
Can you help me?
YES! I'll take the case.
I'm sorry. I can't help.

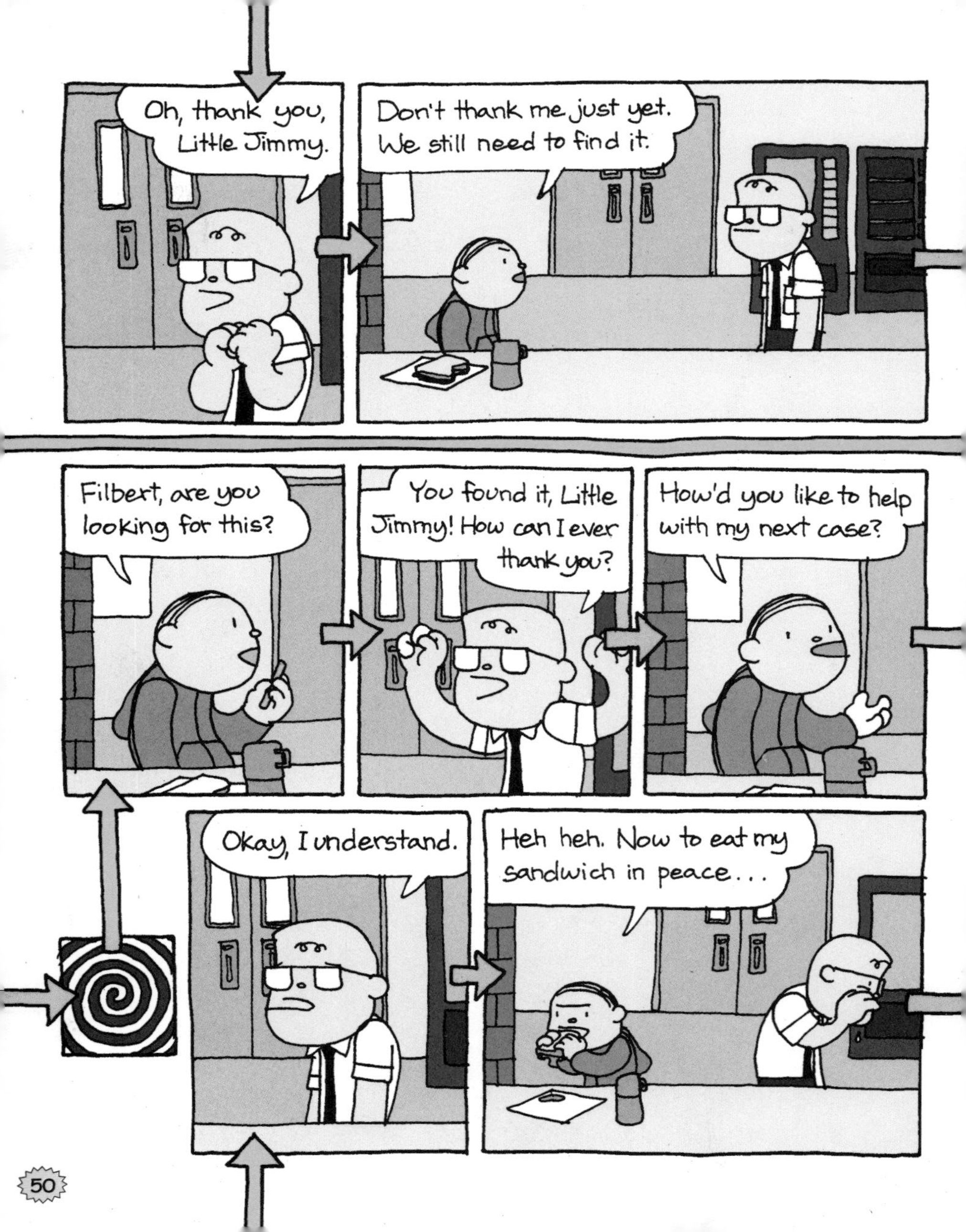
Oh, thank you, Little Jimmy.
Don't thank me just yet. We still need to find it.
Filbert, are you looking for this?
You found it, Little Jimmy! How can I ever thank you?
How'd you like to help with my next case?
Okay, I understand.
Heh heh. Now to eat my sandwich in peace...

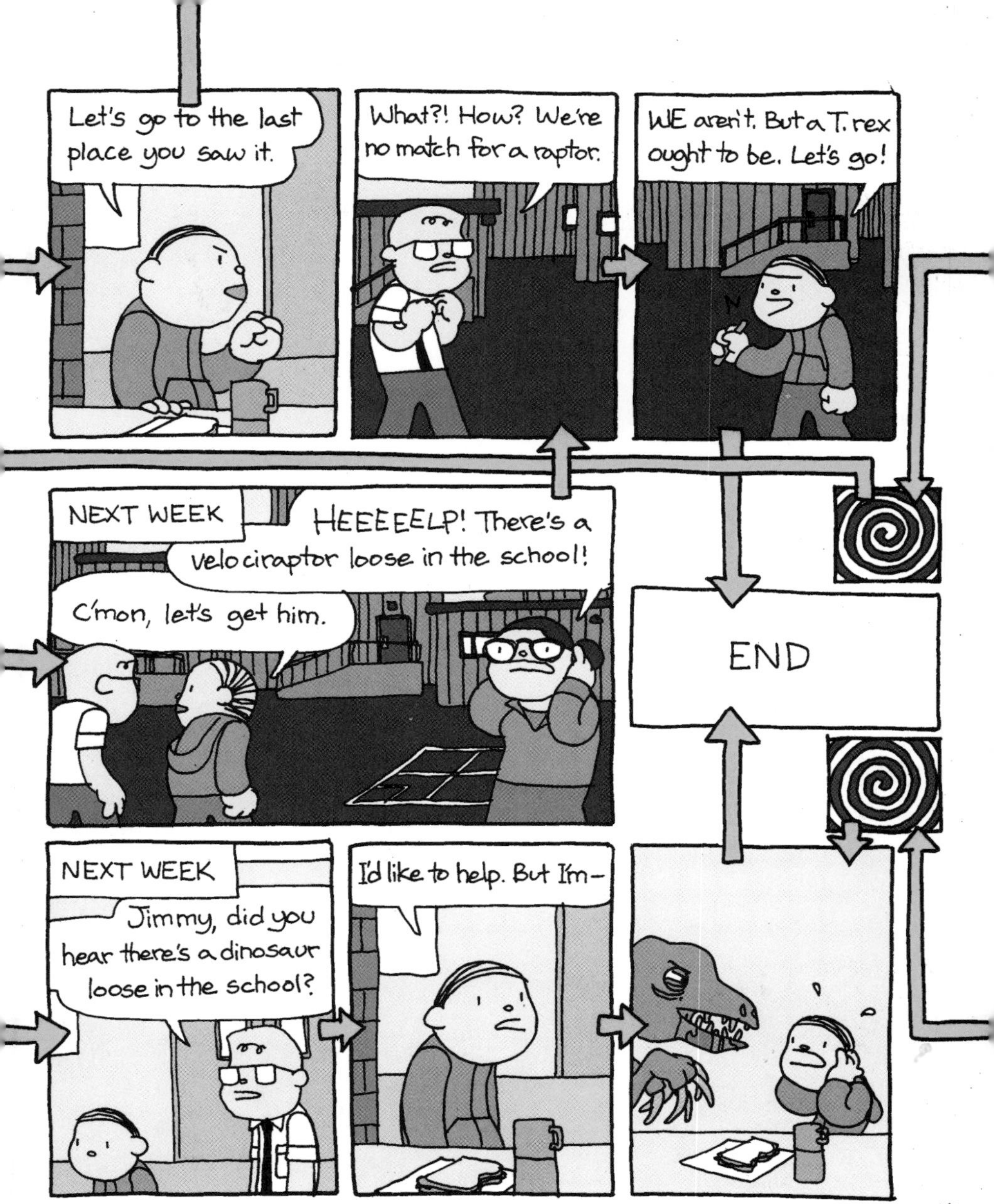
Let's go to the last place you saw it.
What?! How? We're no match for a raptor.
WE aren't. But a T. rex ought to be. Let's go!
NEXT WEEK
HEEEEELP! There's a velociraptor loose in the school!
C'mon, let's get him.
END
NEXT WEEK
Jimmy, did you hear there's a dinosaur loose in the school?
I'd like to help. But I'm—

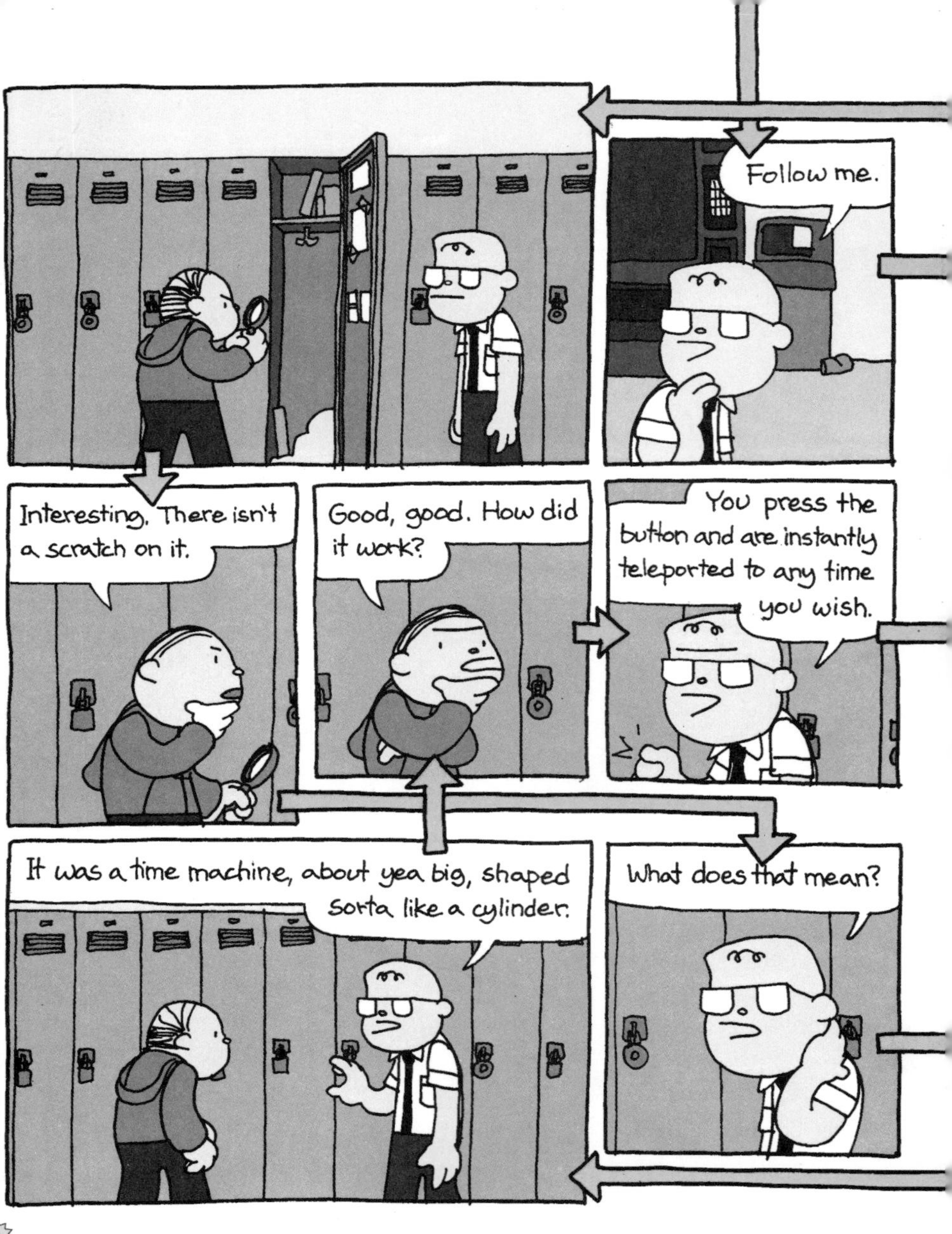
Follow me.
Interesting. There isn't a scratch on it.
Good, good. How did it work?
You press the button and are instantly teleported to any time you wish.
It was a time machine, about yea big, shaped sorta like a cylinder.
What does that mean?

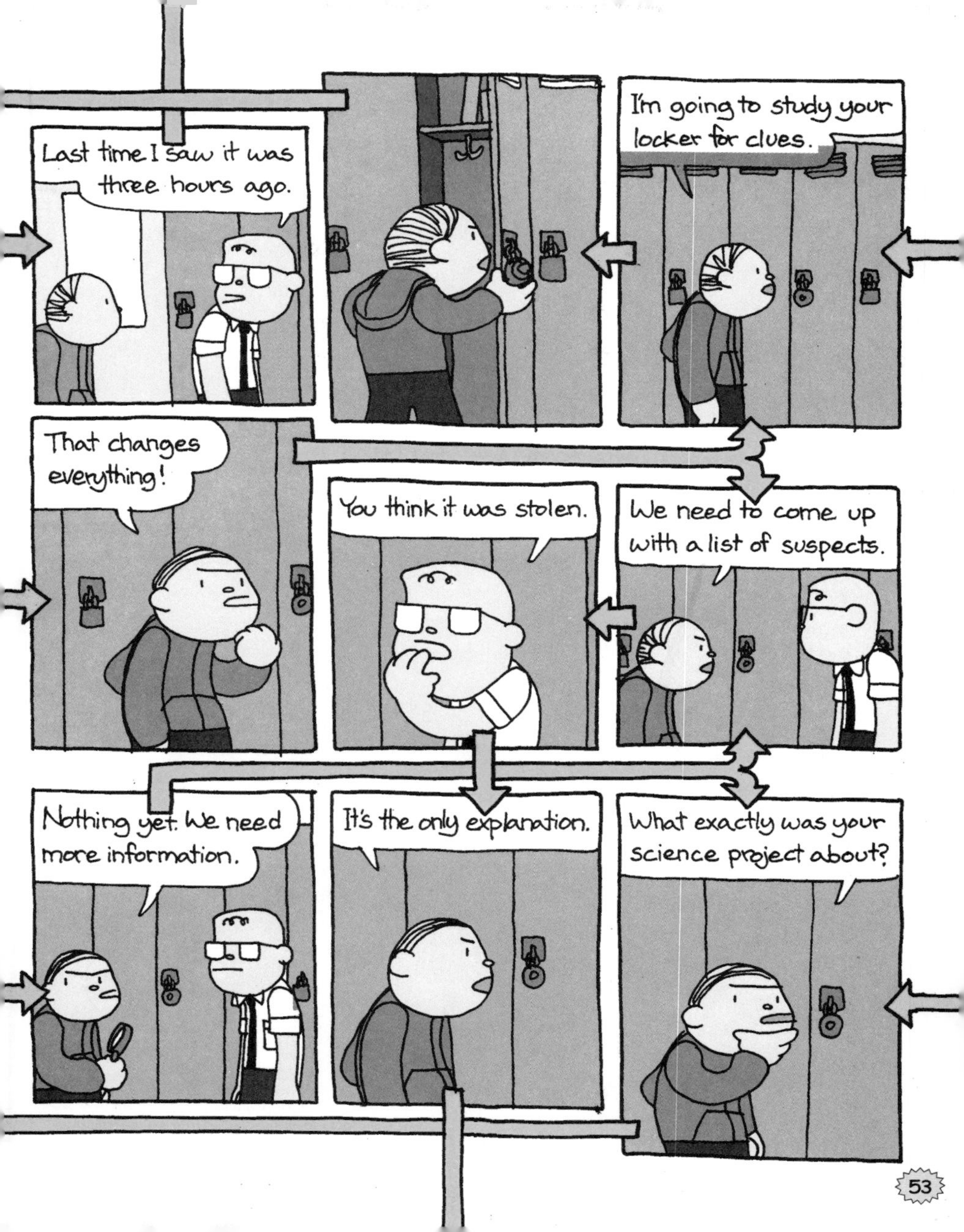

Last time I saw it was three hours ago.
I'm going to study your locker for clues.
That changes everything!
You think it was stolen.
We need to come up with a list of suspects.
Nothing yet. We need more information.
It's the only explanation.
What exactly was your science project about?

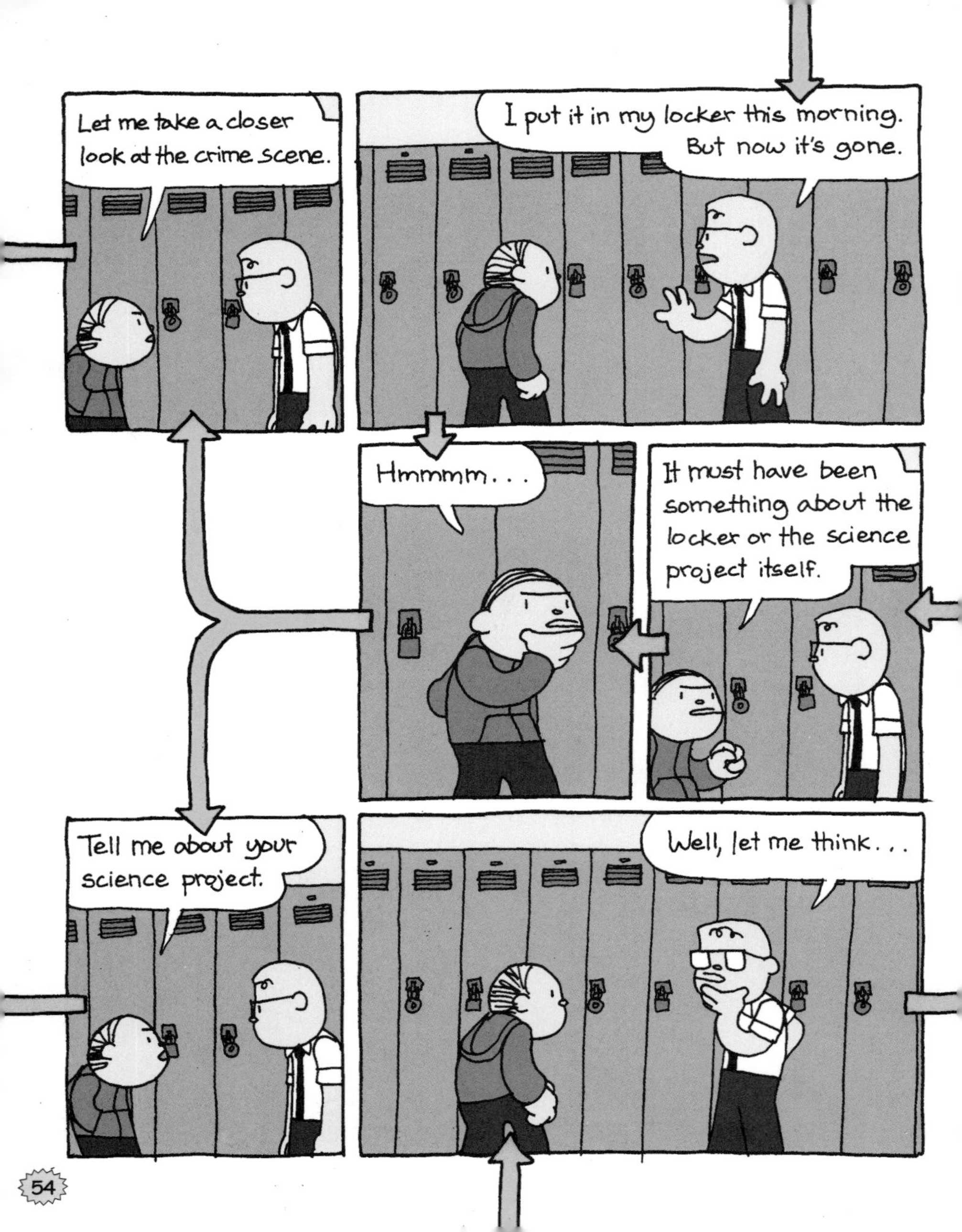
Let me take a closer look at the crime scene.
I put it in my locker this morning. But now it's gone.
Hmmmm. . .
It must have been something about the locker or the science project itself.
Tell me about your science project.
Well, let me think. . .

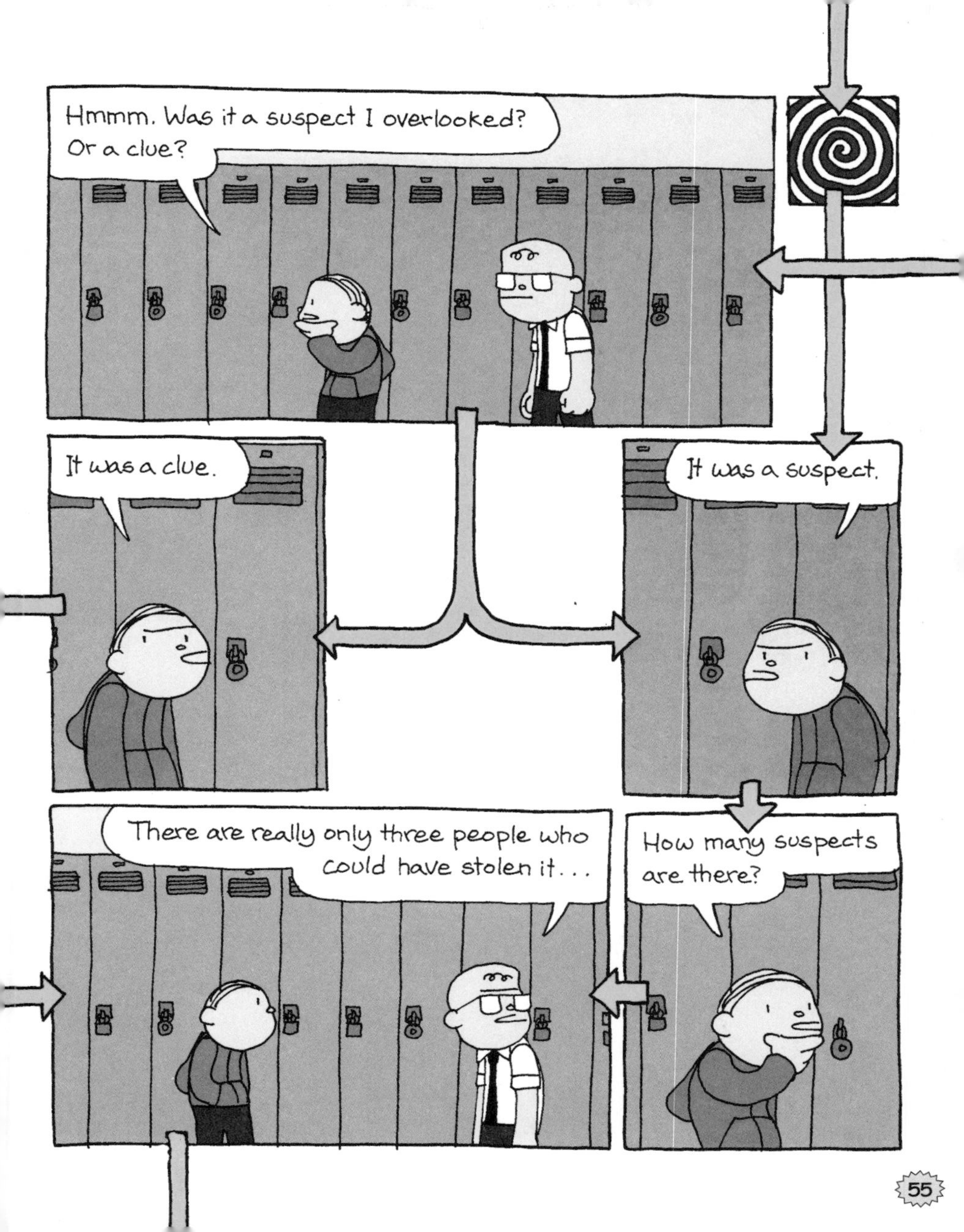
Hmmm. Was it a suspect I overlooked? Or a clue?
It was a clue.
It was a suspect.
How many suspects are there?
There are really only three people who could have stolen it . . .

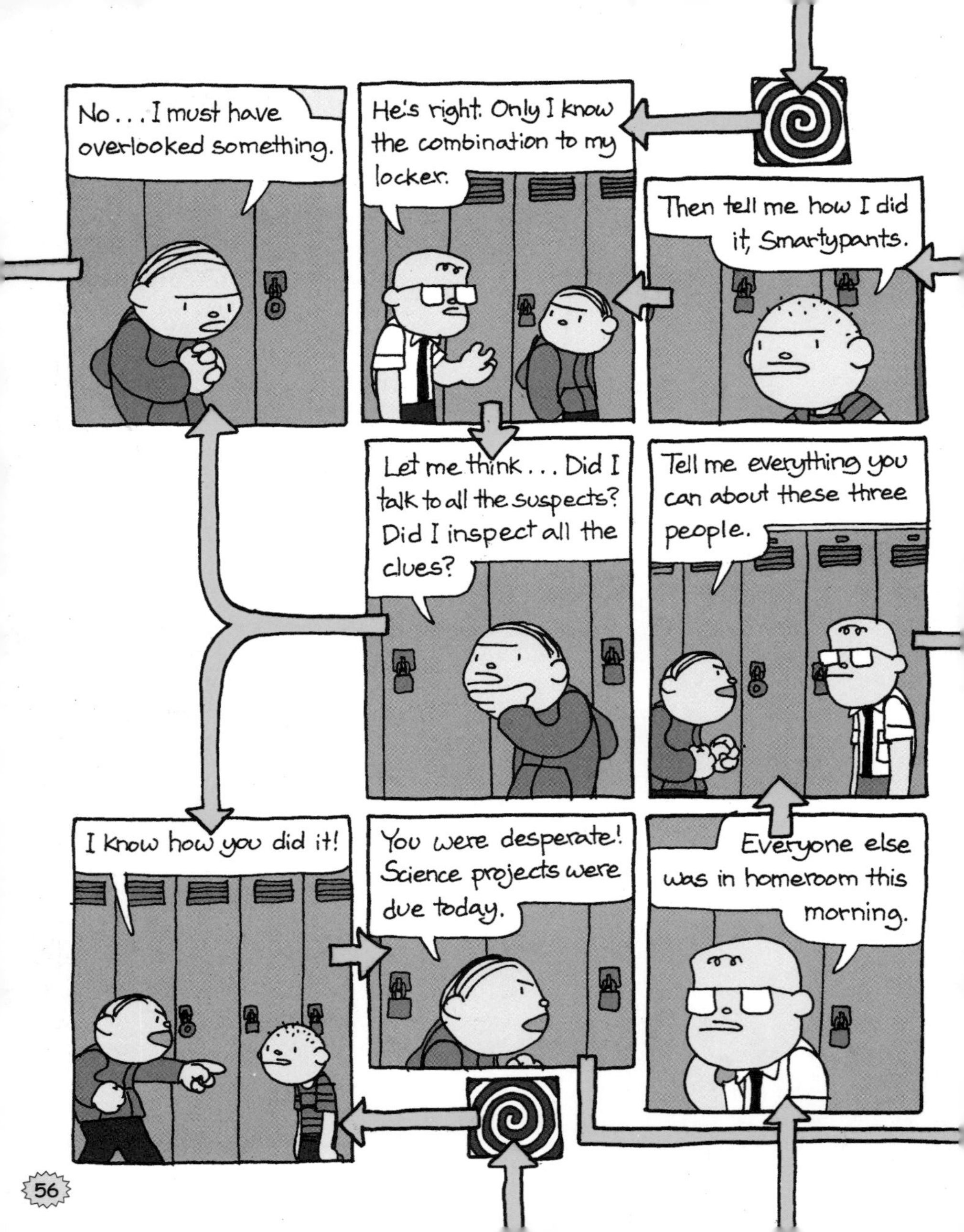
No . . . I must have overlooked something.
He's right. Only I know the combination to my locker.
Then tell me how I did it, Smartypants.
Let me think . . . Did I talk to all the suspects? Did I inspect all the clues?
Tell me everything you can about these three people.
I know how you did it!
You were desperate! Science projects were due today.
Everyone else was in homeroom this morning.

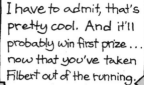
I have to admit, that's pretty cool. And it'll probably win first prize... now that you've taken Filbert out of the running.

Aha! Your science project is a dinosaur egg. But dinosaurs are extinct.

Have a look.

Well, there's Linda. She's been my best friend since second grade.

There's Blane, the most popular kid in school.

And there's Darius. I don't know much about him other than he's not very organized.

But due to your complete lack of organization, you hadn't even started.

So you did the only logical thing you could.... You broke into Filbert's locker and used his time machine to find a dinosaur egg.

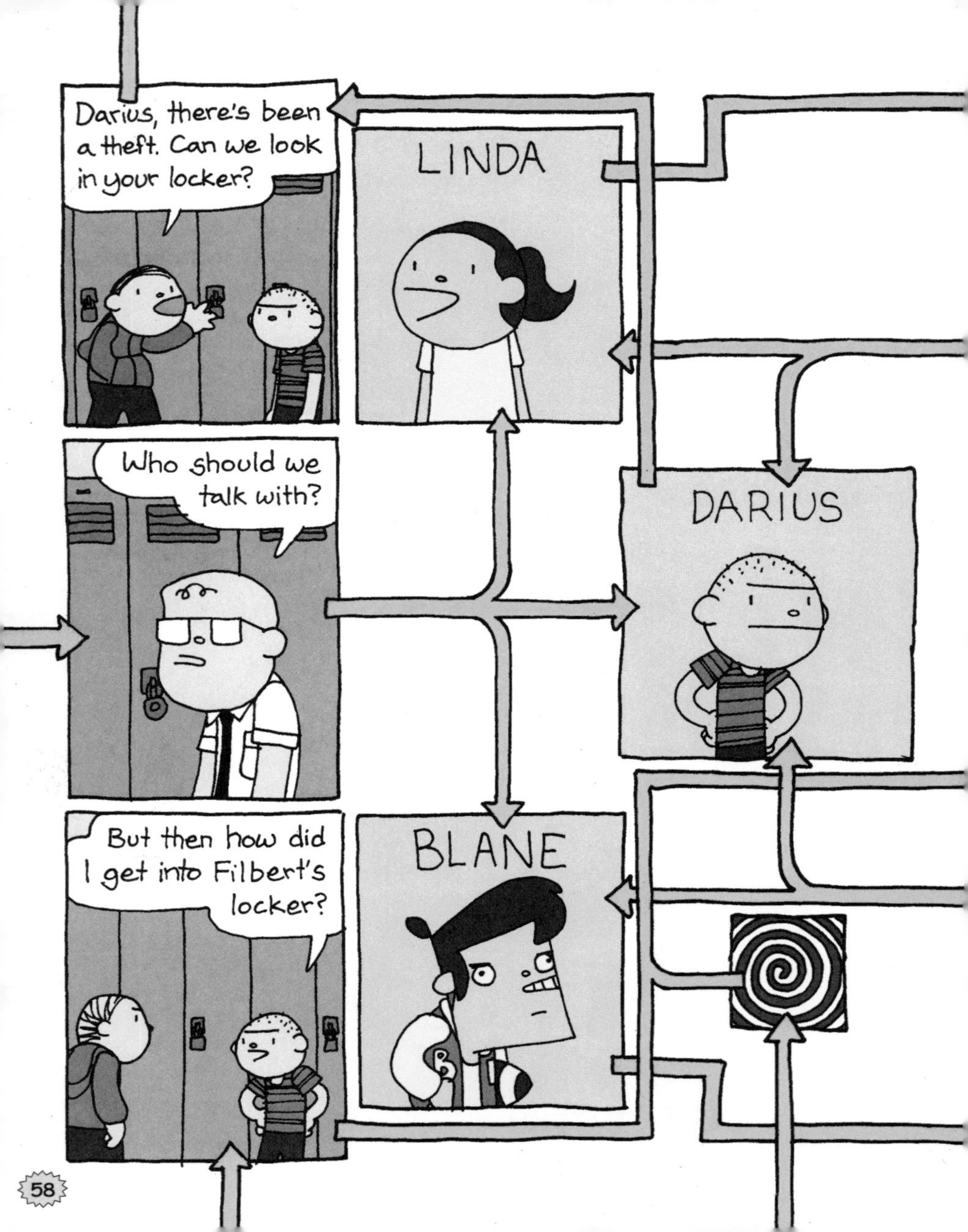
Darius, there's been a theft. Can we look in your locker?
LINDA
Who should we talk with?
DARIUS
But then how did I get into Filbert's locker?
BLANE

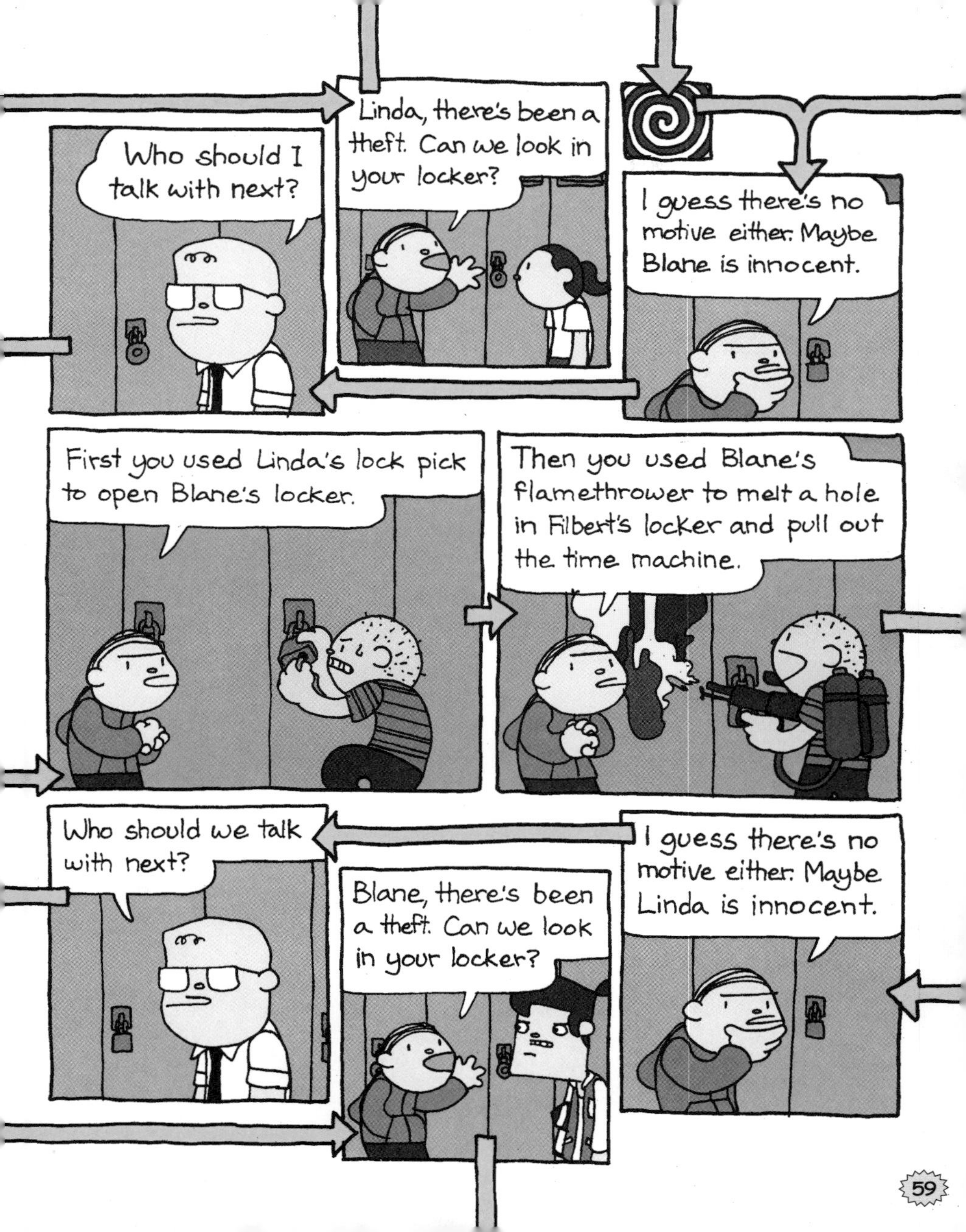
Linda, there's been a theft. Can we look in your locker?
Who should I talk with next?
I guess there's no motive either. Maybe Blane is innocent.
First you used Linda's lock pick to open Blane's locker.
Then you used Blane's flamethrower to melt a hole in Filbert's locker and pull out the time machine.
I guess there's no motive either. Maybe Linda is innocent.
Who should we talk with next?
Blane, there's been a theft. Can we look in your locker?

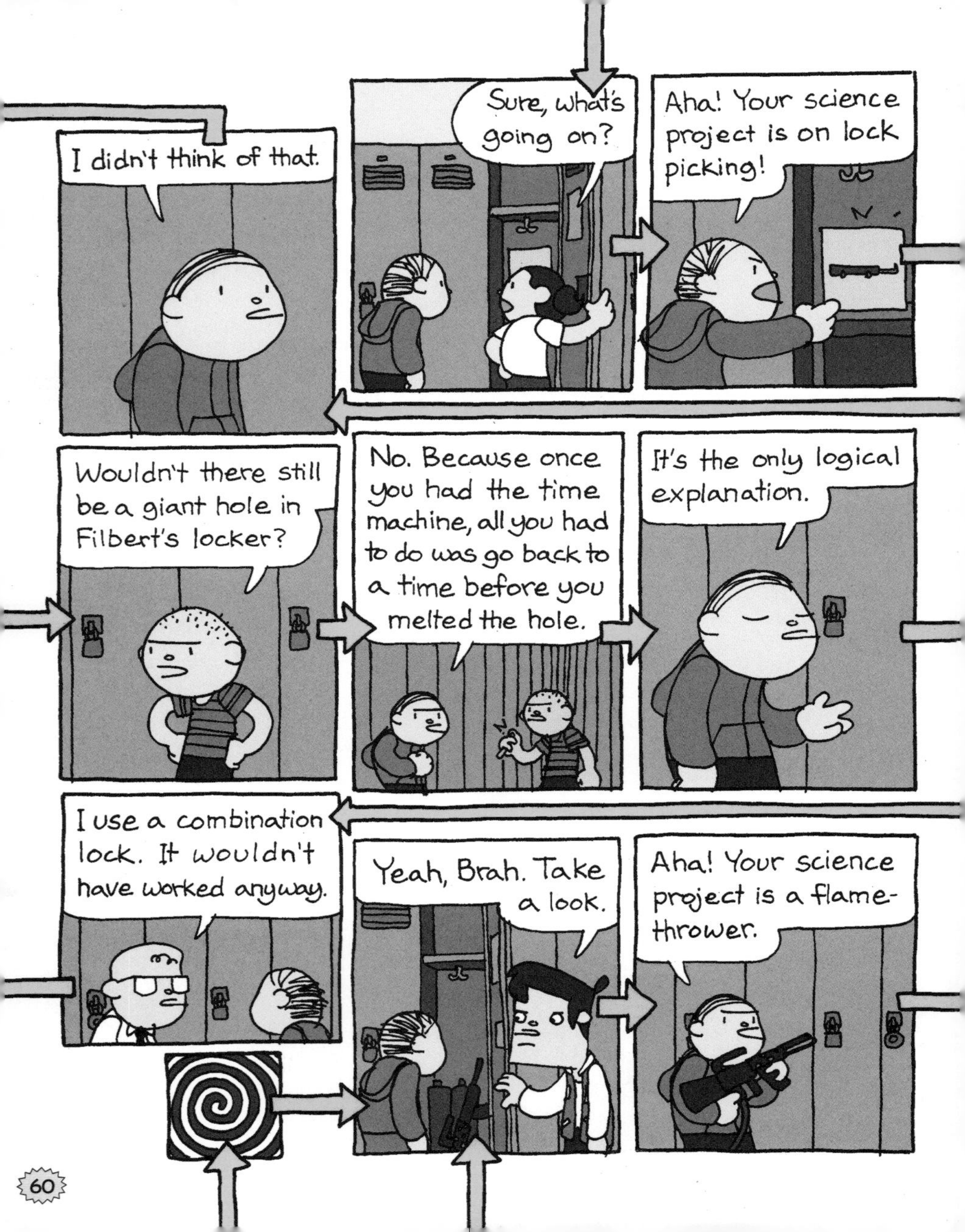

I didn't think of that.
Sure, what's going on?
Aha! Your science project is on lock picking!
Wouldn't there still be a giant hole in Filbert's locker?
No. Because once you had the time machine, all you had to do was go back to a time before you melted the hole.
It's the only logical explanation.
I use a combination lock. It wouldn't have worked anyway.
Yeah, Brah. Take a look.
Aha! Your science project is a flame-thrower.

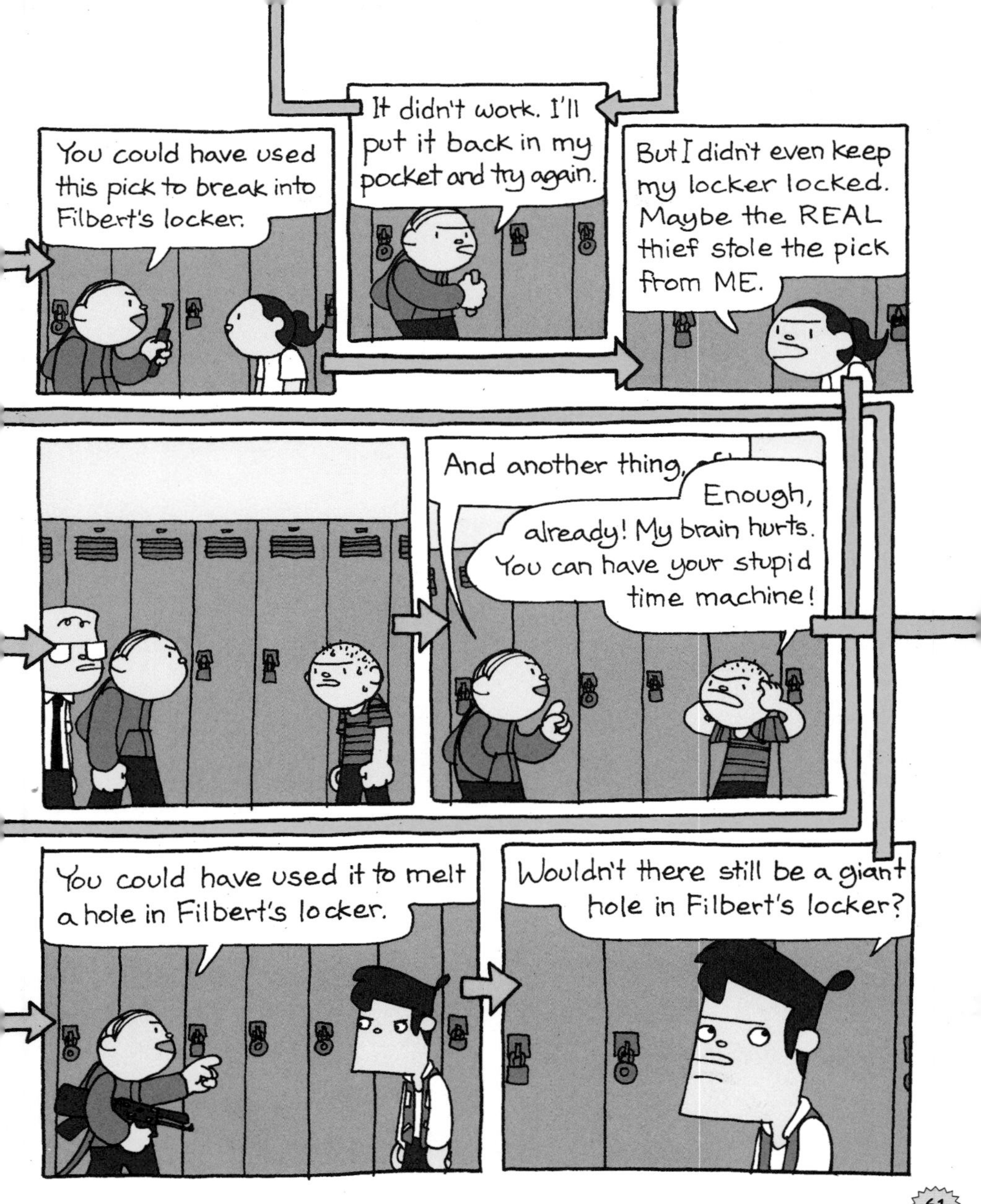
You could have used this pick to break into Filbert's locker.
It didn't work. I'll put it back in my pocket and try again.
But I didn't even keep my locker locked. Maybe the REAL thief stole the pick from ME.
And another thing,
Enough, already! My brain hurts. You can have your stupid time machine!
You could have used it to melt a hole in Filbert's locker.
Wouldn't there still be a giant hole in Filbert's locker?

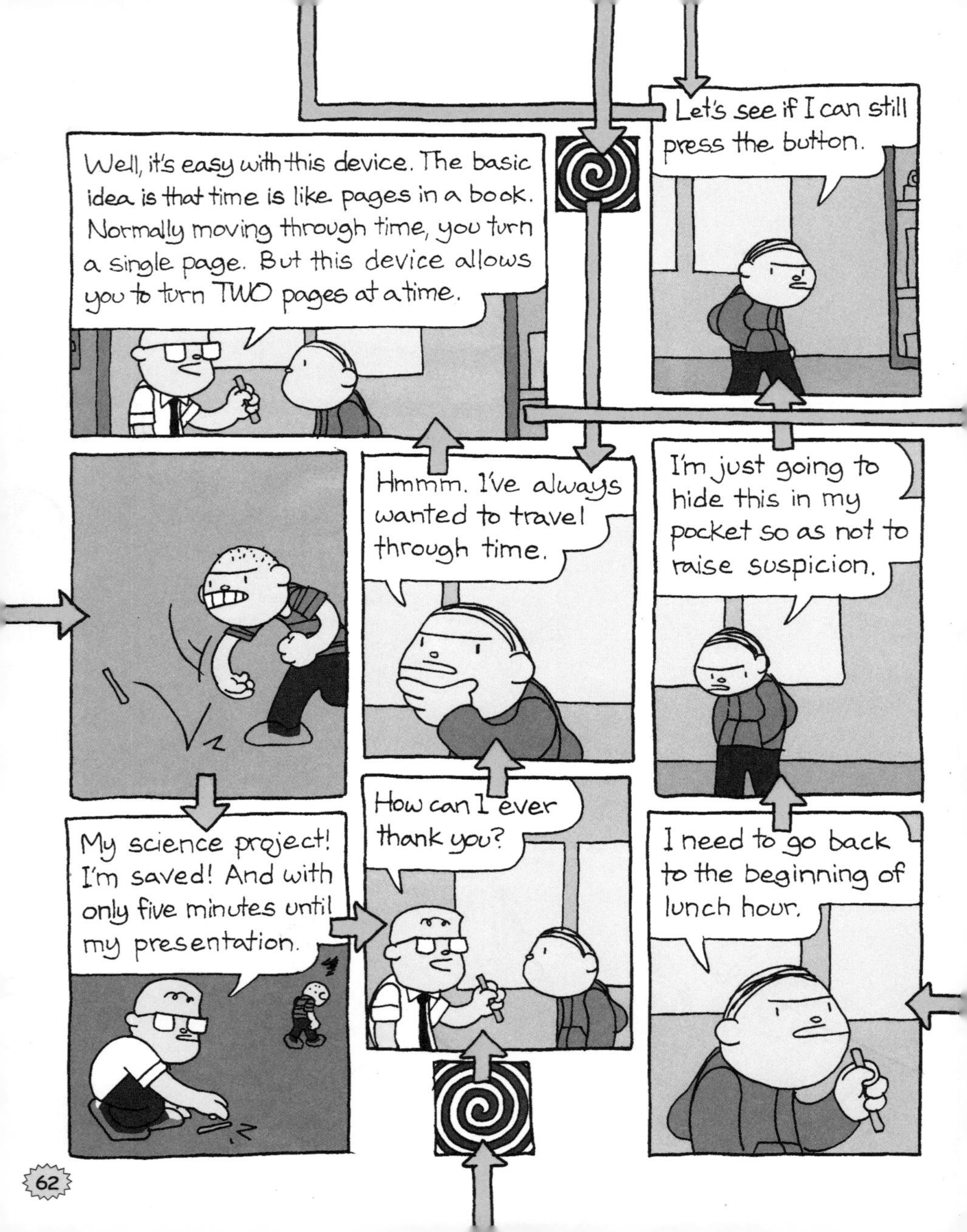
Let's see if I can still press the button.
Well, it's easy with this device. The basic idea is that time is like pages in a book. Normally moving through time, you turn a single page. But this device allows you to turn TWO pages at a time.
Hmmm. I've always wanted to travel through time.
I'm just going to hide this in my pocket so as not to raise suspicion.
My science project! I'm saved! And with only five minutes until my presentation.
How can I ever thank you?
I need to go back to the beginning of lunch hour.

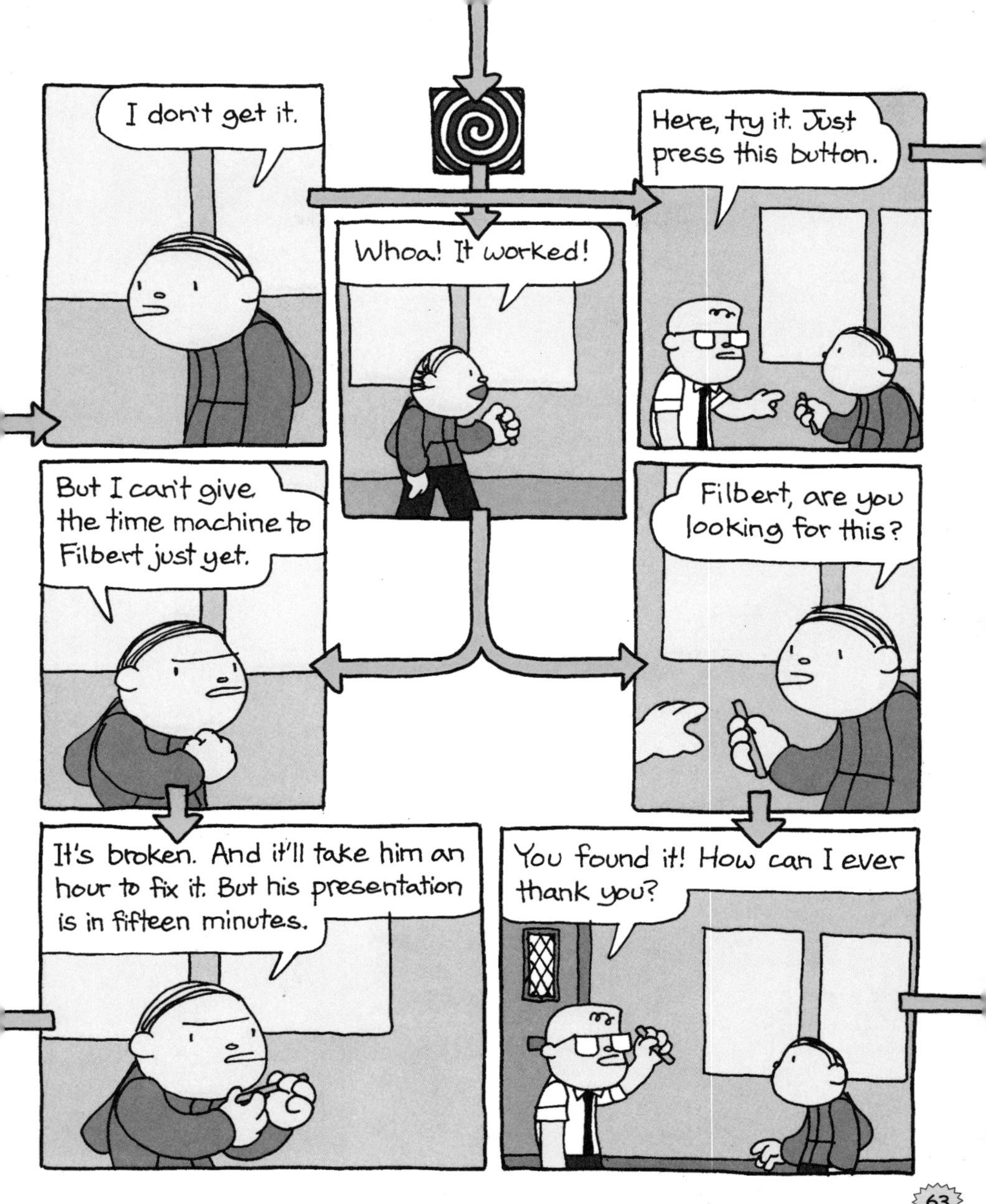
I don't get it.
Here, try it. Just press this button.
Whoa! It worked!
But I can't give the time machine to Filbert just yet.
Filbert, are you looking for this?
It's broken. And it'll take him an hour to fix it. But his presentation is in fifteen minutes.
You found it! How can I ever thank you?

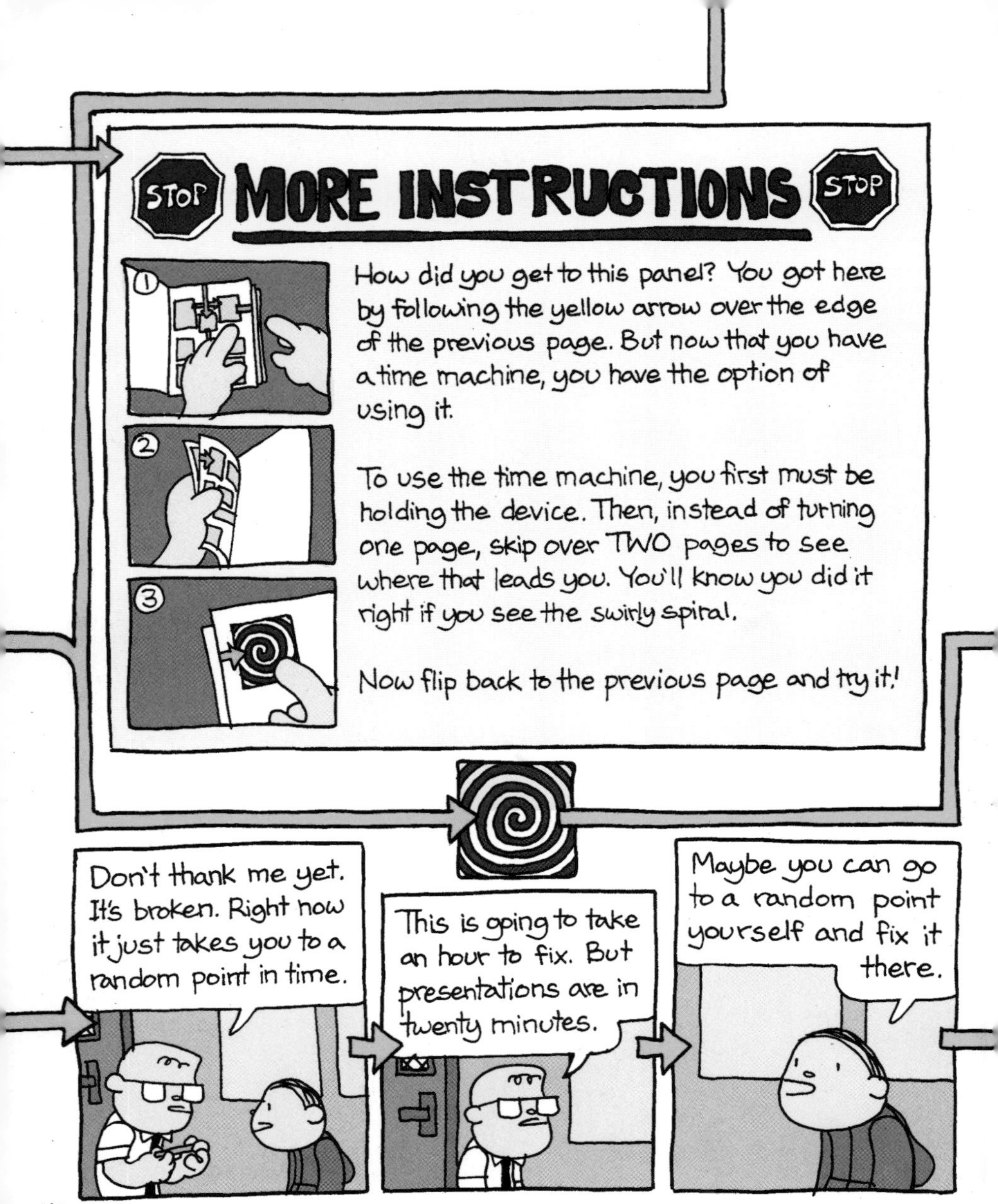
STOP MORE INSTRUCTIONS STOP
①
②
③
How did you get to this panel? You got here by following the yellow arrow over the edge of the previous page. But now that you have a time machine, you have the option of using it.
To use the time machine, you first must be holding the device. Then, instead of turning one page, skip over TWO pages to see where that leads you. You'll know you did it right if you see the swirly spiral.
Now flip back to the previous page and try it!
Don't thank me yet. It's broken. Right now it just takes you to a random point in time.
This is going to take an hour to fix. But presentations are in twenty minutes.
Maybe you can go to a random point yourself and fix it there.

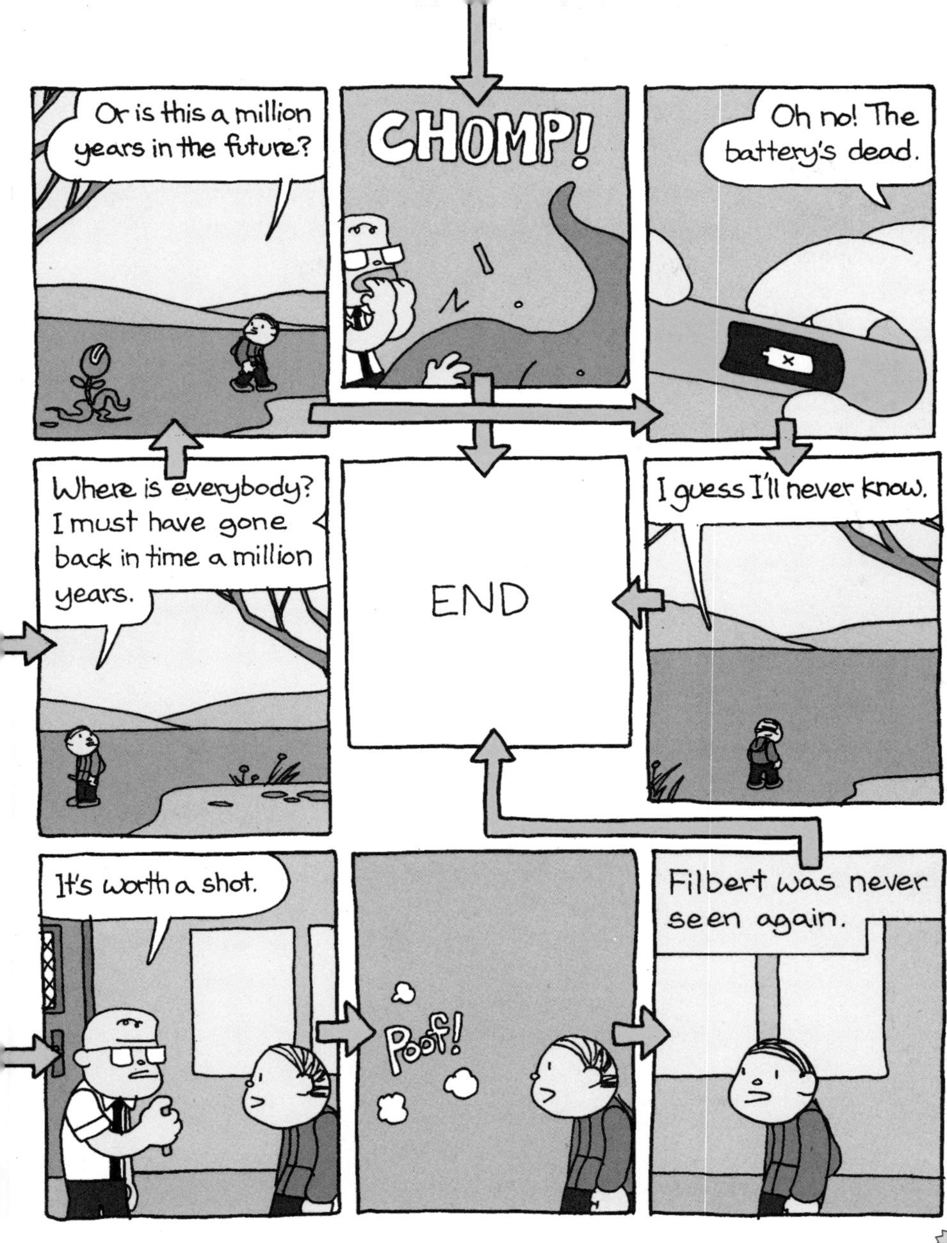
Or is this a million years in the future?
CHOMP!
Oh no! The battery's dead.
Where is everybody? I must have gone back in time a million years.
END
I guess I'll never know.
It's worth a shot.
Poof!
Filbert was never seen again.

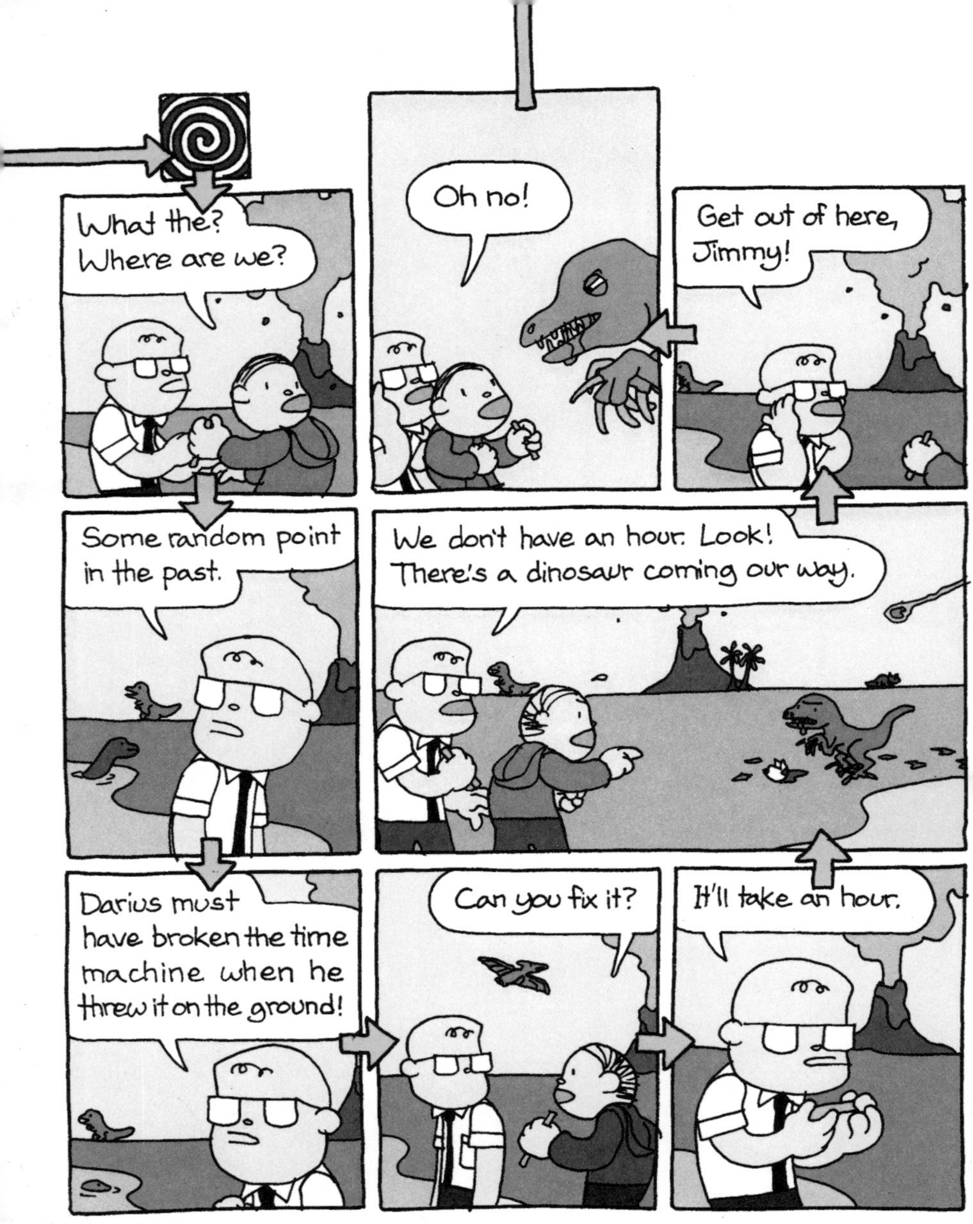
What the? Where are we?
Some random point in the past.
Darius must have broken the time machine when he threw it on the ground!
Can you fix it?
It'll take an hour.
We don't have an hour. Look! There's a dinosaur coming our way.
Get out of here, Jimmy!
Oh no!

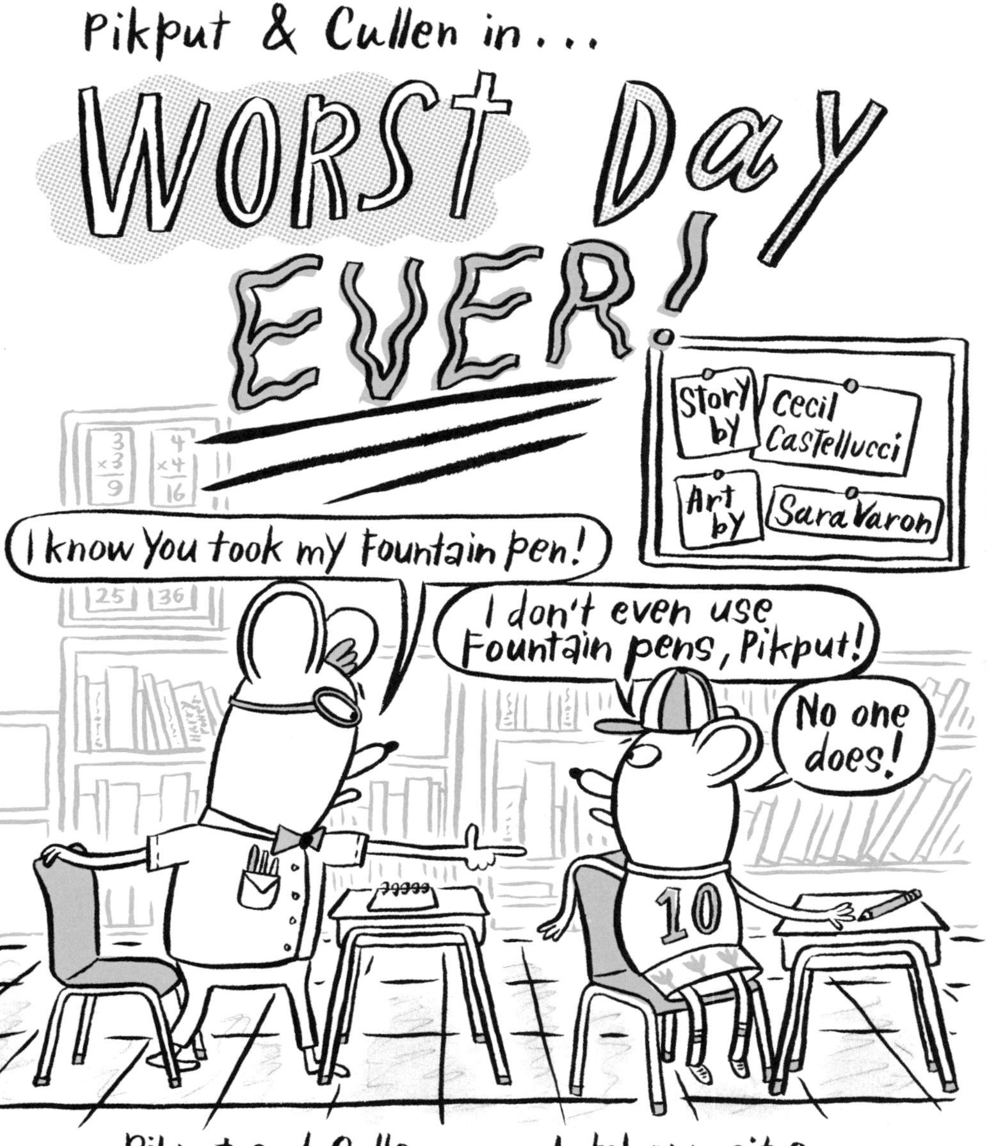
Pikput & Cullen in...
WORST Day EVER!
Story by Cecil Castellucci
Art by Sara Varon
I know You took my Fountain pen!
I don't even use Fountain pens, Pikput!
No one does!
10

Pikput and Cullen were total opposites.

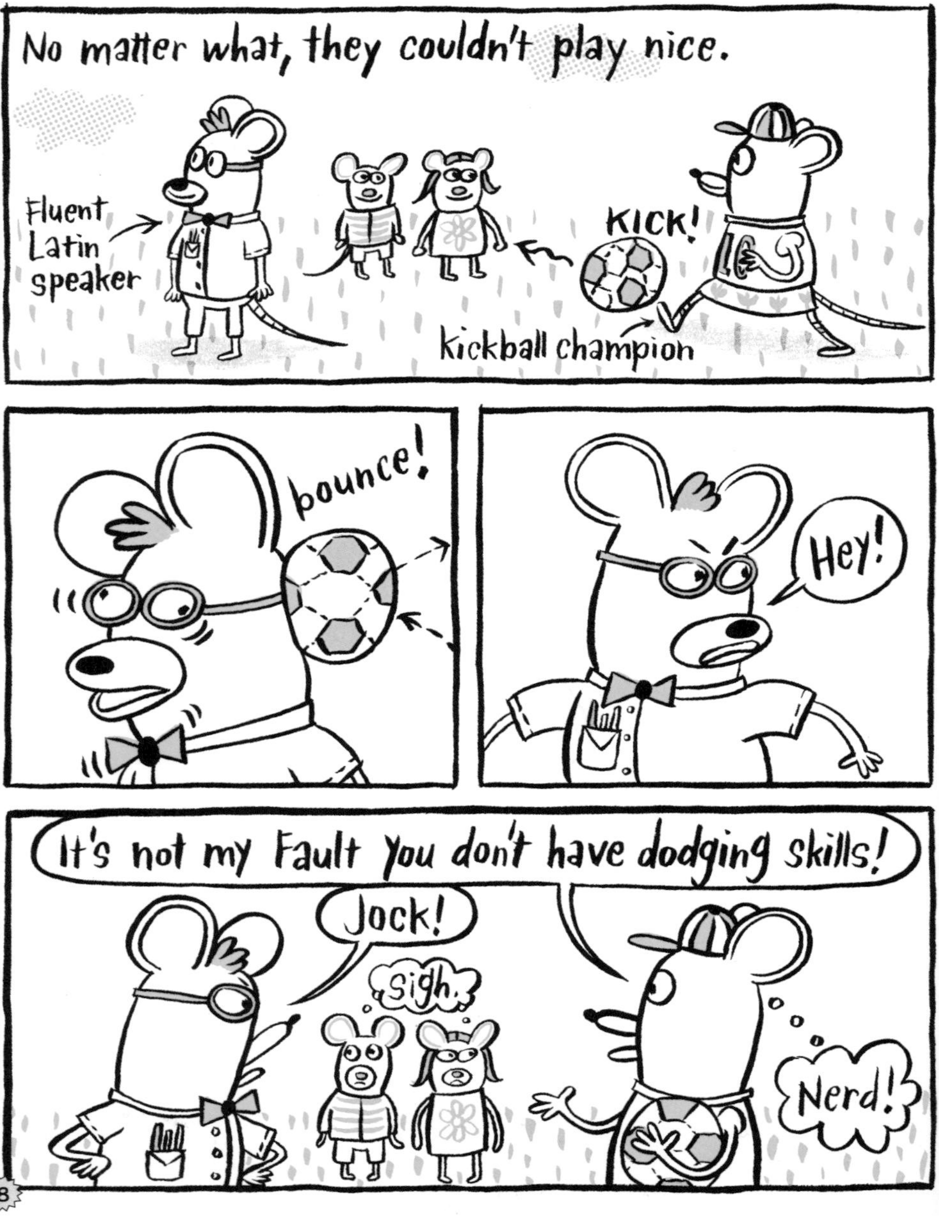
No matter what, they couldn't play nice.
Fluent Latin speaker
KICK!
kickball champion
bounce!
Hey!
It's not my Fault you don't have dodging skills!
Jock!
sigh.
Nerd!

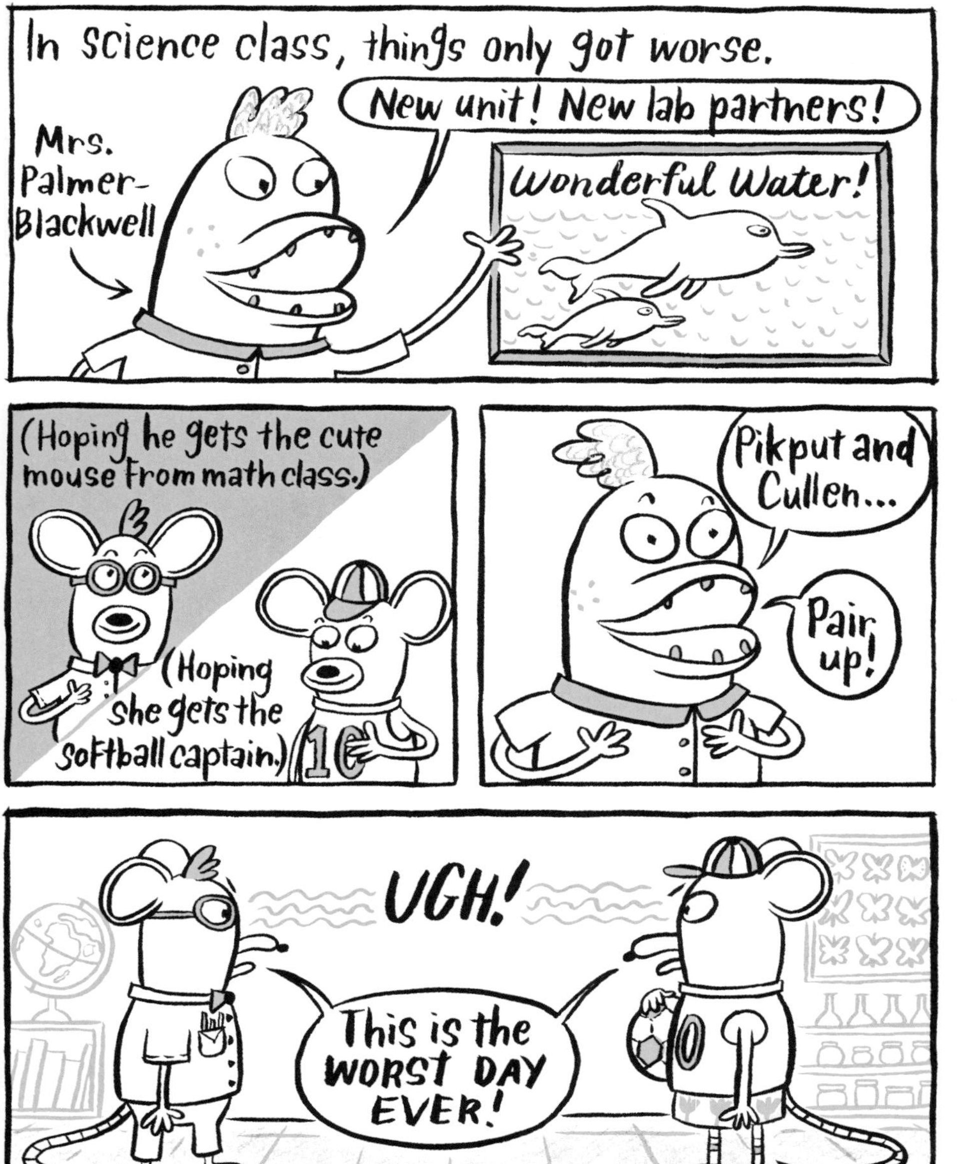
In science class, things only got worse.
Mrs. Palmer-Blackwell
New unit! New lab partners!
Wonderful Water!
(Hoping he gets the cute mouse from math class.)
(Hoping she gets the softball captain.)
Pikput and Cullen...
Pair up!
UGH!
This is the WORST DAY EVER!

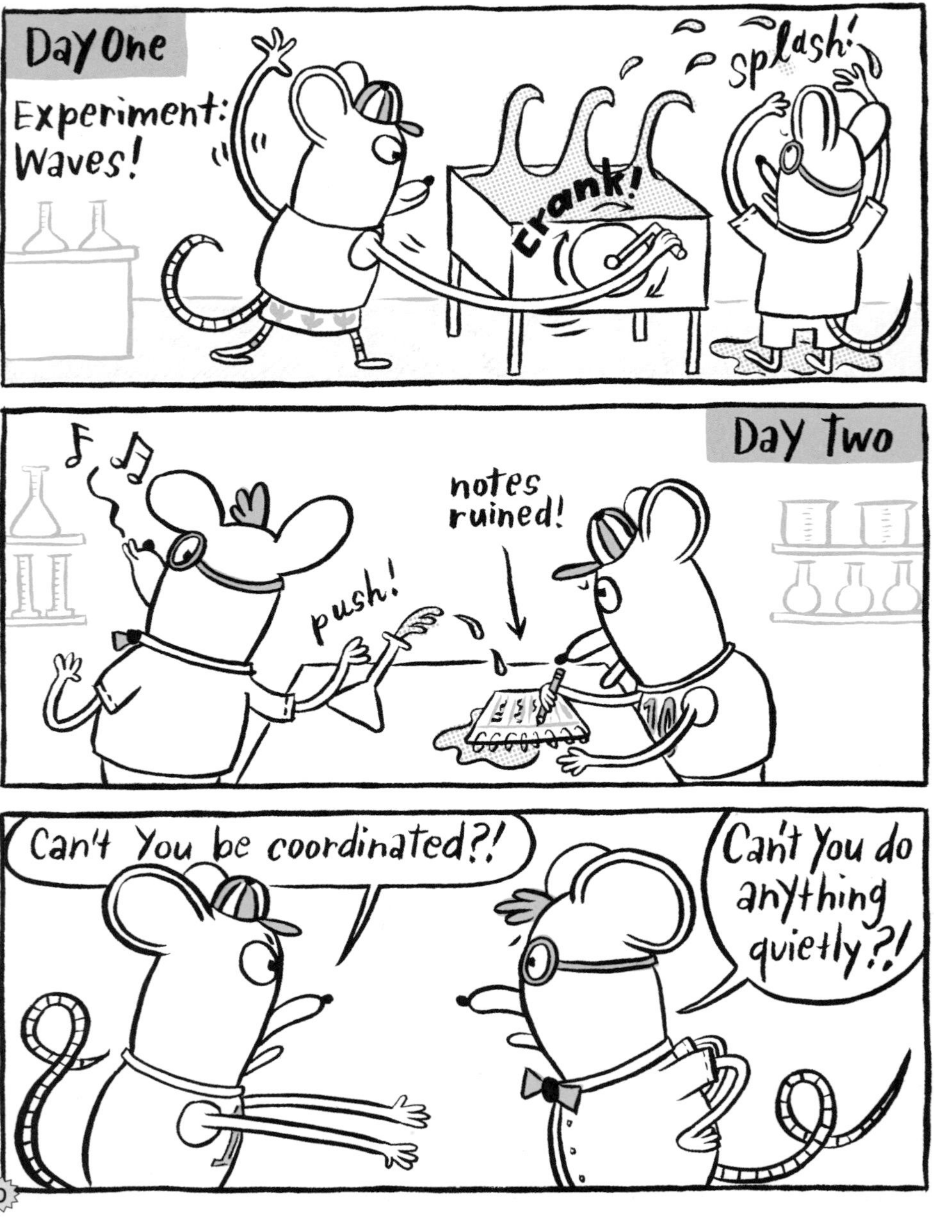
Day One
Experiment: Waves!
crank!
splash!
Day Two
notes ruined!
push!
Can't You be coordinated?!
Can't You do anything quietly?!

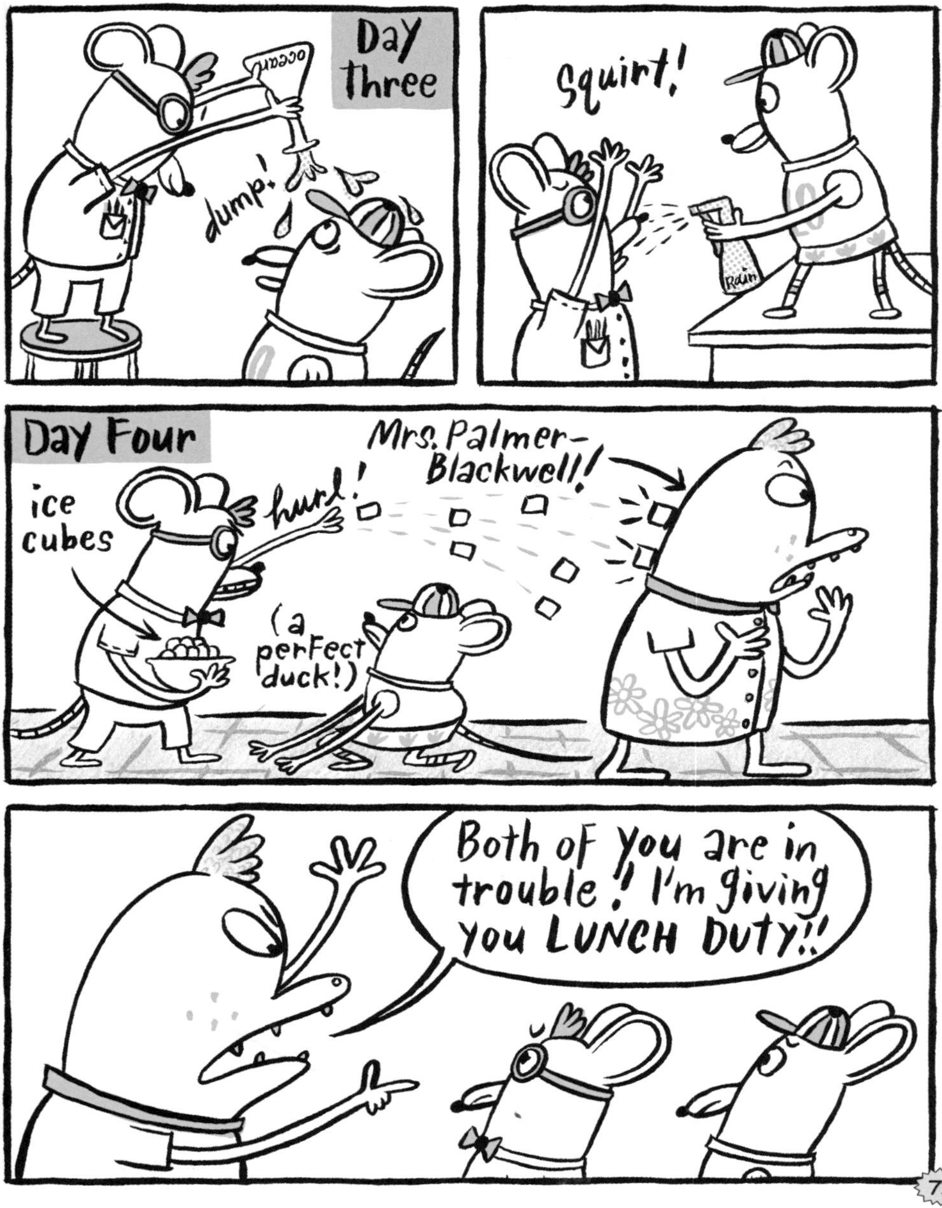
Day Three
ocean
dump!
Squirt!
Rain
Day Four
ice cubes
hurl!
Mrs. Palmer-Blackwell!
(a perfect duck!)
Both of you are in trouble! I'm giving you LUNCH DUTY!!

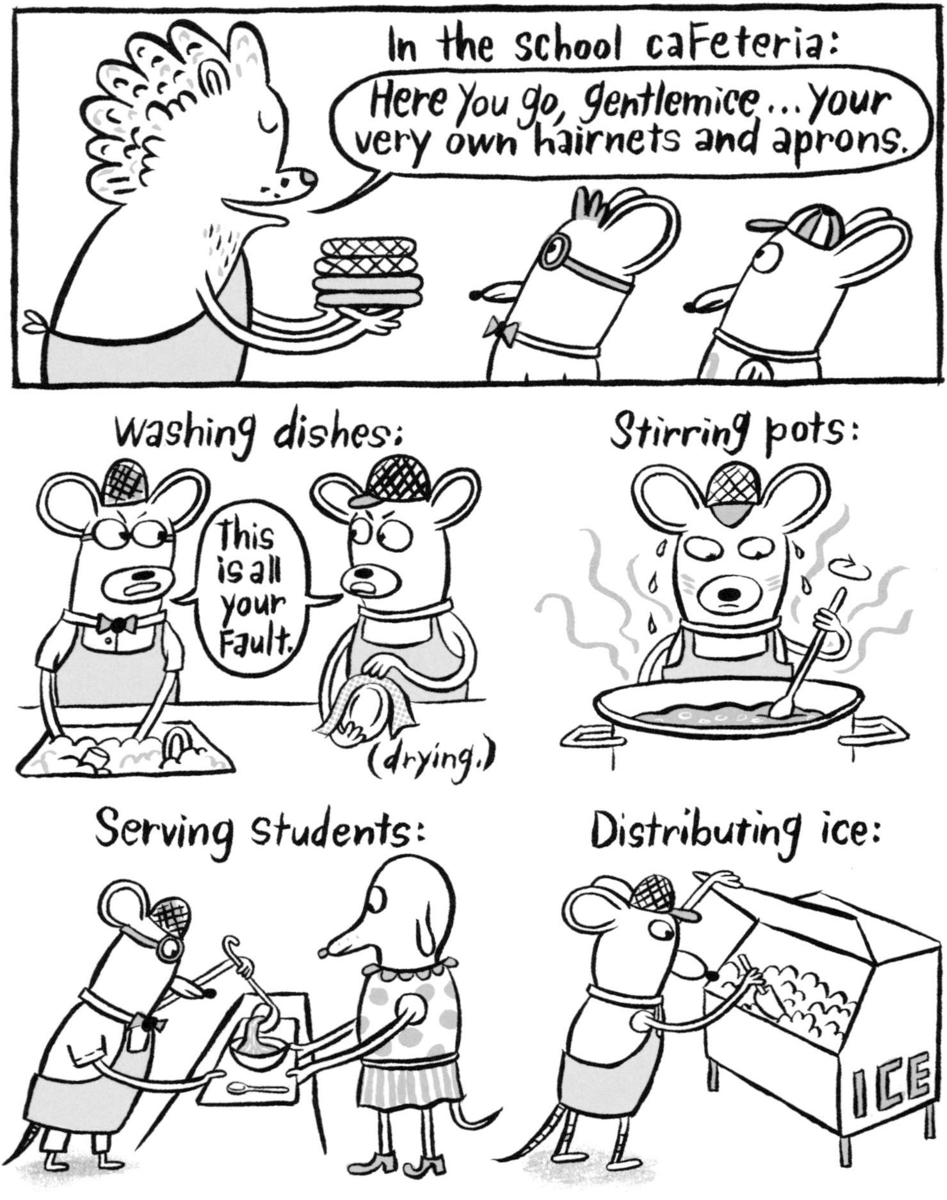
In the school cafeteria:
Here you go, gentlemice... your very own hairnets and aprons.
Washing dishes:
This is all your fault.
(drying.)
Stirring pots:
Serving students:
Distributing ice:
ICE

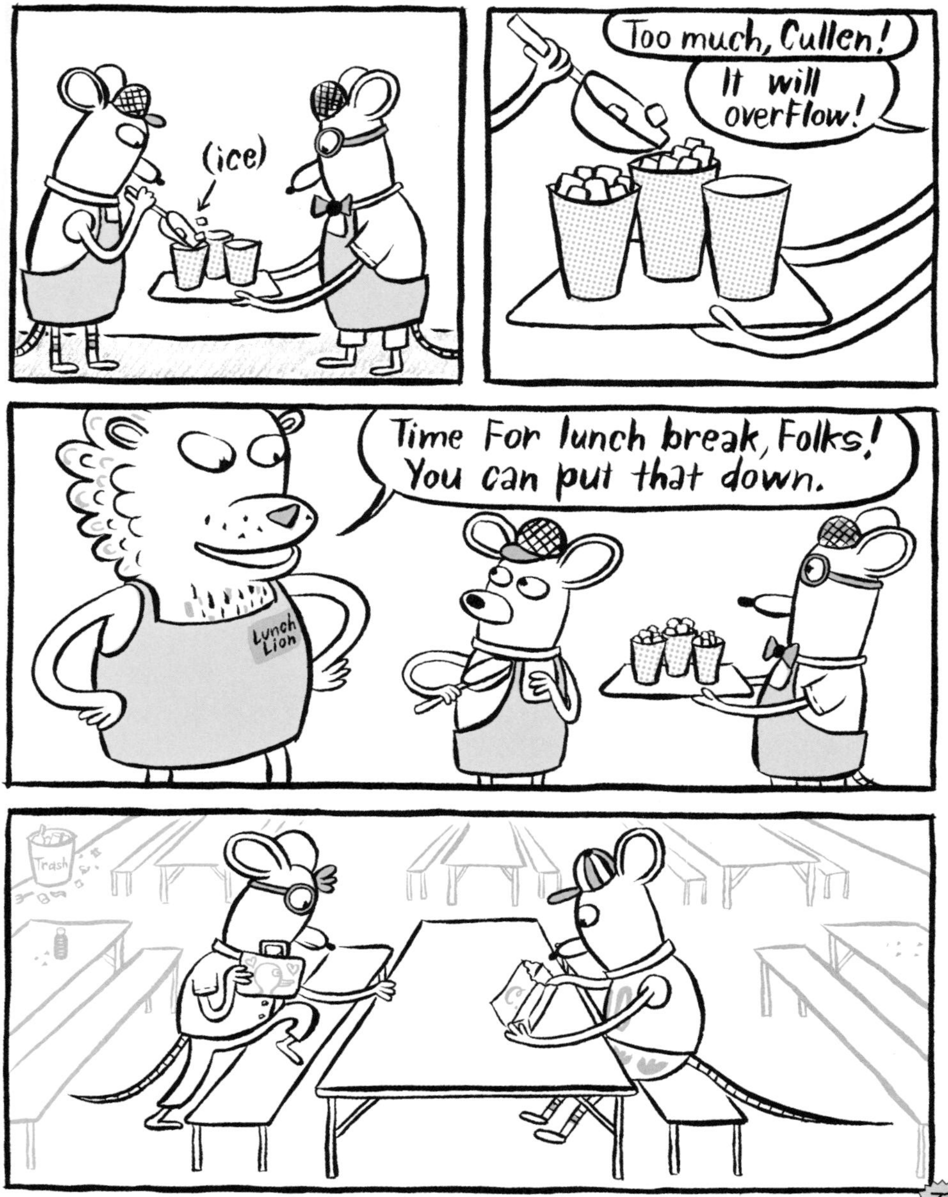
(ice)
Too much, Cullen!
It will overflow!
Time for lunch break, folks! You can put that down.
Lunch Lion
Trash

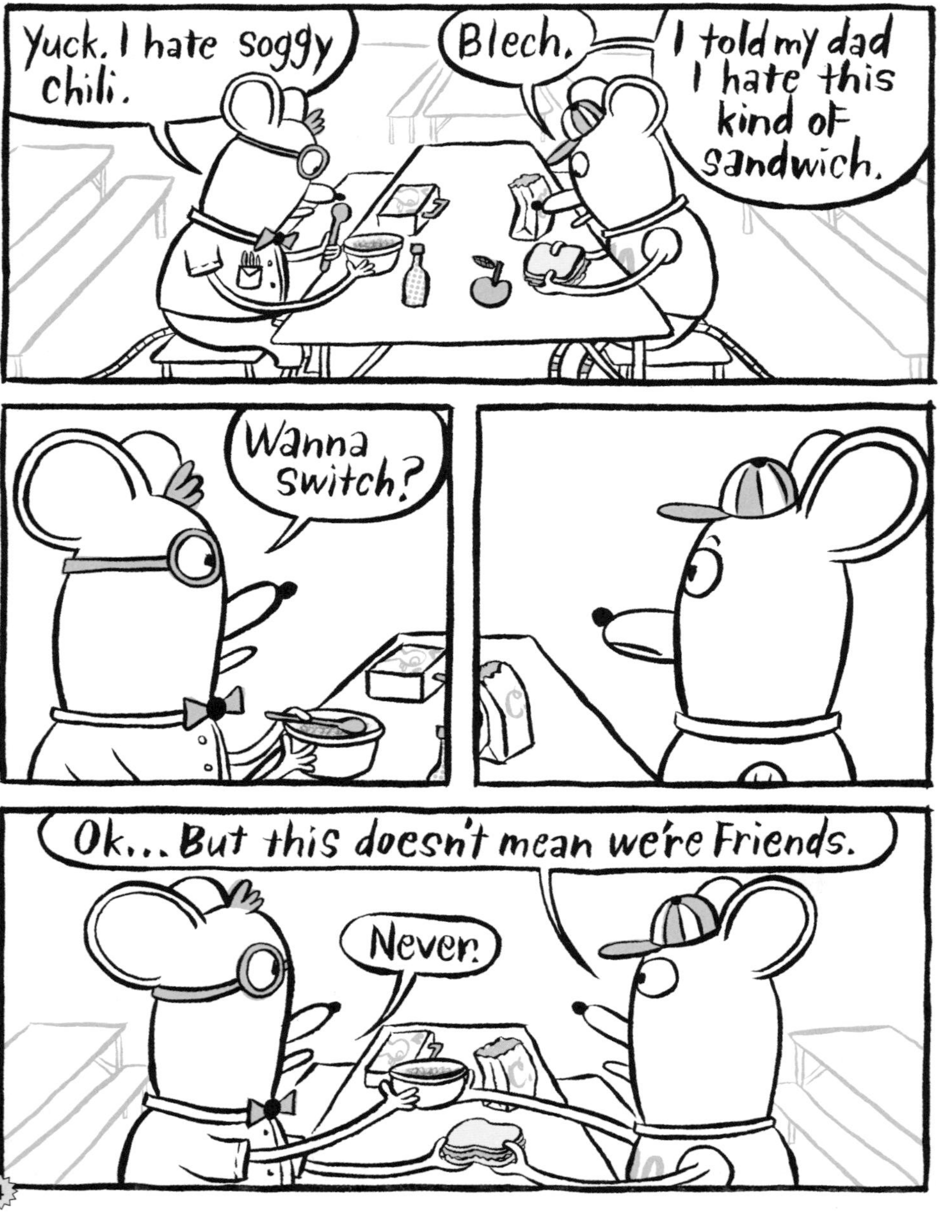
Yuck. I hate soggy chili.
Blech.
I told my dad I hate this kind of sandwich.
Wanna switch?
Ok... But this doesn't mean we're Friends.
Never.

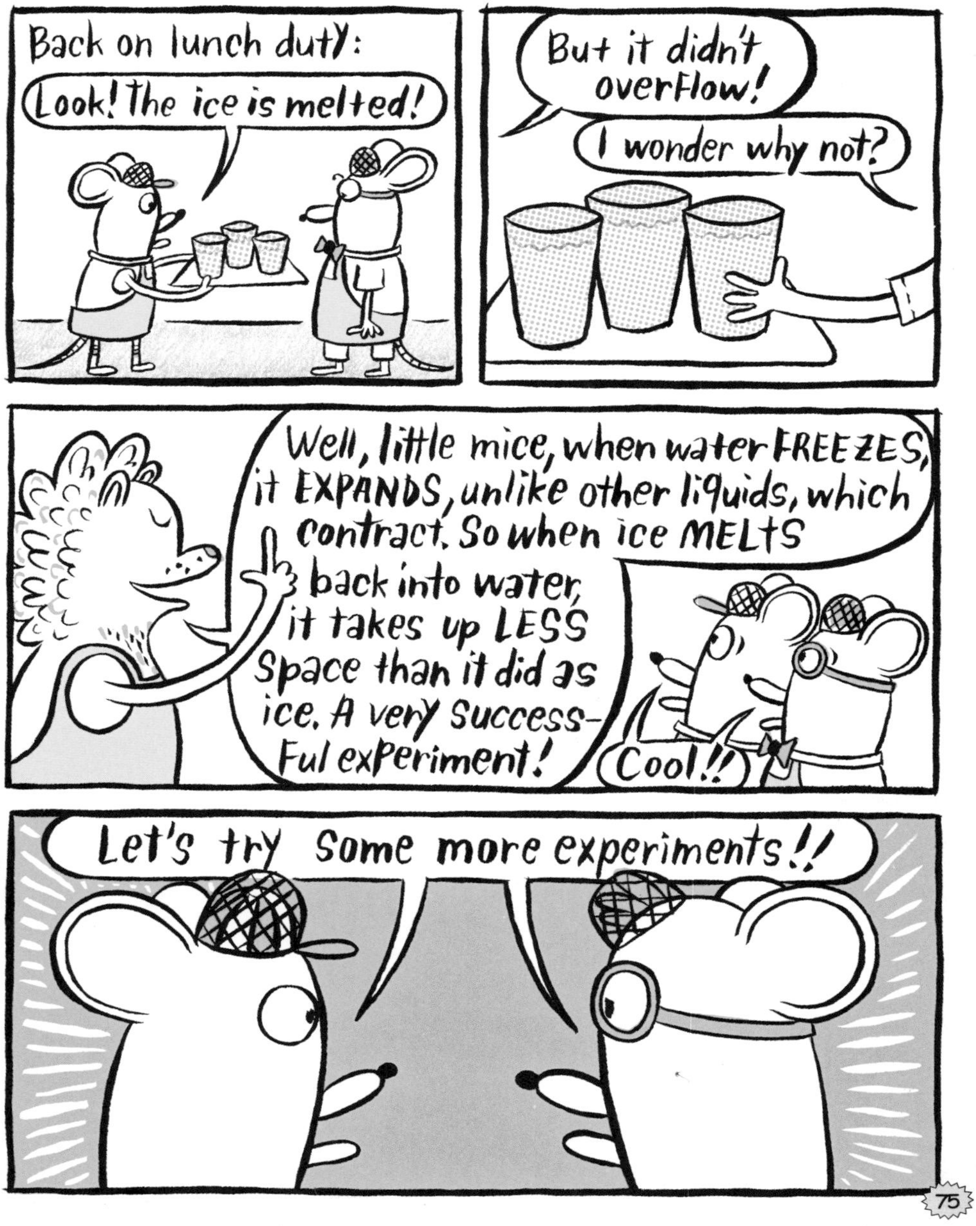
Back on lunch duty:
Look! The ice is melted!
But it didn't overflow!
I wonder why not?
Well, little mice, when water FREEZES, it EXPANDS, unlike other liquids, which contract. So when ice MELTS back into water, it takes up LESS space than it did as ice. A very success-ful experiment!
Cool!!
Let's try some more experiments!!

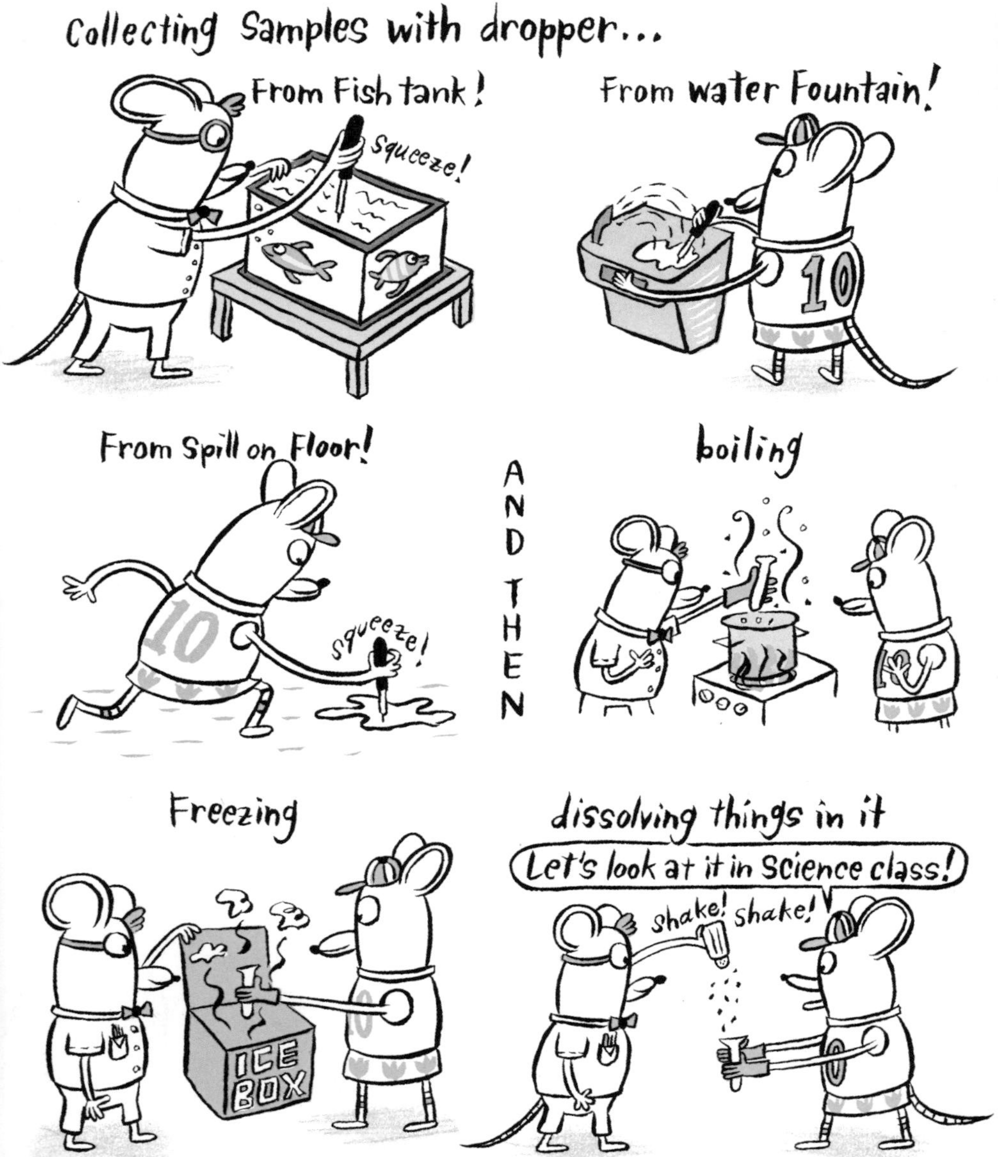
Collecting Samples with dropper...
From Fish tank!
Squeeze!
From water Fountain!
From Spill on Floor!
squeeze!
AND THEN
boiling
Freezing
ICE BOX
dissolving things in it
Let's look at it in Science class!
shake! shake!

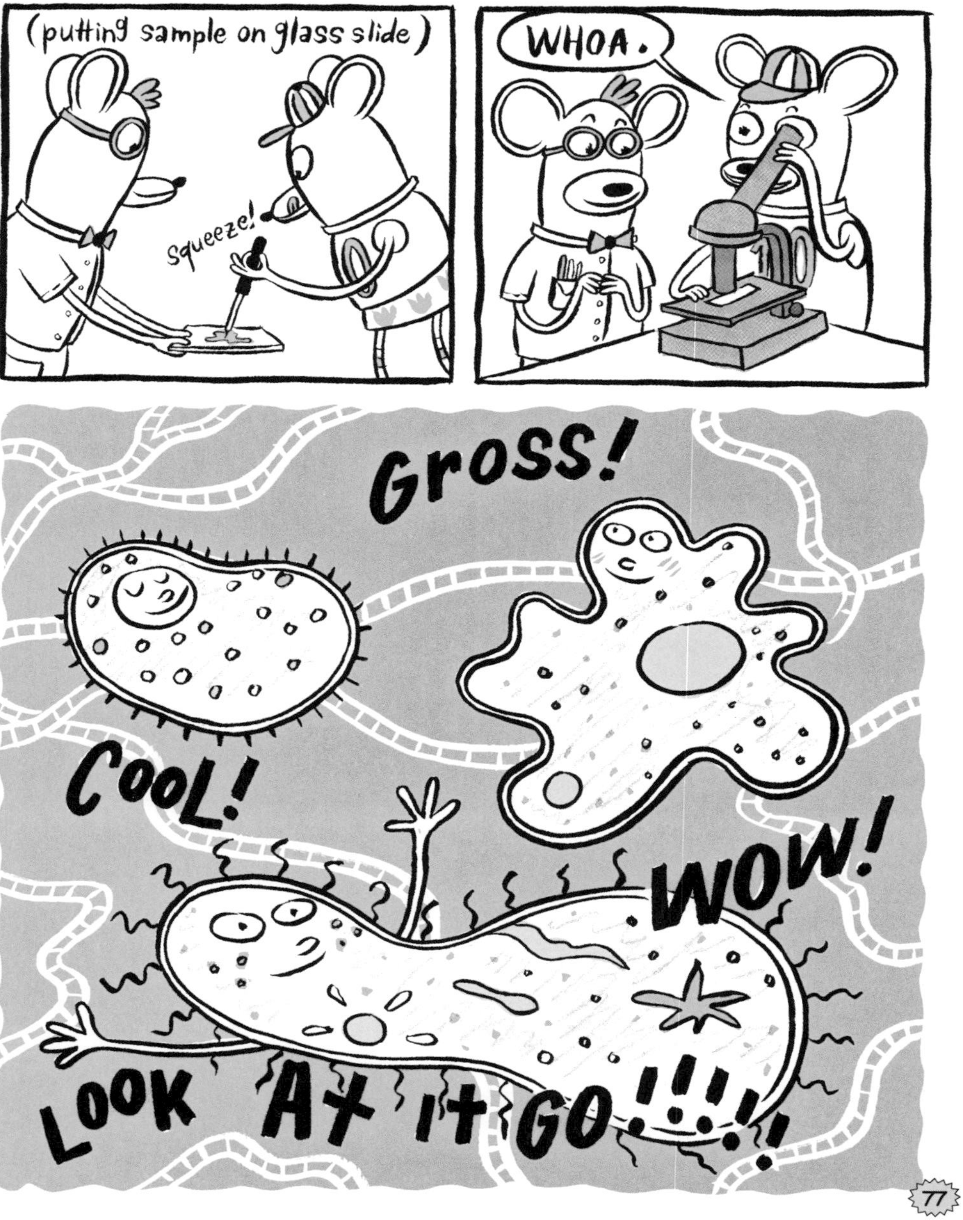
(putting sample on glass slide)
squeeze!
WHOA.
GROSS!
COOL!
WOW!
LOOK AT IT GO!!!!!

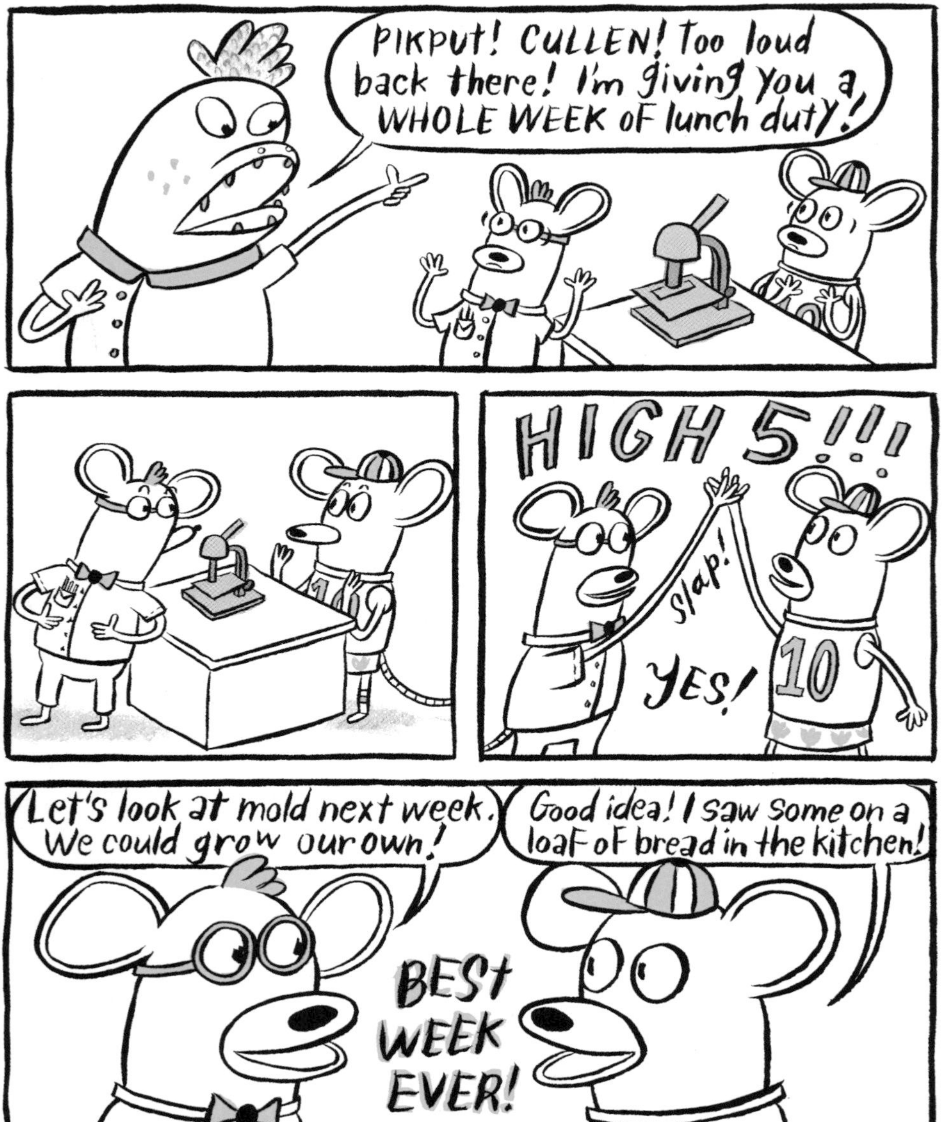
PIKPUT! CULLEN! Too loud back there! I'm giving you a WHOLE WEEK OF lunch duty!
HIGH 5!!!
slap!
YES!
10
Let's look at mold next week. We could grow our own!
Good idea! I saw some on a loaf of bread in the kitchen!
BEST WEEK EVER!

Sometimes the worst day leads to a best friend.

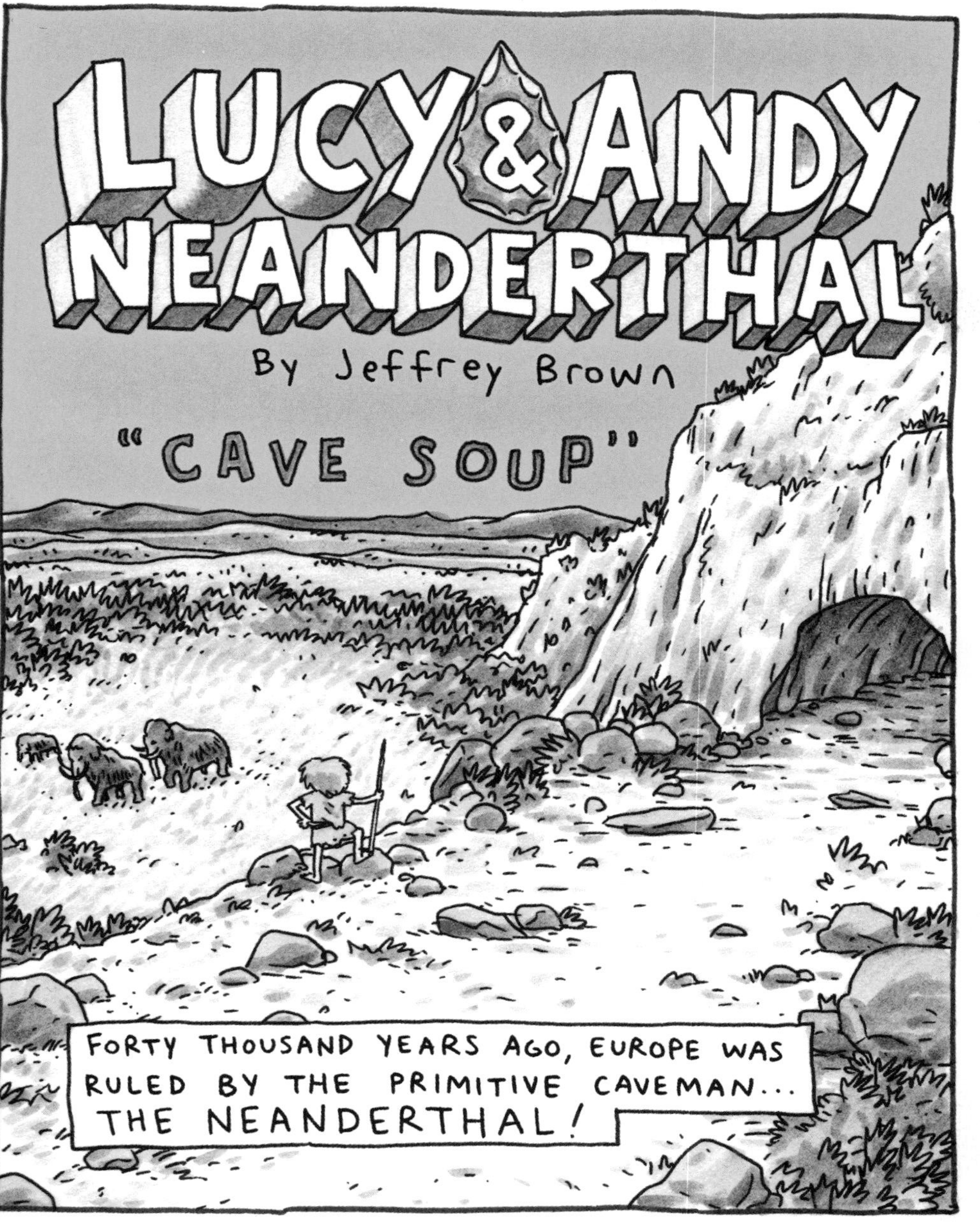
LUCY & ANDY NEANDERTHAL
By Jeffrey Brown
"CAVE SOUP"
FORTY THOUSAND YEARS AGO, EUROPE WAS RULED BY THE PRIMITIVE CAVEMAN... THE NEANDERTHAL!

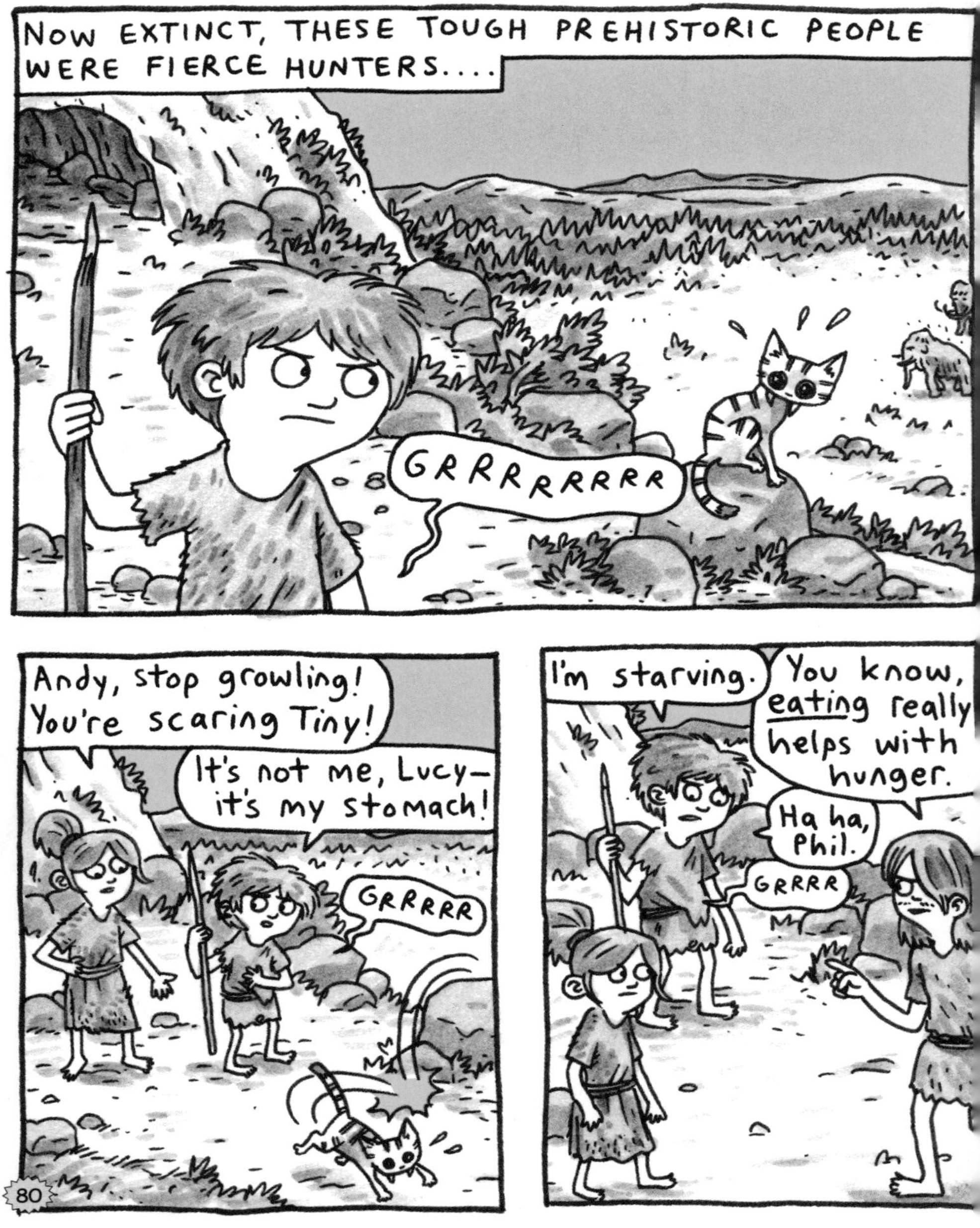
NOW EXTINCT, THESE TOUGH PREHISTORIC PEOPLE WERE FIERCE HUNTERS....
GRRRRRRRRR
Andy, stop growling! You're scaring Tiny!
It's not me, Lucy— it's my stomach!
GRRRRR
I'm starving.
You know, eating really helps with hunger.
Ha ha, Phil.
GRRRR

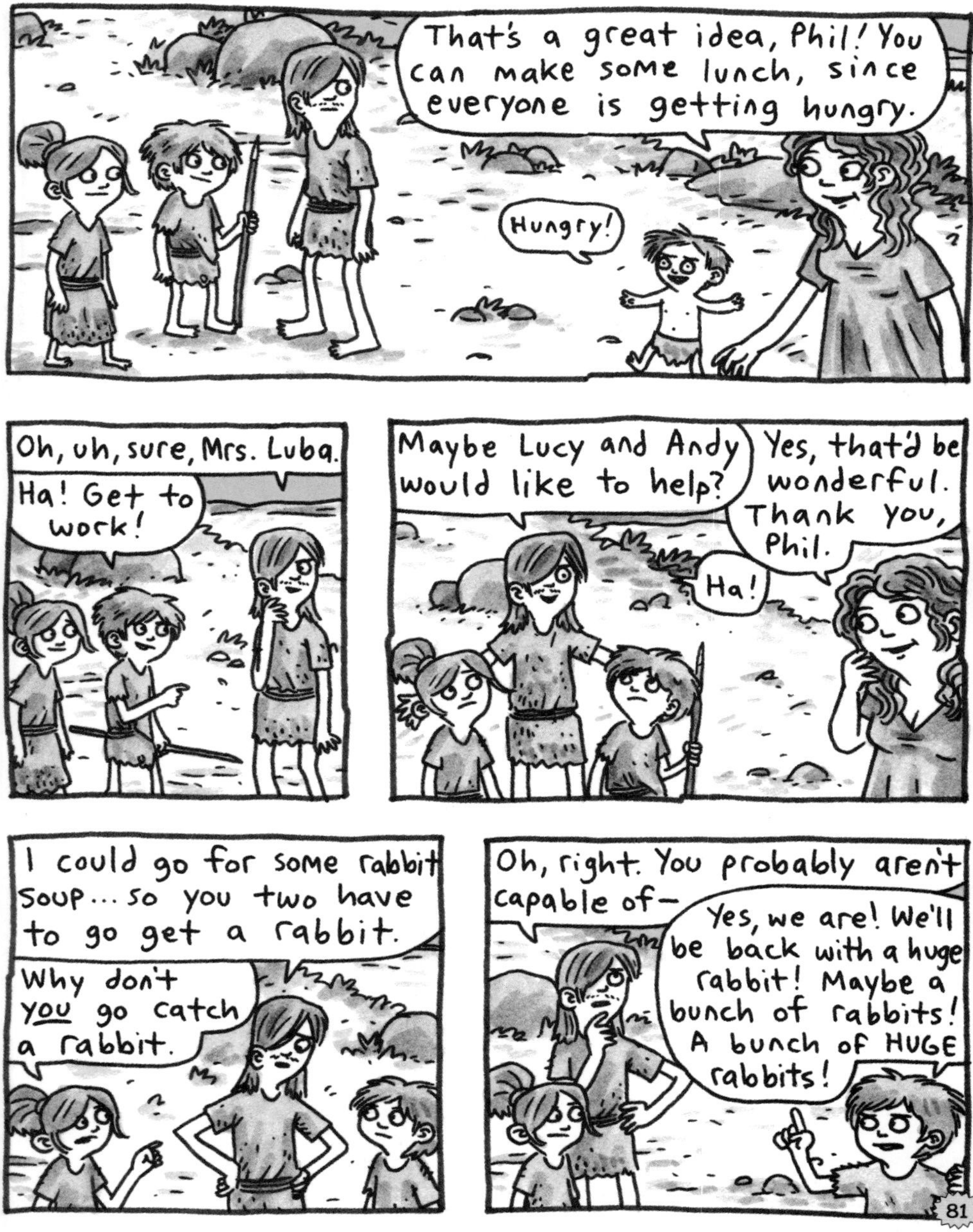
That's a great idea, Phil! You can make some lunch, since everyone is getting hungry.
Hungry!
Oh, uh, sure, Mrs. Luba.
Ha! Get to work!
Maybe Lucy and Andy would like to help?
Yes, that'd be wonderful. Thank you, Phil.
Ha!
I could go for some rabbit soup... so you two have to go get a rabbit.
Why don't YOU go catch a rabbit.
Oh, right. You probably aren't capable of—
Yes, we are! We'll be back with a huge rabbit! Maybe a bunch of rabbits! A bunch of HUGE rabbits!

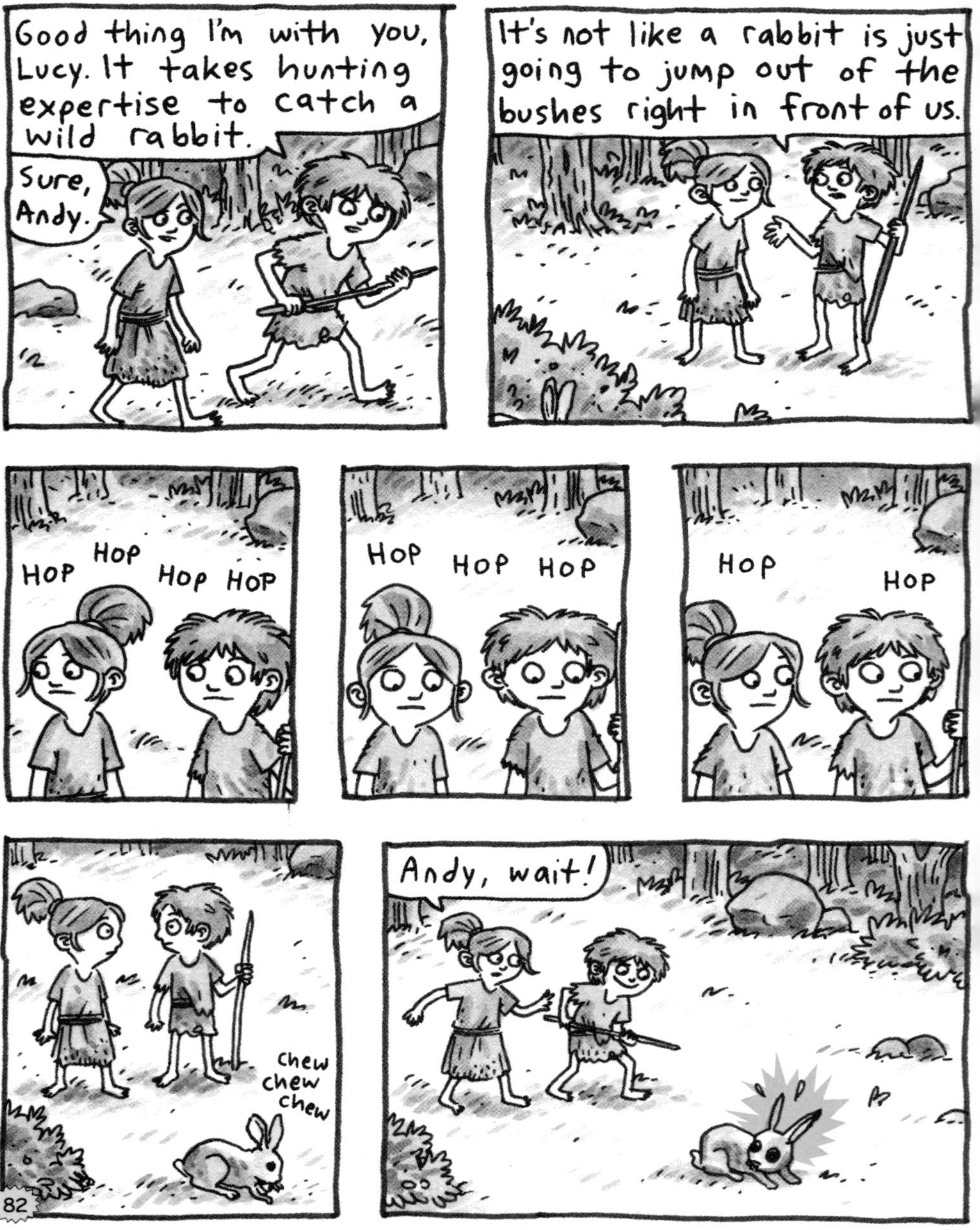
Good thing I'm with you, Lucy. It takes hunting expertise to catch a wild rabbit.
Sure, Andy.
It's not like a rabbit is just going to jump out of the bushes right in front of us.
HOP
HOP
HOP HOP
HOP
HOP HOP
HOP
HOP
chew chew chew
Andy, wait!

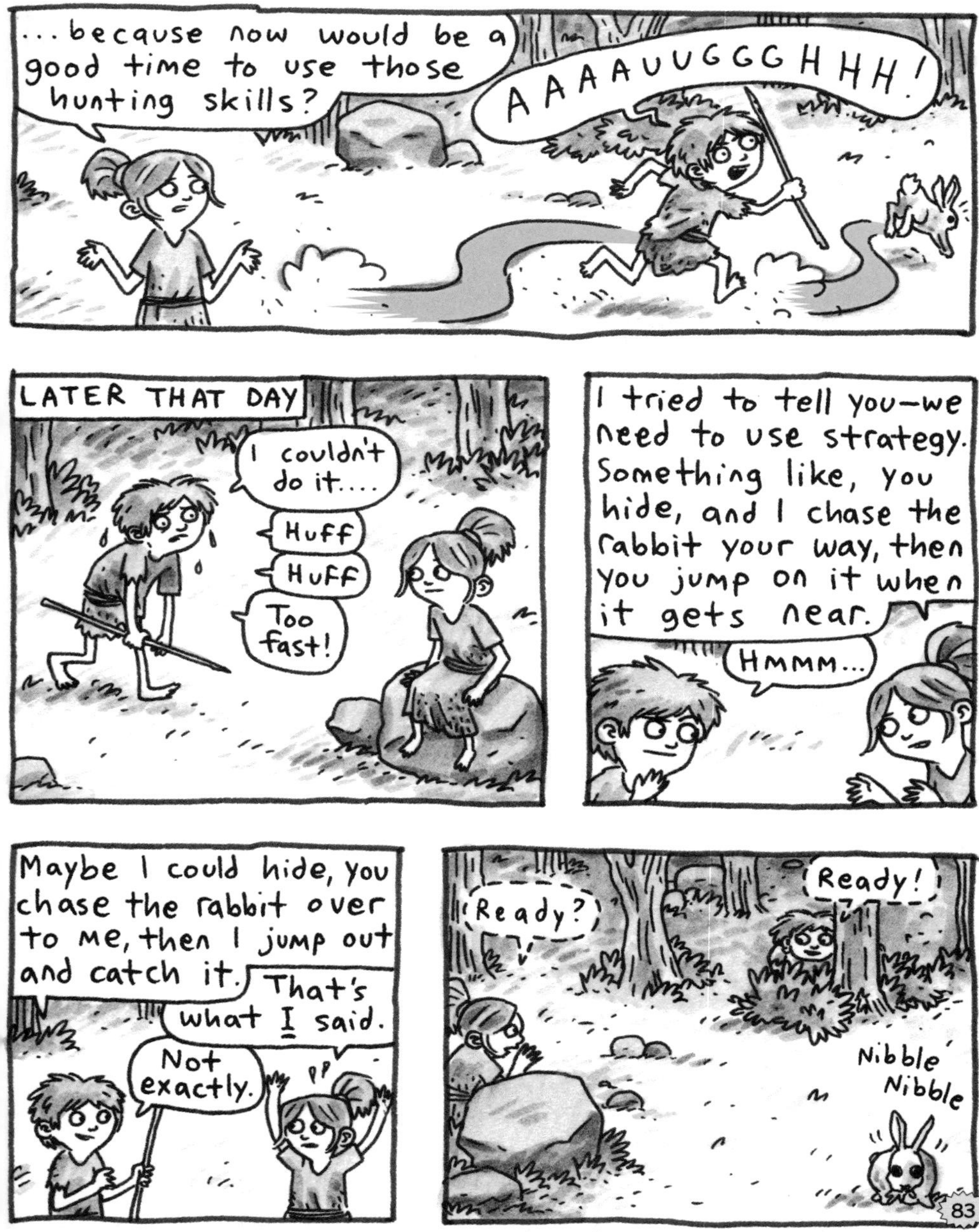
...because now would be a good time to use those hunting skills?
AAAAUUGGGHHHH!
LATER THAT DAY
I couldn't do it....
Huff
Huff
Too fast!
I tried to tell you—we need to use strategy. Something like, you hide, and I chase the rabbit your way, then you jump on it when it gets near.
HMMM...
Maybe I could hide, you chase the rabbit over to me, then I jump out and catch it.
That's what I said.
Not exactly.
Ready?
Ready!
Nibble
Nibble

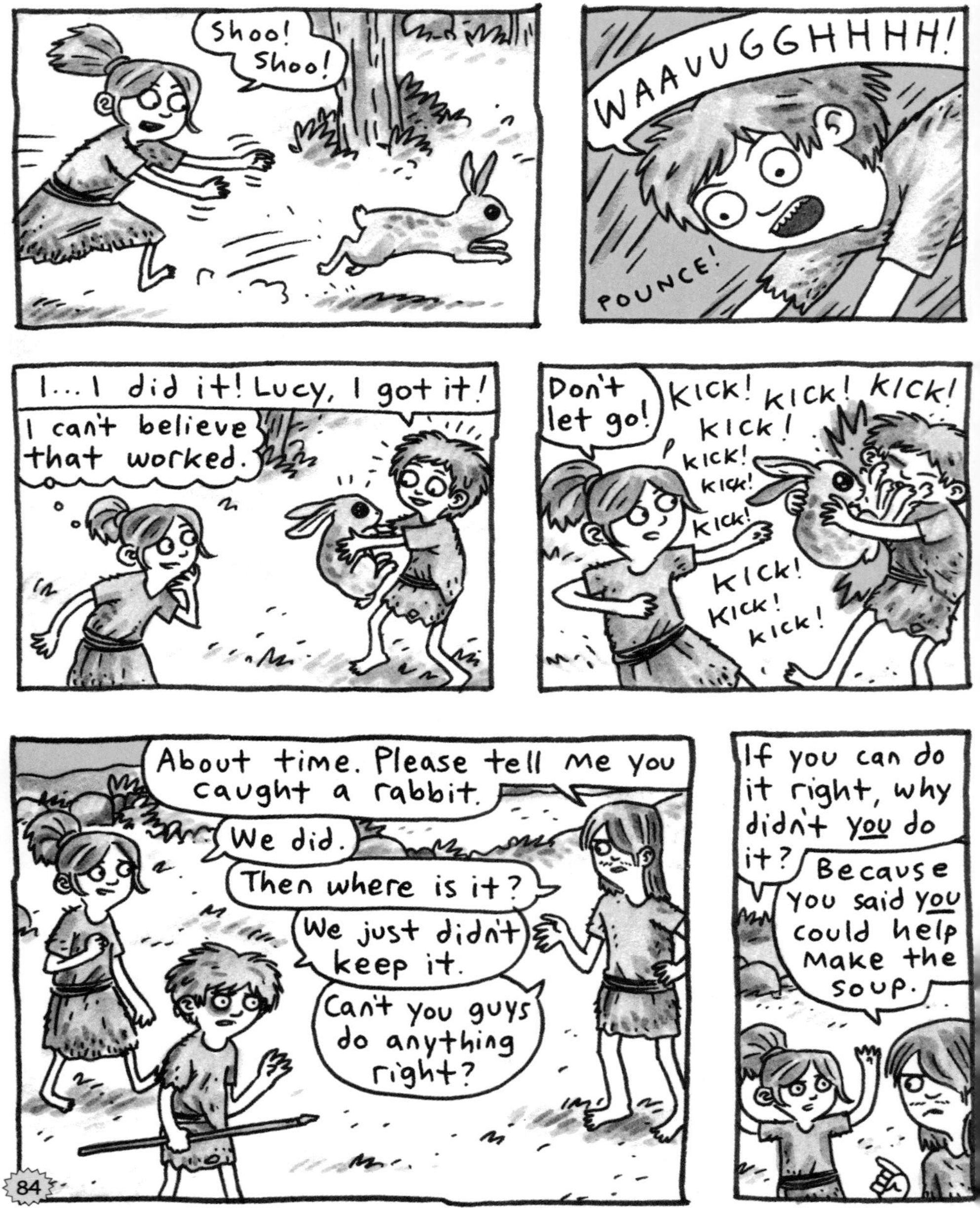
Shoo! Shoo!
WAAUUGGHHHH!
POUNCE!
I... I did it! Lucy, I got it!
I can't believe that worked.
Don't let go!
KICK! KICK! KICK! KICK! KICK! KICK! KICK! KICK! KICK! KICK!
About time. Please tell me you caught a rabbit.
We did.
Then where is it?
We just didn't keep it.
Can't you guys do anything right?
If you can do it right, why didn't you do it?
Because you said you could help make the soup.

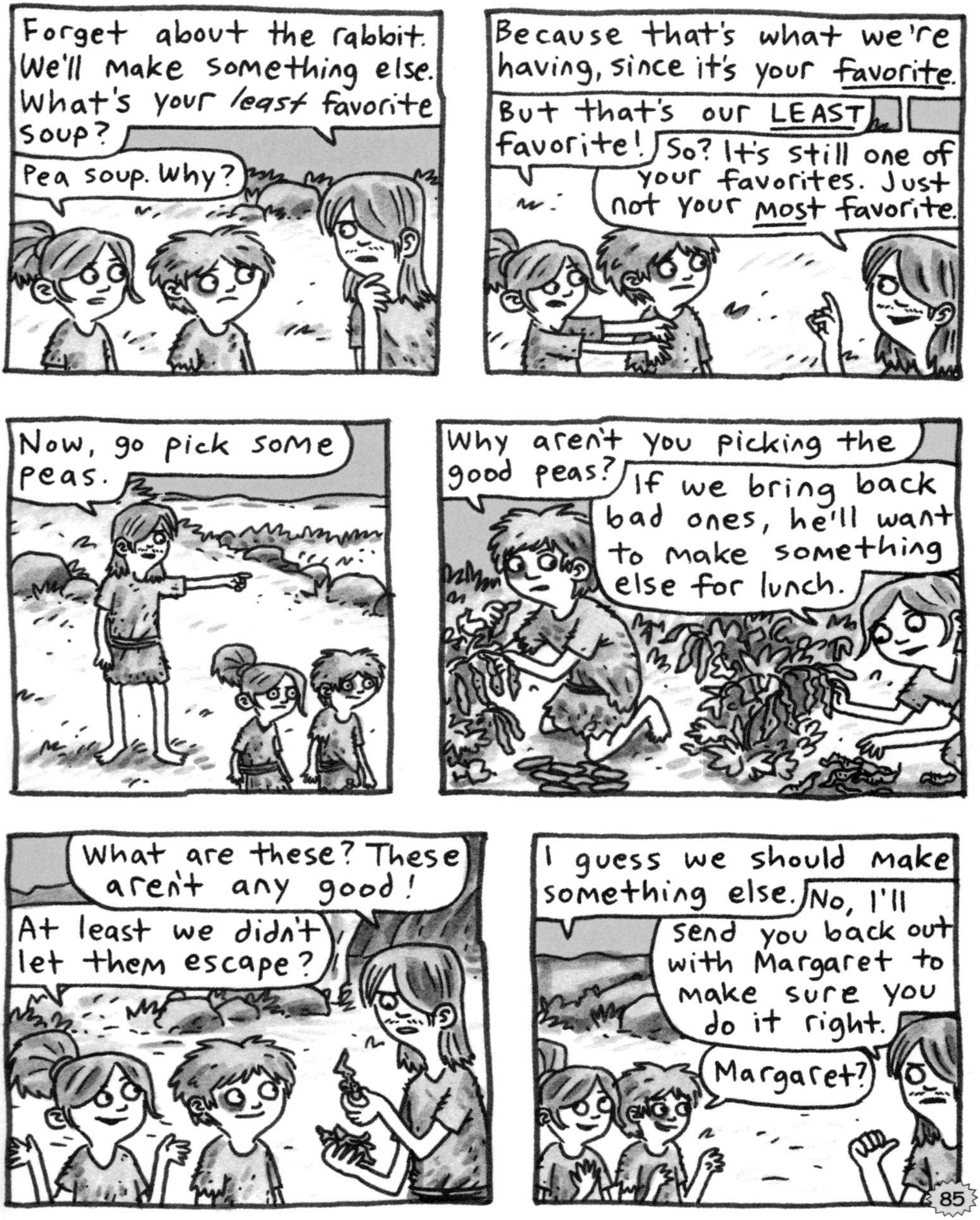
Forget about the rabbit. We'll make something else. What's your *least* favorite soup?
Pea soup. Why?
Because that's what we're having, since it's your favorite.
But that's our LEAST favorite!
So? It's still one of your favorites. Just not your MOST favorite.
Now, go pick some peas.
Why aren't you picking the good peas?
If we bring back bad ones, he'll want to make something else for lunch.
What are these? These aren't any good!
At least we didn't let them escape?
I guess we should make something else.
No, I'll send you back out with Margaret to make sure you do it right.
Margaret?

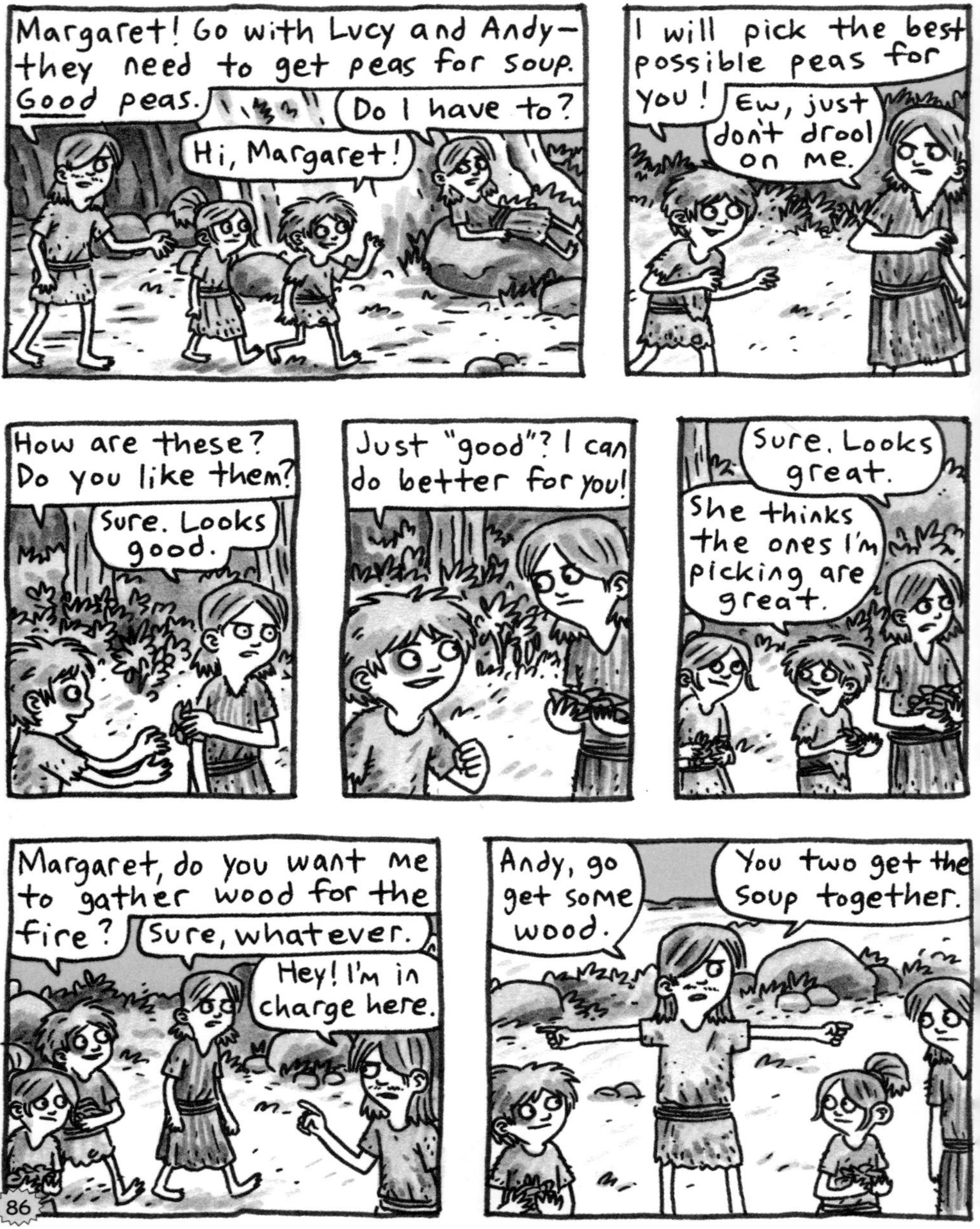
Margaret! Go with Lucy and Andy—they need to get peas for soup. Good peas.
Hi, Margaret!
Do I have to?
I will pick the best possible peas for you!
Ew, just don't drool on me.
How are these? Do you like them?
Sure. Looks good.
Just "good"? I can do better for you!
Sure. Looks great.
She thinks the ones I'm picking are great.
Margaret, do you want me to gather wood for the fire?
Sure, whatever.
Hey! I'm in charge here.
Andy, go get some wood.
You two get the soup together.

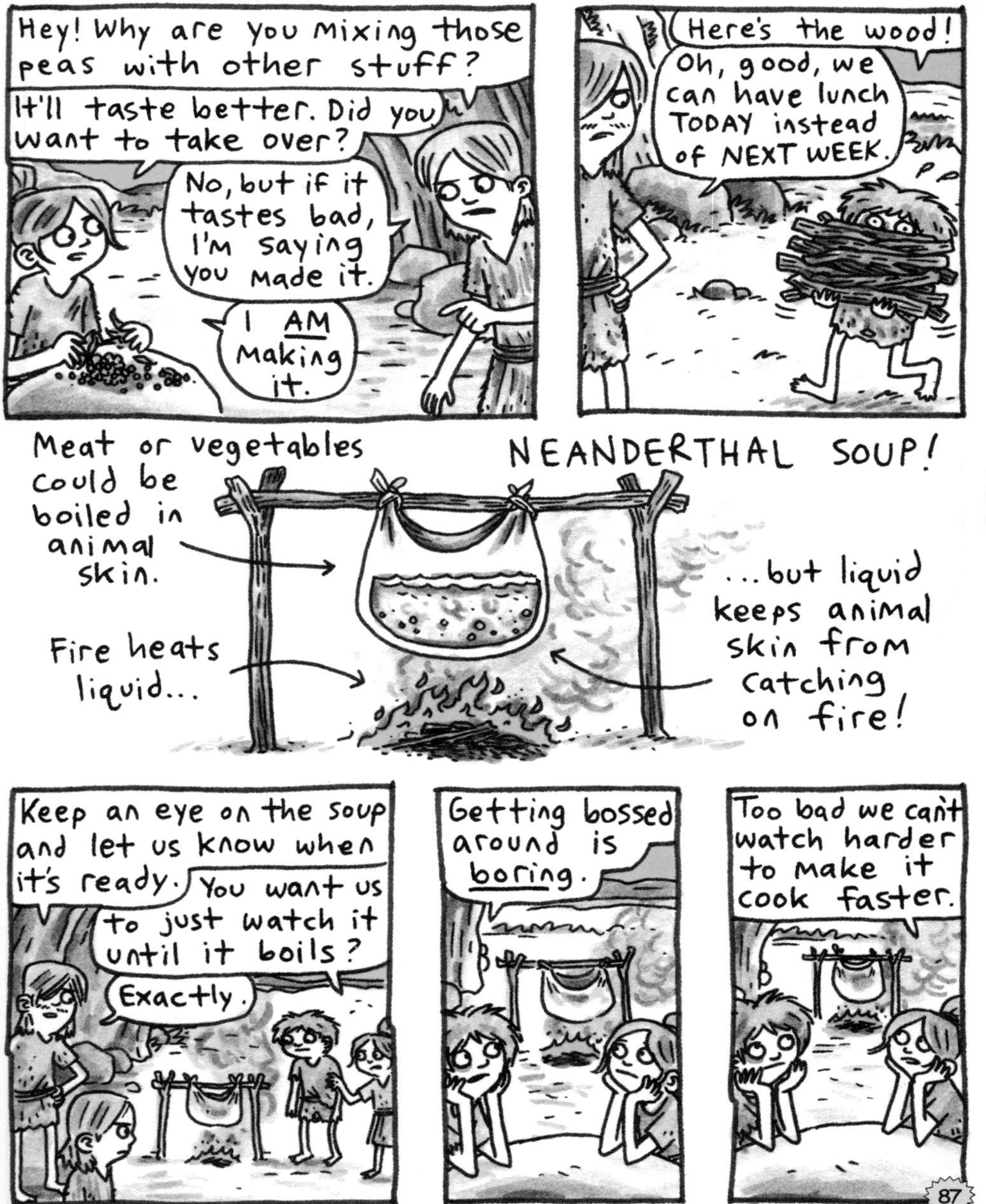
Hey! Why are you mixing those peas with other stuff?
It'll taste better. Did you want to take over?
No, but if it tastes bad, I'm saying you made it.
I AM making it.
Here's the wood!
Oh, good, we can have lunch TODAY instead of NEXT WEEK.
NEANDERTHAL SOUP!
Meat or vegetables could be boiled in animal skin.
Fire heats liquid...
...but liquid keeps animal skin from catching on fire!
Keep an eye on the soup and let us know when it's ready.
You want us to just watch it until it boils?
Exactly.
Getting bossed around is boring.
Too bad we can't watch harder to make it cook faster.

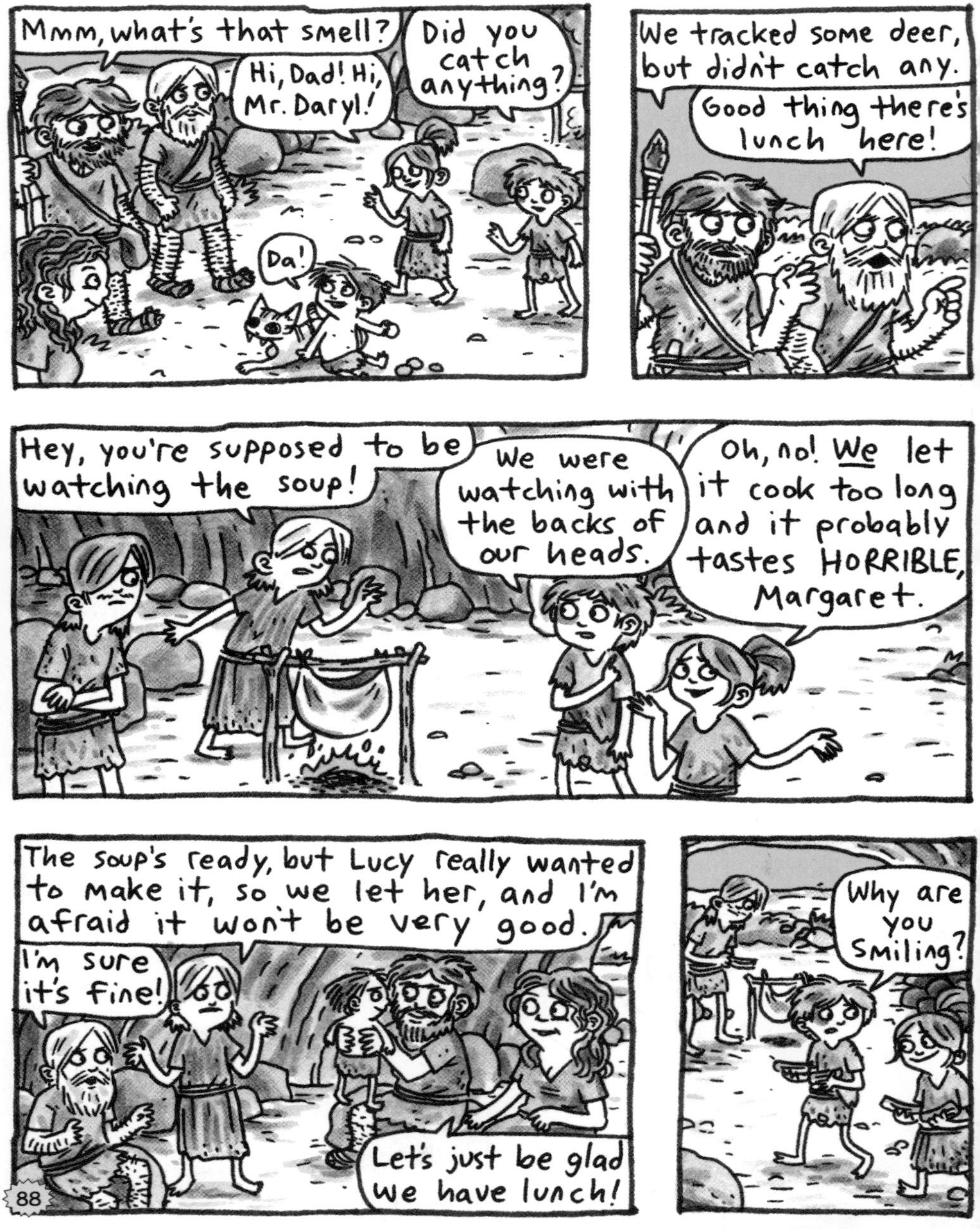
Mmm, what's that smell?
Hi, Dad! Hi, Mr. Daryl!
Did you catch anything?
Da!
We tracked some deer, but didn't catch any.
Good thing there's lunch here!
Hey, you're supposed to be watching the soup!
We were watching with the backs of our heads.
Oh, no! We let it cook too long and it probably tastes HORRIBLE, Margaret.
The soup's ready, but Lucy really wanted to make it, so we let her, and I'm afraid it won't be very good.
I'm sure it's fine!
Let's just be glad we have lunch!
Why are you smiling?

Since they didn't have bowls or spoons, Neanderthals would have to eat their soup out of something else — like a piece of tree bark!

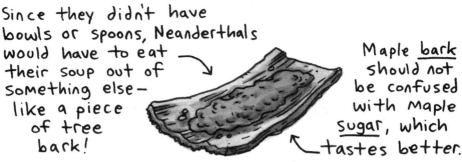

Maple <u>bark</u> should not be confused with maple <u>sugar</u>, which tastes better.

Lucy, you shouldn't have been worried, this is delicious!

Do you want me to get you some more, Margaret?

Mmmm!

Good work, Lucy!

Not bad.

Yum!

Thanks for making the soup, Lucy!

Good job, Lucy!

Why don't you adults take it easy? I'll clean up.

Oh, thank you, Margaret.

Burp!

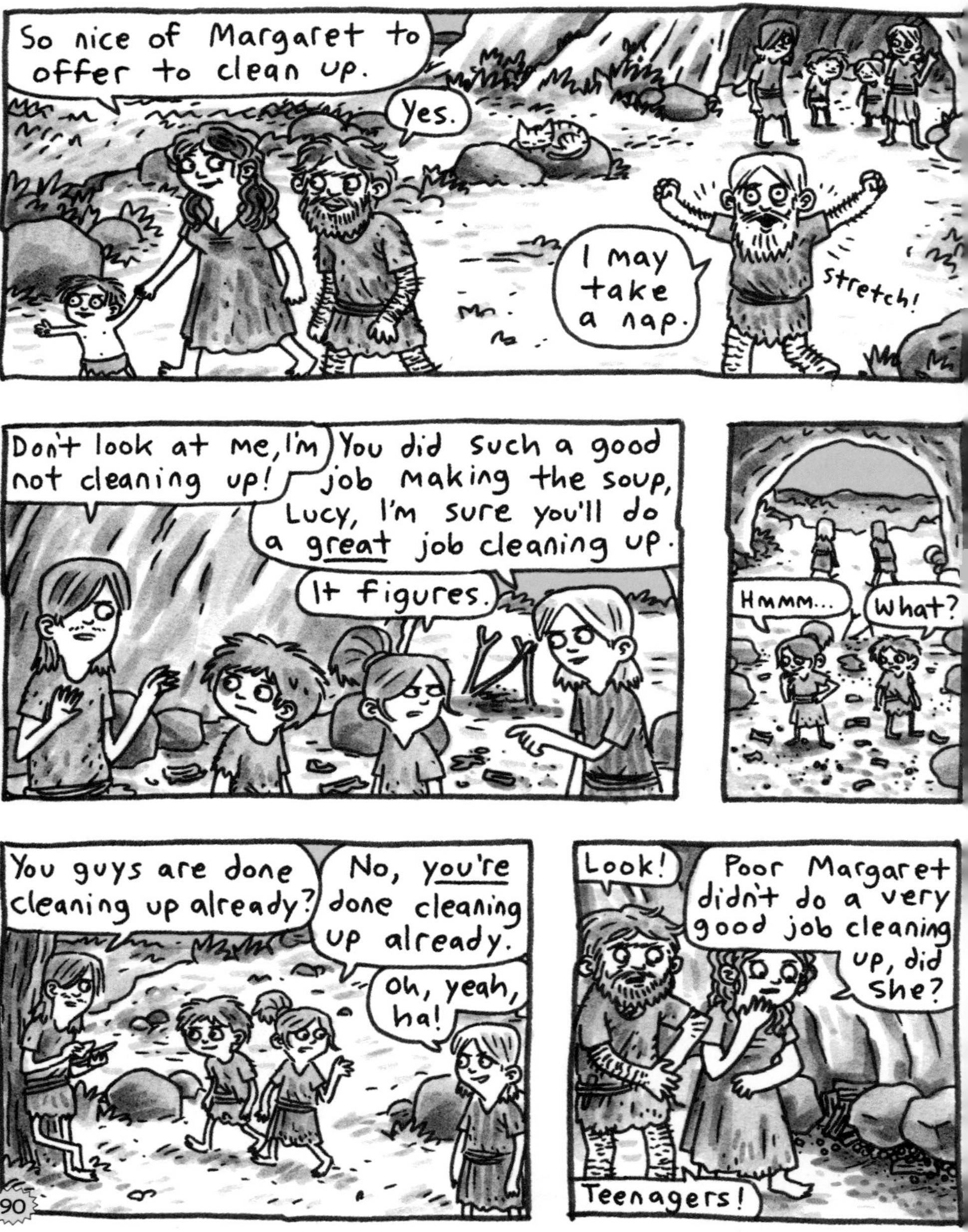
So nice of Margaret to offer to clean up.
Yes.
I may take a nap.
stretch!
Don't look at me, I'm not cleaning up!
You did such a good job making the soup, Lucy, I'm sure you'll do a great job cleaning up.
It figures.
Hmmm...
What?
You guys are done cleaning up already?
No, you're done cleaning up already.
Oh, yeah, ha!
Look!
Poor Margaret didn't do a very good job cleaning up, did she?
Teenagers!

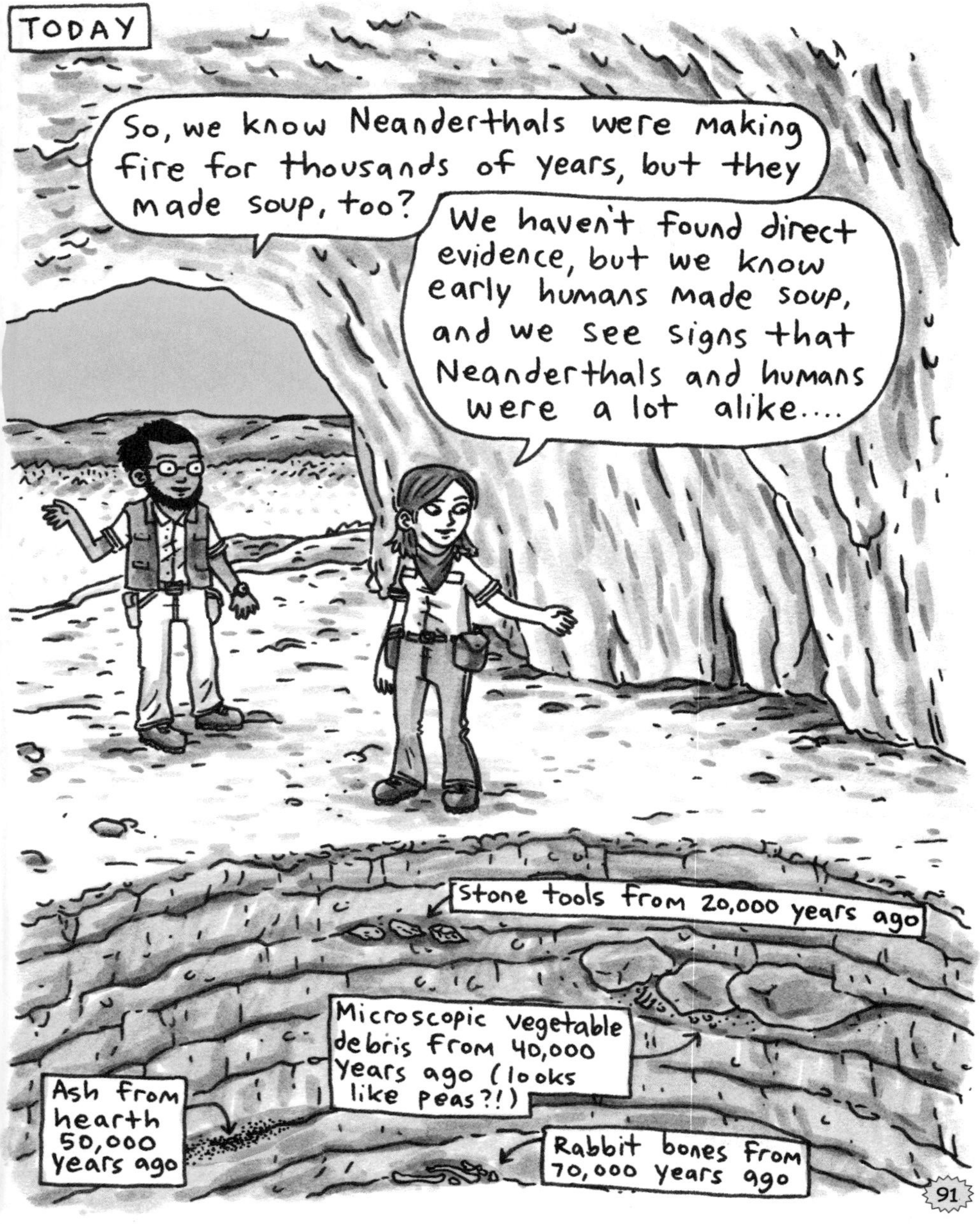
TODAY
So, we know Neanderthals were making fire for thousands of years, but they made soup, too?
We haven't found direct evidence, but we know early humans made soup, and we see signs that Neanderthals and humans were a lot alike....
Stone tools from 20,000 years ago
Microscopic vegetable debris from 40,000 years ago (looks like peas?!)
Ash from hearth 50,000 years ago
Rabbit bones from 70,000 years ago

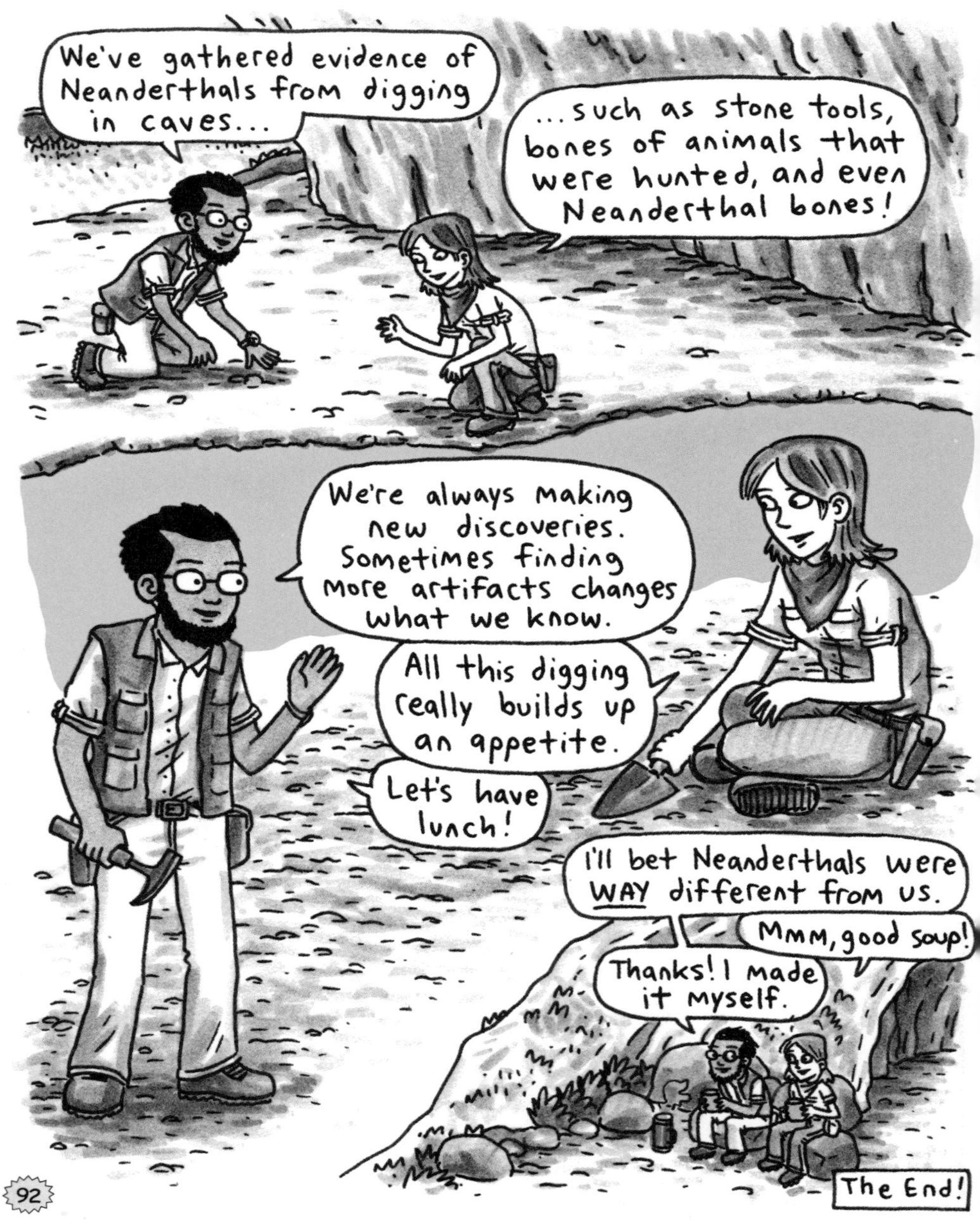
We've gathered evidence of Neanderthals from digging in caves...
...such as stone tools, bones of animals that were hunted, and even Neanderthal bones!
We're always making new discoveries. Sometimes finding more artifacts changes what we know.
All this digging really builds up an appetite.
Let's have lunch!
I'll bet Neanderthals were WAY different from us.
MMM, good soup!
Thanks! I made it myself.
The End!

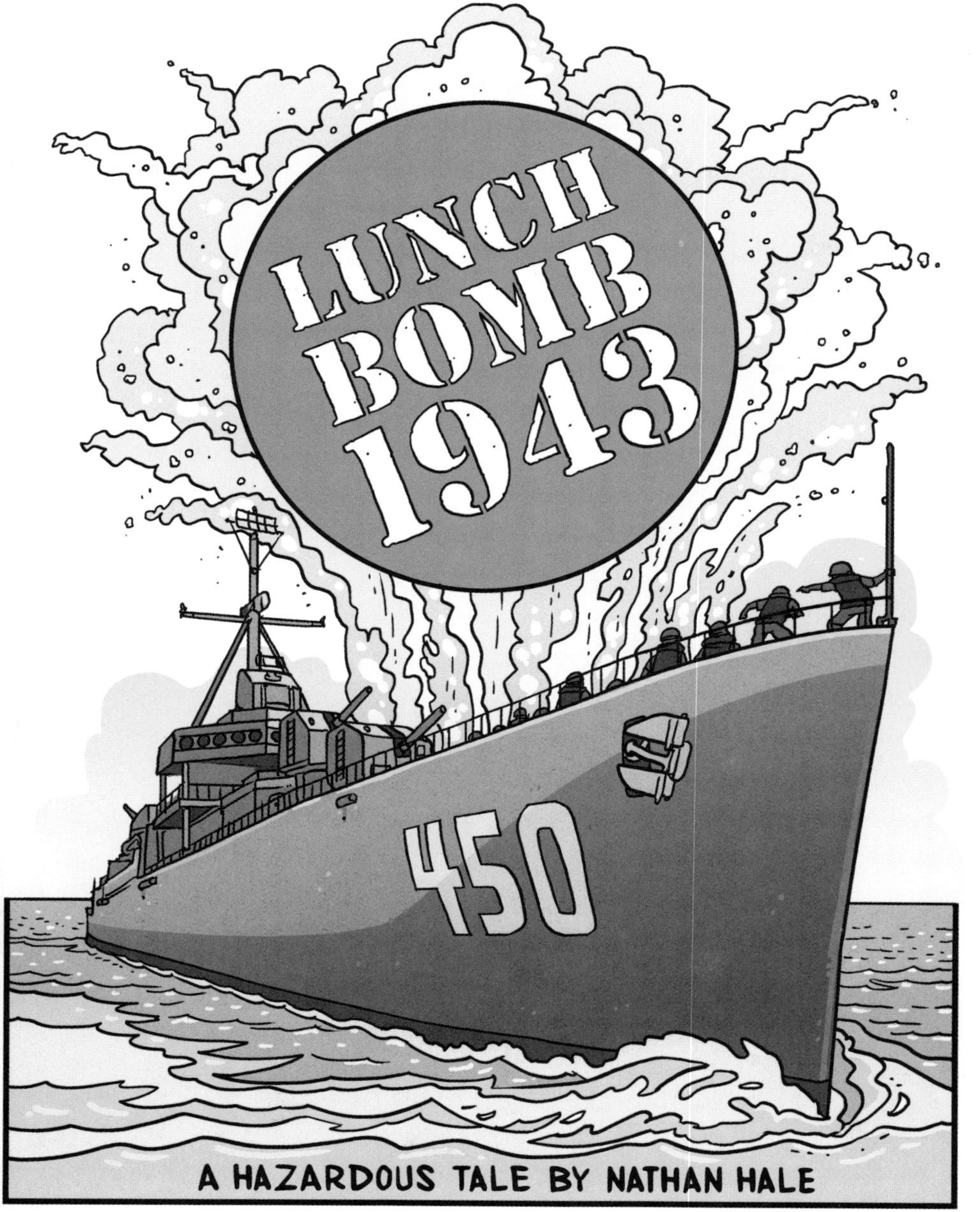
LUNCH
BOMB
1943
450
A HAZARDOUS TALE BY NATHAN HALE

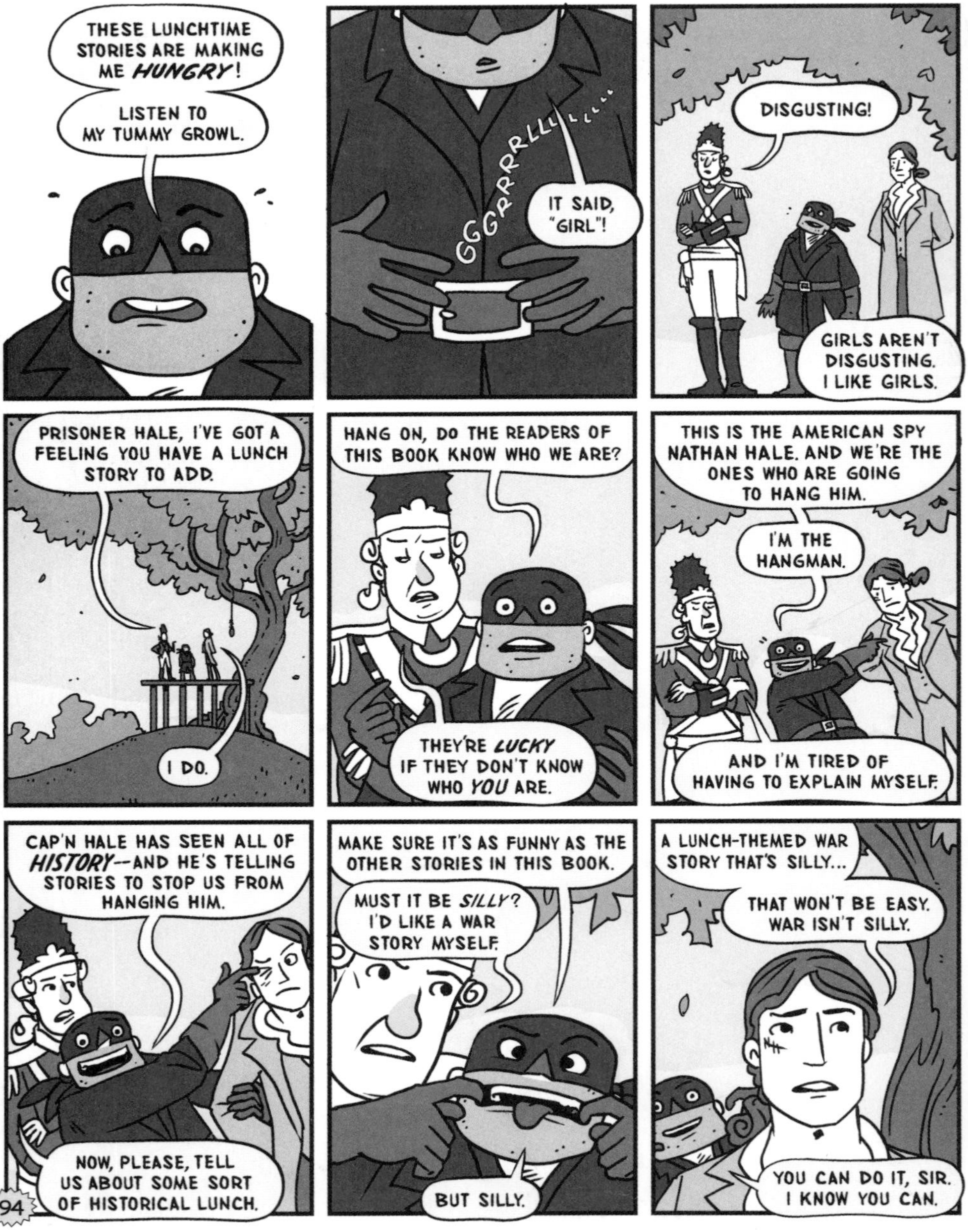

THESE LUNCHTIME STORIES ARE MAKING ME HUNGRY!
LISTEN TO MY TUMMY GROWL.
GGGRRRRLLLLLLLL
IT SAID, "GIRL"!
DISGUSTING!
GIRLS AREN'T DISGUSTING. I LIKE GIRLS.
PRISONER HALE, I'VE GOT A FEELING YOU HAVE A LUNCH STORY TO ADD.
I DO.
HANG ON, DO THE READERS OF THIS BOOK KNOW WHO WE ARE?
THEY'RE LUCKY IF THEY DON'T KNOW WHO YOU ARE.
THIS IS THE AMERICAN SPY NATHAN HALE. AND WE'RE THE ONES WHO ARE GOING TO HANG HIM.
I'M THE HANGMAN.
AND I'M TIRED OF HAVING TO EXPLAIN MYSELF.
CAP'N HALE HAS SEEN ALL OF HISTORY--AND HE'S TELLING STORIES TO STOP US FROM HANGING HIM.
NOW, PLEASE, TELL US ABOUT SOME SORT OF HISTORICAL LUNCH.
MAKE SURE IT'S AS FUNNY AS THE OTHER STORIES IN THIS BOOK.
MUST IT BE SILLY? I'D LIKE A WAR STORY MYSELF.
BUT SILLY.
A LUNCH-THEMED WAR STORY THAT'S SILLY...
THAT WON'T BE EASY. WAR ISN'T SILLY.
YOU CAN DO IT, SIR. I KNOW YOU CAN.

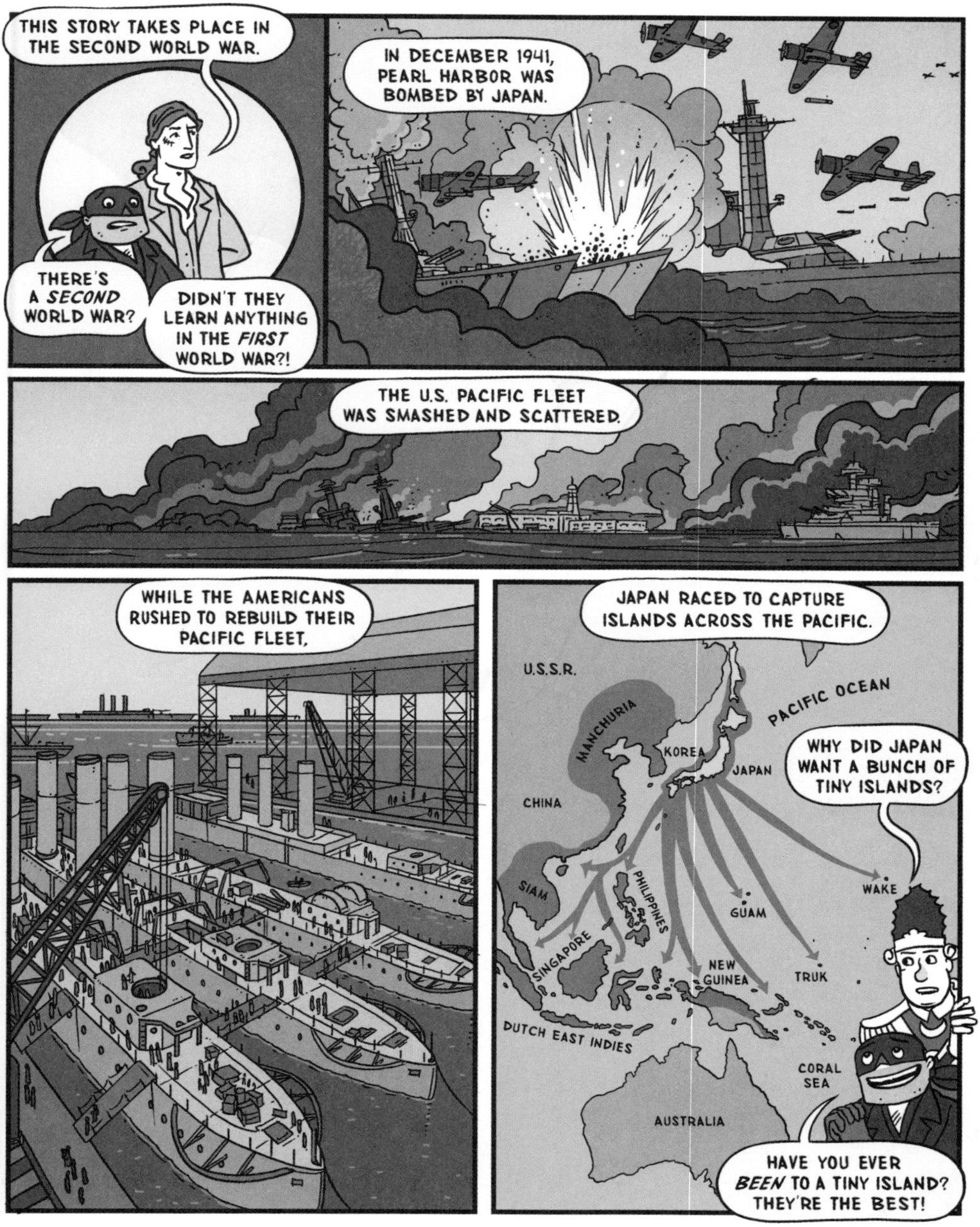
THIS STORY TAKES PLACE IN THE SECOND WORLD WAR.
THERE'S A *SECOND* WORLD WAR?
DIDN'T THEY LEARN ANYTHING IN THE *FIRST* WORLD WAR?!
IN DECEMBER 1941, PEARL HARBOR WAS BOMBED BY JAPAN.
THE U.S. PACIFIC FLEET WAS SMASHED AND SCATTERED.
WHILE THE AMERICANS RUSHED TO REBUILD THEIR PACIFIC FLEET,
JAPAN RACED TO CAPTURE ISLANDS ACROSS THE PACIFIC.
U.S.S.R.
MANCHURIA
PACIFIC OCEAN
KOREA
JAPAN
CHINA
SIAM
PHILIPPINES
GUAM
WAKE
SINGAPORE
NEW GUINEA
TRUK
DUTCH EAST INDIES
CORAL SEA
AUSTRALIA
WHY DID JAPAN WANT A BUNCH OF TINY ISLANDS?
HAVE YOU EVER *BEEN* TO A TINY ISLAND? THEY'RE THE BEST!

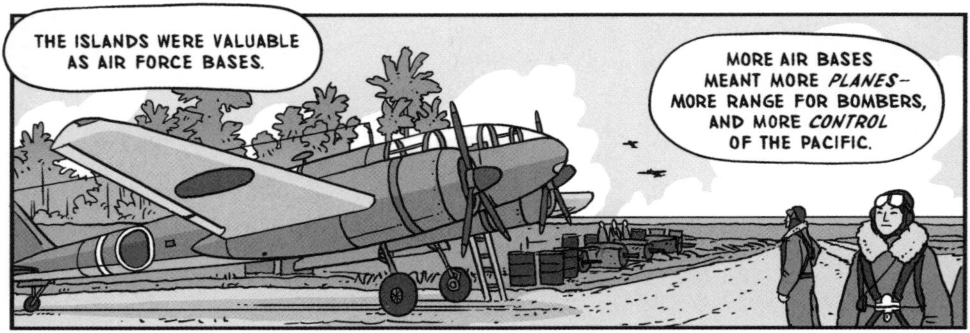
THE ISLANDS WERE VALUABLE AS AIR FORCE BASES.
MORE AIR BASES MEANT MORE *PLANES*— MORE RANGE FOR BOMBERS, AND MORE *CONTROL* OF THE PACIFIC.

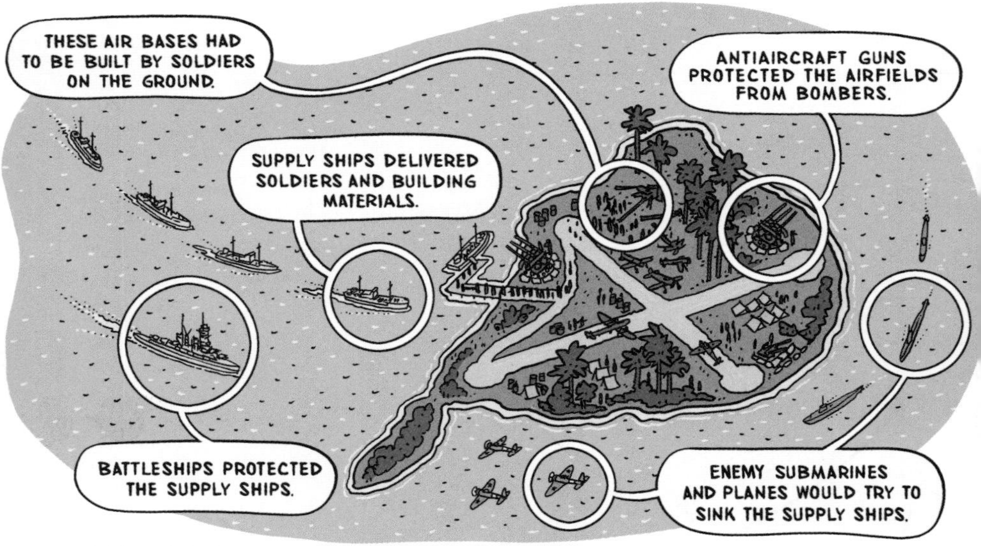
THESE AIR BASES HAD TO BE BUILT BY SOLDIERS ON THE GROUND.
ANTIAIRCRAFT GUNS PROTECTED THE AIRFIELDS FROM BOMBERS.
SUPPLY SHIPS DELIVERED SOLDIERS AND BUILDING MATERIALS.
BATTLESHIPS PROTECTED THE SUPPLY SHIPS.
ENEMY SUBMARINES AND PLANES WOULD TRY TO SINK THE SUPPLY SHIPS.

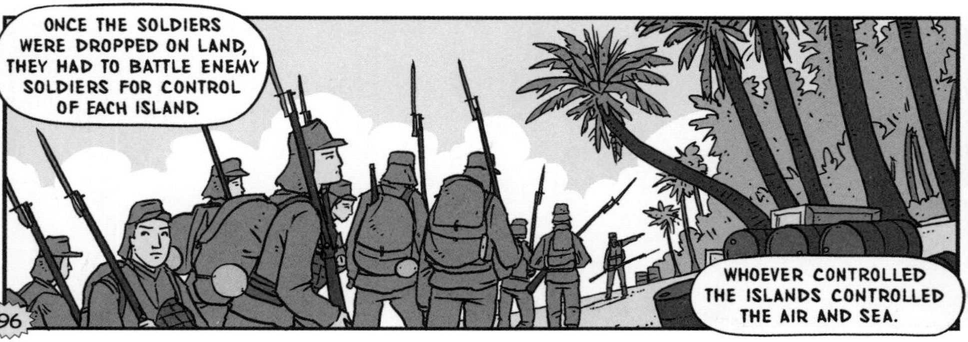
ONCE THE SOLDIERS WERE DROPPED ON LAND, THEY HAD TO BATTLE ENEMY SOLDIERS FOR CONTROL OF EACH ISLAND.
WHOEVER CONTROLLED THE ISLANDS CONTROLLED THE AIR AND SEA.

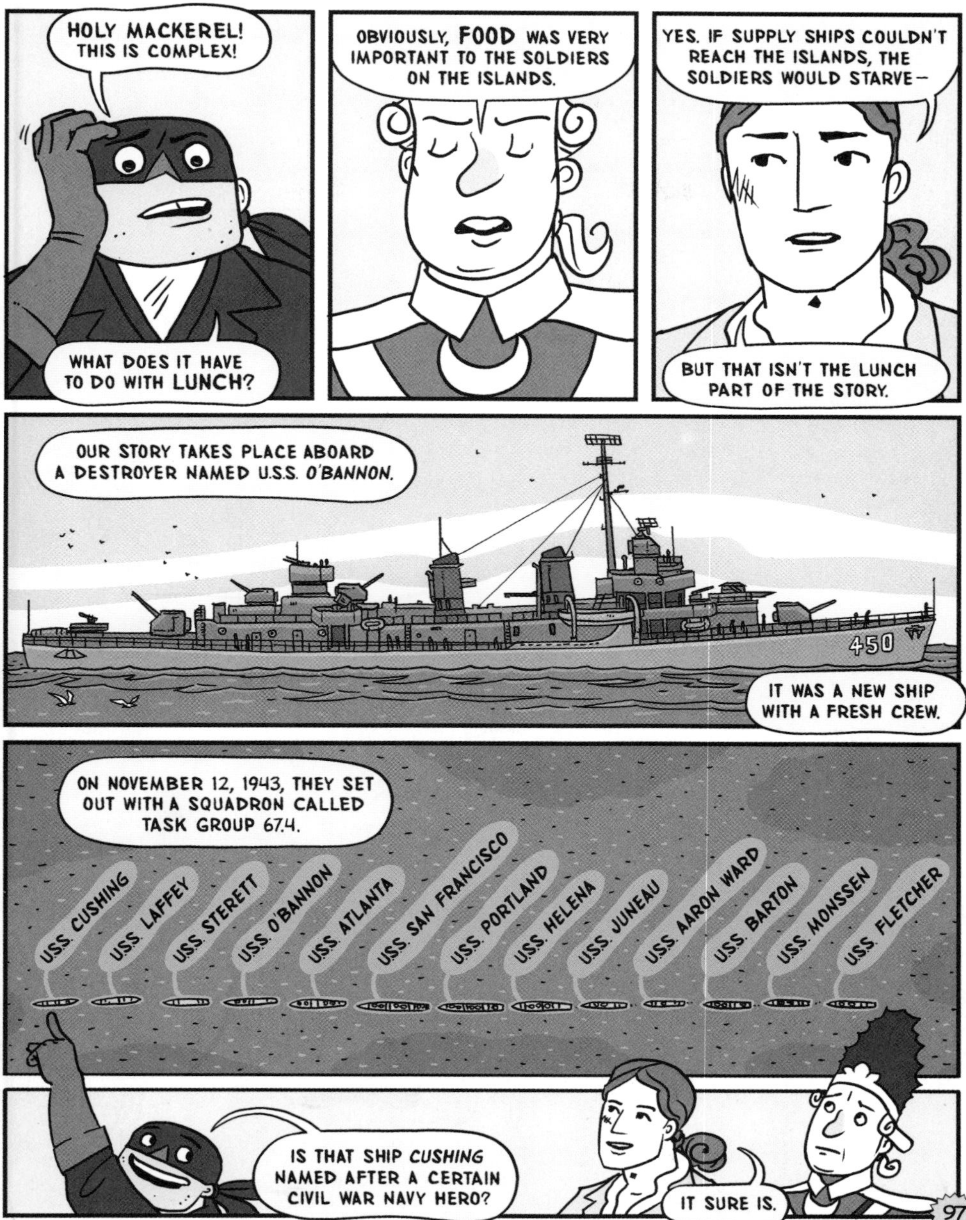
HOLY MACKEREL! THIS IS COMPLEX!
WHAT DOES IT HAVE TO DO WITH LUNCH?
OBVIOUSLY, FOOD WAS VERY IMPORTANT TO THE SOLDIERS ON THE ISLANDS.
YES. IF SUPPLY SHIPS COULDN'T REACH THE ISLANDS, THE SOLDIERS WOULD STARVE—
BUT THAT ISN'T THE LUNCH PART OF THE STORY.
OUR STORY TAKES PLACE ABOARD A DESTROYER NAMED U.S.S. O'BANNON.
450
IT WAS A NEW SHIP WITH A FRESH CREW.
ON NOVEMBER 12, 1943, THEY SET OUT WITH A SQUADRON CALLED TASK GROUP 67.4.
U.S.S. CUSHING
U.S.S. LAFFEY
U.S.S. STERETT
U.S.S. O'BANNON
U.S.S. ATLANTA
U.S.S. SAN FRANCISCO
U.S.S. PORTLAND
U.S.S. HELENA
U.S.S. JUNEAU
U.S.S. AARON WARD
U.S.S. BARTON
U.S.S. MONSSEN
U.S.S. FLETCHER
IS THAT SHIP CUSHING NAMED AFTER A CERTAIN CIVIL WAR NAVY HERO?
IT SURE IS.

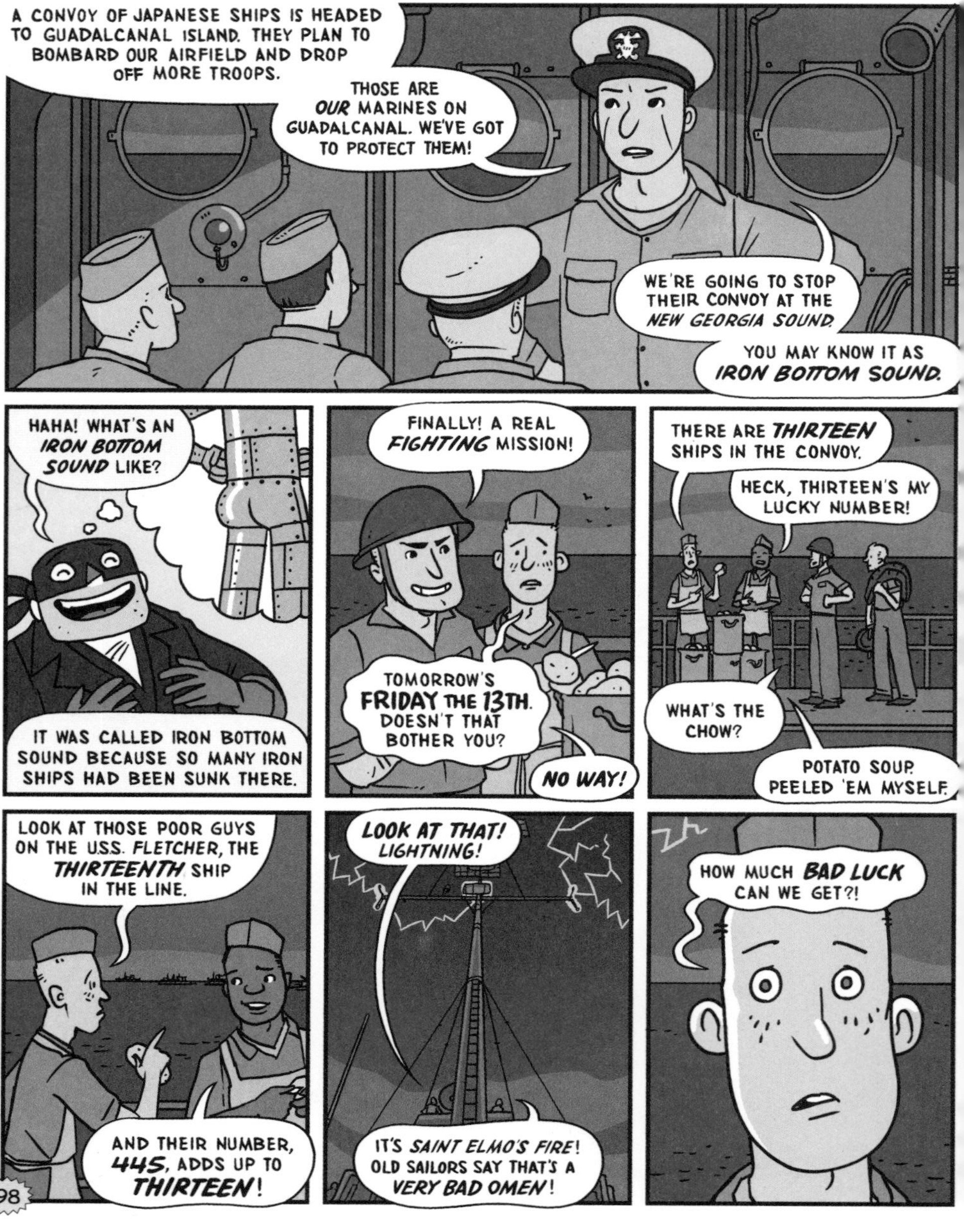
A CONVOY OF JAPANESE SHIPS IS HEADED TO GUADALCANAL ISLAND. THEY PLAN TO BOMBARD OUR AIRFIELD AND DROP OFF MORE TROOPS.
THOSE ARE *OUR* MARINES ON GUADALCANAL. WE'VE GOT TO PROTECT THEM!
WE'RE GOING TO STOP THEIR CONVOY AT THE *NEW GEORGIA SOUND.*
YOU MAY KNOW IT AS ***IRON BOTTOM SOUND.***
HAHA! WHAT'S AN ***IRON BOTTOM SOUND*** LIKE?
IT WAS CALLED IRON BOTTOM SOUND BECAUSE SO MANY IRON SHIPS HAD BEEN SUNK THERE.
FINALLY! A REAL ***FIGHTING*** MISSION!
TOMORROW'S **FRIDAY THE 13TH.** DOESN'T THAT BOTHER YOU?
NO WAY!
THERE ARE ***THIRTEEN*** SHIPS IN THE CONVOY.
HECK, THIRTEEN'S MY LUCKY NUMBER!
WHAT'S THE CHOW?
POTATO SOUP. PEELED 'EM MYSELF.
LOOK AT THOSE POOR GUYS ON THE U.S.S. *FLETCHER*, THE ***THIRTEENTH*** SHIP IN THE LINE.
AND THEIR NUMBER, ***445***, ADDS UP TO ***THIRTEEN***!
LOOK AT THAT! LIGHTNING!
IT'S *SAINT ELMO'S FIRE*! OLD SAILORS SAY THAT'S A *VERY BAD OMEN*!
HOW MUCH ***BAD LUCK*** CAN WE GET?!

THE U.S.S. *O'BANNON* HAD A NEW, TOP-SECRET TECHNOLOGY ON BOARD—RADAR.

THIS ALLOWED THEM TO SEE ENEMY SHIPS APPROACHING.

IT WAS SO NEW THAT ONLY A FEW SHIPS IN TASK GROUP 67.4 HAD IT.

SIR, CONTACT! INCOMING SHIPS! THREE GROUPS!

WHAT DOES REAR ADMIRAL CALLAGHAN SAY?

WE HAVEN'T BEEN GIVEN ORDERS TO CHANGE COURSE.

ANY CLOSER AND RADAR WON'T DO US ANY GOOD.

ORDERS ARE TO GO STRAIGHT AHEAD.

HOLY SMOKES! I CAN *SEE* THEM OUT THERE. WE'RE GONNA GO RIGHT THROUGH 'EM.

SHHH.

I HOPE ADMIRAL CALLAGHAN KNOWS WHAT HE'S DOING.

WHAT *IS* HE DOING?

HARD TO PORT! *TURN!*

THE *CUSHING'S* TURNING! WE'VE GOTTA TURN TOO!

TURN! HARD TO PORT!

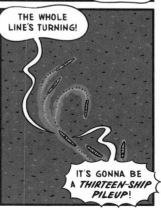

THE WHOLE LINE'S TURNING!

IT'S GONNA BE A *THIRTEEN-SHIP PILEUP!*

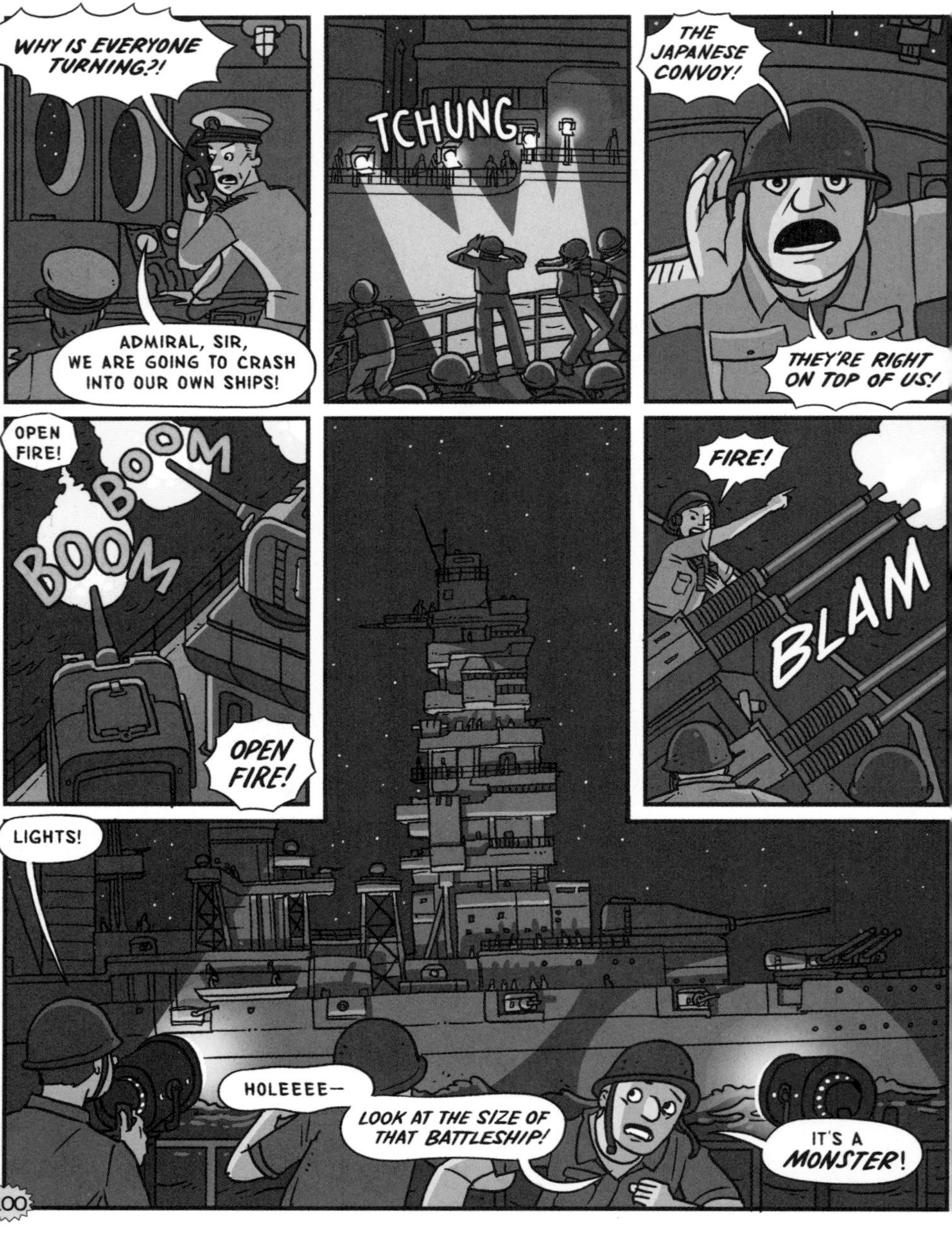
WHY IS EVERYONE TURNING?!
ADMIRAL, SIR, WE ARE GOING TO CRASH INTO OUR OWN SHIPS!
TCHUNG
THE JAPANESE CONVOY!
THEY'RE RIGHT ON TOP OF US!
OPEN FIRE!
BOOM
BOOM
OPEN FIRE!
FIRE!
BLAM
LIGHTS!
HOLEEEE—
LOOK AT THE SIZE OF THAT BATTLESHIP!
IT'S A MONSTER!

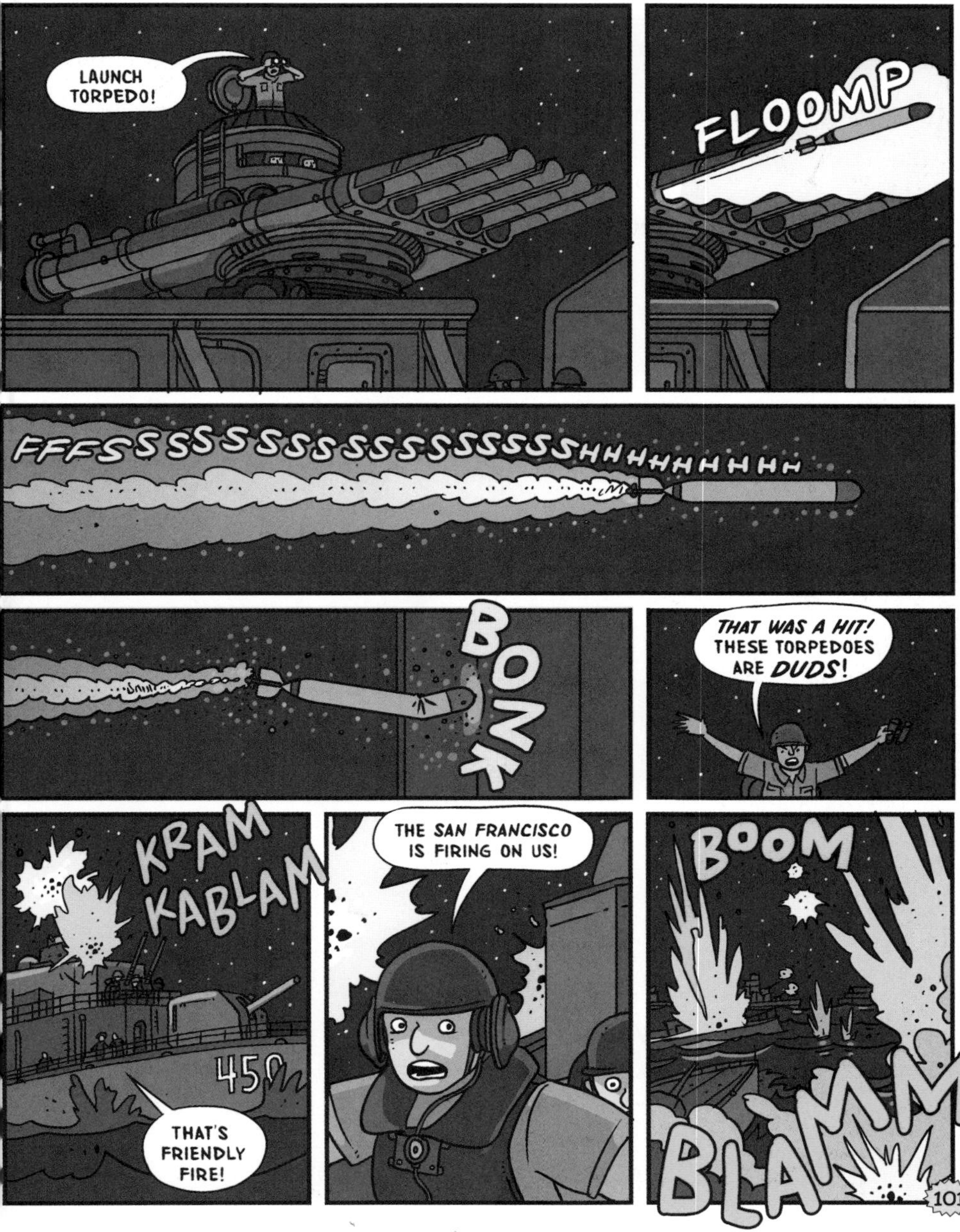
LAUNCH TORPEDO!
FLOOMP
FFFSSSSSSSSSSSSSSSSSHHHHHHHHHH
BONK
THAT WAS A HIT! THESE TORPEDOES ARE DUDS!
KRAM KABLAM
450
THAT'S FRIENDLY FIRE!
THE SAN FRANCISCO IS FIRING ON US!
BOOM
BLAMMM

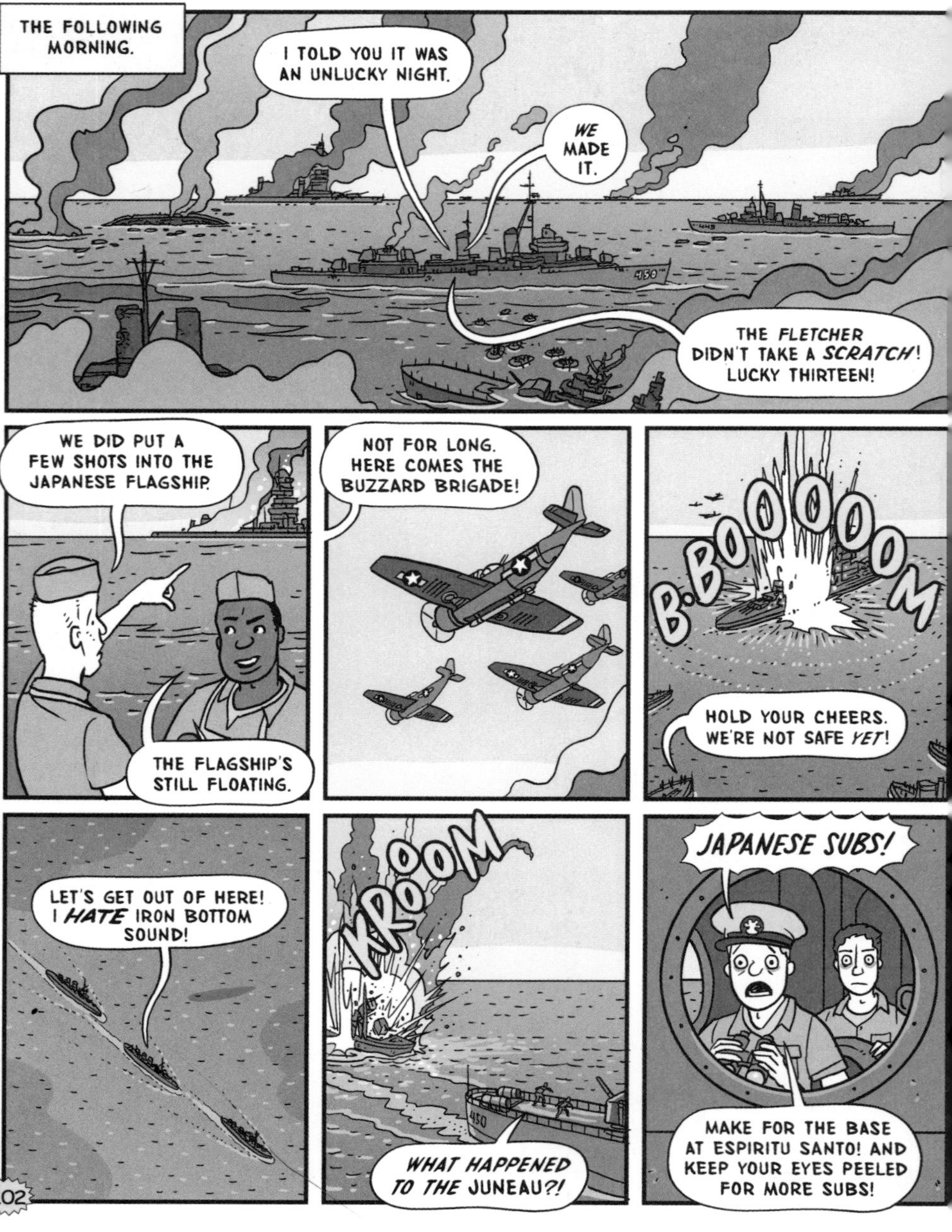
THE FOLLOWING MORNING.
I TOLD YOU IT WAS AN UNLUCKY NIGHT.
WE MADE IT.
THE FLETCHER DIDN'T TAKE A SCRATCH! LUCKY THIRTEEN!
WE DID PUT A FEW SHOTS INTO THE JAPANESE FLAGSHIP.
THE FLAGSHIP'S STILL FLOATING.
NOT FOR LONG. HERE COMES THE BUZZARD BRIGADE!
B-BOOOOOOM
HOLD YOUR CHEERS. WE'RE NOT SAFE YET!
LET'S GET OUT OF HERE! I HATE IRON BOTTOM SOUND!
KROOOOM
WHAT HAPPENED TO THE JUNEAU?!
JAPANESE SUBS!
MAKE FOR THE BASE AT ESPIRITU SANTO! AND KEEP YOUR EYES PEELED FOR MORE SUBS!

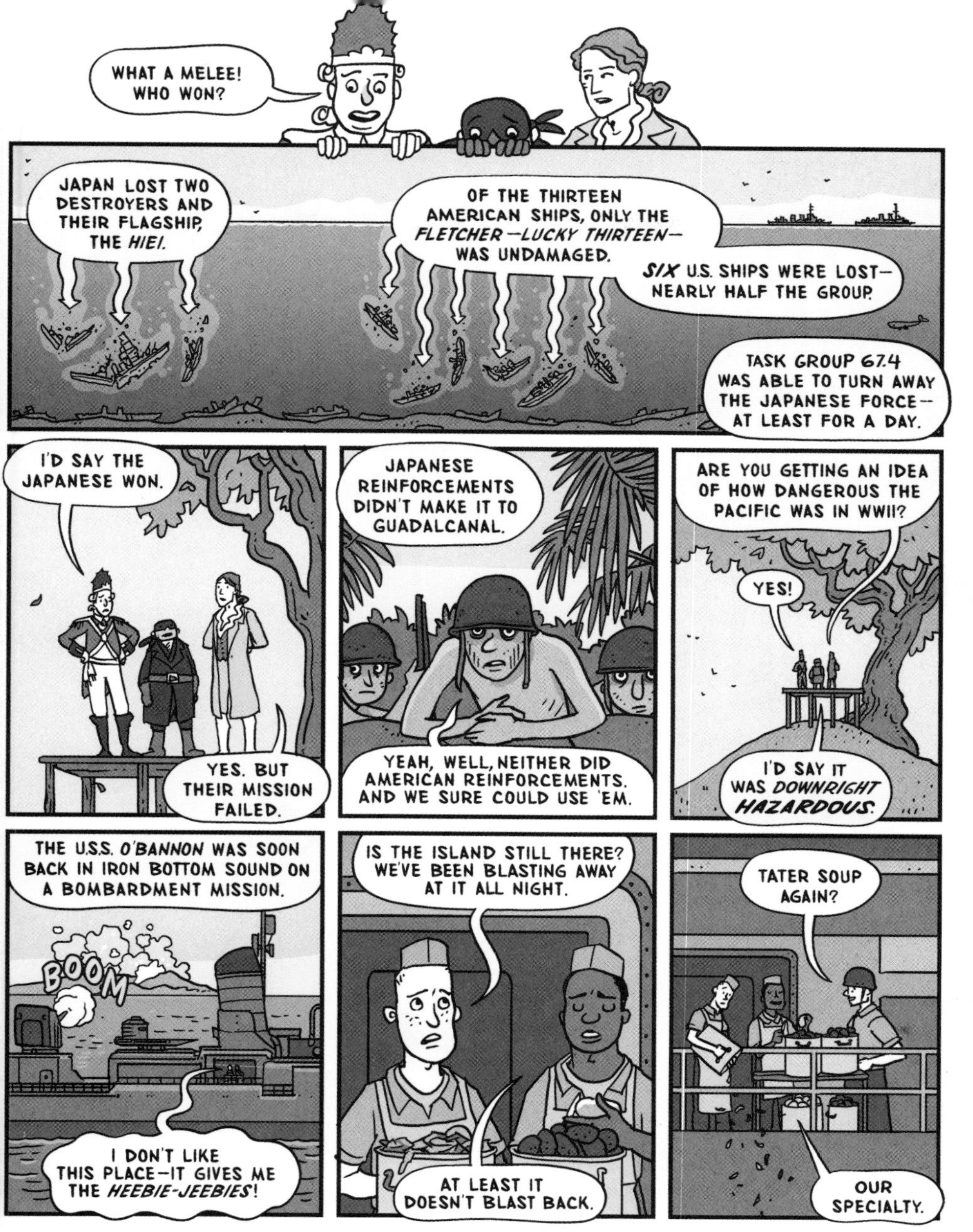
WHAT A MELEE! WHO WON?
JAPAN LOST TWO DESTROYERS AND THEIR FLAGSHIP, THE *HIEI*.
OF THE THIRTEEN AMERICAN SHIPS, ONLY THE *FLETCHER*—*LUCKY THIRTEEN*—WAS UNDAMAGED.
SIX U.S. SHIPS WERE LOST—NEARLY HALF THE GROUP.
TASK GROUP 67.4 WAS ABLE TO TURN AWAY THE JAPANESE FORCE—AT LEAST FOR A DAY.
I'D SAY THE JAPANESE WON.
YES. BUT THEIR MISSION FAILED.
JAPANESE REINFORCEMENTS DIDN'T MAKE IT TO GUADALCANAL.
YEAH, WELL, NEITHER DID AMERICAN REINFORCEMENTS. AND WE SURE COULD USE 'EM.
ARE YOU GETTING AN IDEA OF HOW DANGEROUS THE PACIFIC WAS IN WWII?
YES!
I'D SAY IT WAS *DOWNRIGHT* ***HAZARDOUS***.
THE U.S.S. *O'BANNON* WAS SOON BACK IN IRON BOTTOM SOUND ON A BOMBARDMENT MISSION.
BOOM
I DON'T LIKE THIS PLACE—IT GIVES ME THE *HEEBIE-JEEBIES*!
IS THE ISLAND STILL THERE? WE'VE BEEN BLASTING AWAY AT IT ALL NIGHT.
AT LEAST IT DOESN'T BLAST BACK.
TATER SOUP AGAIN?
OUR SPECIALTY.

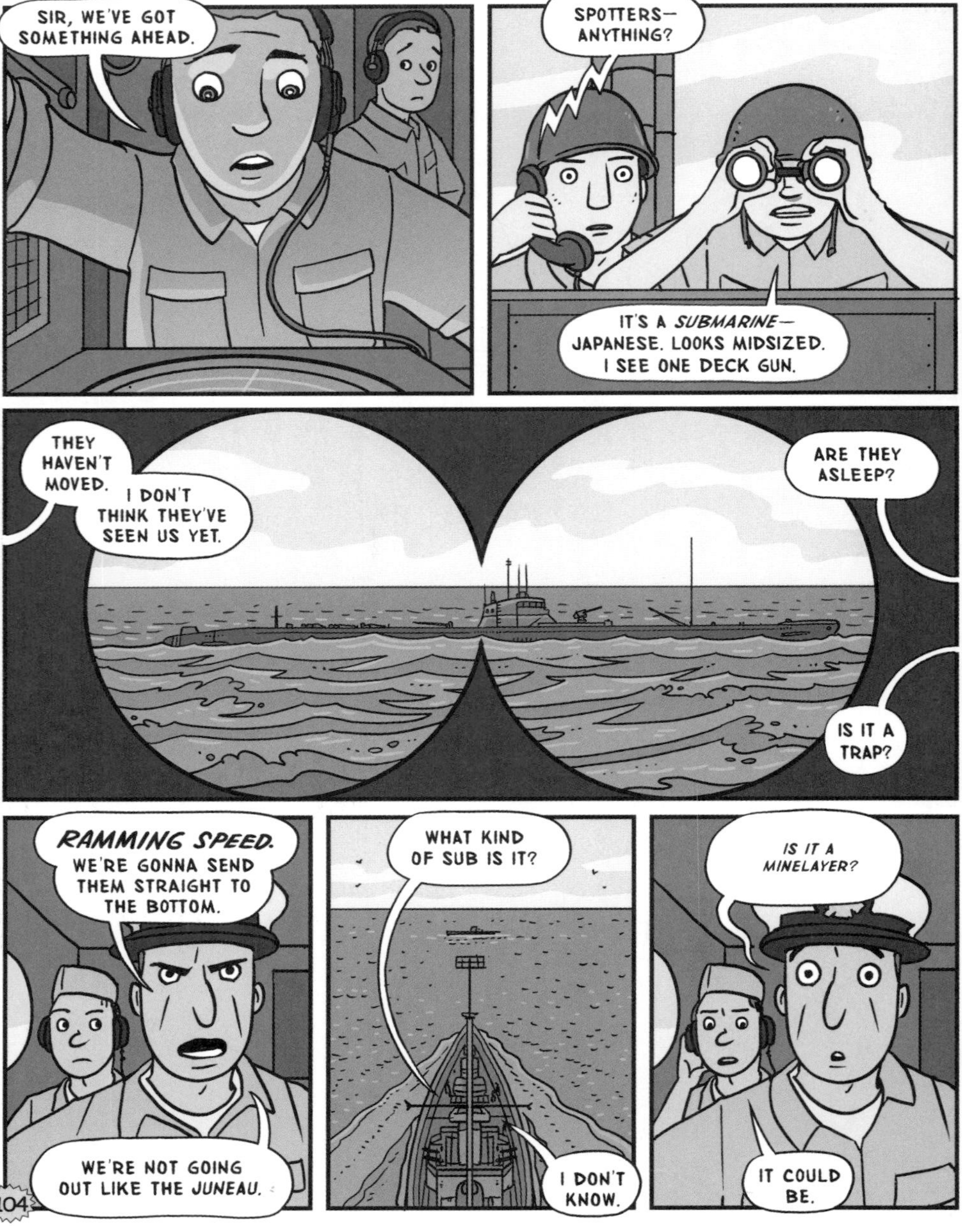
SIR, WE'VE GOT SOMETHING AHEAD.
SPOTTERS— ANYTHING?
IT'S A *SUBMARINE*— JAPANESE. LOOKS MIDSIZED. I SEE ONE DECK GUN.
THEY HAVEN'T MOVED.
I DON'T THINK THEY'VE SEEN US YET.
ARE THEY ASLEEP?
IS IT A TRAP?
RAMMING SPEED. WE'RE GONNA SEND THEM STRAIGHT TO THE BOTTOM.
WE'RE NOT GOING OUT LIKE THE *JUNEAU.*
WHAT KIND OF SUB IS IT?
I DON'T KNOW.
IS IT A MINELAYER?
IT COULD BE.

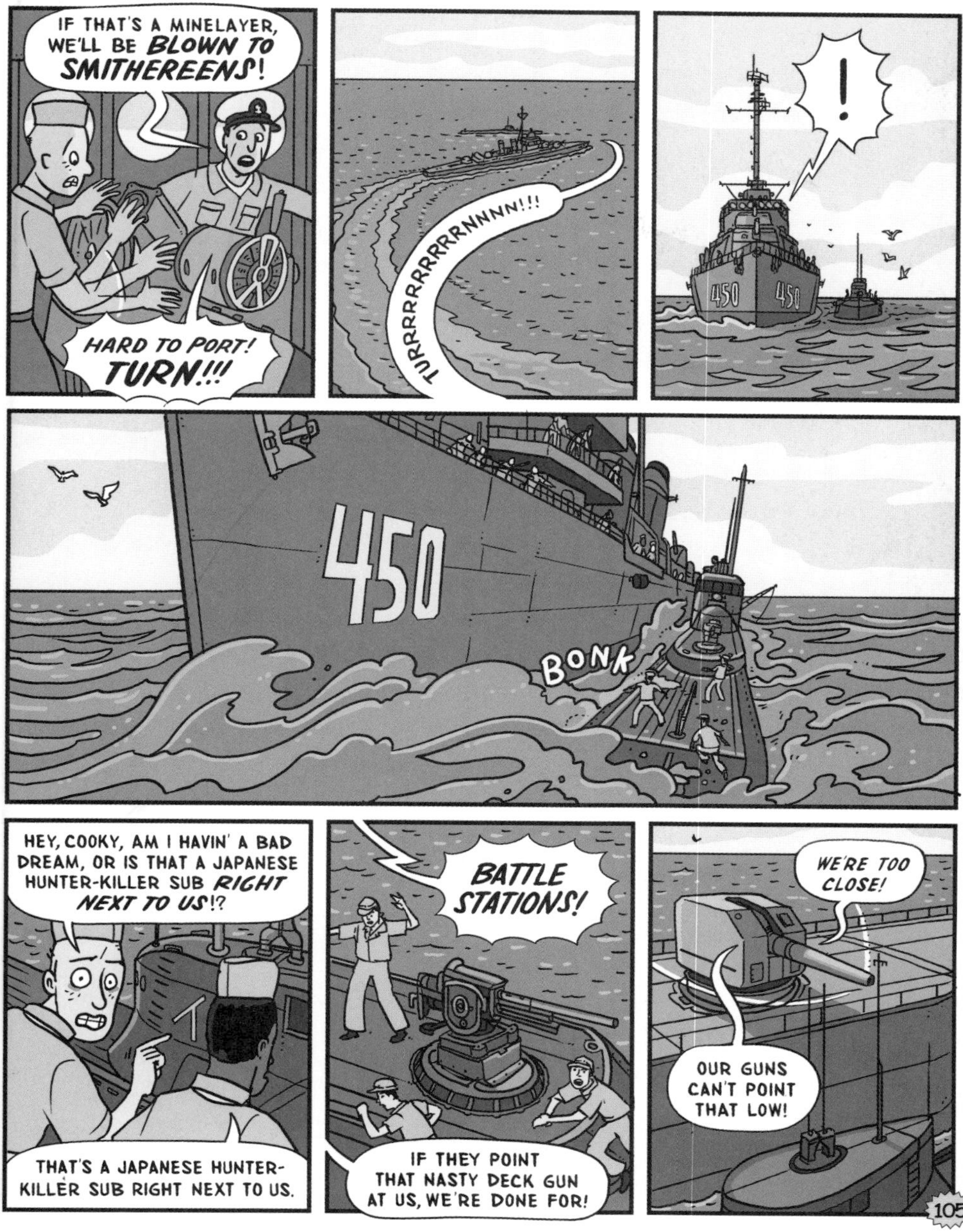

IF THAT'S A MINELAYER, WE'LL BE BLOWN TO SMITHEREENS!
HARD TO PORT! TURN!!!
TURRRRRRRRRNNNNN!!!
!
BONK
HEY, COOKY, AM I HAVIN' A BAD DREAM, OR IS THAT A JAPANESE HUNTER-KILLER SUB RIGHT NEXT TO US!?
THAT'S A JAPANESE HUNTER-KILLER SUB RIGHT NEXT TO US.
BATTLE STATIONS!
IF THEY POINT THAT NASTY DECK GUN AT US, WE'RE DONE FOR!
WE'RE TOO CLOSE!
OUR GUNS CAN'T POINT THAT LOW!

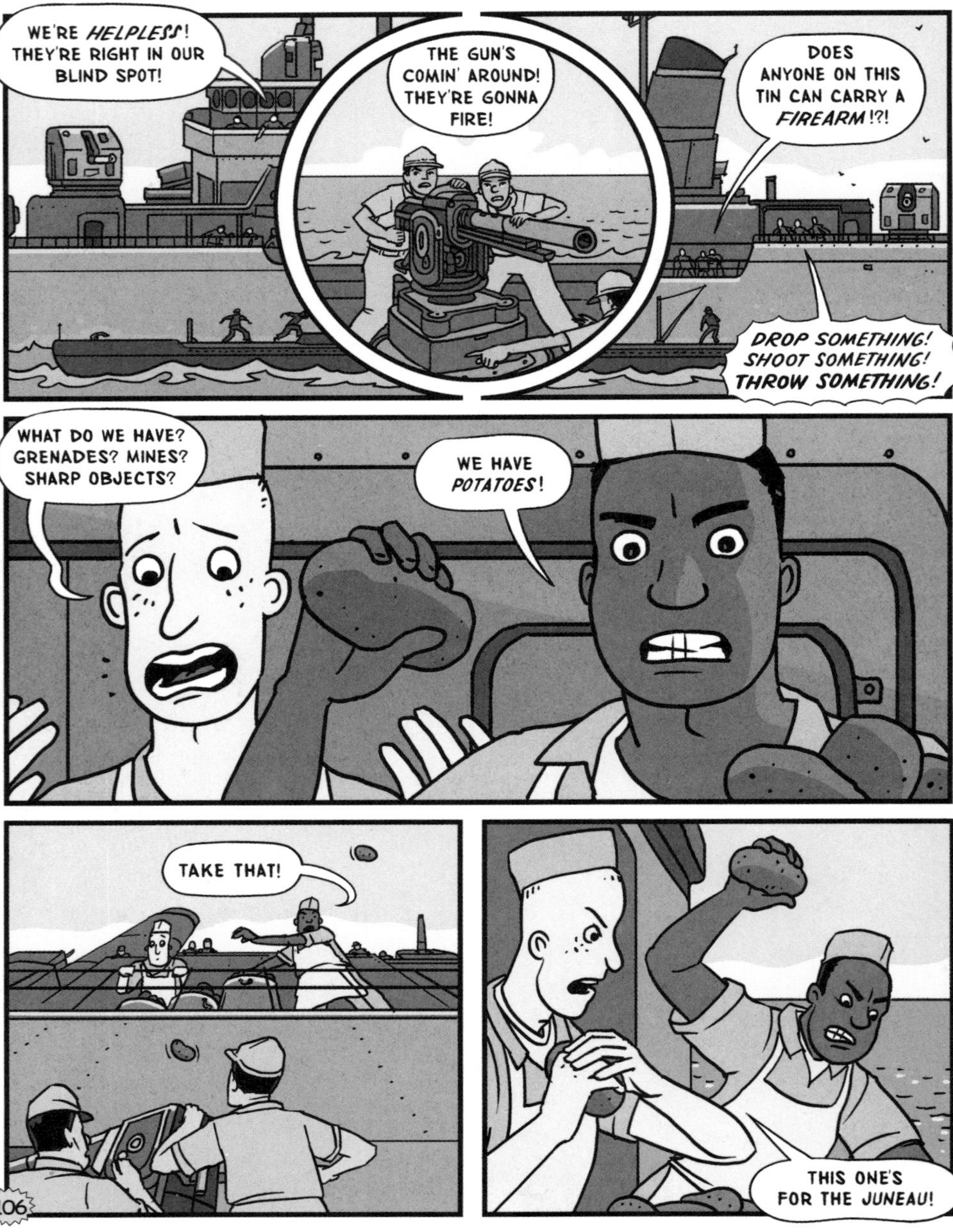
WE'RE HELPLESS! THEY'RE RIGHT IN OUR BLIND SPOT!
THE GUN'S COMIN' AROUND! THEY'RE GONNA FIRE!
DOES ANYONE ON THIS TIN CAN CARRY A FIREARM!?!
DROP SOMETHING! SHOOT SOMETHING! THROW SOMETHING!
WHAT DO WE HAVE? GRENADES? MINES? SHARP OBJECTS?
WE HAVE POTATOES!
TAKE THAT!
THIS ONE'S FOR THE JUNEAU!

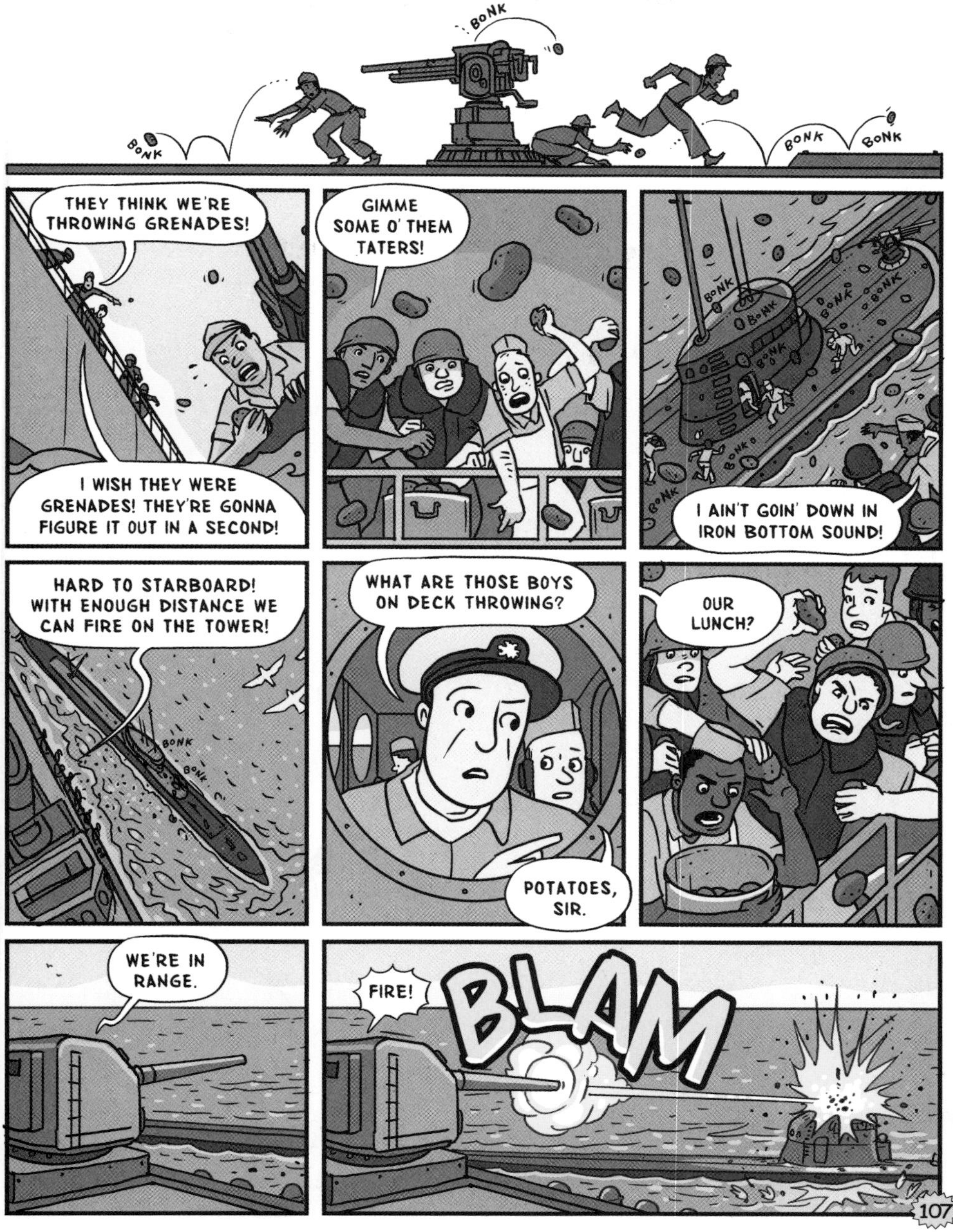
BONK
BONK
BONK
BONK
THEY THINK WE'RE THROWING GRENADES!
I WISH THEY WERE GRENADES! THEY'RE GONNA FIGURE IT OUT IN A SECOND!
GIMME SOME O' THEM TATERS!
BONK
BONK
BONK
BONK
I AIN'T GOIN' DOWN IN IRON BOTTOM SOUND!
HARD TO STARBOARD! WITH ENOUGH DISTANCE WE CAN FIRE ON THE TOWER!
BONK
BONK
WHAT ARE THOSE BOYS ON DECK THROWING?
POTATOES, SIR.
OUR LUNCH?
WE'RE IN RANGE.
FIRE!
BLAM

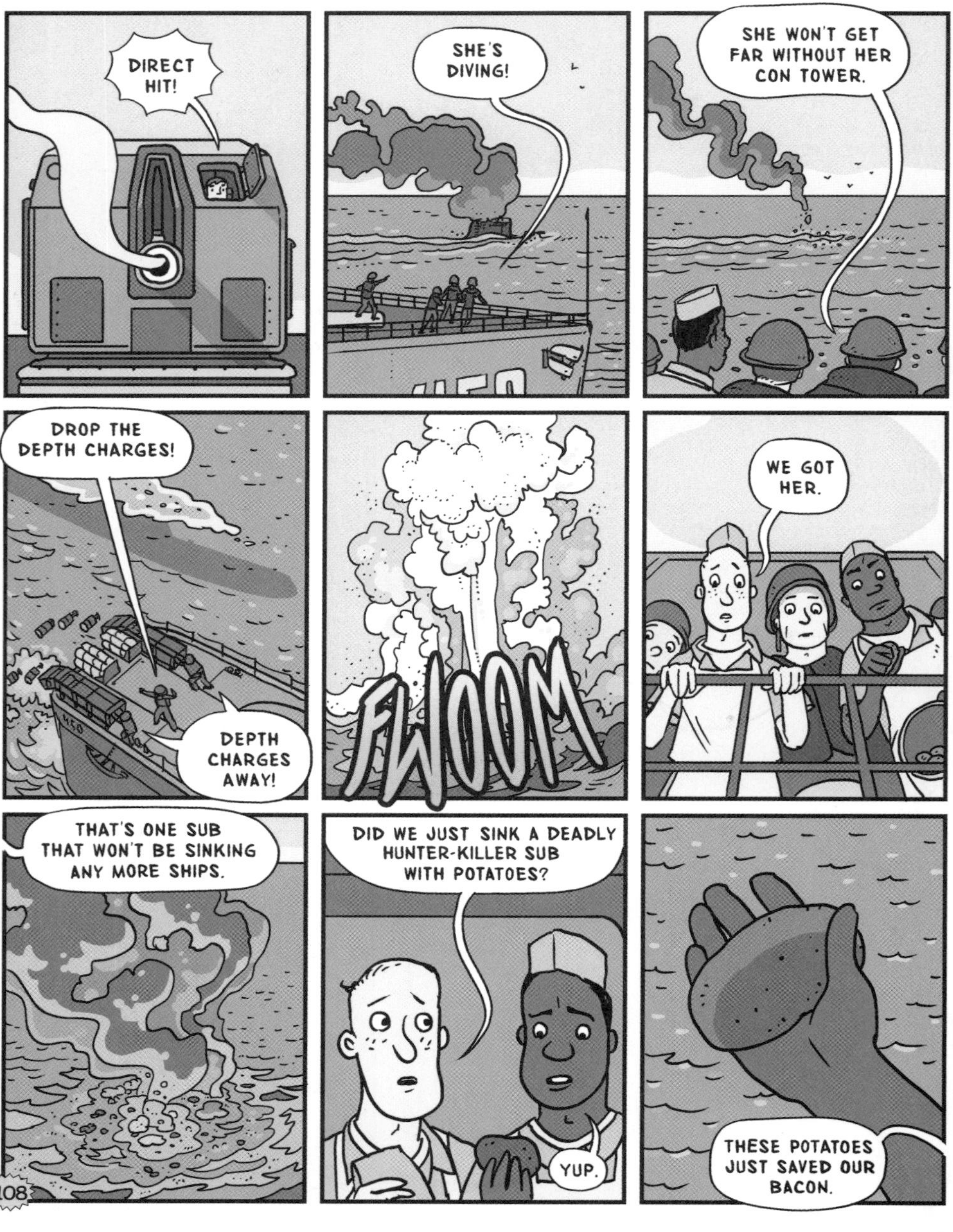
DIRECT HIT!
SHE'S DIVING!
SHE WON'T GET FAR WITHOUT HER CON TOWER.
DROP THE DEPTH CHARGES!
DEPTH CHARGES AWAY!
FWOOM
WE GOT HER.
THAT'S ONE SUB THAT WON'T BE SINKING ANY MORE SHIPS.
DID WE JUST SINK A DEADLY HUNTER-KILLER SUB WITH POTATOES?
YUP.
THESE POTATOES JUST SAVED OUR BACON.

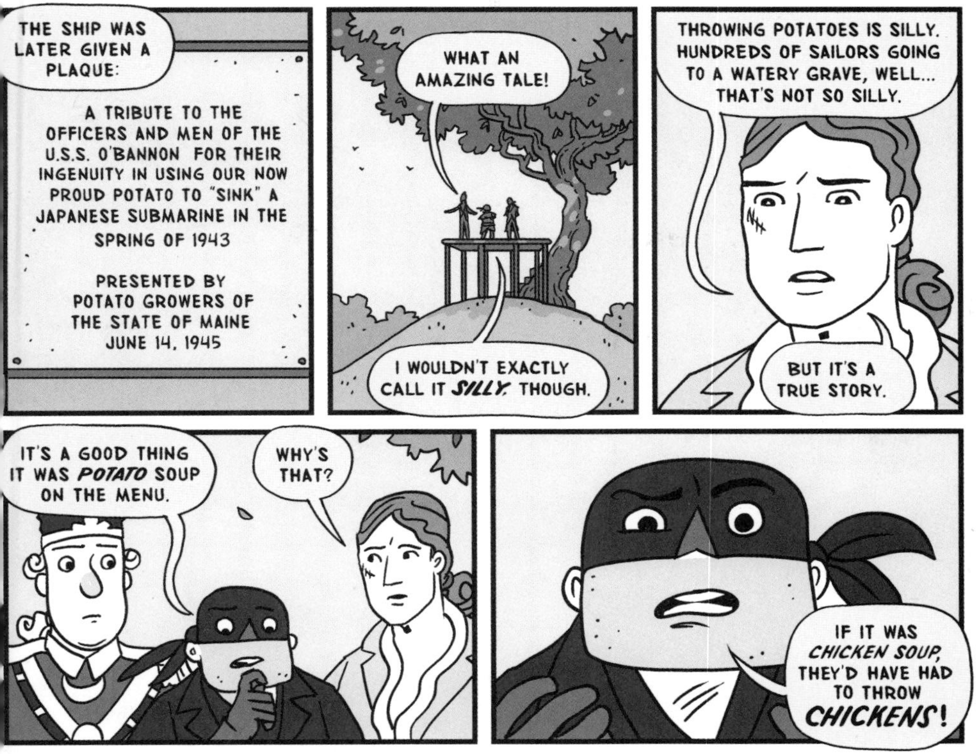
THE SHIP WAS LATER GIVEN A PLAQUE:
A TRIBUTE TO THE OFFICERS AND MEN OF THE U.S.S. O'BANNON FOR THEIR INGENUITY IN USING OUR NOW PROUD POTATO TO "SINK" A JAPANESE SUBMARINE IN THE SPRING OF 1943
PRESENTED BY POTATO GROWERS OF THE STATE OF MAINE JUNE 14, 1945
WHAT AN AMAZING TALE!
I WOULDN'T EXACTLY CALL IT *SILLY,* THOUGH.
THROWING POTATOES IS SILLY. HUNDREDS OF SAILORS GOING TO A WATERY GRAVE, WELL... THAT'S NOT SO SILLY.
BUT IT'S A TRUE STORY.
IT'S A GOOD THING IT WAS *POTATO* SOUP ON THE MENU.
WHY'S THAT?
IF IT WAS *CHICKEN SOUP,* THEY'D HAVE HAD TO THROW *CHICKENS*!

BIBLIOGRAPHY

- *EYEWITNESS PACIFIC THEATER,* D. M. GIANGRECO AND JOHN T. KUEHN, STERLING, 2008
- "HORROR AT GUADALCANAL," ERNEST A. HERR, A FIRSTHAND ESSAY ON THE DESTROYER HISTORY FOUNDATION'S WEBSITE: DESTROYERHISTORY.ORG
- *ISLANDS OF HELL: THE U.S. MARINES IN THE WESTERN PACIFIC, 1944–1945,* ERIC HAMMEL, ZENITH PRESS, 2010
- *NEPTUNE'S INFERNO: THE U.S. NAVY AT GUADALCANAL,* JAMES D. HORNFISCHER, RANDOM HOUSE, 2011
- *THE PACIFIC WAR ATLAS 1941–1945,* DAVID SMURTHWAITE, FACTS ON FILE, 1995

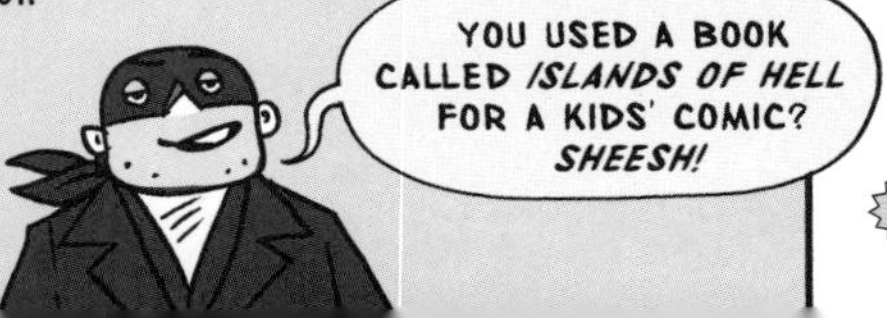
YOU USED A BOOK CALLED *ISLANDS OF HELL* FOR A KIDS' COMIC? *SHEESH!*

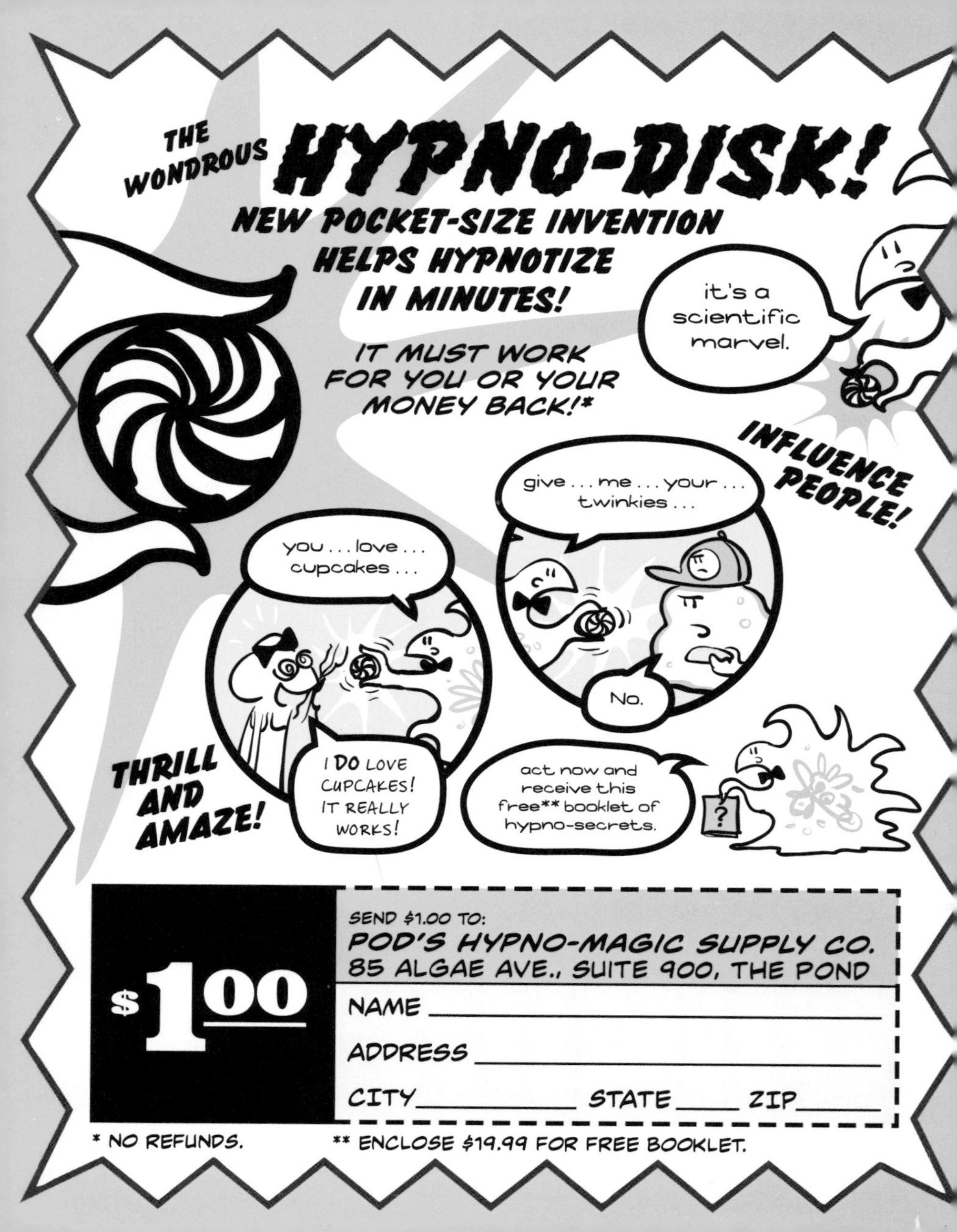

THE WONDROUS HYPNO-DISK!
NEW POCKET-SIZE INVENTION HELPS HYPNOTIZE IN MINUTES!
IT MUST WORK FOR YOU OR YOUR MONEY BACK!*
it's a scientific marvel.
INFLUENCE PEOPLE!
give . . . me . . . your . . . twinkies . . .
you . . . love . . . cupcakes . . .
No.
THRILL AND AMAZE!
I DO LOVE CUPCAKES! IT REALLY WORKS!
act now and receive this free** booklet of hypno-secrets.
?
$1.00
SEND $1.00 TO:
POD'S HYPNO-MAGIC SUPPLY CO.
85 ALGAE AVE., SUITE 900, THE POND
NAME ____
ADDRESS ____
CITY ____ STATE ____ ZIP ____
* NO REFUNDS.
** ENCLOSE $19.99 FOR FREE BOOKLET.

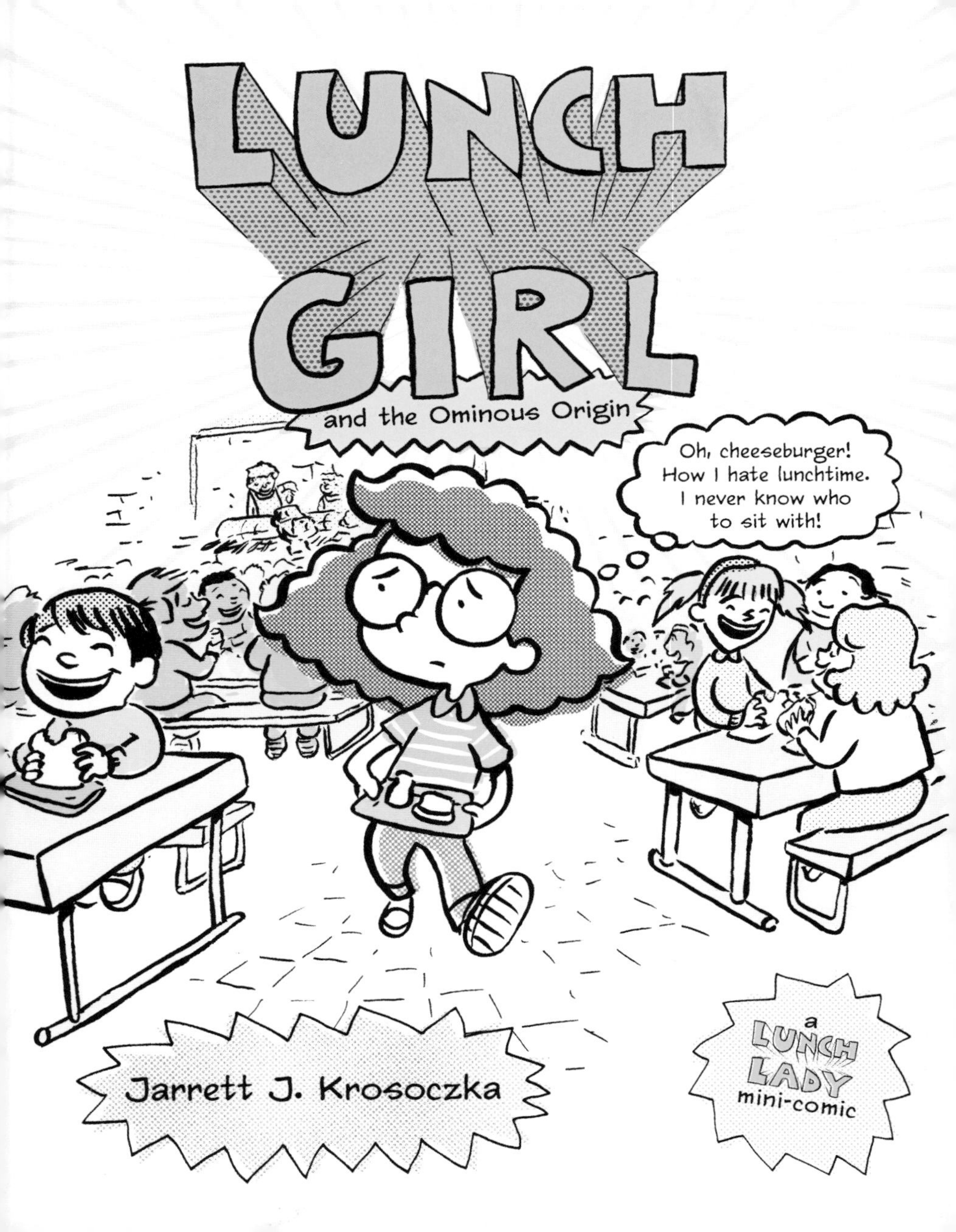
LUNCH GIRL
and the Ominous Origin
Oh, cheeseburger! How I hate lunchtime. I never know who to sit with!
Jarrett J. Krosoczka
a LUNCH LADY mini-comic

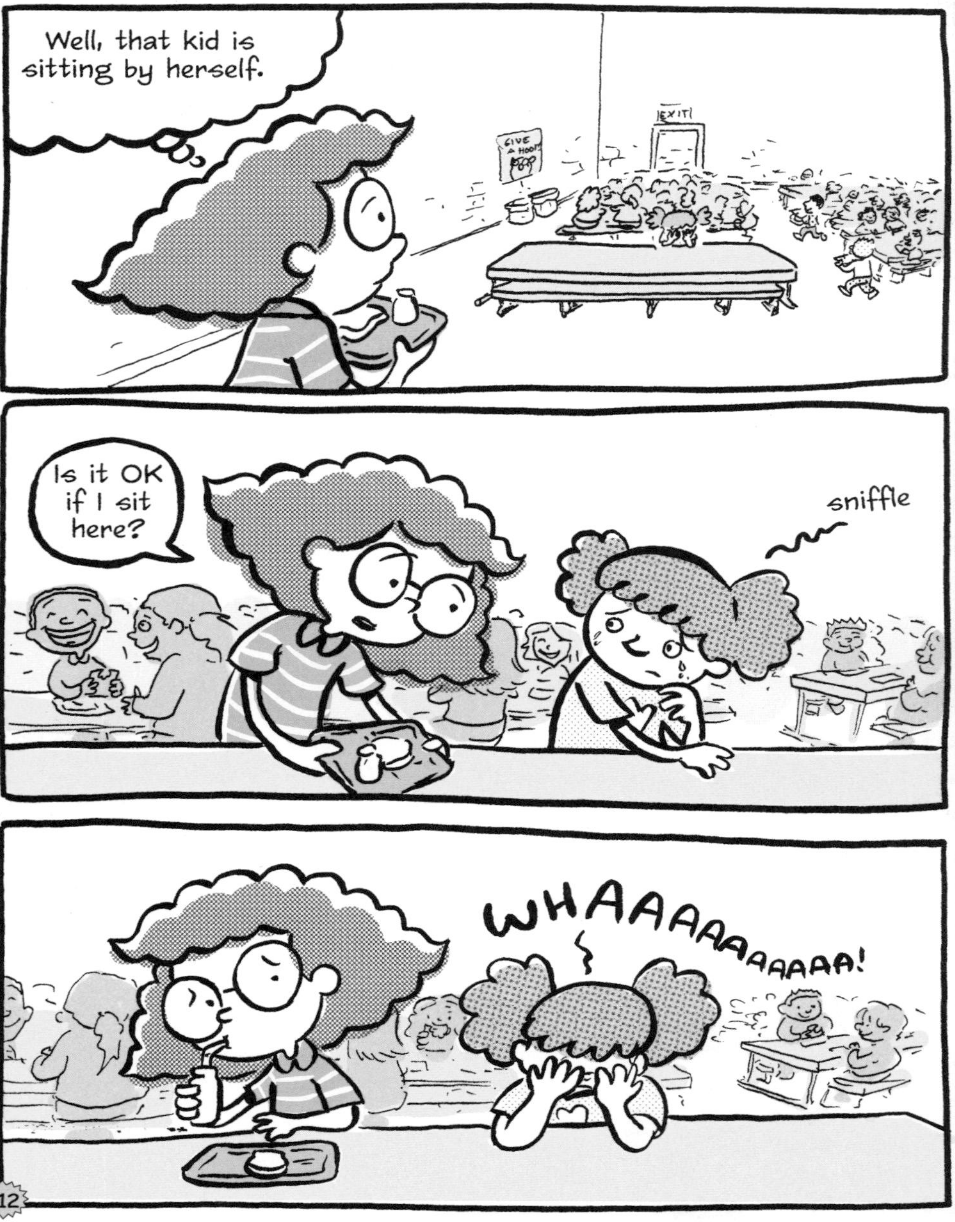
Well, that kid is sitting by herself.
EXIT
Is it OK if I sit here?
sniffle
WHAAAAAAAAAAA!

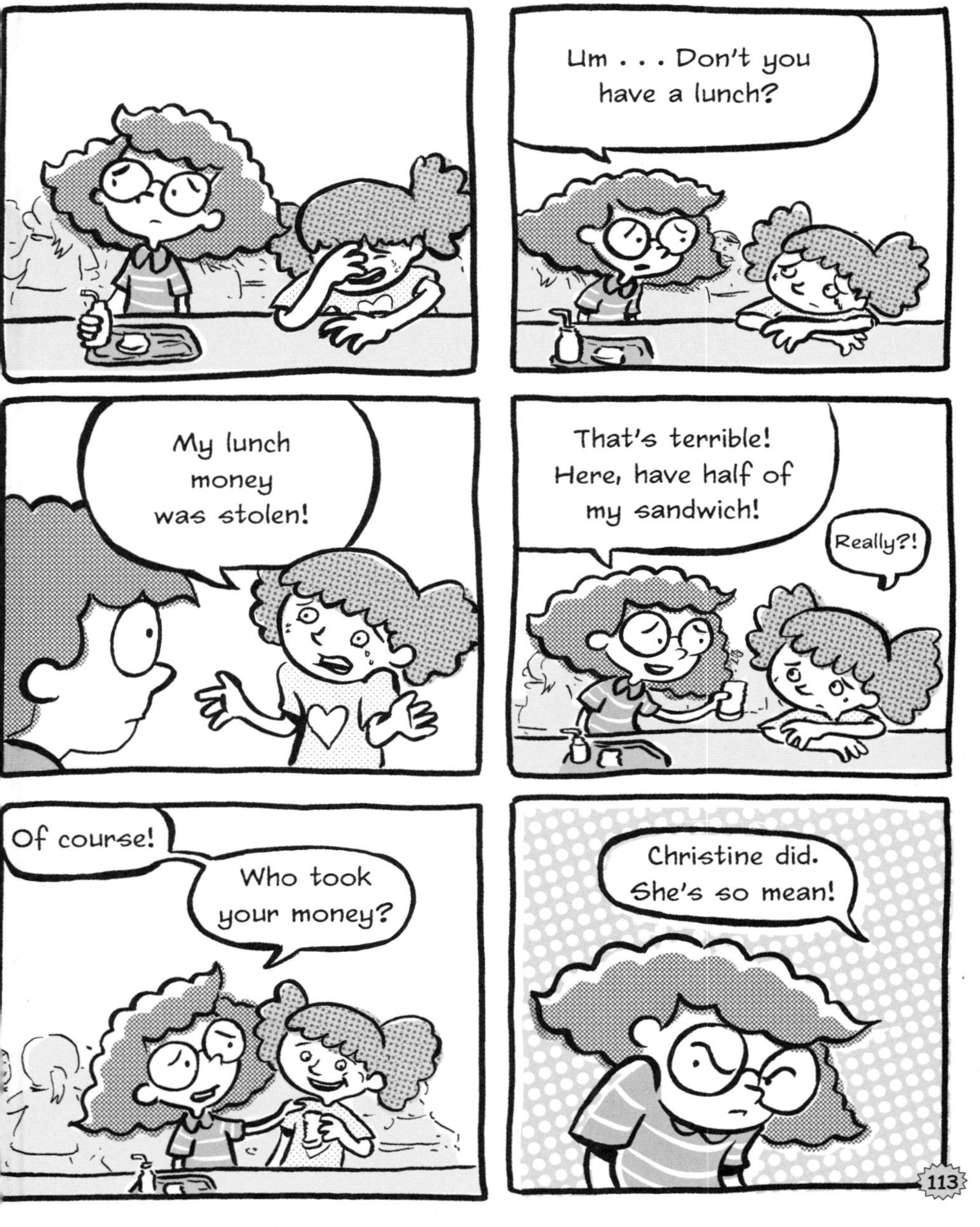
Um . . . Don't you have a lunch?
My lunch money was stolen!
That's terrible! Here, have half of my sandwich!
Really?!
Of course!
Who took your money?
Christine did. She's so mean!

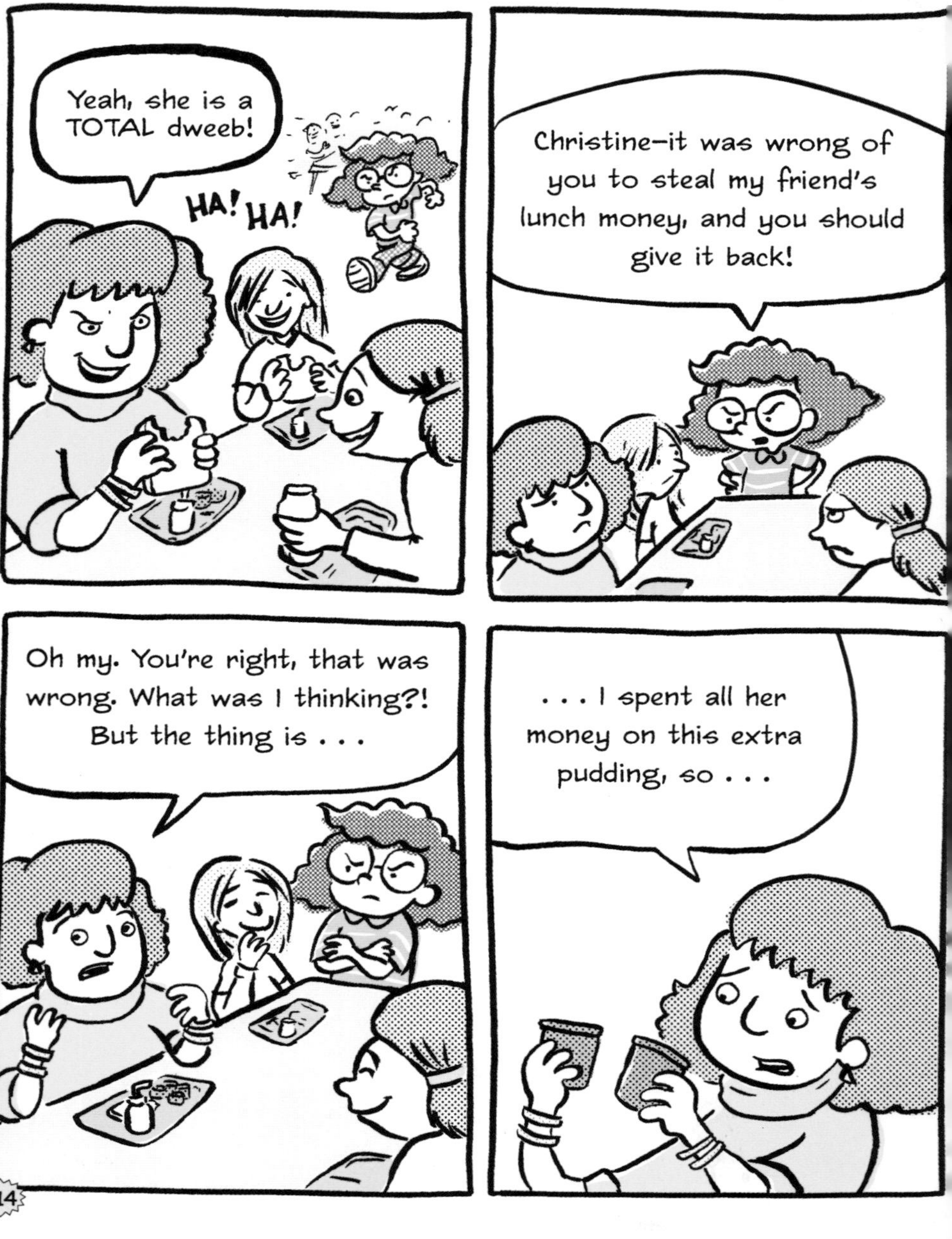
Yeah, she is a TOTAL dweeb!
HA! HA!
Christine—it was wrong of you to steal my friend's lunch money, and you should give it back!
Oh my. You're right, that was wrong. What was I thinking?! But the thing is . . .
. . . I spent all her money on this extra pudding, so . . .

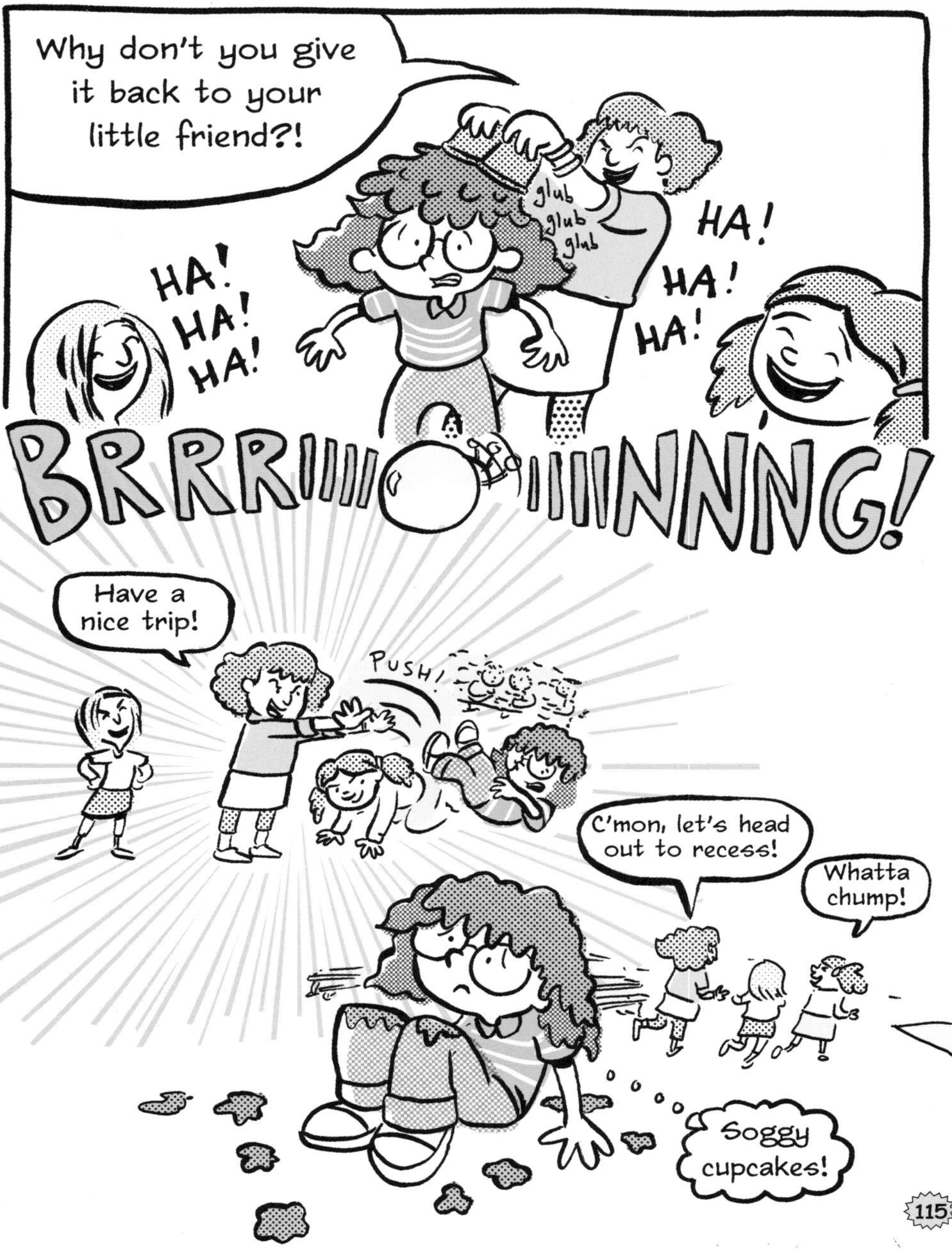
Why don't you give it back to your little friend?!
glub glub glub
HA! HA! HA!
HA! HA! HA!
BRRRIIIIIIIIIIIINNNG!
Have a nice trip!
PUSH!
C'mon, let's head out to recess!
Whatta chump!
Soggy cupcakes!

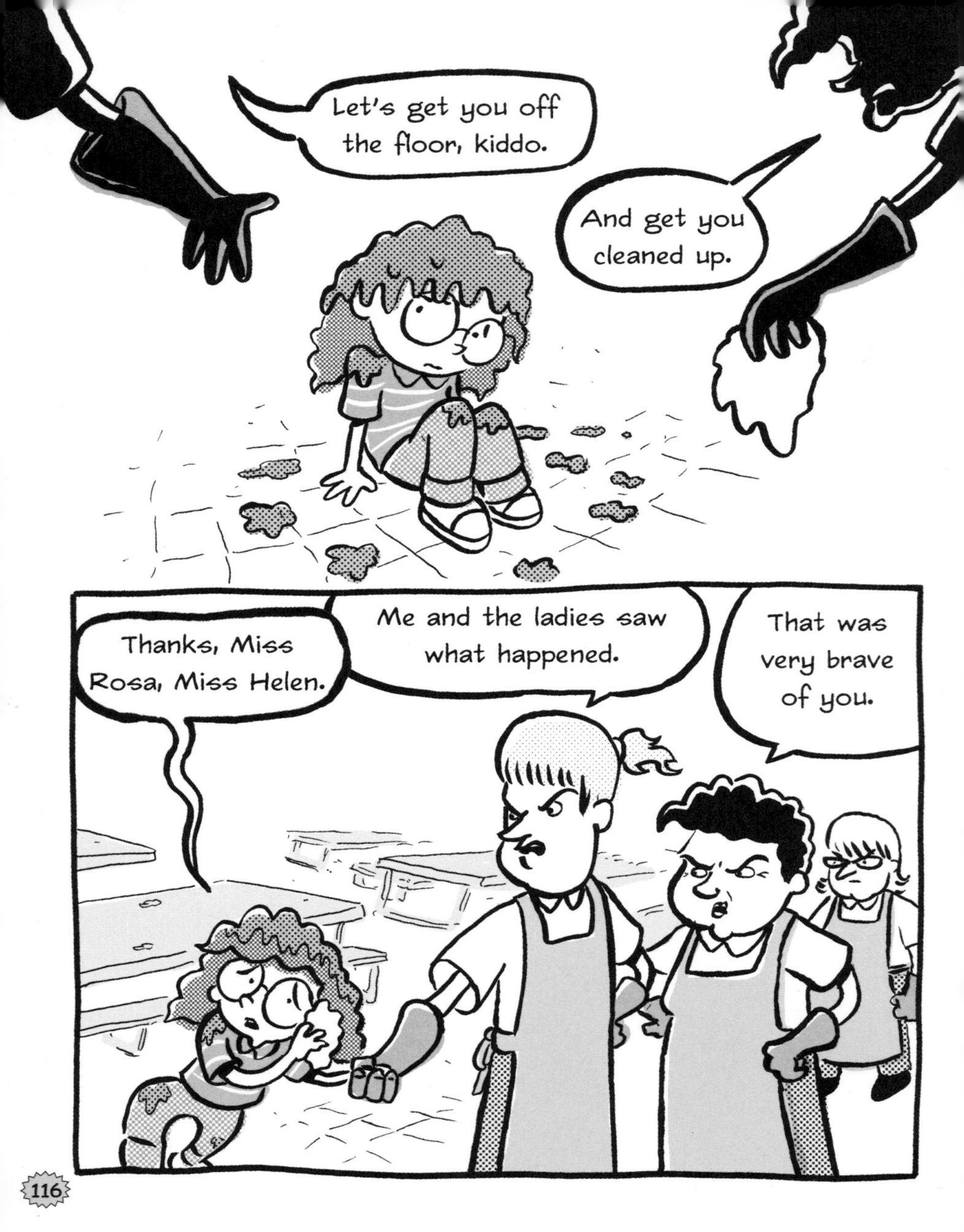
Let's get you off the floor, kiddo.
And get you cleaned up.
Thanks, Miss Rosa, Miss Helen.
Me and the ladies saw what happened.
That was very brave of you.

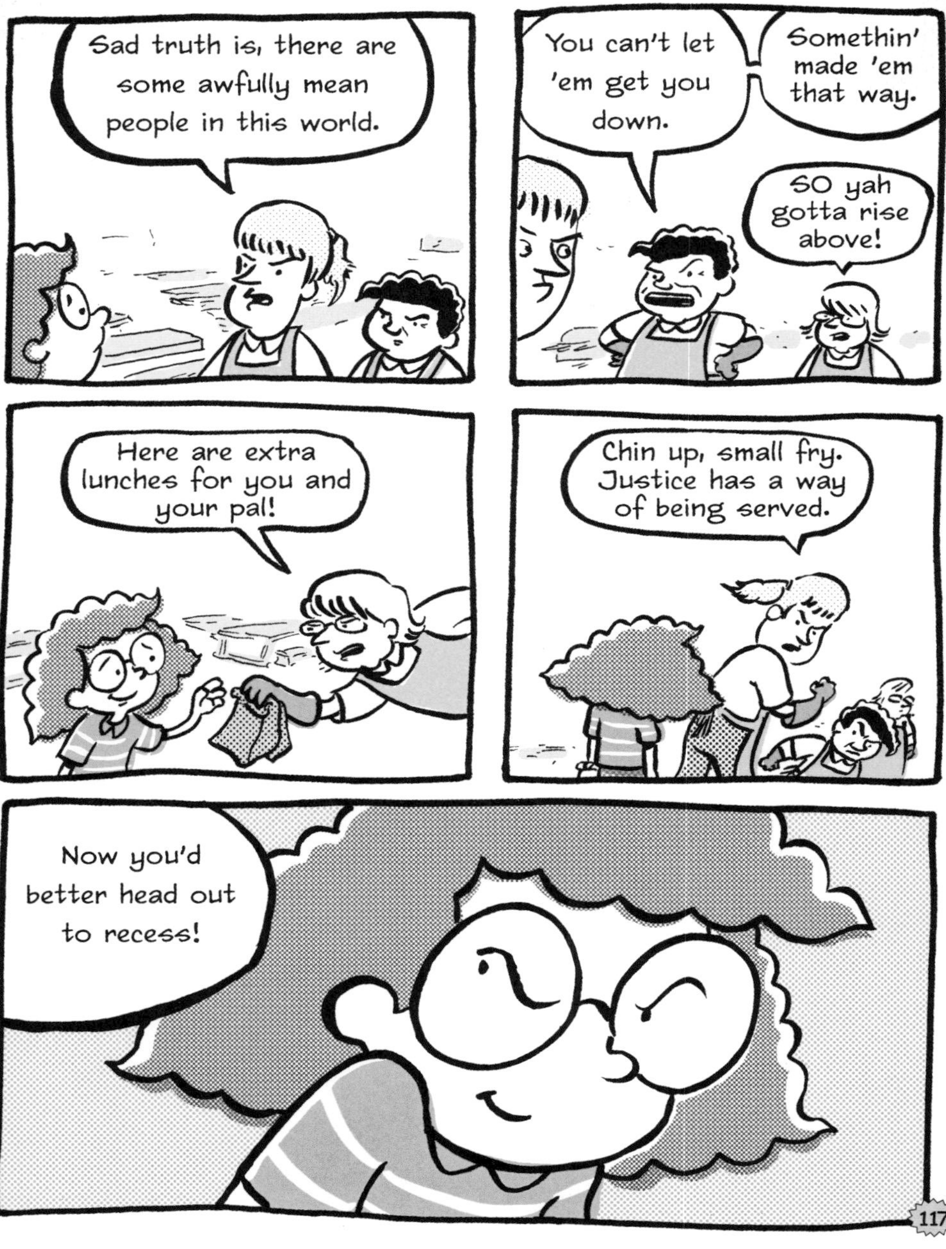
Sad truth is, there are some awfully mean people in this world.
You can't let 'em get you down.
Somethin' made 'em that way.
SO yah gotta rise above!
Here are extra lunches for you and your pal!
Chin up, small fry. Justice has a way of being served.
Now you'd better head out to recess!

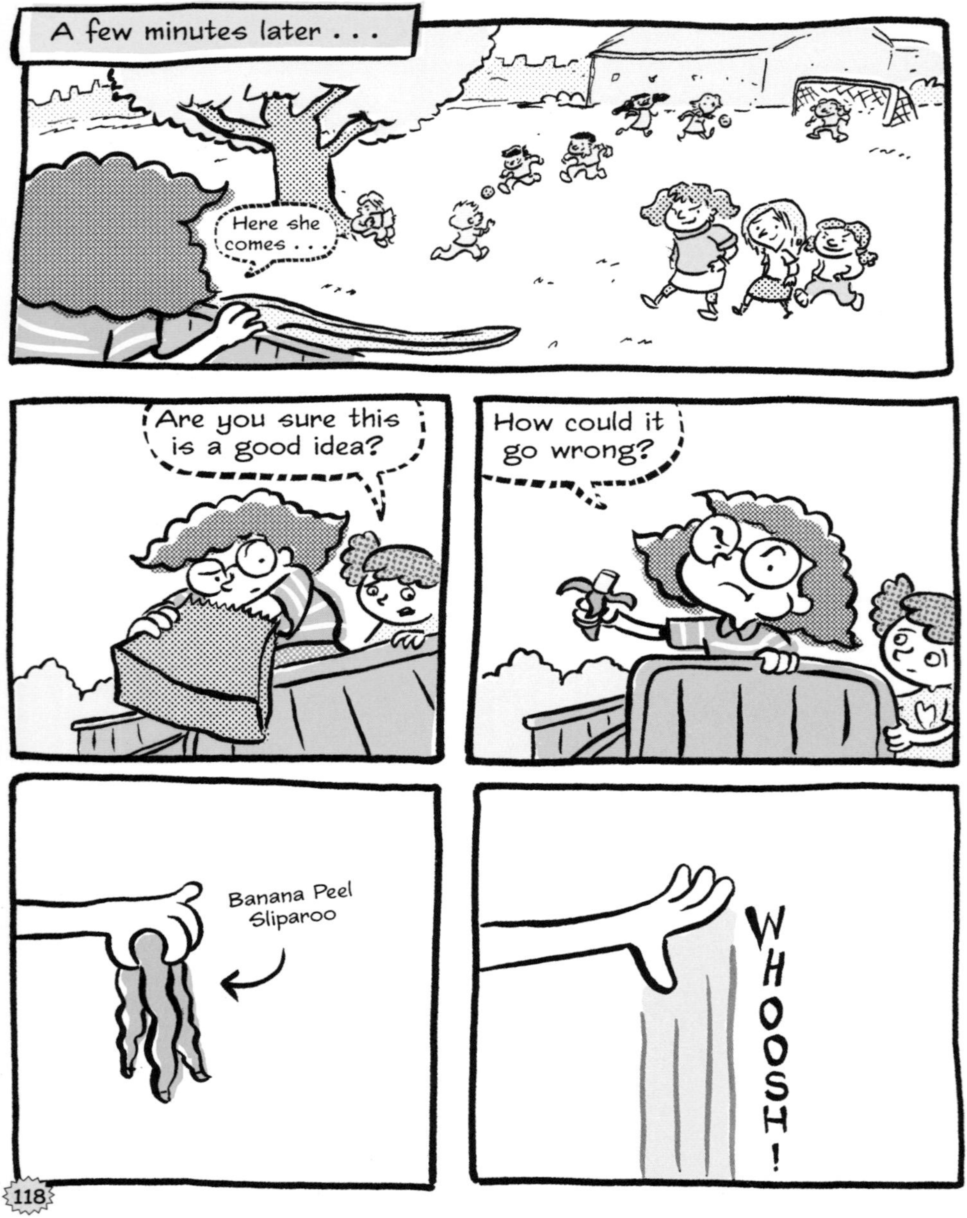
A few minutes later . . .
Here she comes . . .
Are you sure this is a good idea?
How could it go wrong?
Banana Peel Sliparoo
WHOOSH!

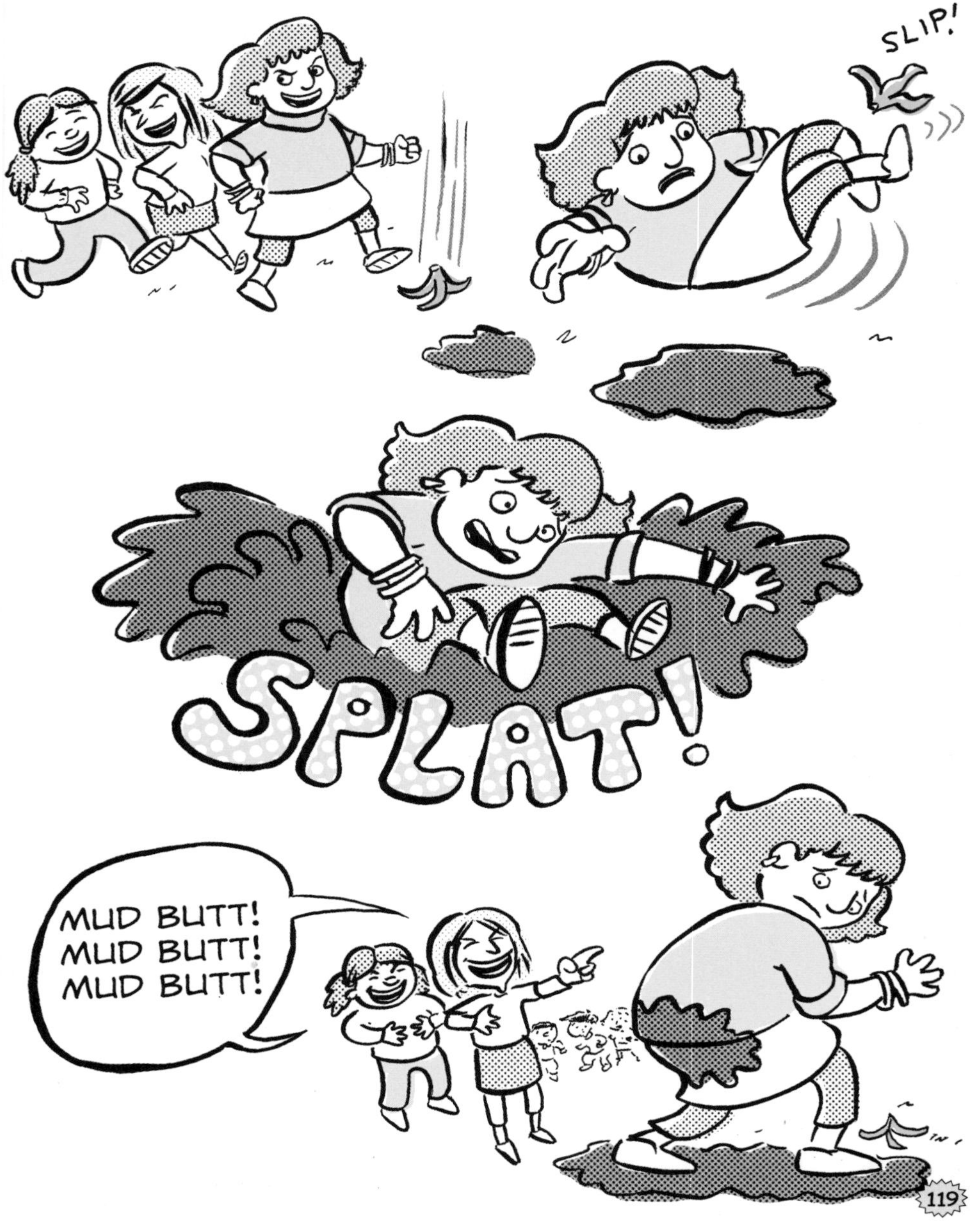
SLIP!
SPLAT!
MUD BUTT!
MUD BUTT!
MUD BUTT!

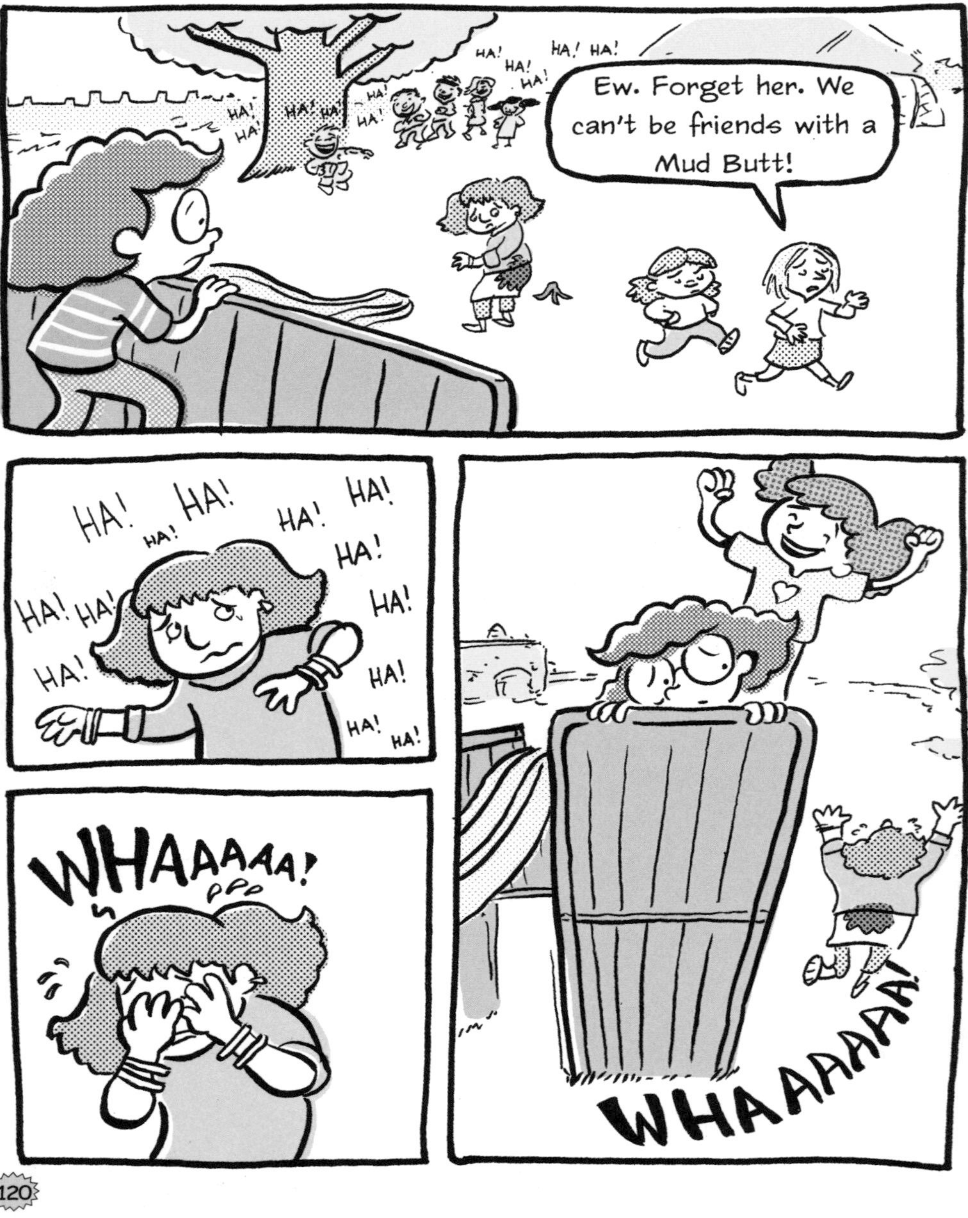
HA! HA!
HA! HA!
HA! HA!
HA!
HA!
HA! HA!
HA! HA! HA!
Ew. Forget her. We can't be friends with a Mud Butt!
HA! HA! HA! HA! HA! HA! HA! HA! HA! HA! HA! HA! HA!
WHAAAAA!
WHAAAAAAA!

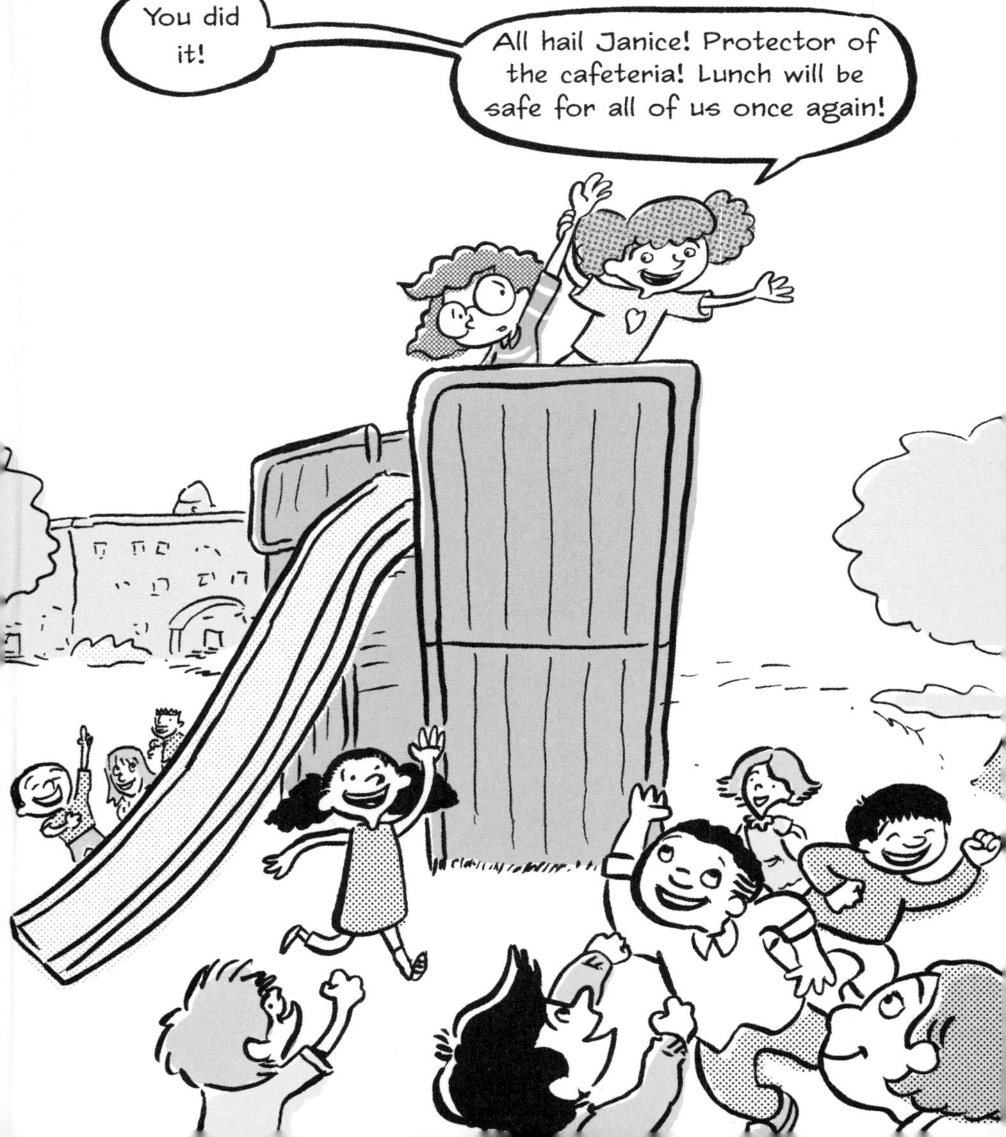
You did it!
All hail Janice! Protector of the cafeteria! Lunch will be safe for all of us once again!

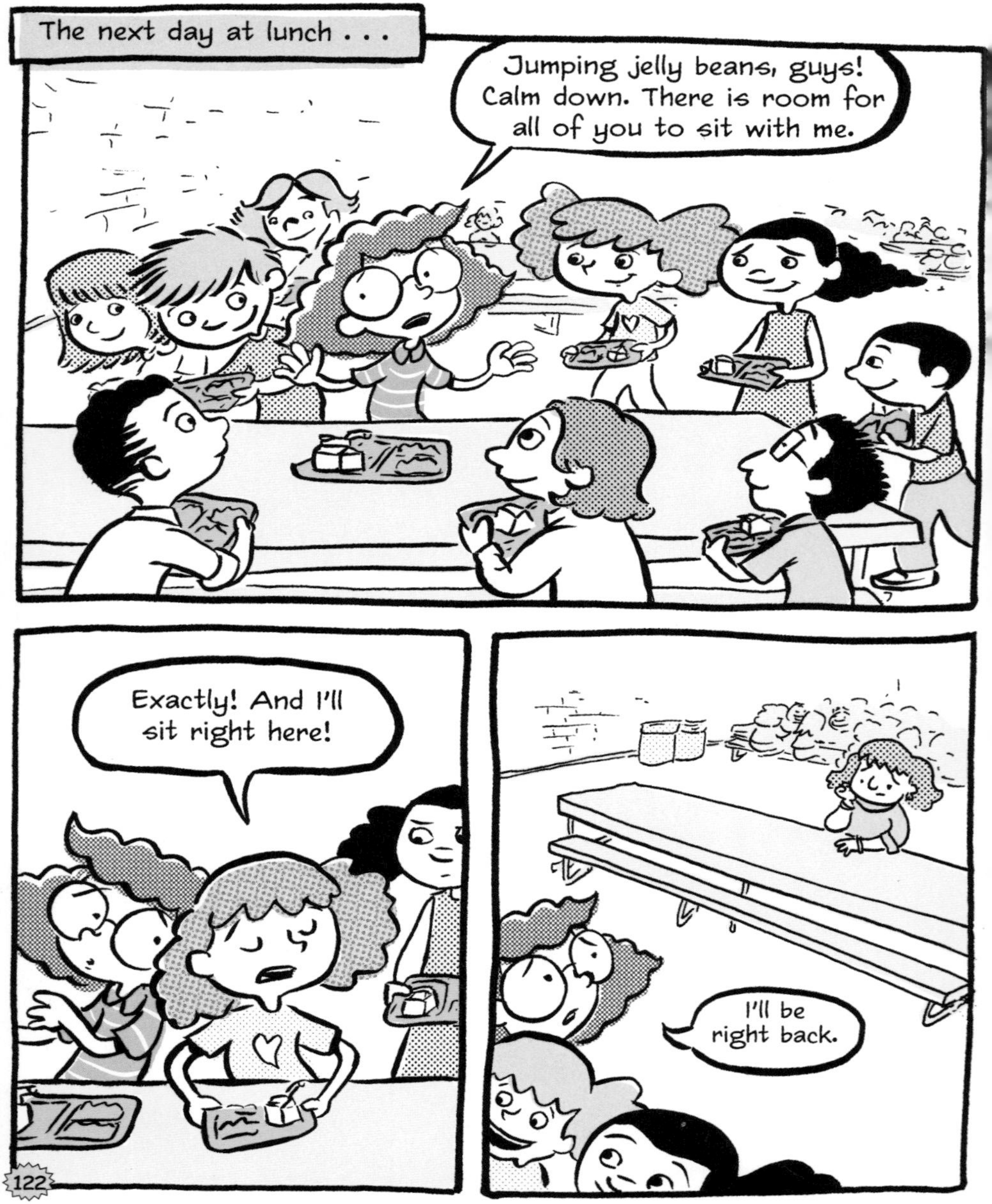
The next day at lunch . . .
Jumping jelly beans, guys! Calm down. There is room for all of you to sit with me.
Exactly! And I'll sit right here!
I'll be right back.

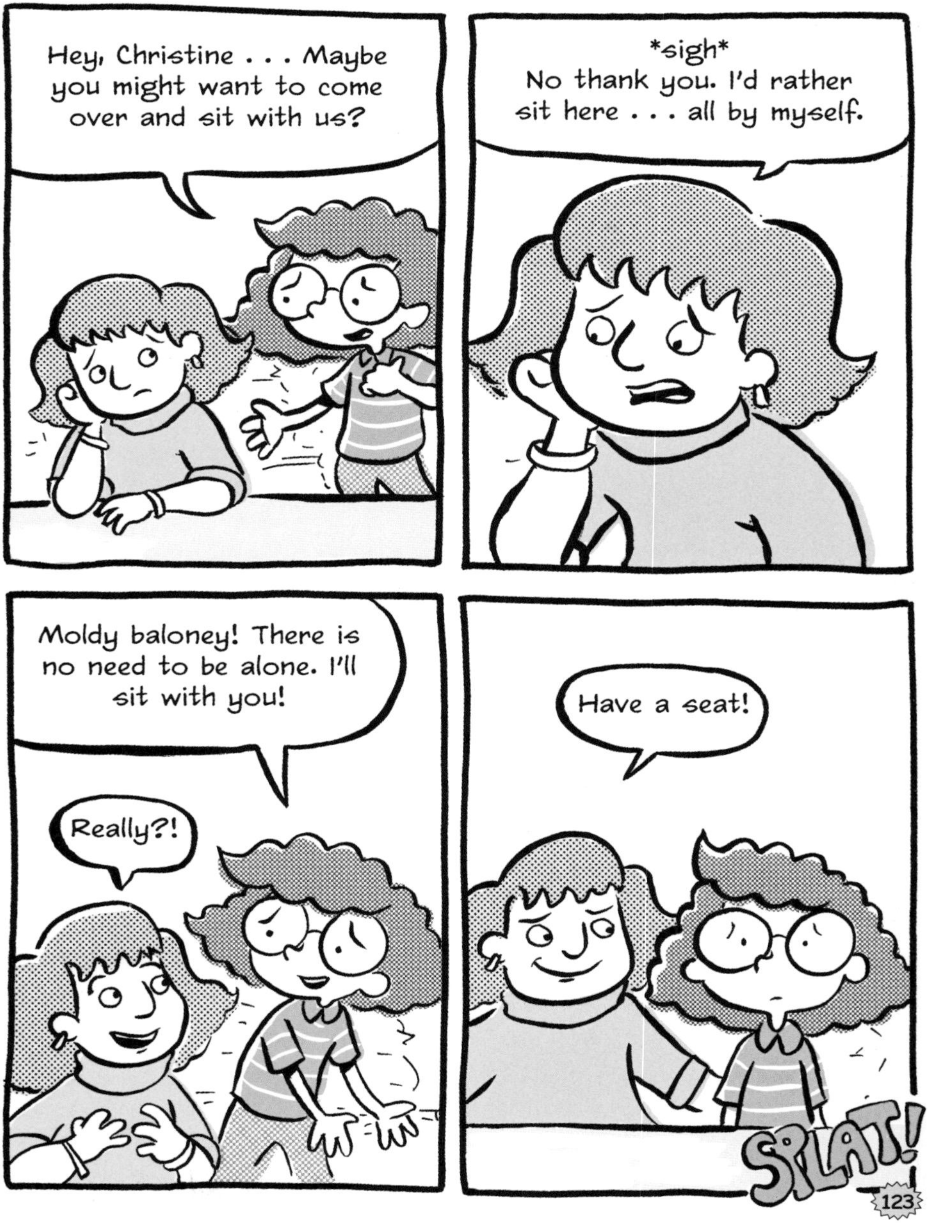

Hey, Christine . . . Maybe you might want to come over and sit with us?
sigh No thank you. I'd rather sit here . . . all by myself.
Moldy baloney! There is no need to be alone. I'll sit with you!
Really?!
Have a seat!
SPLAT!

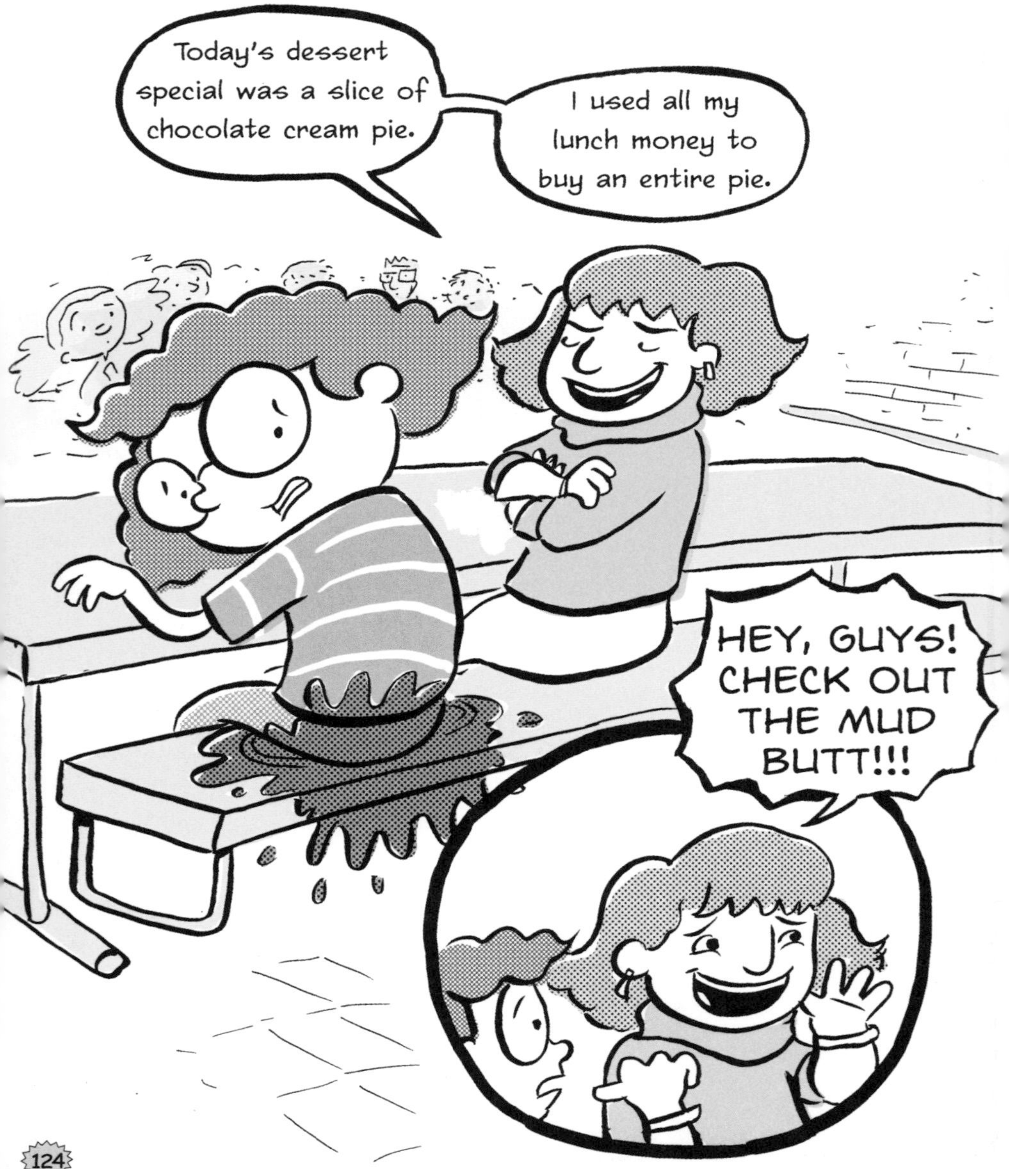
Today's dessert special was a slice of chocolate cream pie.
I used all my lunch money to buy an entire pie.
HEY, GUYS! CHECK OUT THE MUD BUTT!!!

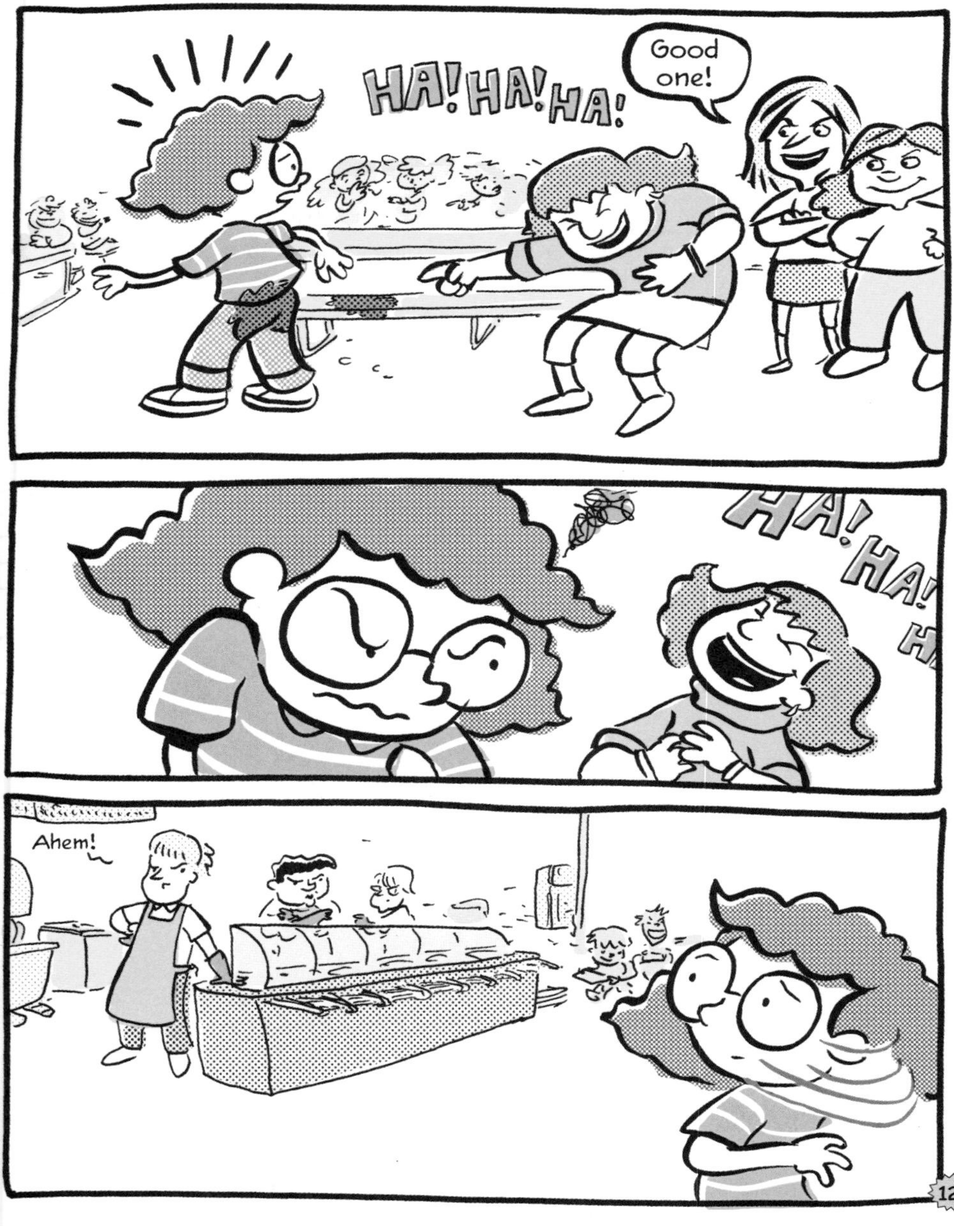
HA! HA! HA!
Good one!
HA! HA! HA! H
Ahem!

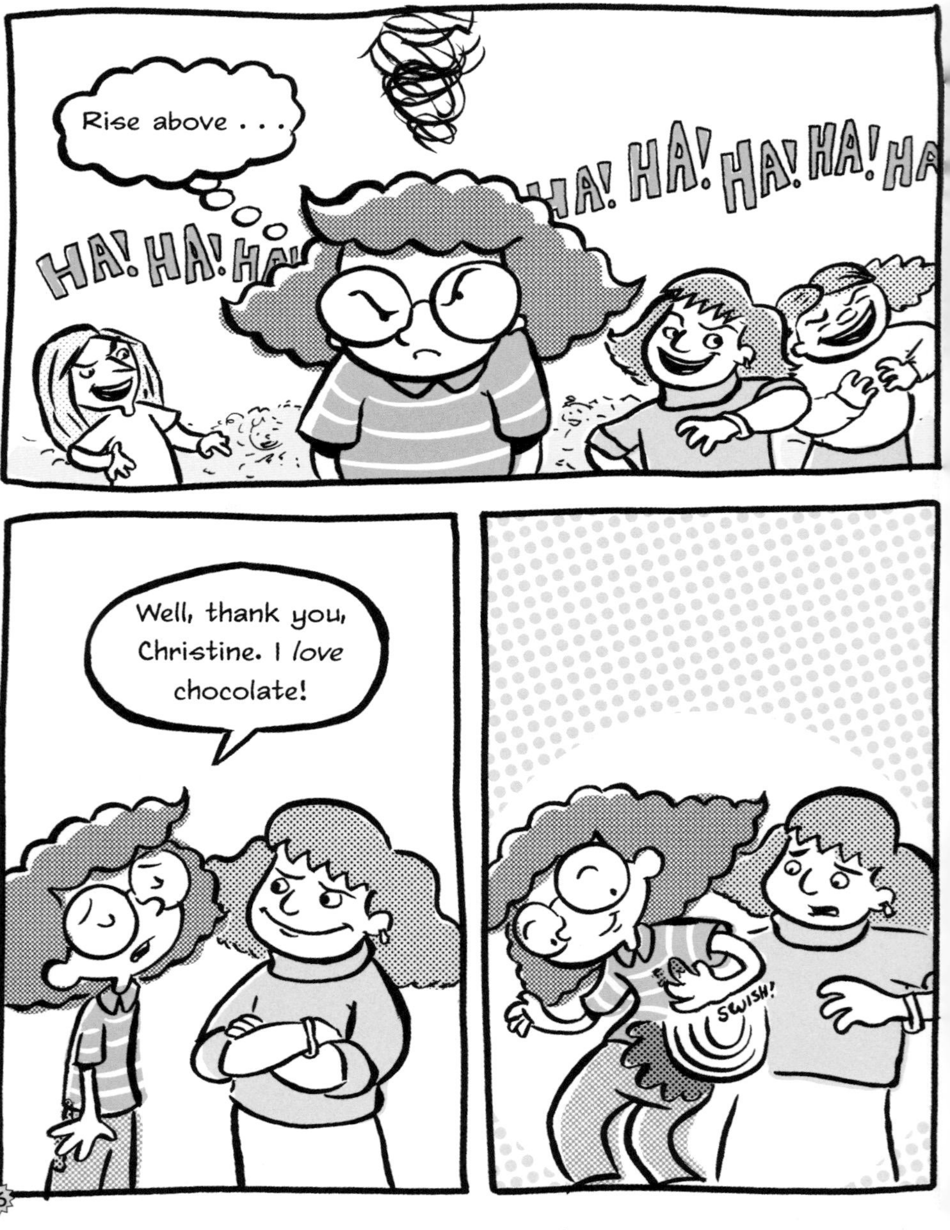
Rise above . . .
HA! HA! HA
HA! HA! HA! HA! HA
Well, thank you, Christine. I *love* chocolate!
SWISH!

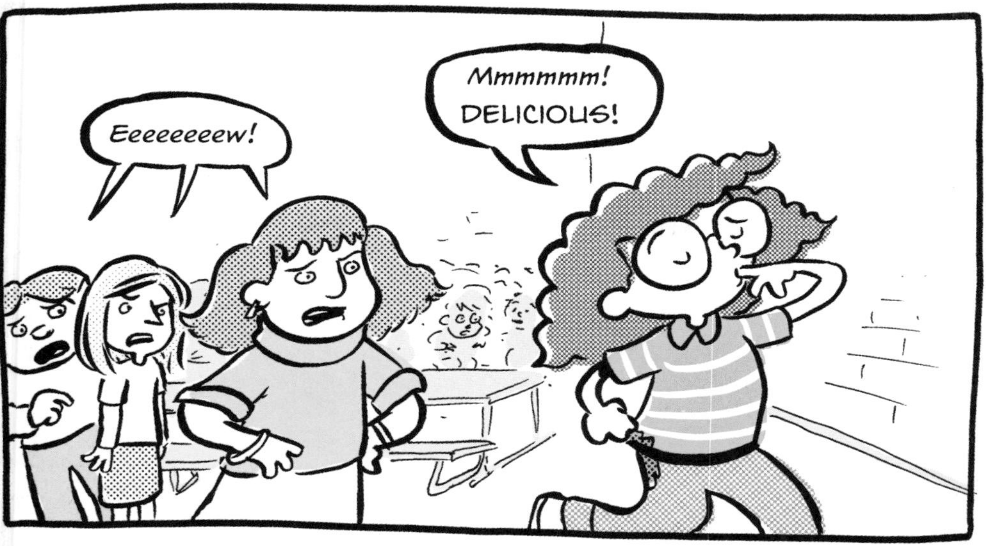
Eeeeeeeew!
Mmmmmm! DELICIOUS!

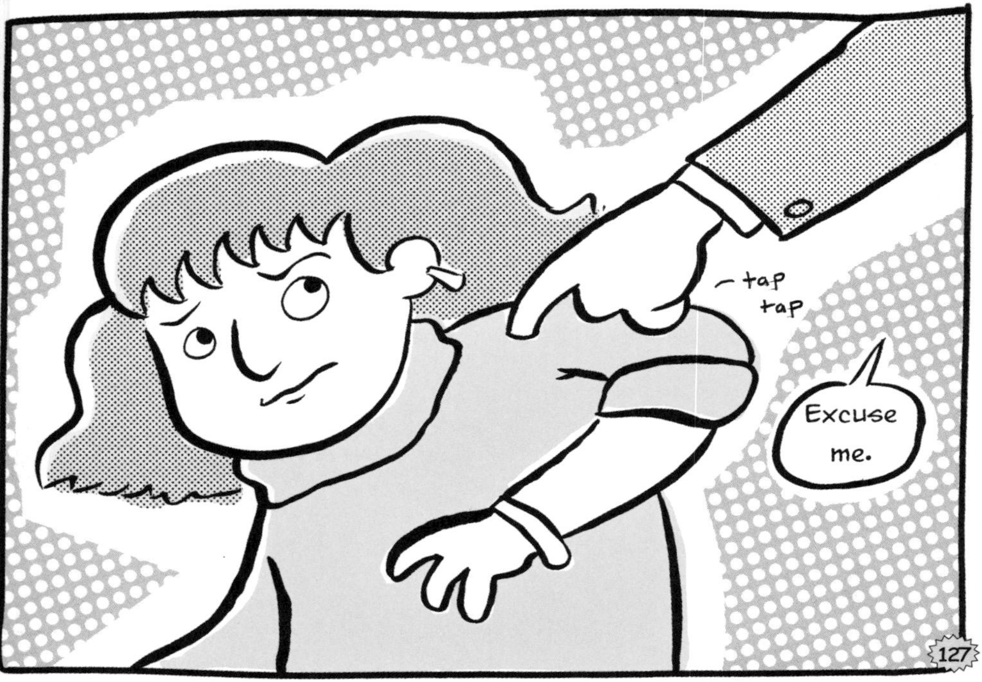
tap tap
Excuse me.

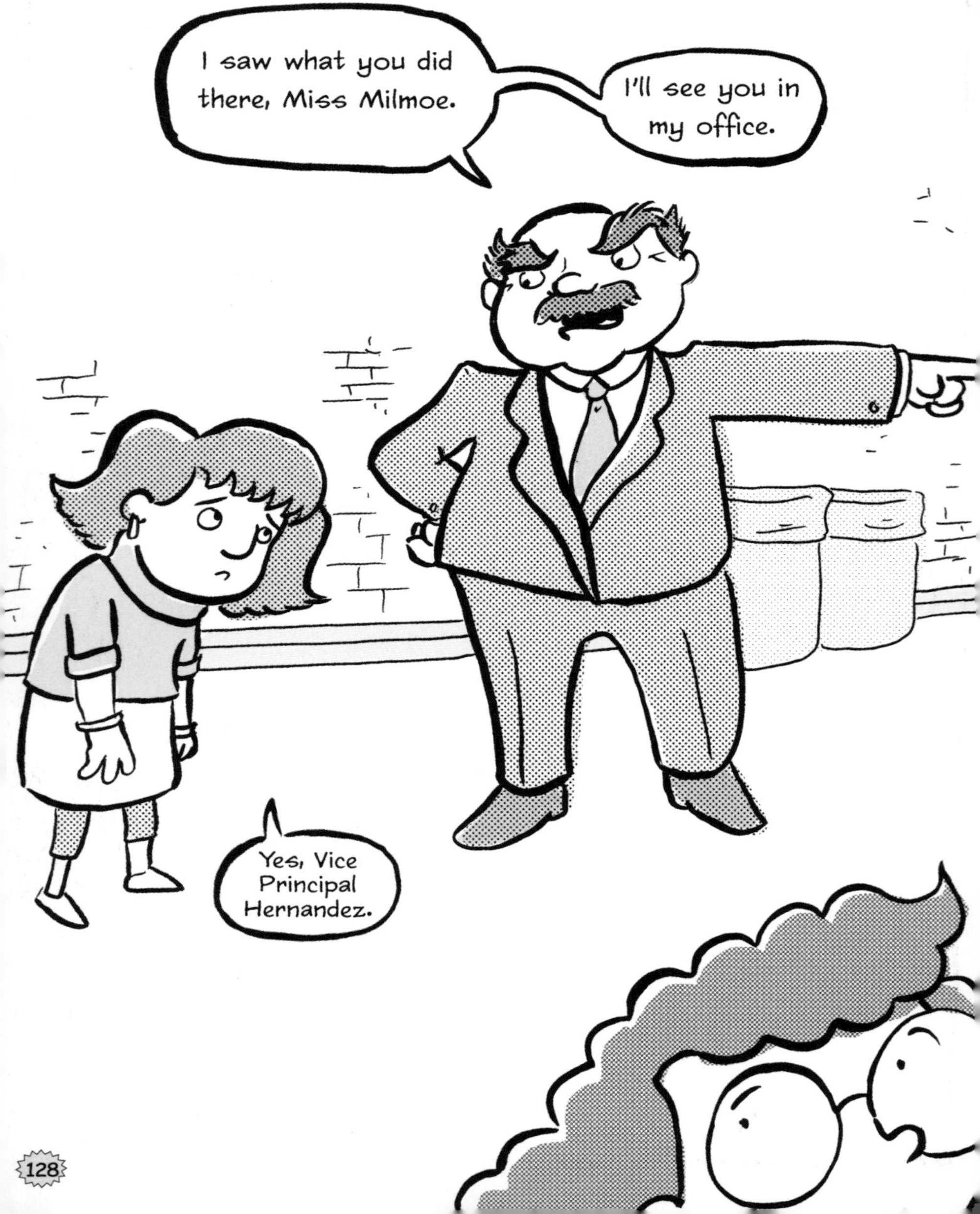
I saw what you did there, Miss Milmoe.
I'll see you in my office.
Yes, Vice Principal Hernandez.

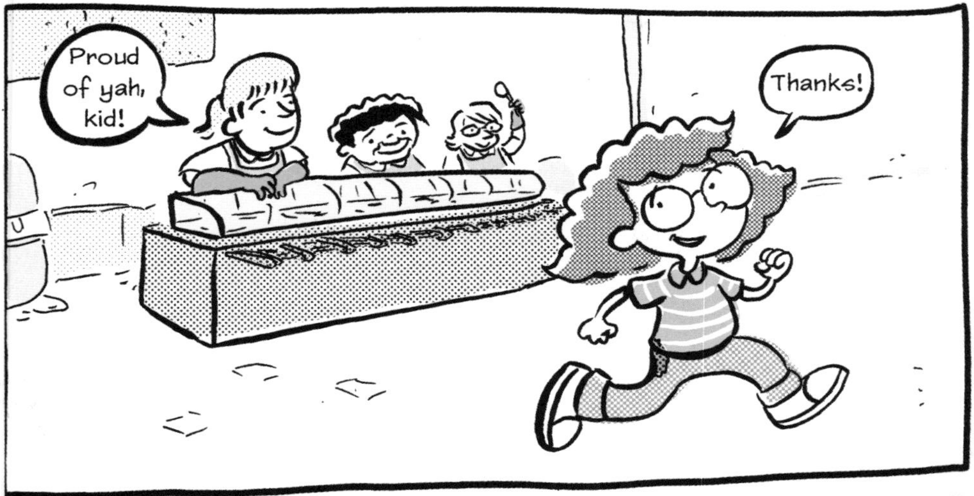
Proud of yah, kid!
Thanks!

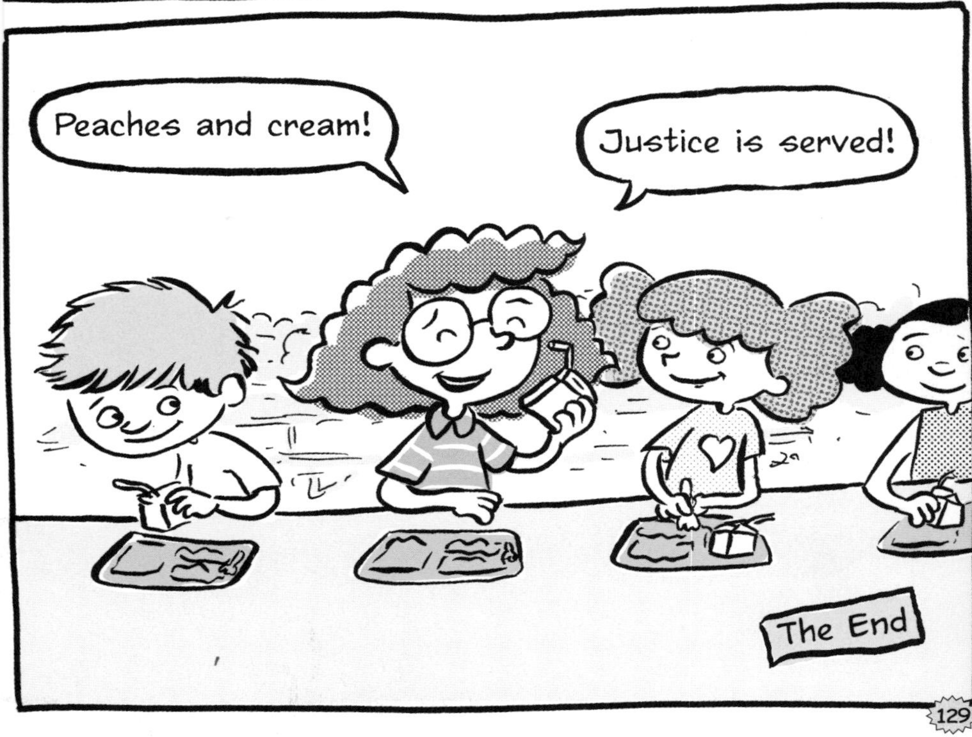
Peaches and cream!
Justice is served!
The End

WRITE YOUR OWN ORIGIN STORY!

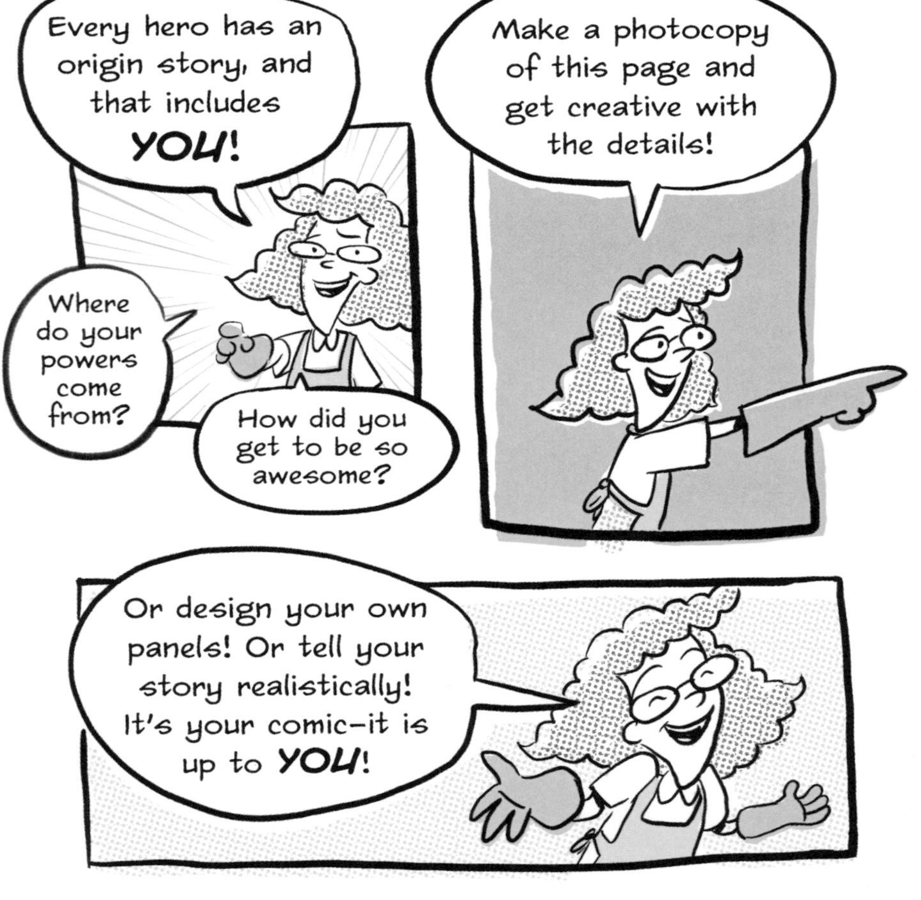
Every hero has an origin story, and that includes YOU!
Where do your powers come from?
How did you get to be so awesome?
Make a photocopy of this page and get creative with the details!
Or design your own panels! Or tell your story realistically! It's your comic–it is up to YOU!

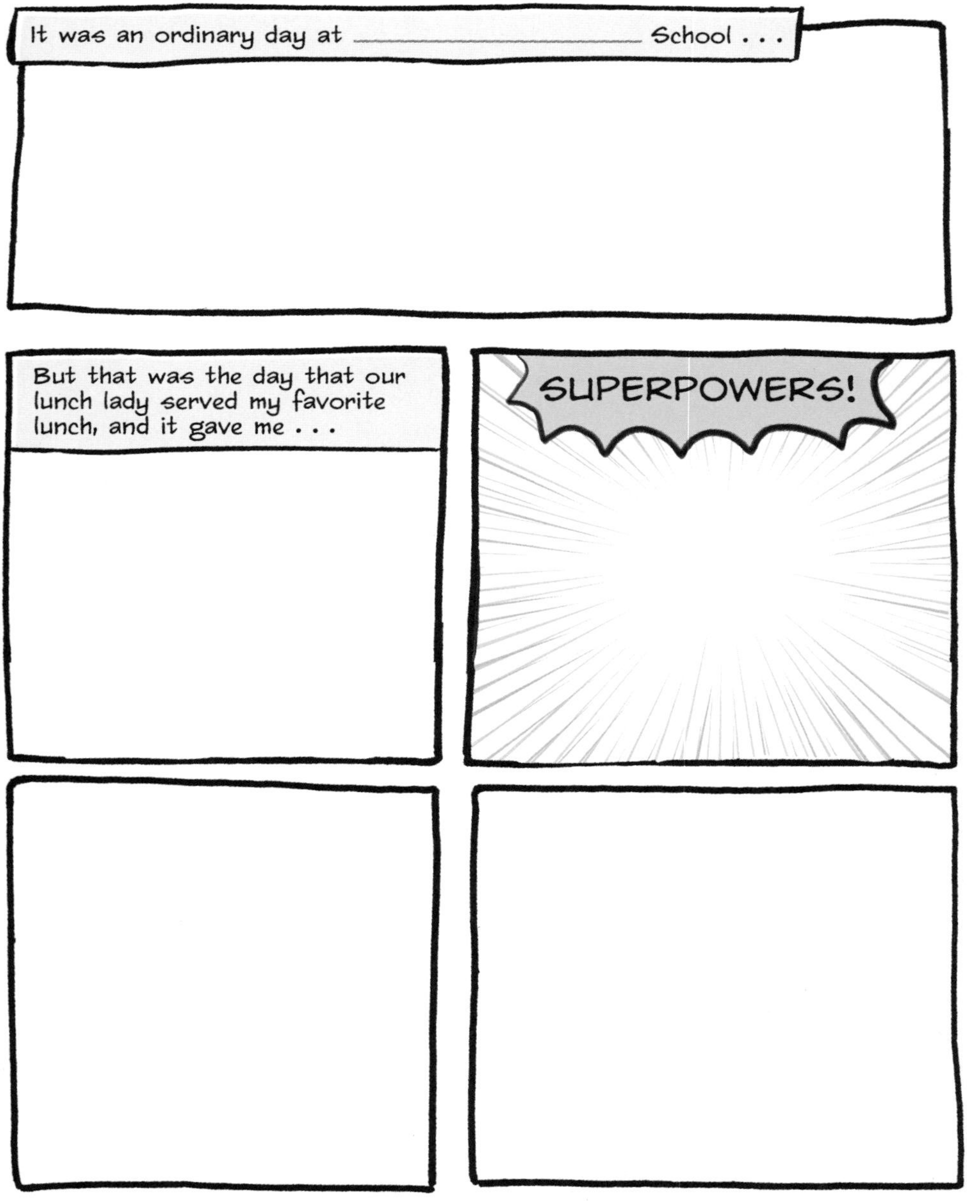
It was an ordinary day at ________________ School . . .
But that was the day that our lunch lady served my favorite lunch, and it gave me . . .
SUPERPOWERS!

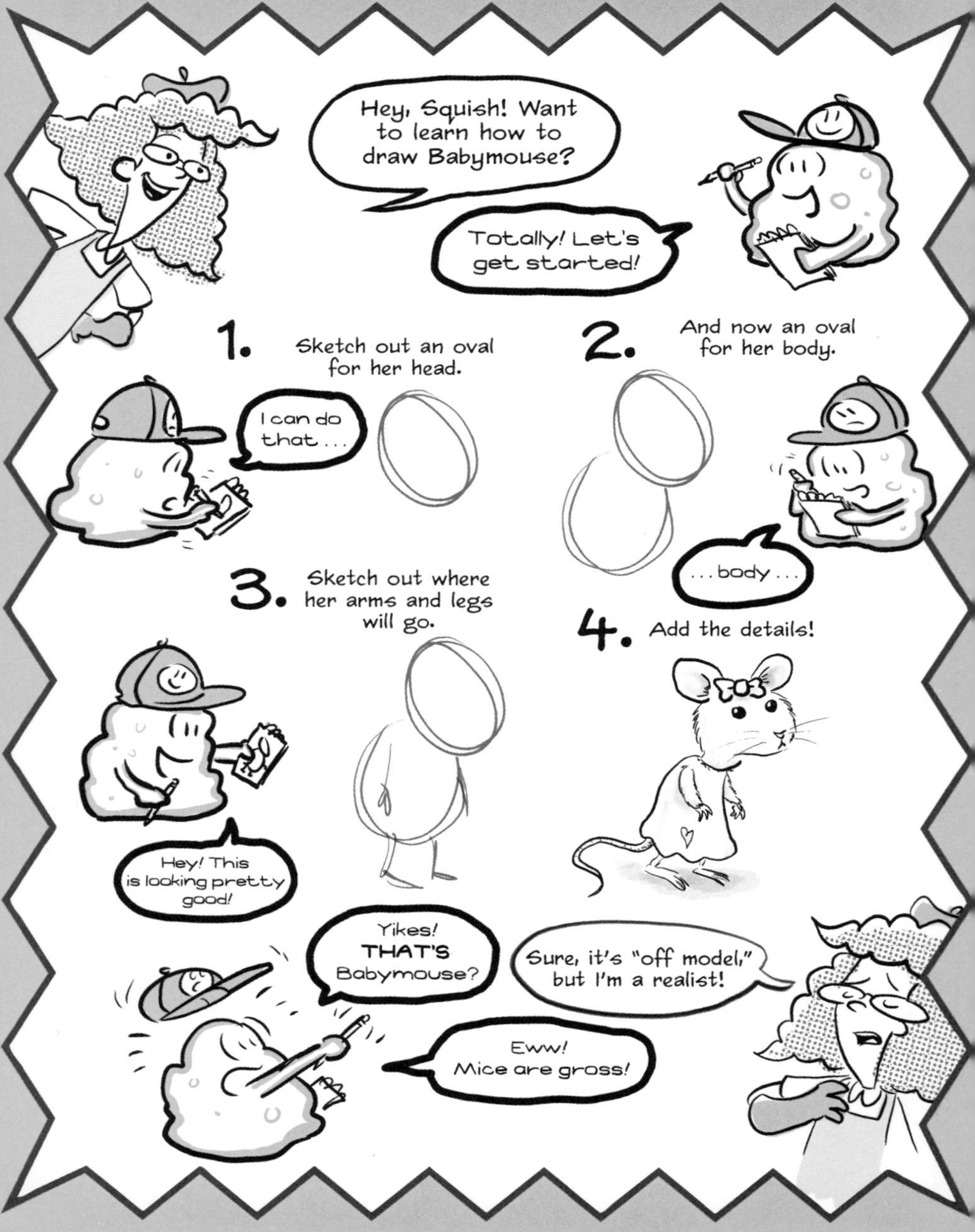
Hey, Squish! Want to learn how to draw Babymouse?
Totally! Let's get started!
1. Sketch out an oval for her head.
I can do that . . .
2. And now an oval for her body.
. . . body . . .
3. Sketch out where her arms and legs will go.
Hey! This is looking pretty good!
4. Add the details!
Yikes! THAT'S Babymouse?
Sure, it's "off model," but I'm a realist!
Eww! Mice are gross!

★ ABOUT THE AUTHORS ★

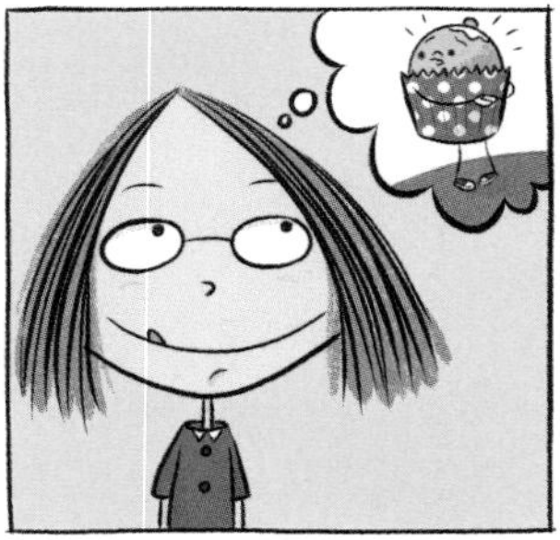

CECE BELL

is the author and illustrator of lots of books for kids, including the autobiographical novel *El Deafo.* She gets to eat lunch with her husband, author Tom Angleberger, practically every day. (cecebell.com)

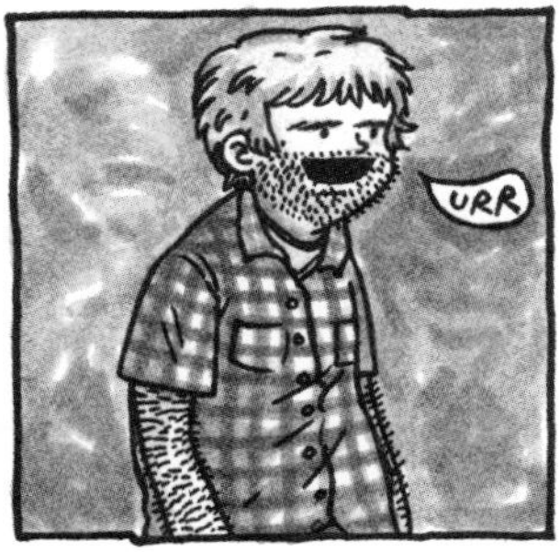
URR

JEFFREY BROWN

is the author of the bestselling Jedi Academy series and is currently working on his new series, Lucy & Andy Neanderthal. According to DNA testing, he is approximately 2.2% Neanderthal. (jeffreybrowncomics.com)

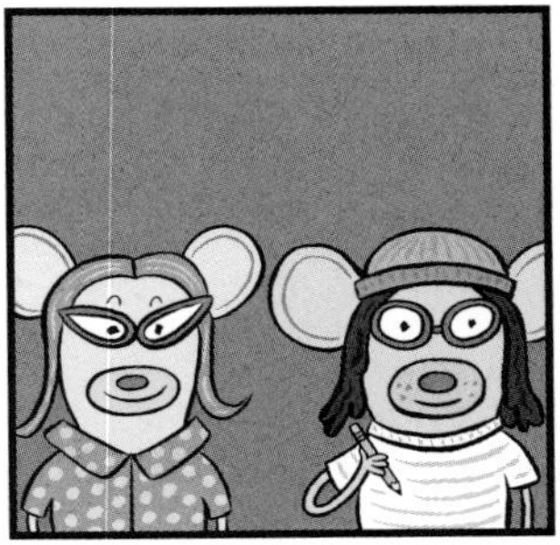

CECIL CASTELLUCCI & SARA VARON

are the author and illustrator of the Eisner-nominated graphic novel *Odd Duck*. Cecil is also the author of *Boy Proof, The Plain Janes,* and *Tin Star.* Sara's other books include *Bake Sale, Robot Dreams,* and *Chicken and Cat.* Like Pikput and Cullen, they both enjoy science. (misscecil.com and chickenopolis.com)

NATHAN HALE

is the author and illustrator of the Hazardous Tales series—gross and amazing true stories about history! He has also illustrated the graphic novels *Rapunzel's Revenge* and *Calamity Jack*. His favorite lunch is a huge burrito. (hazardoustales.com)

JENNIFER L. HOLM & MATTHEW HOLM

are the brother-sister team behind two graphic novel series, Babymouse and Squish. They grew up reading lots of comics, and they turned out just fine. (babymouse.com)

JARRETT J. KROSOCZKA

is the author and illustrator of the Lunch Lady graphic novel series, which chronicles the adventures of a spatula-wielding crime fighter. He has been reading and drawing comics since he was a kid, and he now has thirty books published. He has given two TED Talks and can be heard weekly on SiriusXM's Kids Place Live. (studiojjk.com)

PEANUTS

Charles M. Schulz once described himself as "born to draw comic strips." In 1950, Schulz launched his daily newspapaer comic strip, *Peanuts,* which he drew for the next fifty years. The story that appears here was created by the Schulz Studio and was written

and drawn by Vicki Scott, inked by Paige Braddock, and lettered and colored by Donna Almendrala. (Peanuts.com)

JASON SHIGA

is the author of *Meanwhile* and over twenty other comic books and graphic novels. He is also the creator of the world's second-largest interactive comic. His comics have a geeky side and often feature exciting uses of math.

★ DON'T MISS THESE OTHER GREAT ★ GRAPHIC NOVELS FROM RANDOM HOUSE!

BABYMOUSE

HER DREAMS ARE BIG! HER IMAGINATION IS WILD! HER WHISKERS ARE ALWAYS A MESS.

IT'S GREEN... IT'S BLOBBY... IT'S GROSS... IT'S squish

LUNCH LADY

Serving justice! And serving lunch!

© 2013 Jarrett J. Krosoczka

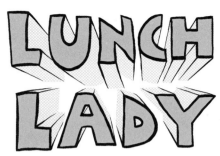

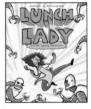

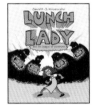

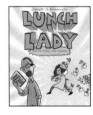

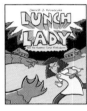

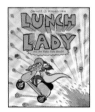

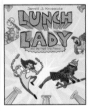

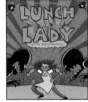

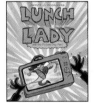

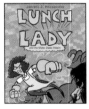

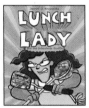

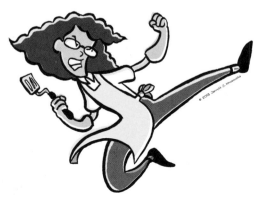

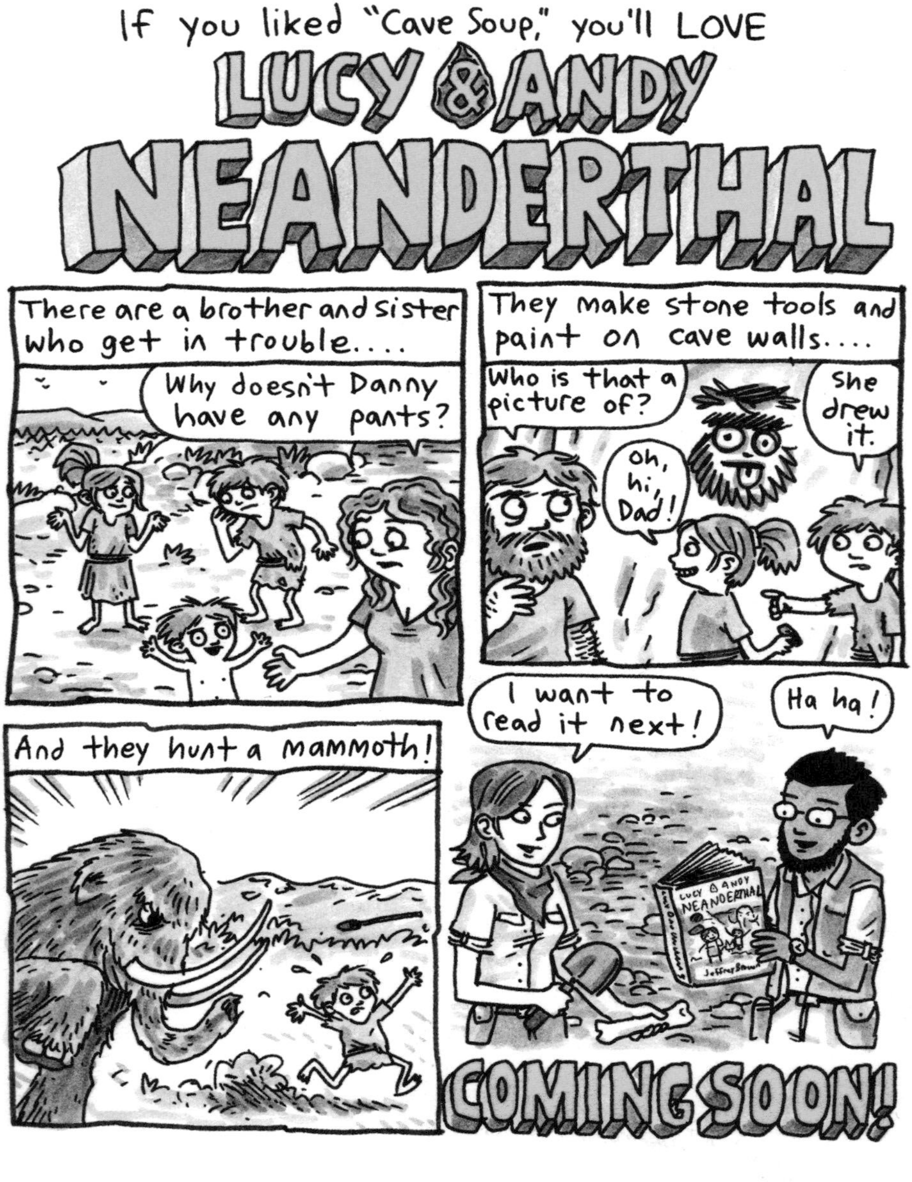
If you liked "Cave Soup," you'll LOVE
LUCY & ANDY
NEANDERTHAL
There are a brother and sister who get in trouble....
Why doesn't Danny have any pants?
They make stone tools and paint on cave walls....
Who is that a picture of?
Oh, hi, Dad!
She drew it.
And they hunt a mammoth!
I want to read it next!
Ha ha!
COMING SOON!